WICKED LOVELY
DESERT TALES
RESOLVE

Wicked Lovely: Desert Tales
Volume 3: Resolve

Story by Melissa Marr

Art by Xian Nu Studio: Irene Diaz & Laura Moreno

Visual Storytelling Consultant - Barbara Randall Kesel
Cover Design - Al-Insan Lashley
Lettering - John Hunt

Senior Editor - Lillian Diaz-Przybyl
Print Production Manager - Lucas Rivera
Managing Editor - Vy Nguyen
Senior Designer - Louis Csontos
Art Director - Al-Insan Lashley
Director of Sales and Manufacturing - Allyson De Simone
Associate Publisher - Marco F. Pavia
President and C.O.O. - John Parker
C.E.O. and Chief Creative Officer - Stu Levy

A TOKYOPOP® Manga

TOKYOPOP Inc.
5900 Wilshire Blvd. Suite 2000
Los Angeles, CA 90036

E-mail: info@TOKYOPOP.com
Come visit us online at www.TOKYOPOP.com

For information address HarperCollins Children's Books, a division of HarperCollins Publishers,
10 East 53rd Street, New York, NY 10022.
www.harperteen.com

Library of Congress catalog card number: 2010941915
ISBN 978-0-06-149350-8

11 12 13 14 15 LP/BV 10 9 8 7 6 5 4 3 2 1

First Edition

WICKED LOVELY
DESERT TALES
RESOLVE

STORY BY
MELISSA MARR

ART BY
XIAN NU STUDIO

TOKYOPOP®

HAMBURG // LONDON // LOS ANGELES // TOKYO

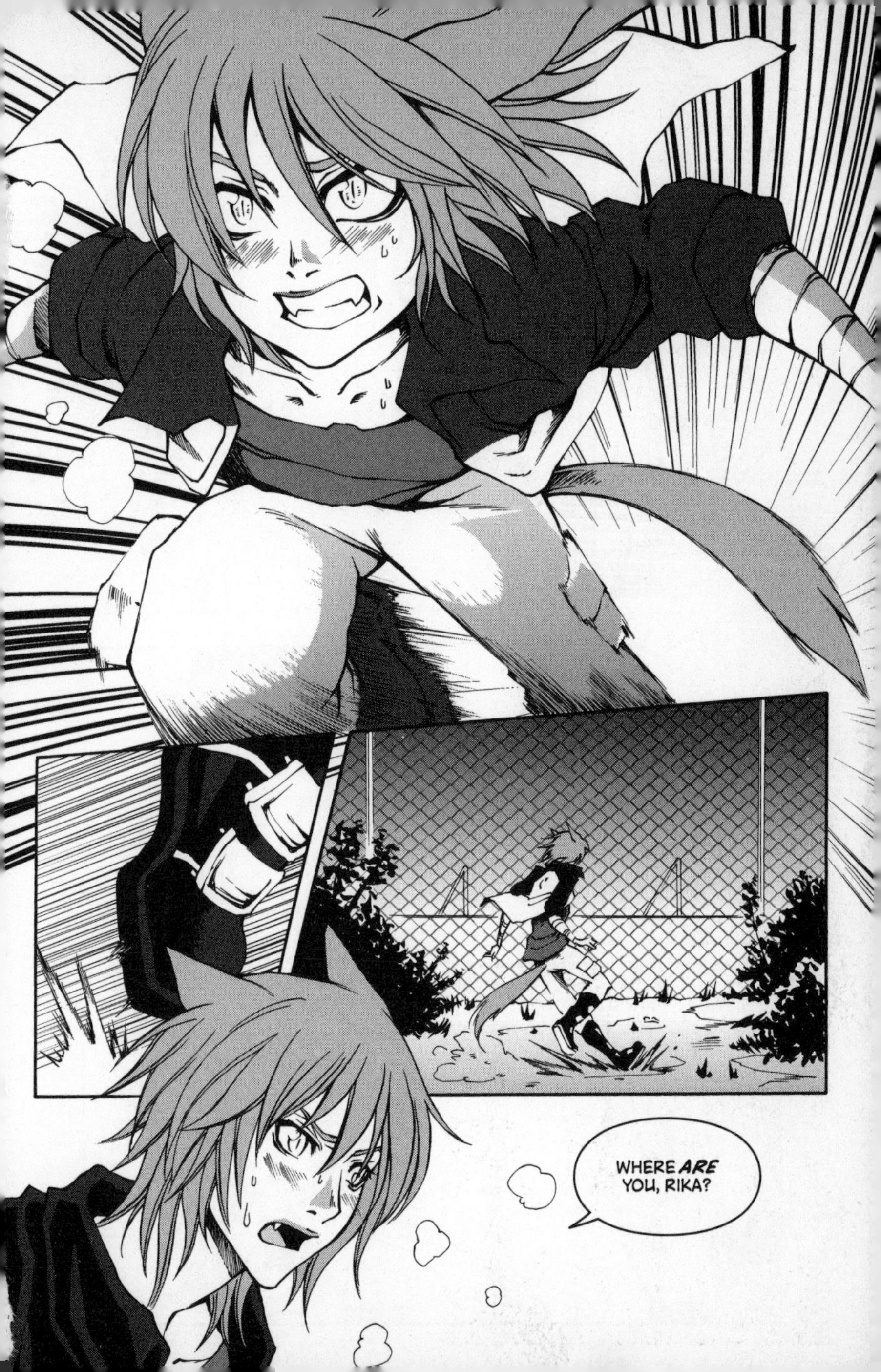
WHERE ARE YOU, RIKA?

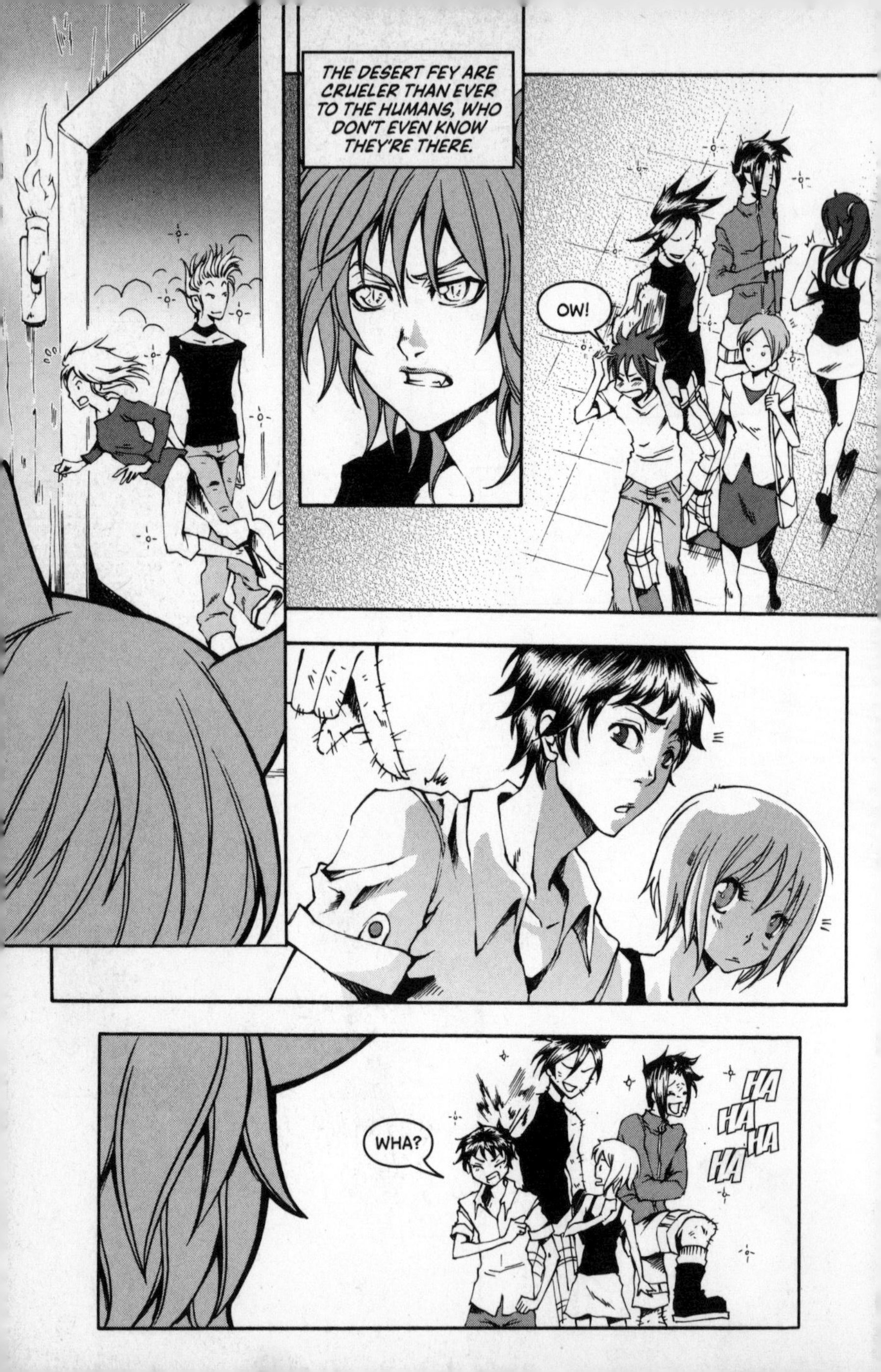
THE DESERT FEY ARE CRUELER THAN EVER TO THE HUMANS, WHO DON'T EVEN KNOW THEY'RE THERE.
OW!
WHA?
HA HA HA HA

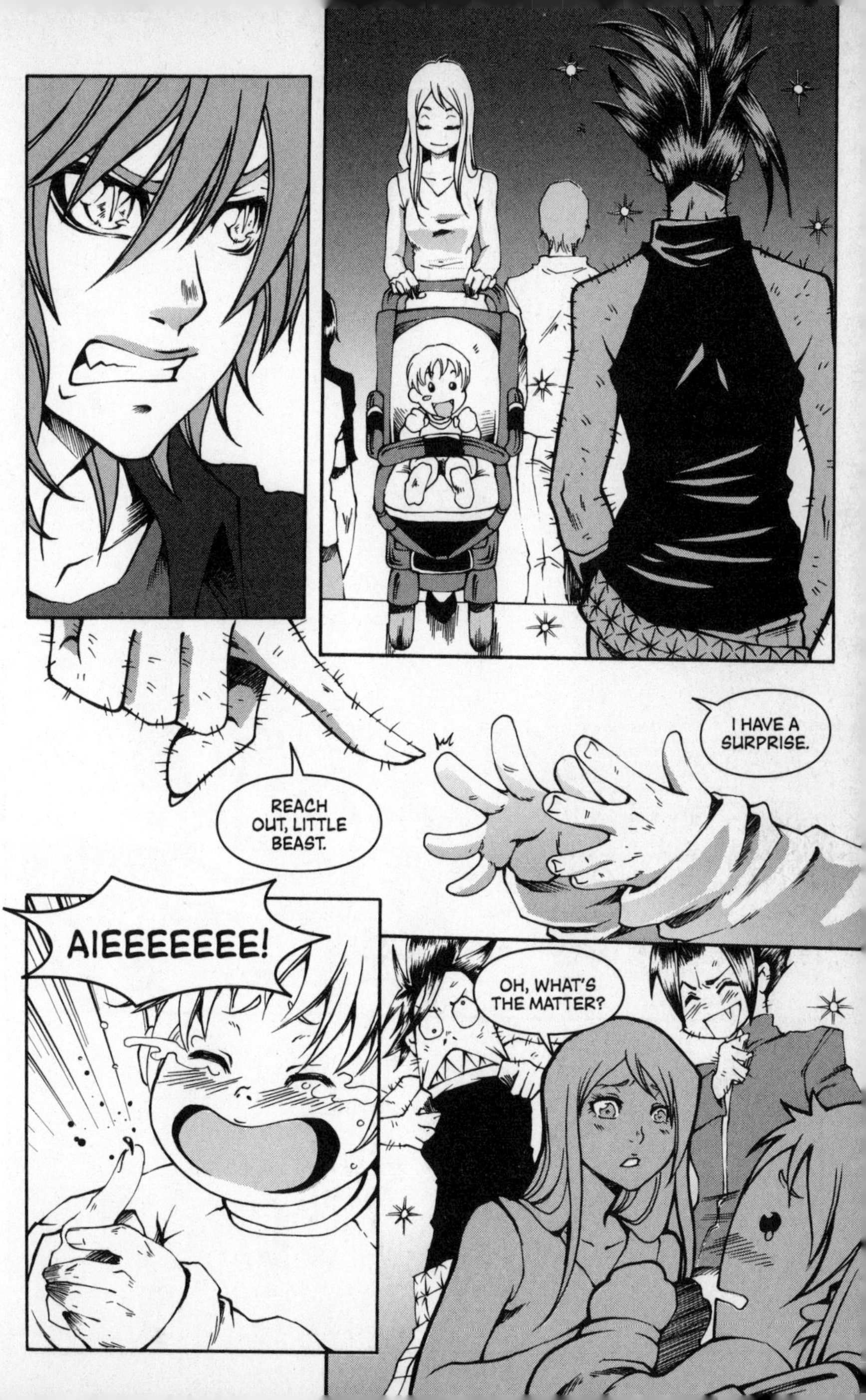
I HAVE A SURPRISE.
REACH OUT, LITTLE BEAST.
AIEEEEEEEE!
OH, WHAT'S THE MATTER?

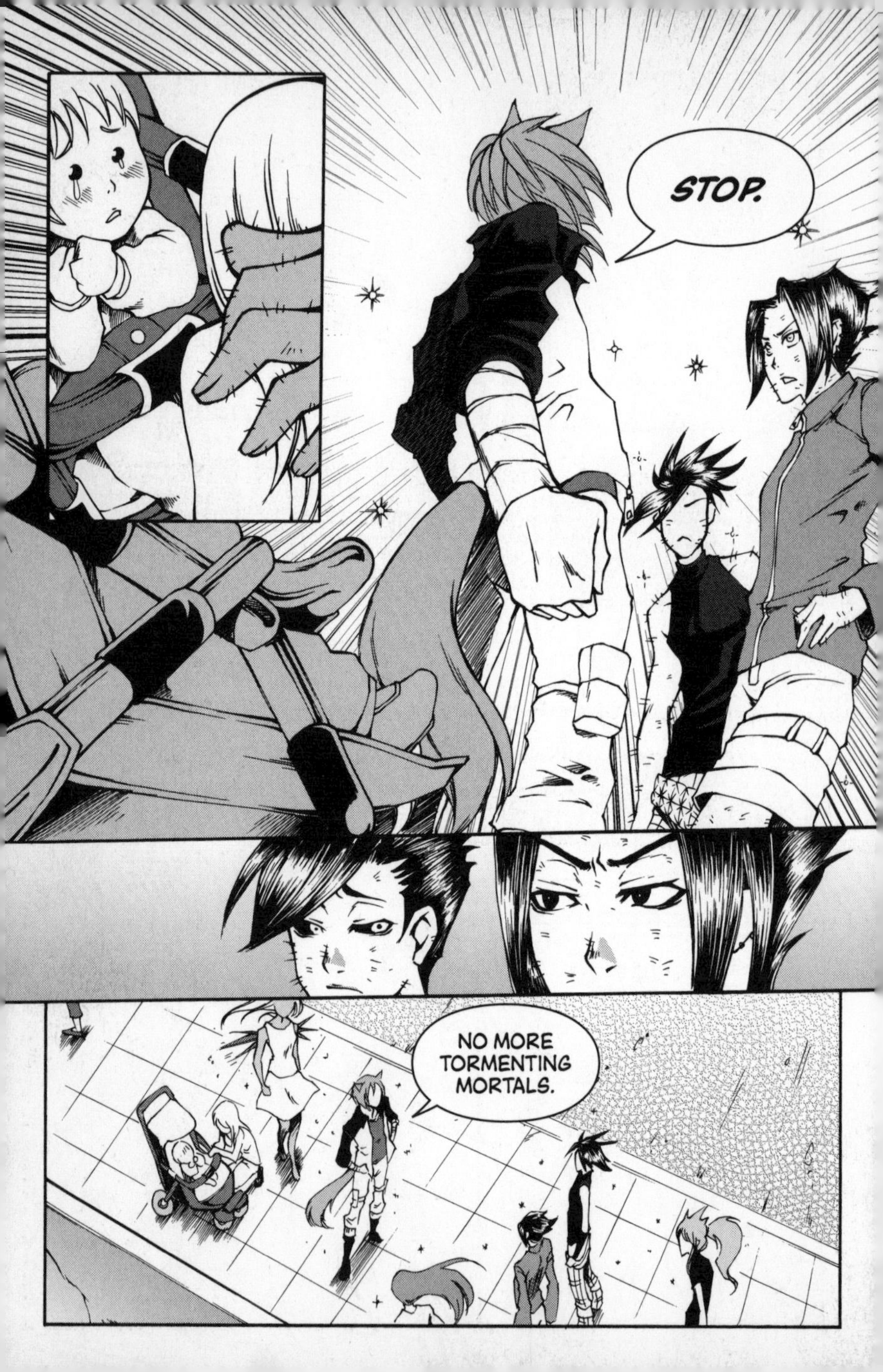
STOP.
NO MORE TORMENTING MORTALS.

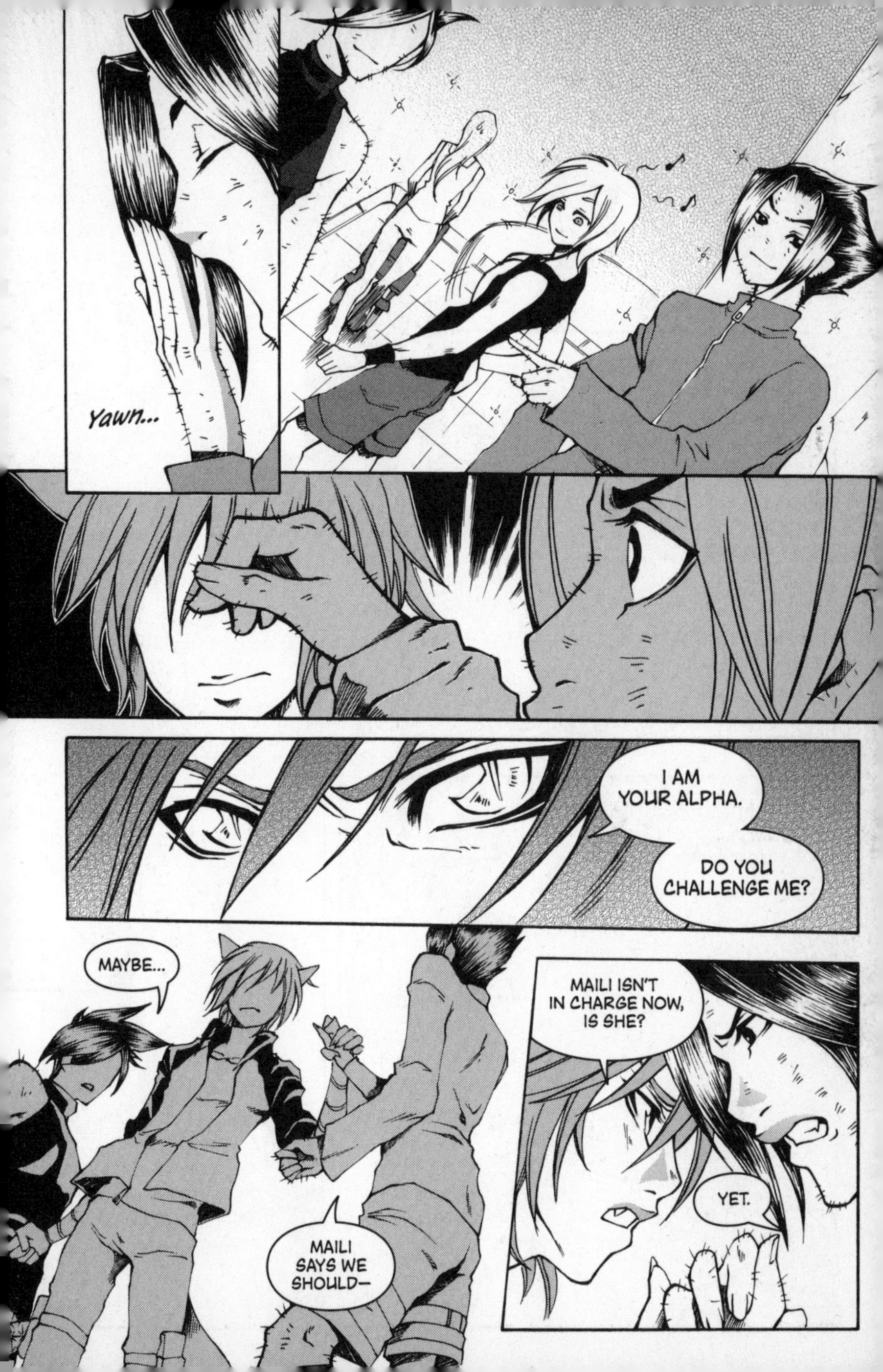
Yawn...
I AM YOUR ALPHA.
DO YOU CHALLENGE ME?
MAYBE...
MAILI SAYS WE SHOULD—
MAILI ISN'T IN CHARGE NOW, IS SHE?
YET.

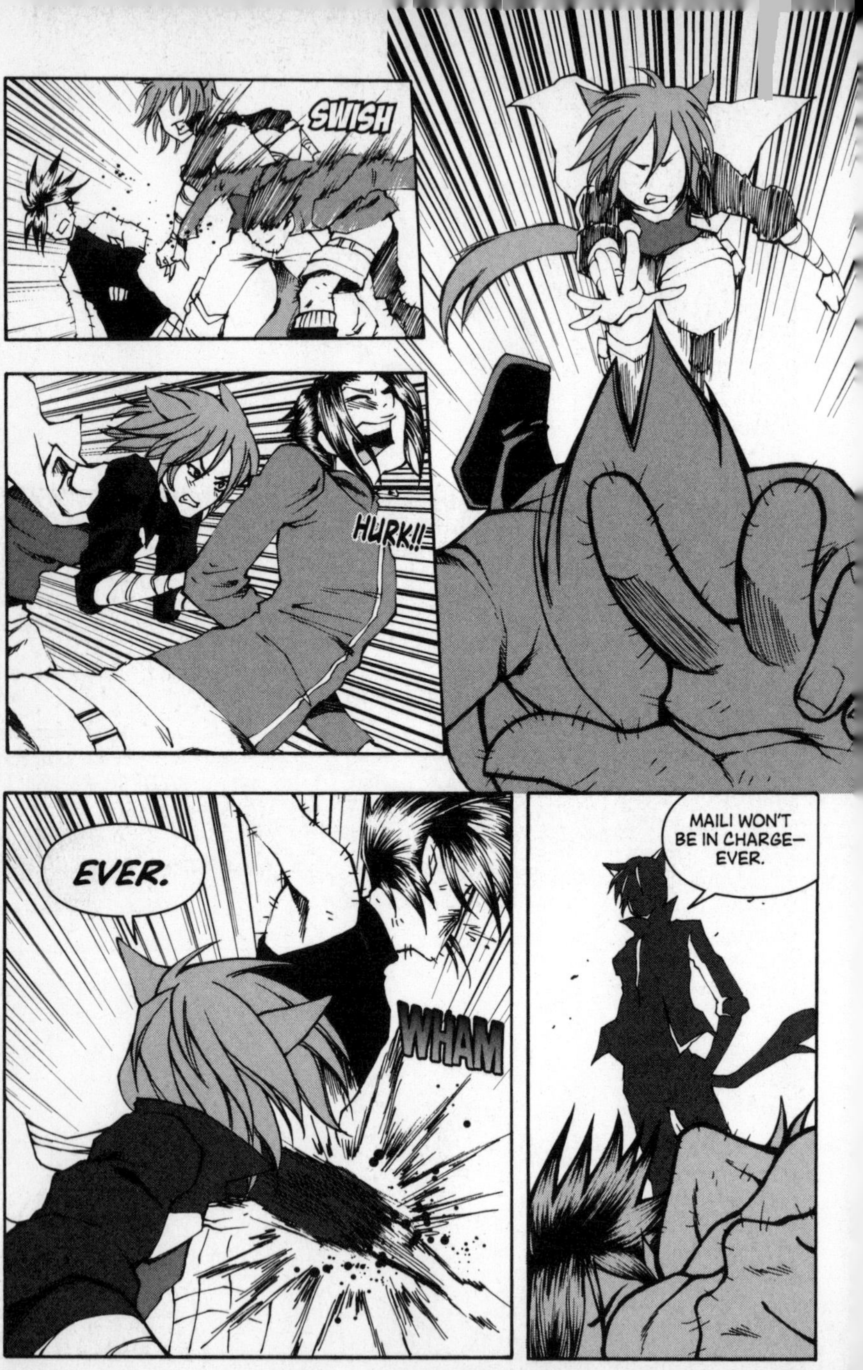
SWISH
HURK!!
EVER.
WHAM
MAILI WON'T BE IN CHARGE—EVER.

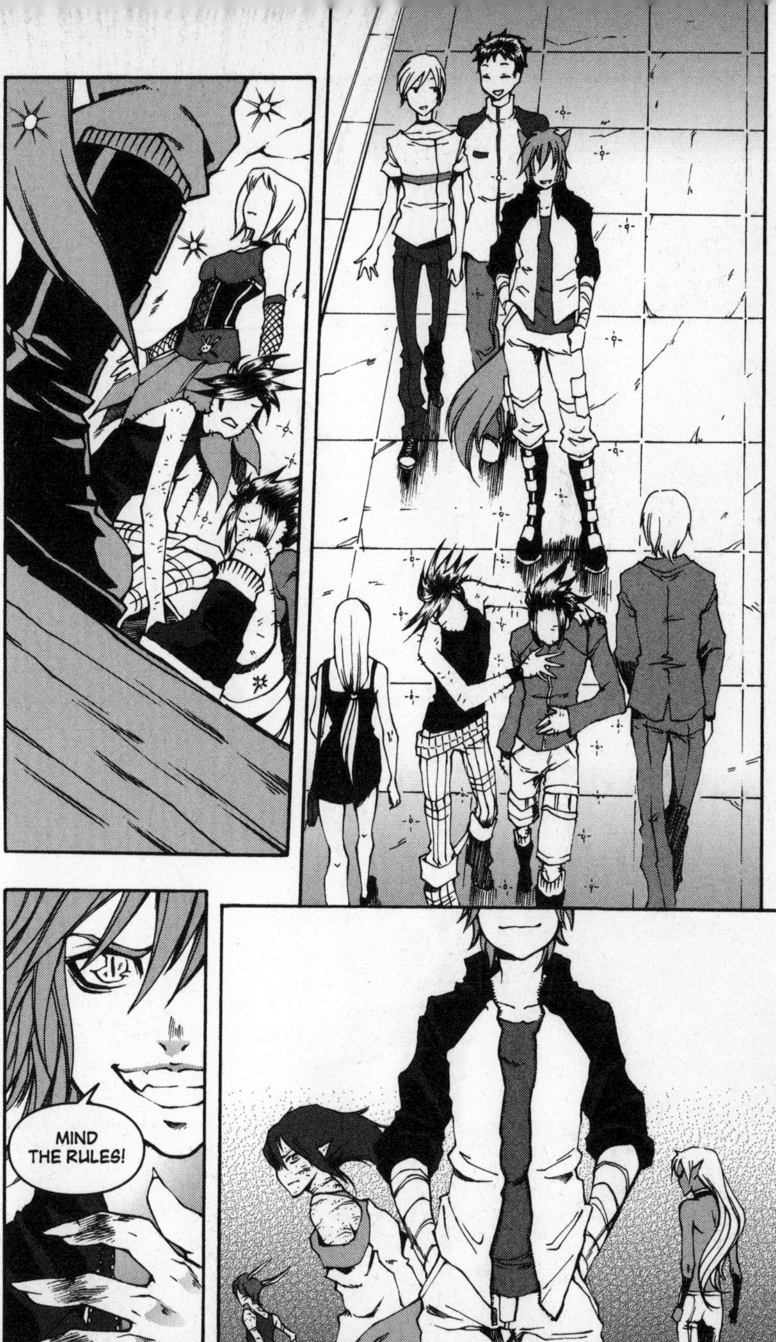
MIND THE RULES!

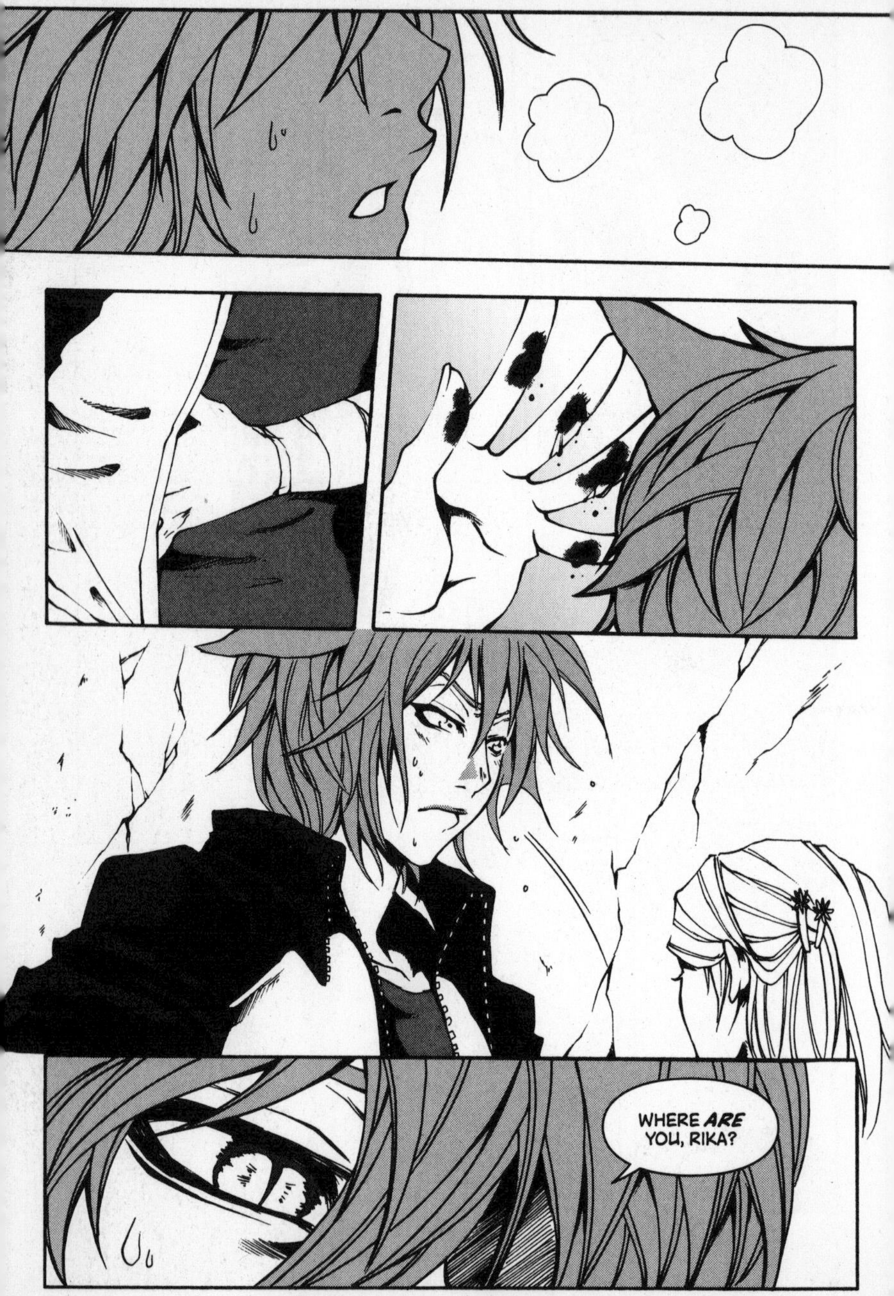
WHERE *ARE* YOU, RIKA?

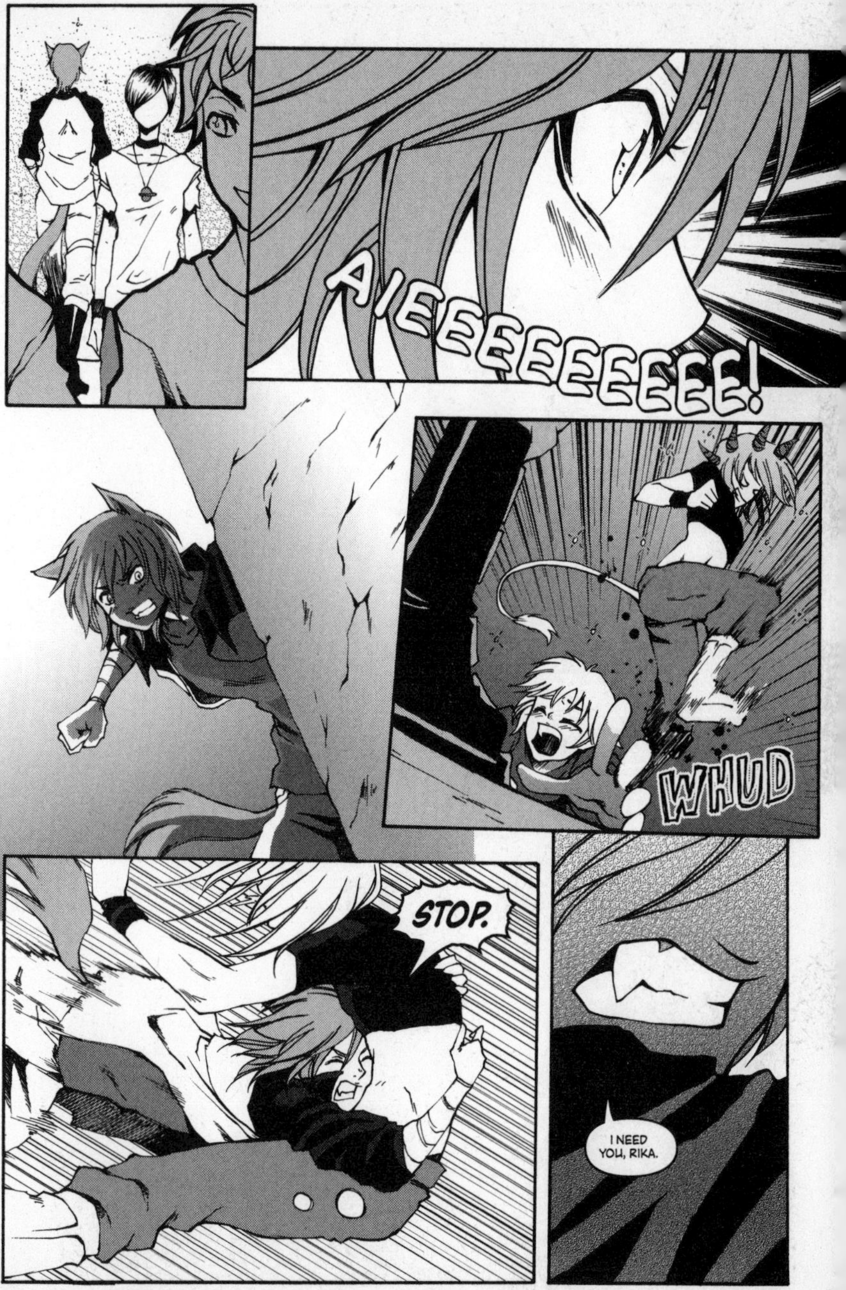
AIEEEEEEEEEEE!
WHUD
STOP.
I NEED YOU, RIKA.

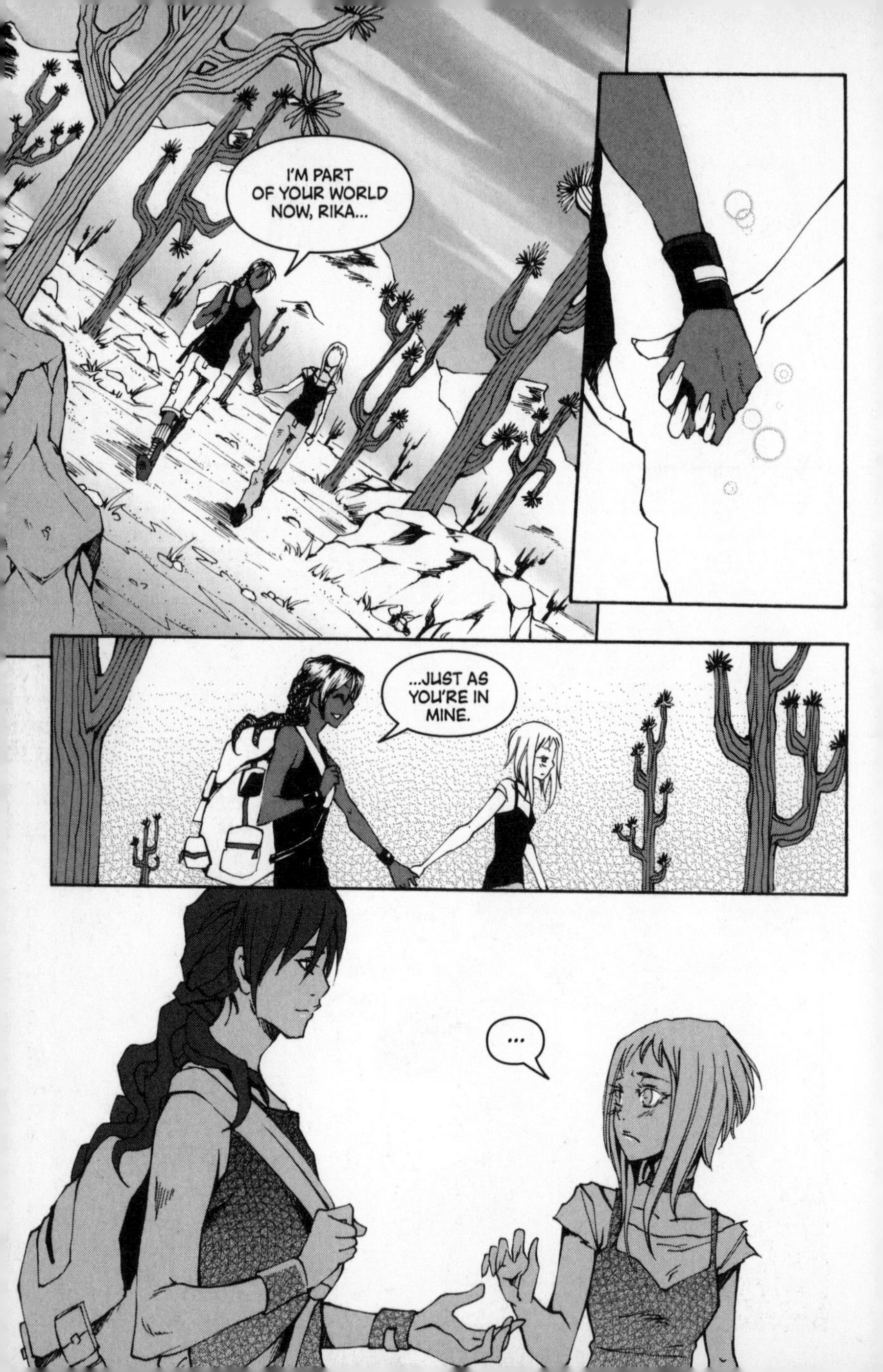
I'M PART OF YOUR WORLD NOW, RIKA...
...JUST AS YOU'RE IN MINE.
...

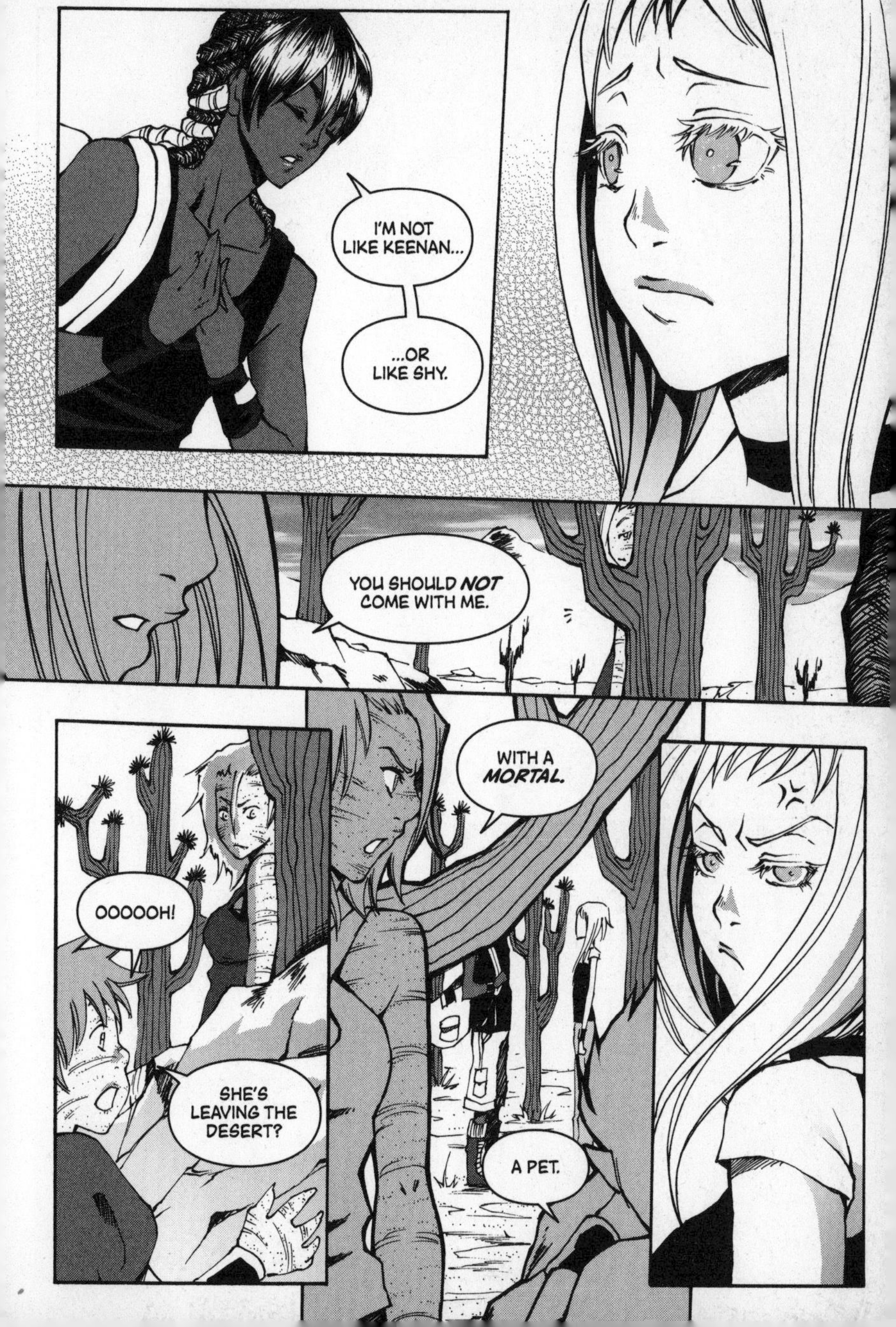
I'M NOT LIKE KEENAN...
...OR LIKE SHY.
YOU SHOULD *NOT* COME WITH ME.
OOOOOH!
SHE'S LEAVING THE DESERT?
WITH A *MORTAL.*
A PET.

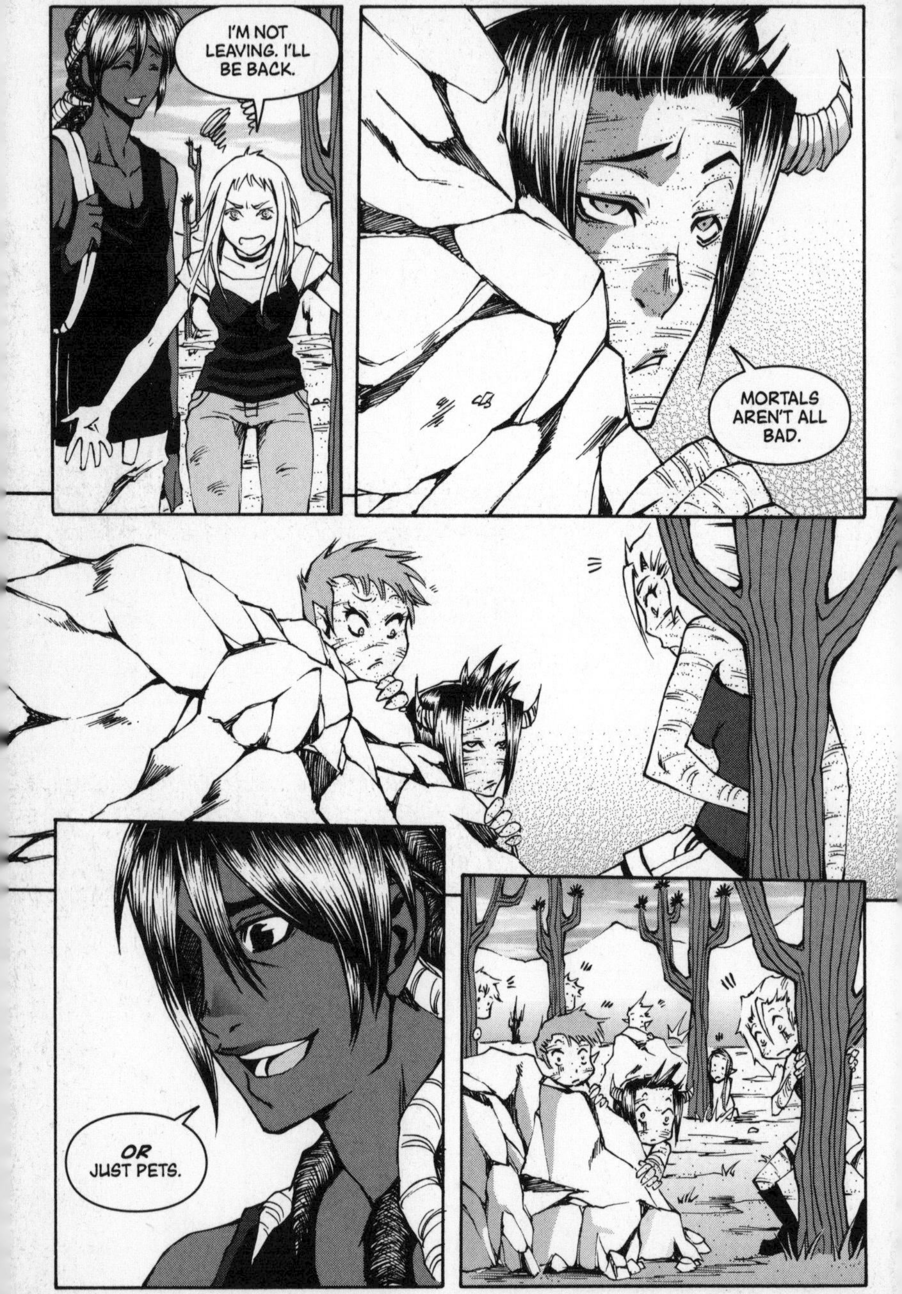
I'M NOT LEAVING. I'LL BE BACK.
MORTALS AREN'T ALL BAD.
OR JUST PETS.

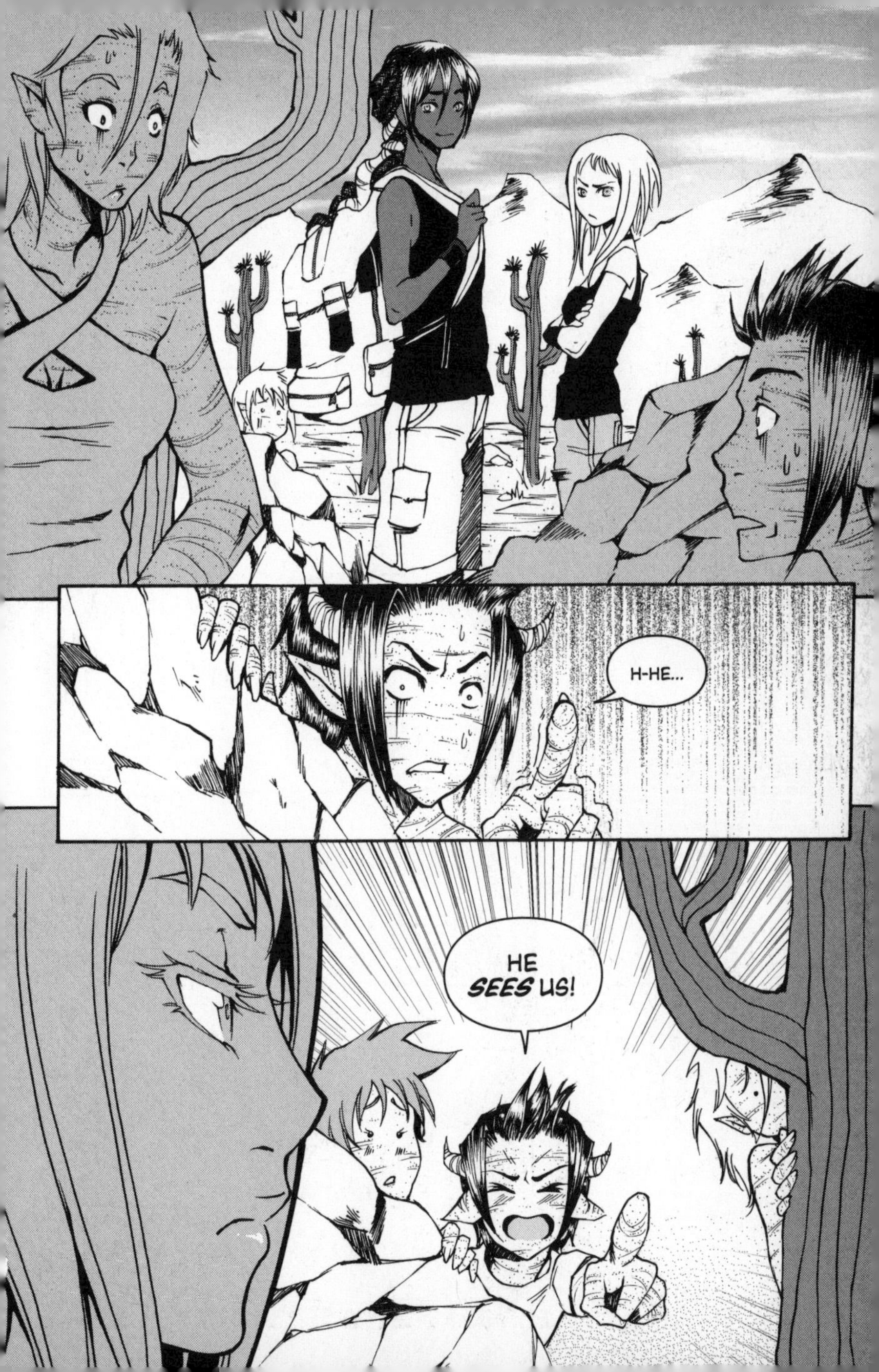
H-HE...
HE *SEES* US!

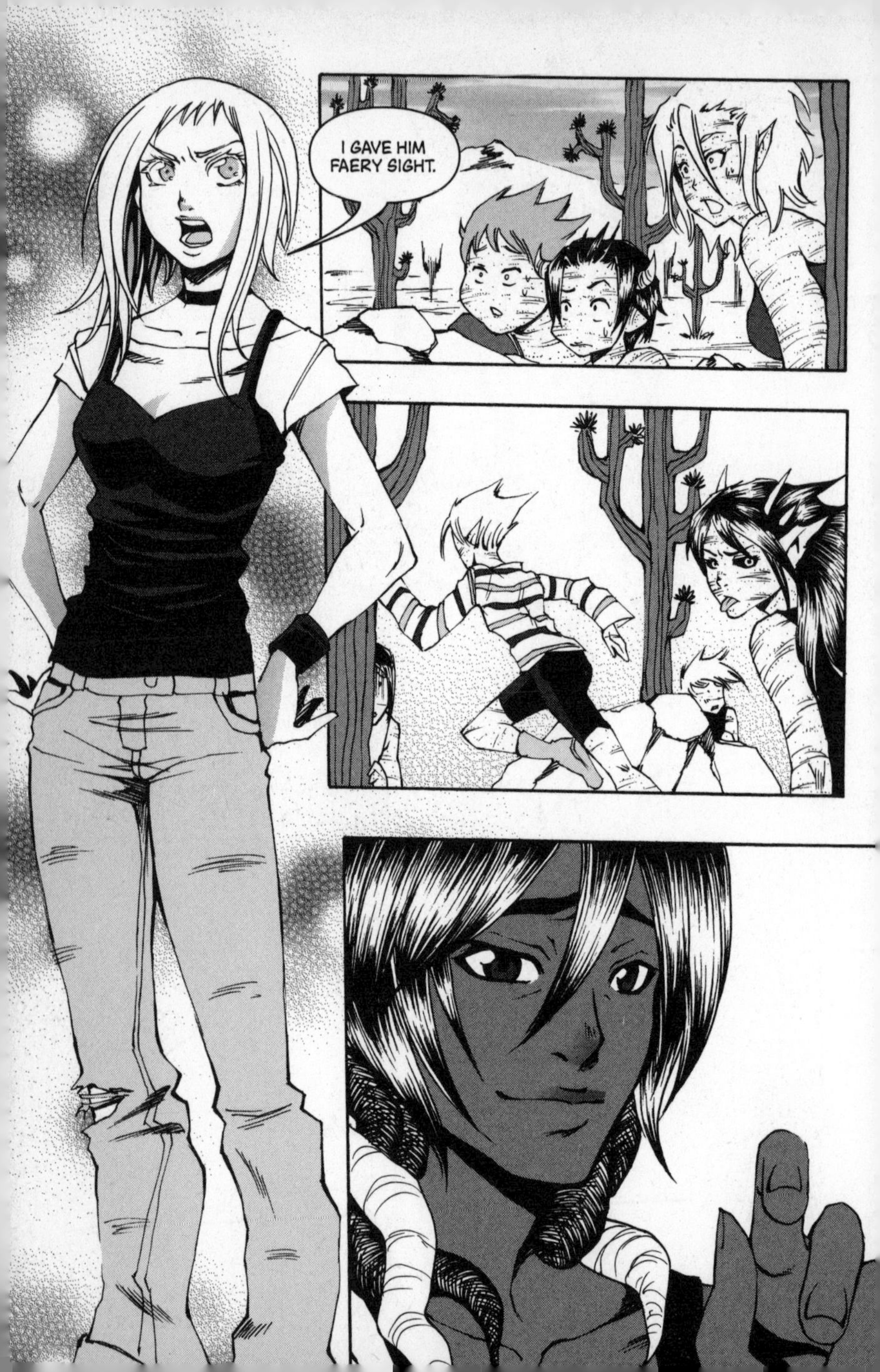
I GAVE HIM
FAERY SIGHT.

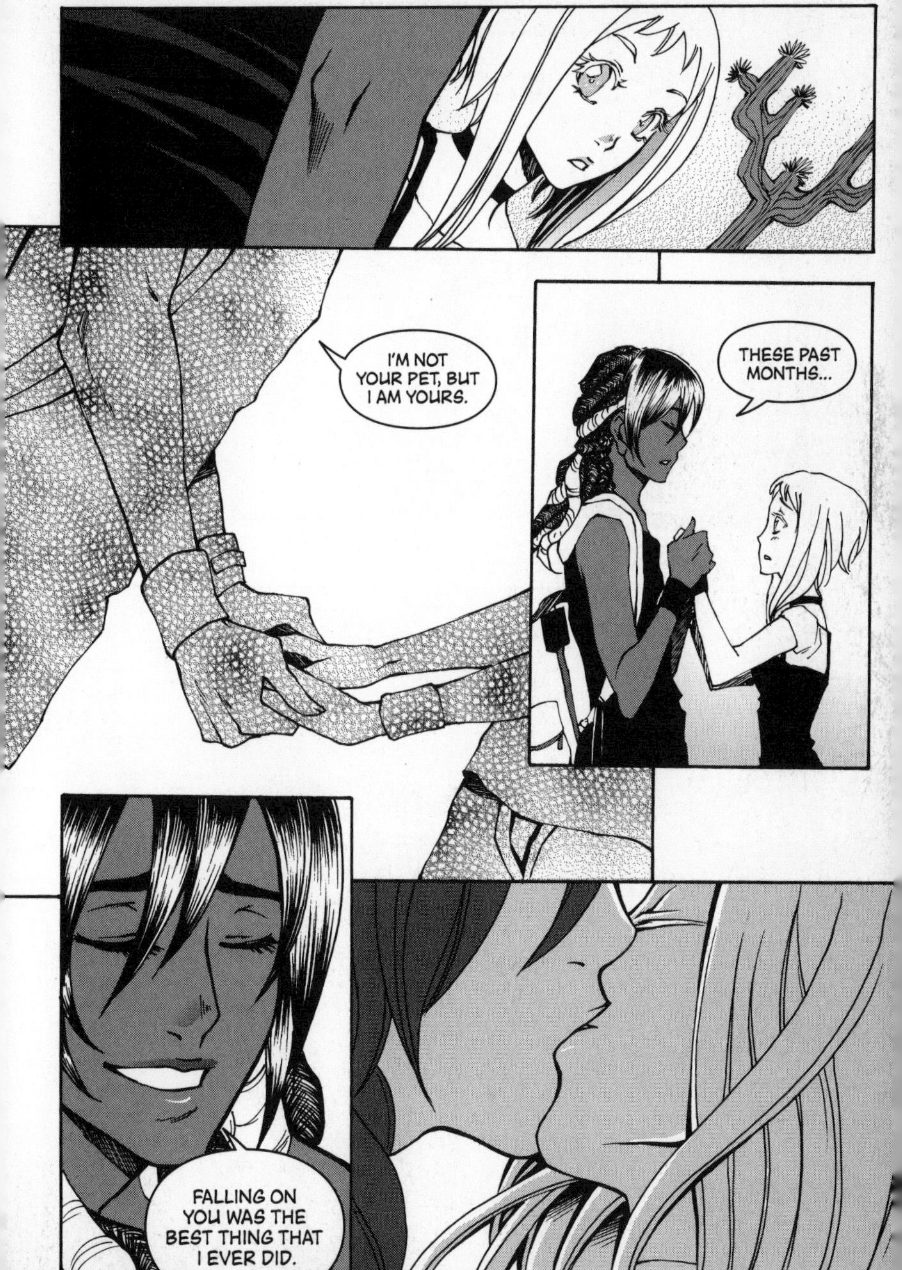
I'M NOT YOUR PET, BUT I AM YOURS.
THESE PAST MONTHS...
FALLING ON YOU WAS THE BEST THING THAT I EVER DID.

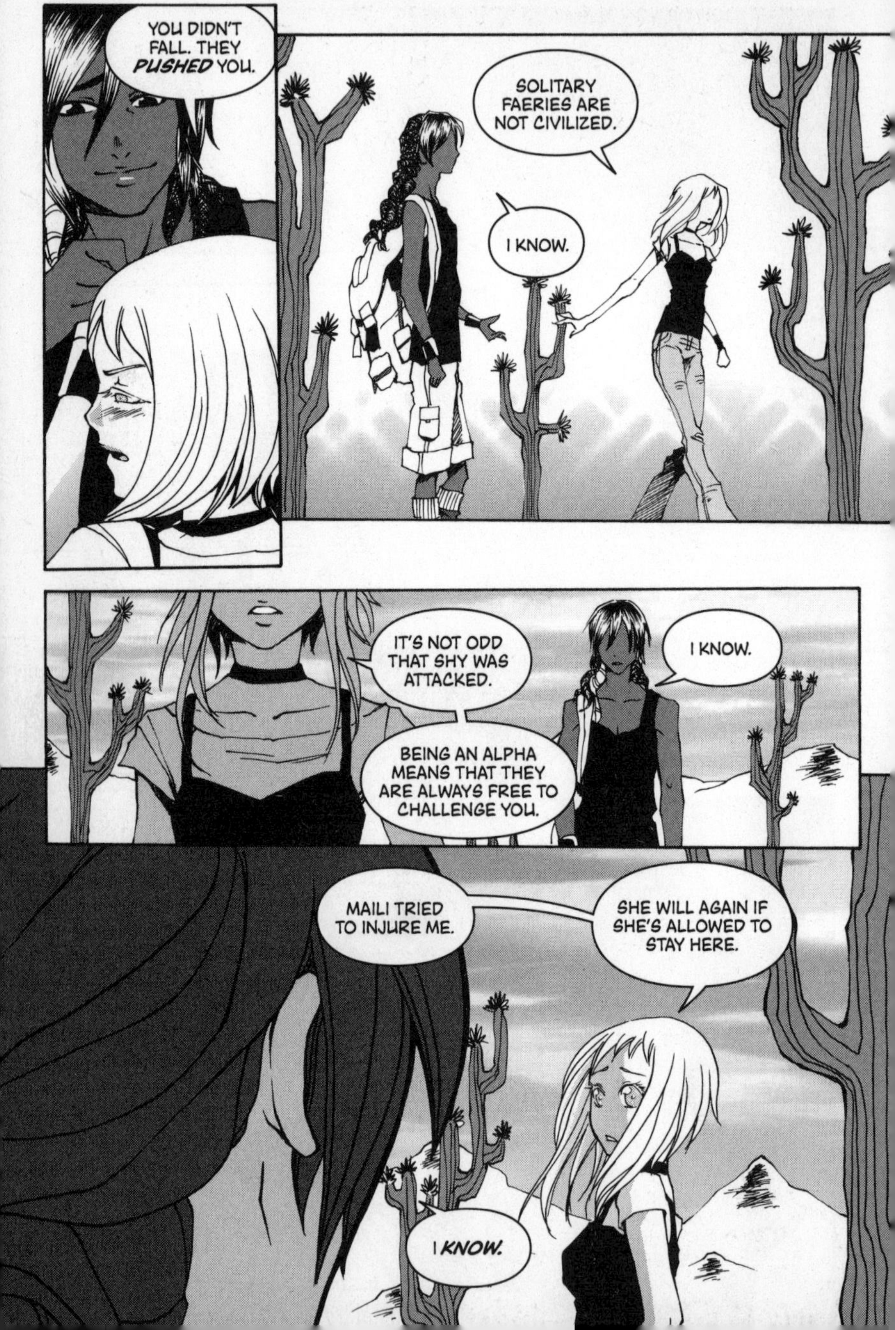
YOU DIDN'T FALL. THEY *PUSHED* YOU.
SOLITARY FAERIES ARE NOT CIVILIZED.
I KNOW.
IT'S NOT ODD THAT SHY WAS ATTACKED.
BEING AN ALPHA MEANS THAT THEY ARE ALWAYS FREE TO CHALLENGE YOU.
I KNOW.
MAILI TRIED TO INJURE ME.
SHE WILL AGAIN IF SHE'S ALLOWED TO STAY HERE.
I *KNOW.*

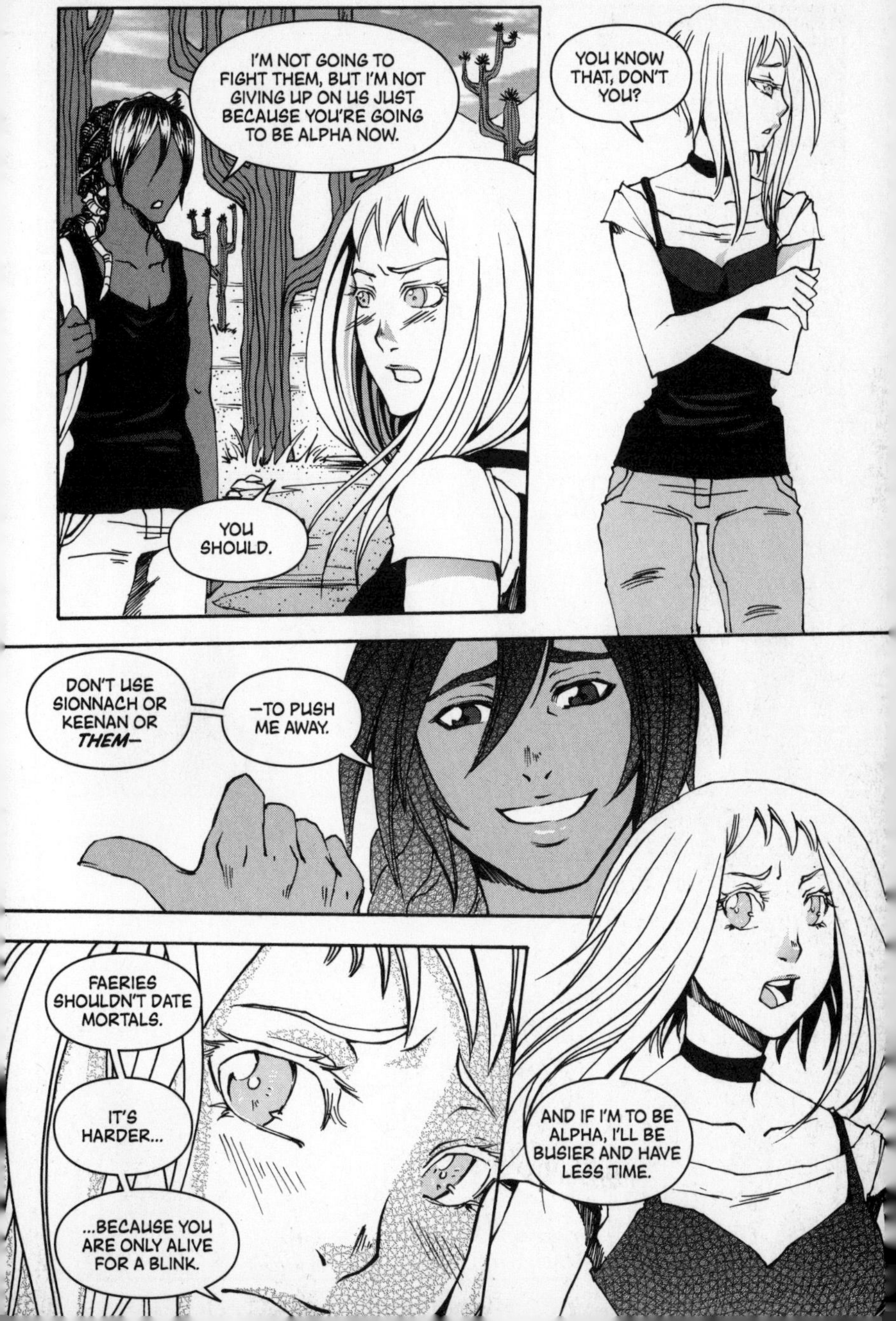
I'M NOT GOING TO FIGHT THEM, BUT I'M NOT GIVING UP ON US JUST BECAUSE YOU'RE GOING TO BE ALPHA NOW.
YOU SHOULD.
YOU KNOW THAT, DON'T YOU?
DON'T USE SIONNACH OR KEENAN OR *THEM*—
—TO PUSH ME AWAY.
FAERIES SHOULDN'T DATE MORTALS.
IT'S HARDER...
...BECAUSE YOU ARE ONLY ALIVE FOR A BLINK.
AND IF I'M TO BE ALPHA, I'LL BE BUSIER AND HAVE LESS TIME.

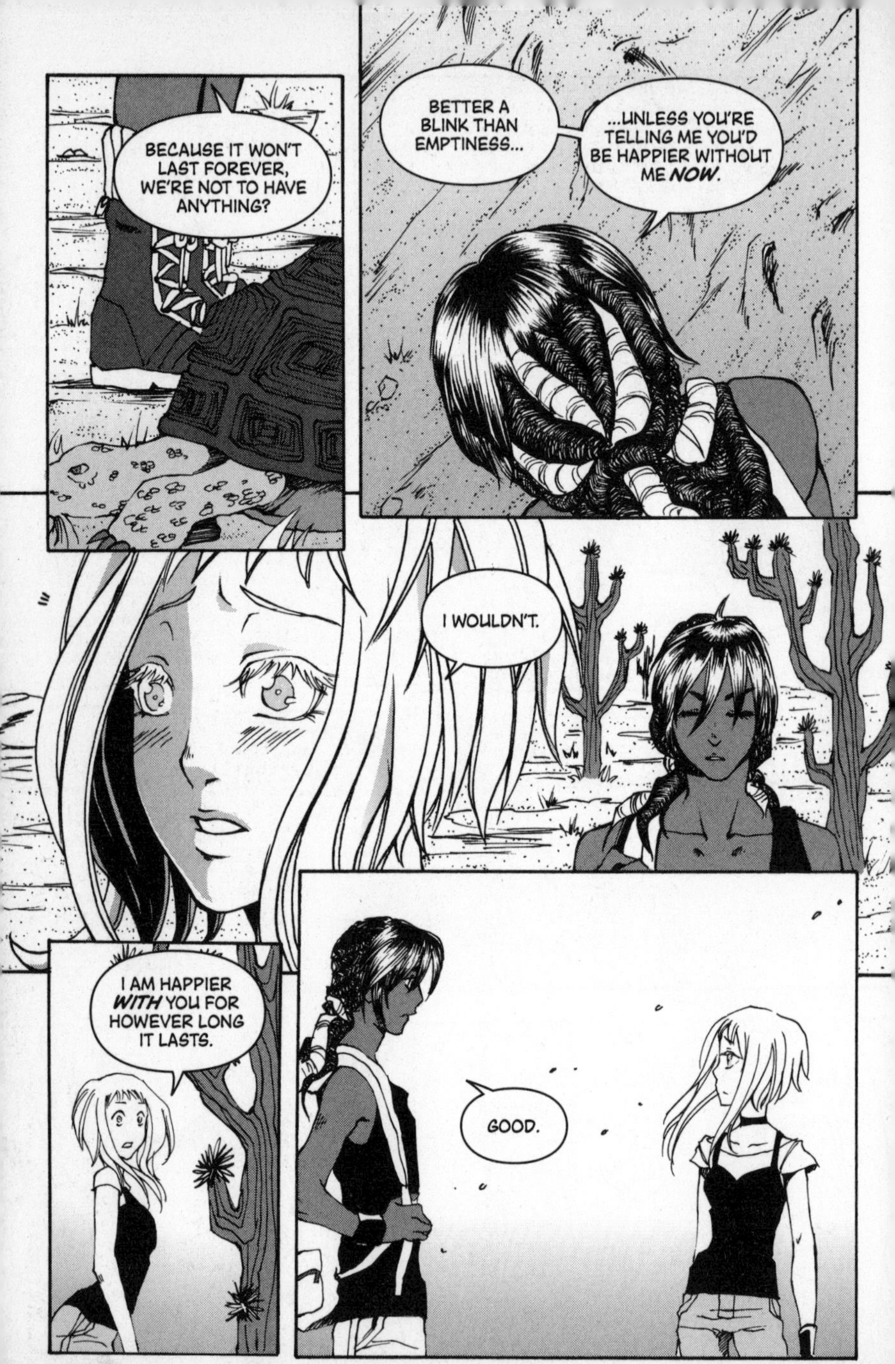
BECAUSE IT WON'T LAST FOREVER, WE'RE NOT TO HAVE ANYTHING?
BETTER A BLINK THAN EMPTINESS...
...UNLESS YOU'RE TELLING ME YOU'D BE HAPPIER WITHOUT ME *NOW*.
I WOULDN'T.
I AM HAPPIER *WITH* YOU FOR HOWEVER LONG IT LASTS.
GOOD.

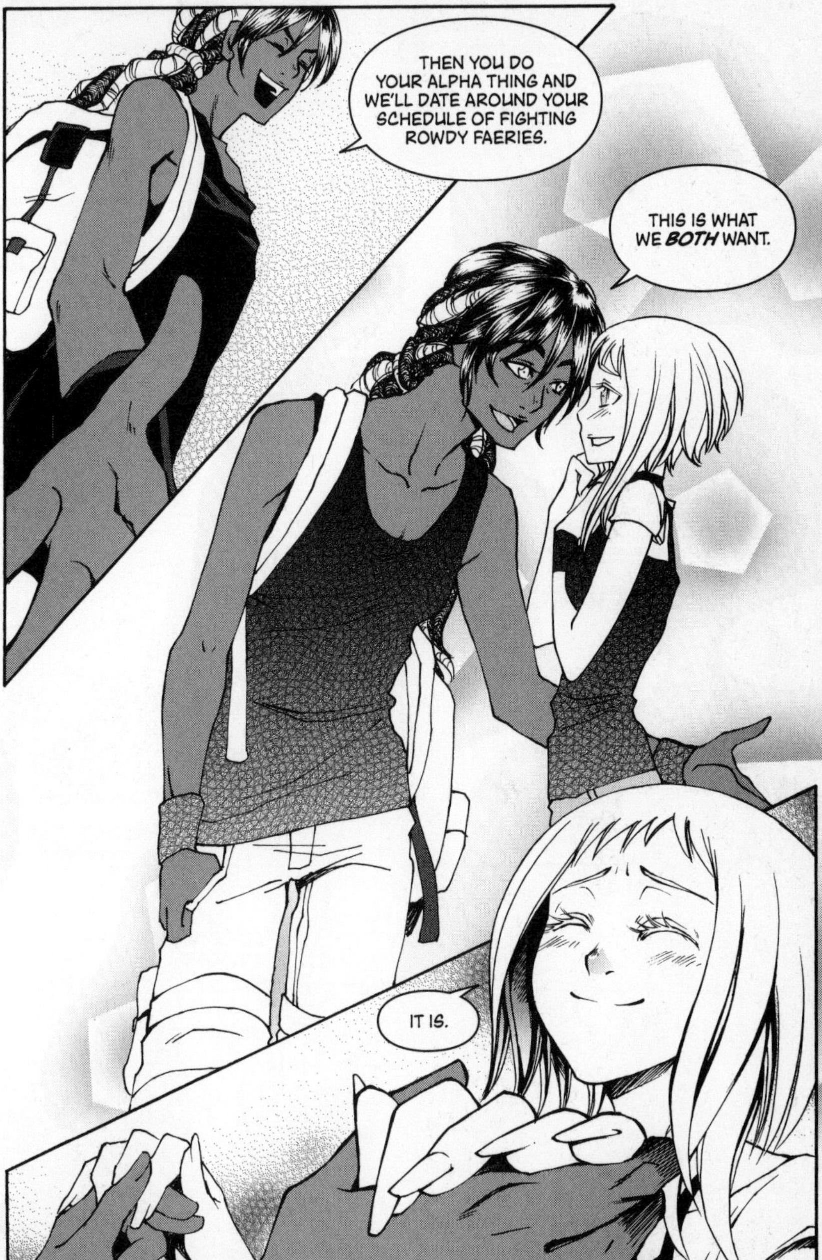
THEN YOU DO YOUR ALPHA THING AND WE'LL DATE AROUND YOUR SCHEDULE OF FIGHTING ROWDY FAERIES.
THIS IS WHAT WE *BOTH* WANT.
IT IS.

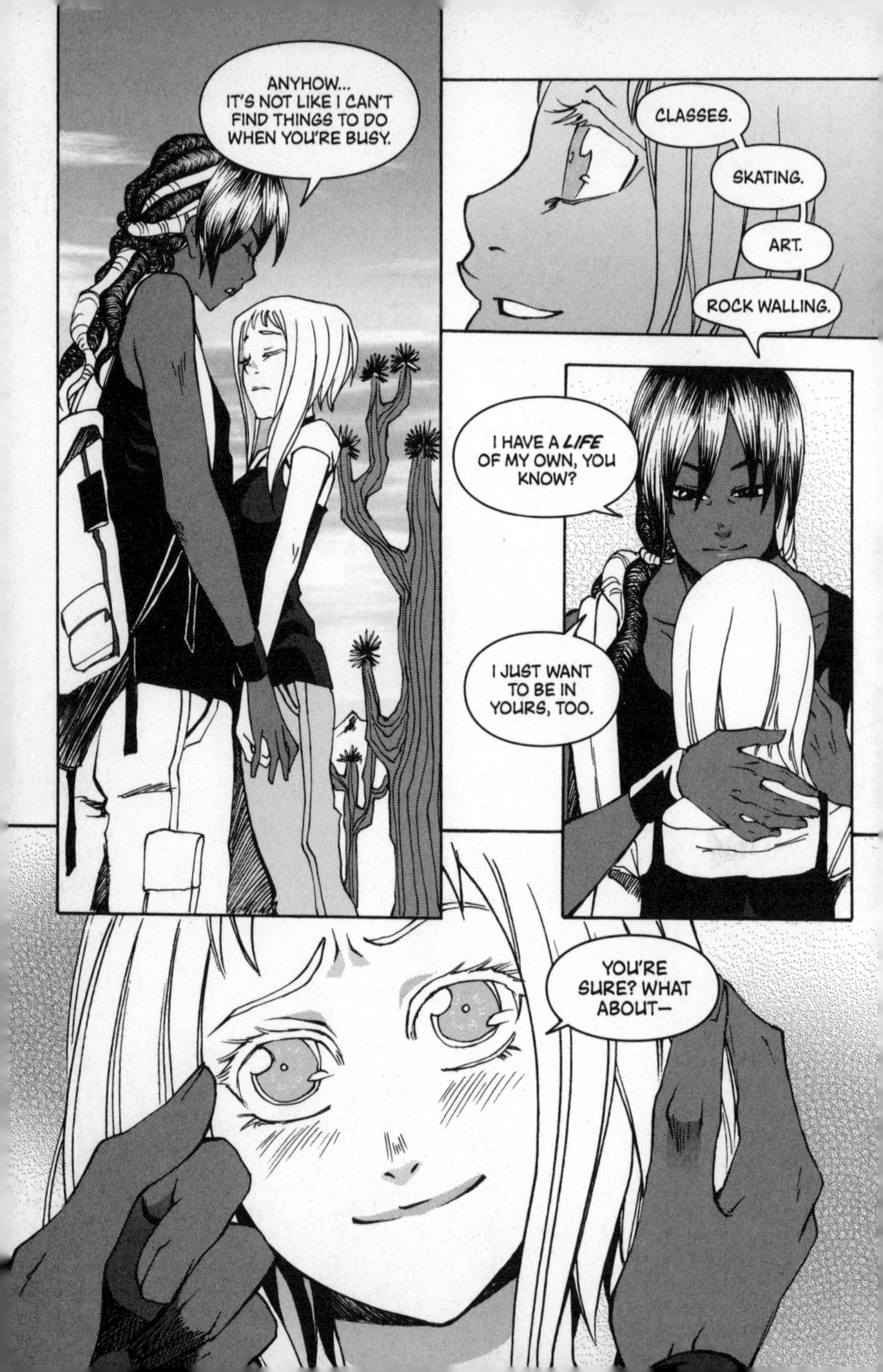
ANYHOW... IT'S NOT LIKE I CAN'T FIND THINGS TO DO WHEN YOU'RE BUSY.
CLASSES.
SKATING.
ART.
ROCK WALLING.
I HAVE A *LIFE* OF MY OWN, YOU KNOW?
I JUST WANT TO BE IN YOURS, TOO.
YOU'RE SURE? WHAT ABOUT–

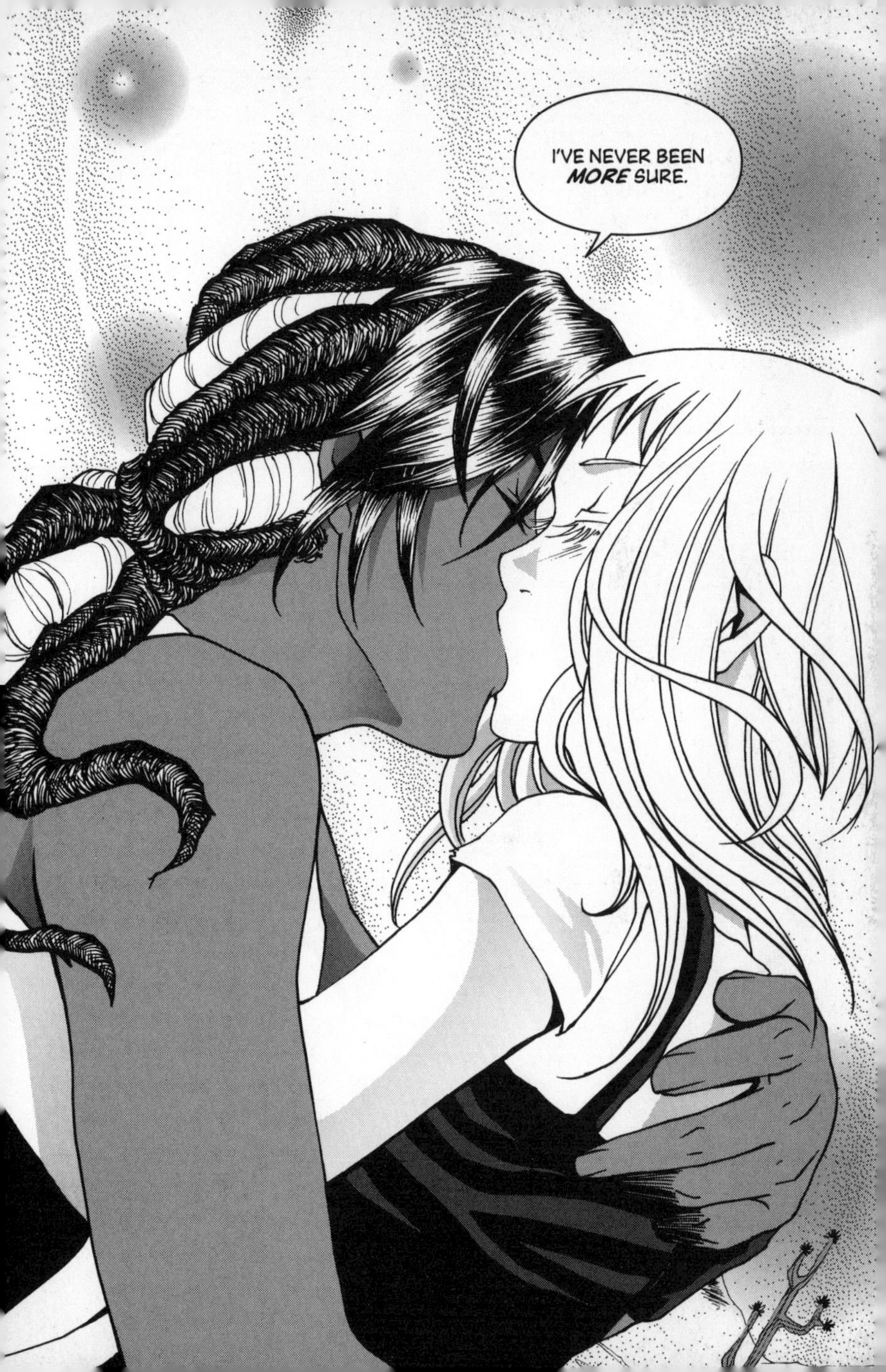
I'VE NEVER BEEN *MORE* SURE.

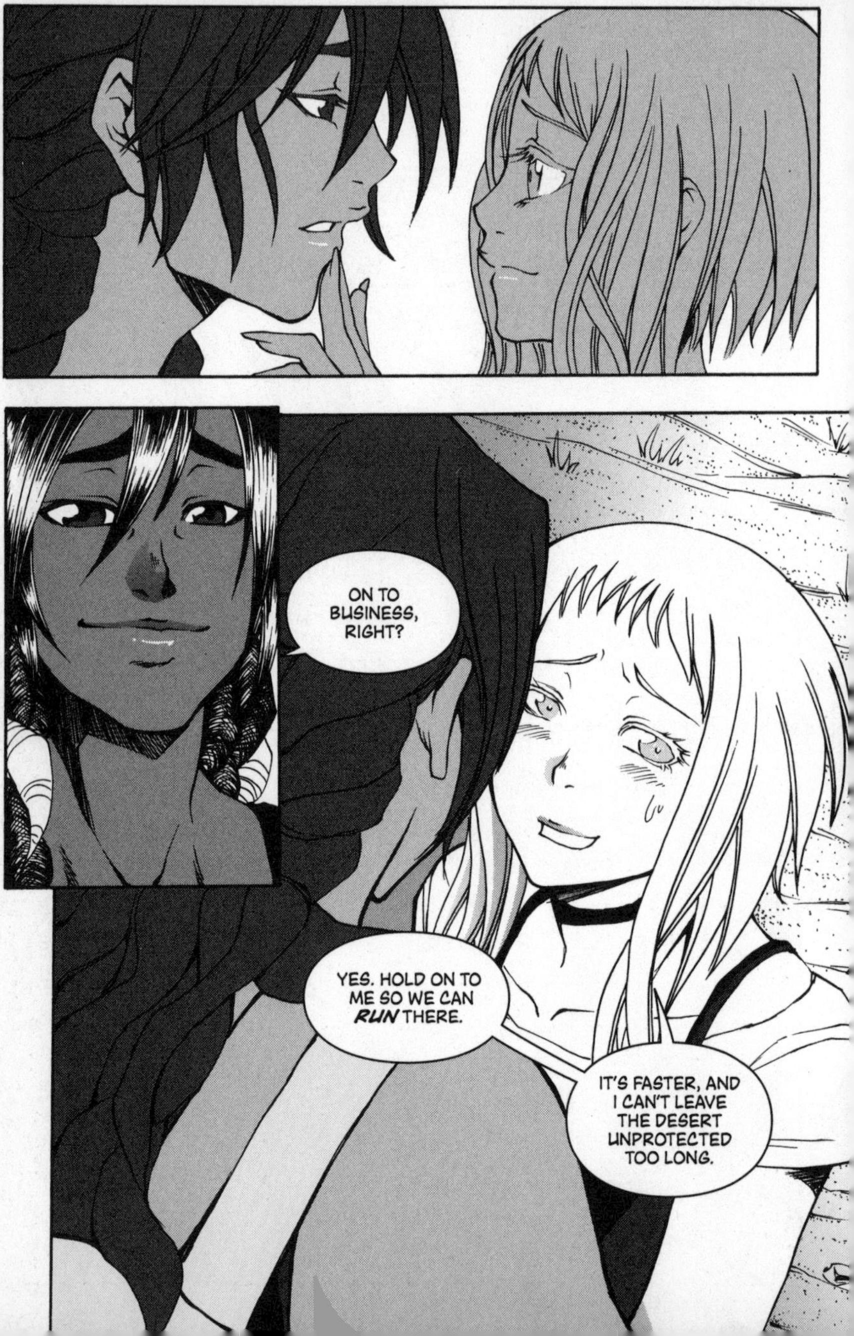
ON TO BUSINESS, RIGHT?
YES. HOLD ON TO ME SO WE CAN *RUN* THERE.
IT'S FASTER, AND I CAN'T LEAVE THE DESERT UNPROTECTED TOO LONG.

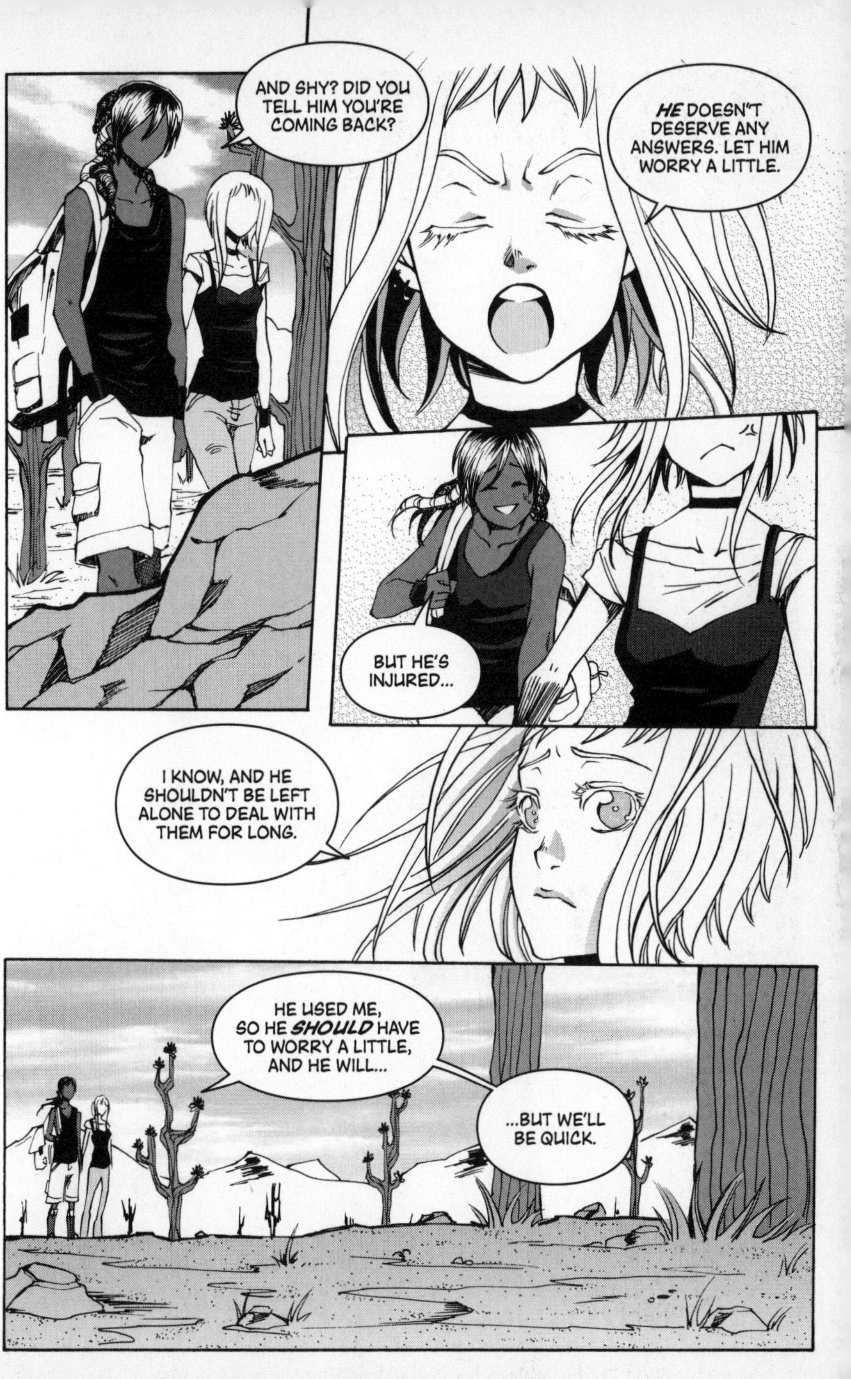
AND SHY? DID YOU TELL HIM YOU'RE COMING BACK?
HE DOESN'T DESERVE ANY ANSWERS. LET HIM WORRY A LITTLE.
BUT HE'S INJURED...
I KNOW, AND HE SHOULDN'T BE LEFT ALONE TO DEAL WITH THEM FOR LONG.
HE USED ME, SO HE SHOULD HAVE TO WORRY A LITTLE, AND HE WILL...
...BUT WE'LL BE QUICK.

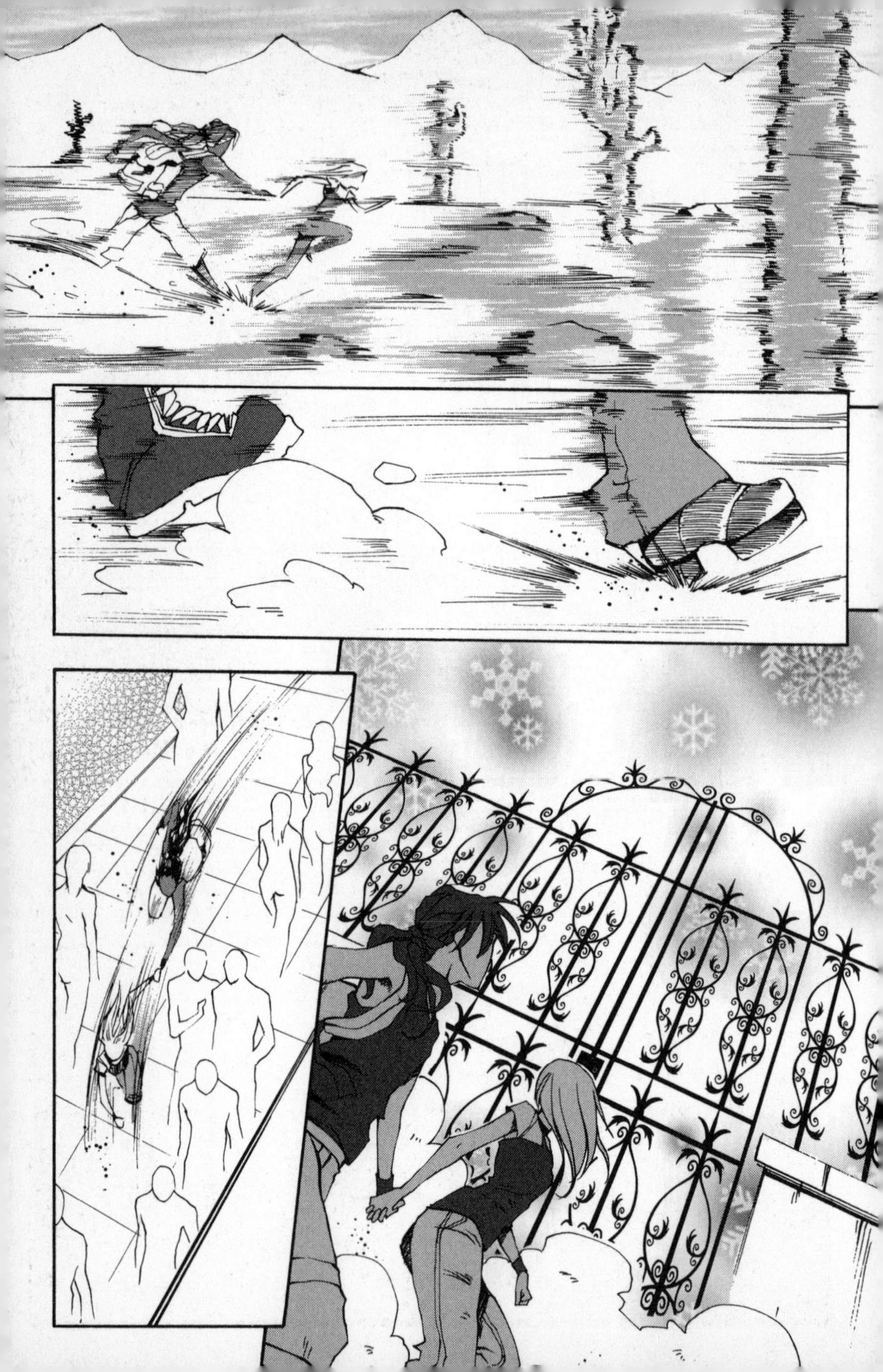

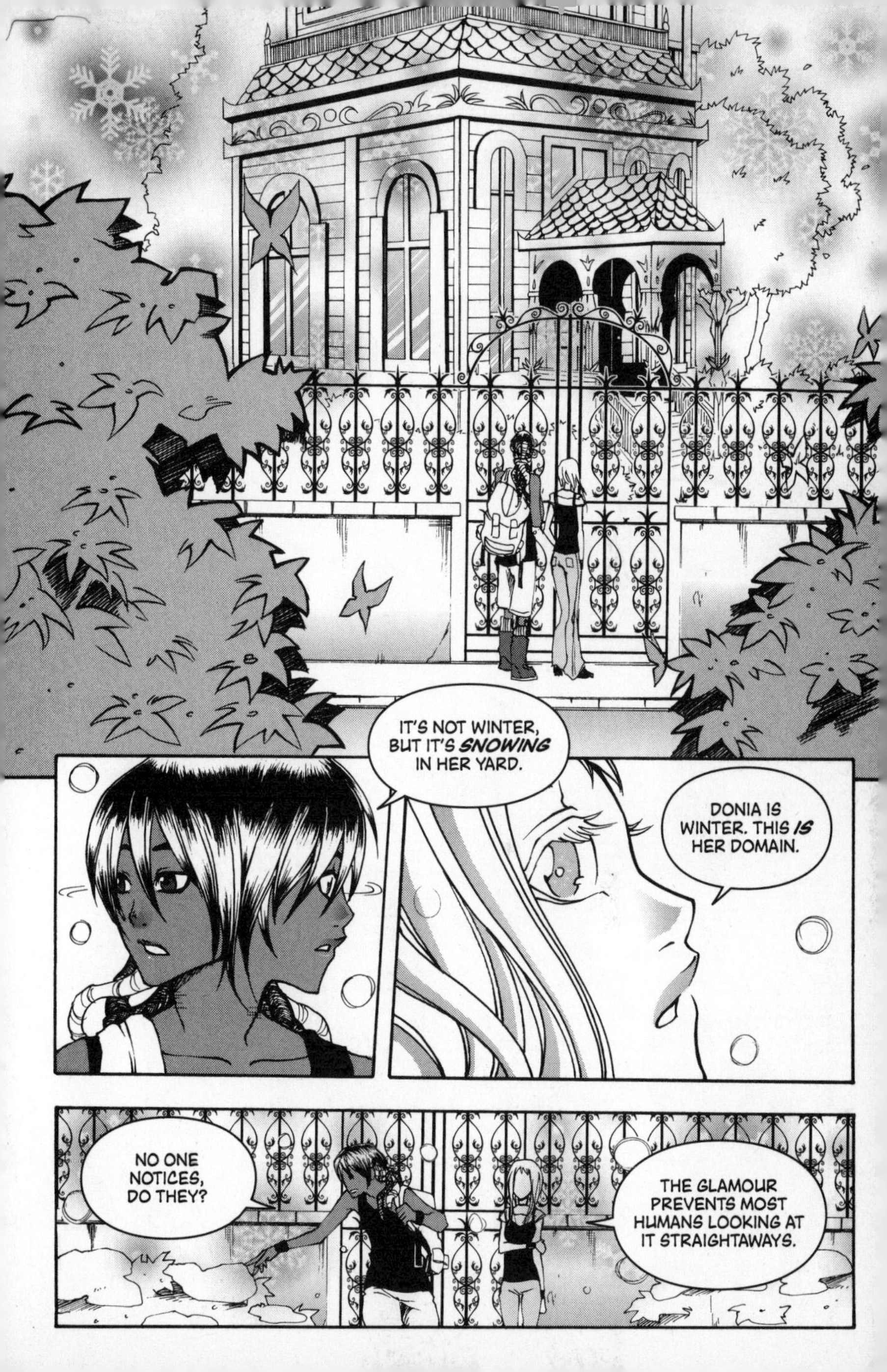
IT'S NOT WINTER, BUT IT'S *SNOWING* IN HER YARD.
DONIA IS WINTER. THIS *IS* HER DOMAIN.
NO ONE NOTICES, DO THEY?
THE GLAMOUR PREVENTS MOST HUMANS LOOKING AT IT STRAIGHTAWAYS.

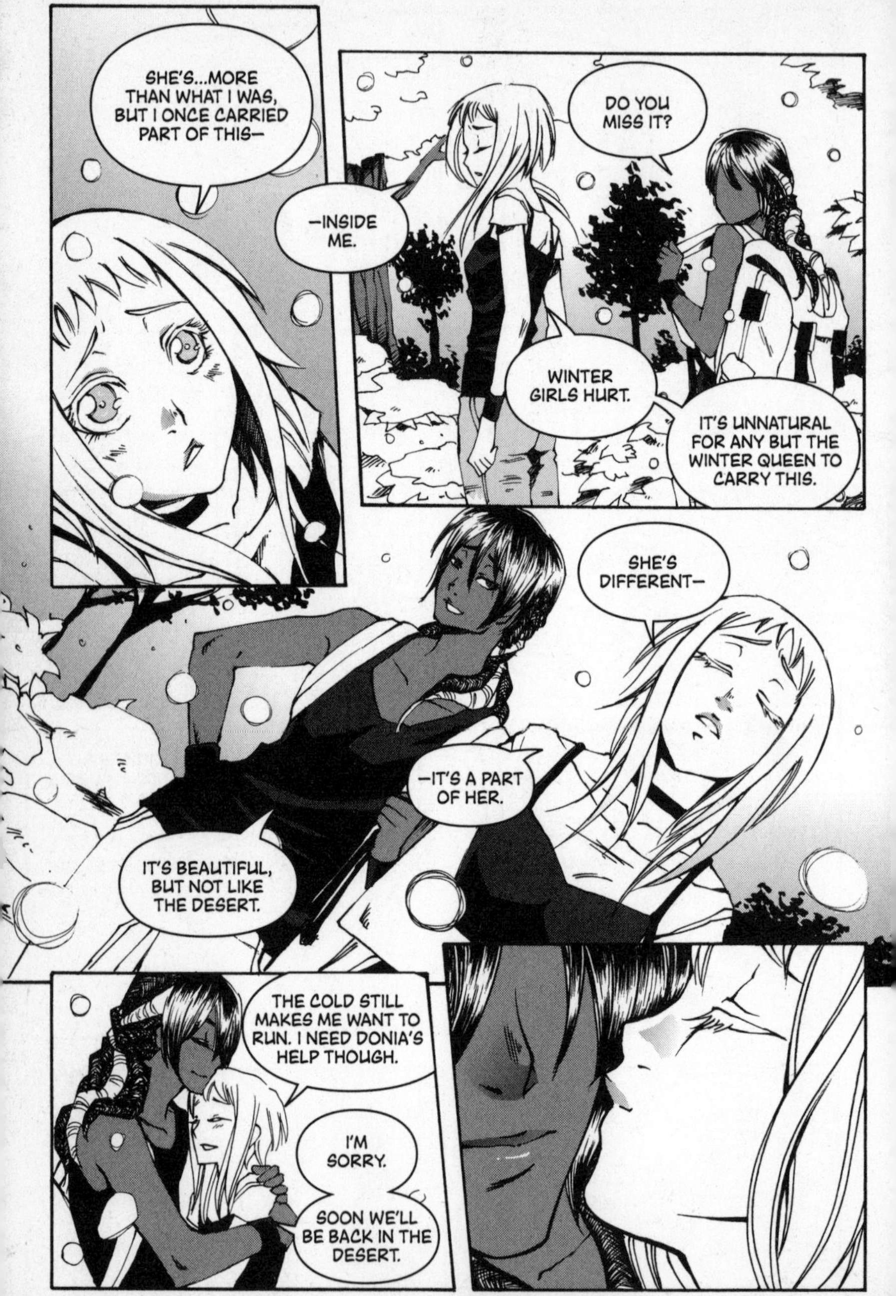
SHE'S...MORE THAN WHAT I WAS, BUT I ONCE CARRIED PART OF THIS—
—INSIDE ME.
DO YOU MISS IT?
WINTER GIRLS HURT.
IT'S UNNATURAL FOR ANY BUT THE WINTER QUEEN TO CARRY THIS.
SHE'S DIFFERENT—
—IT'S A PART OF HER.
IT'S BEAUTIFUL, BUT NOT LIKE THE DESERT.
THE COLD STILL MAKES ME WANT TO RUN. I NEED DONIA'S HELP THOUGH.
I'M SORRY.
SOON WE'LL BE BACK IN THE DESERT.

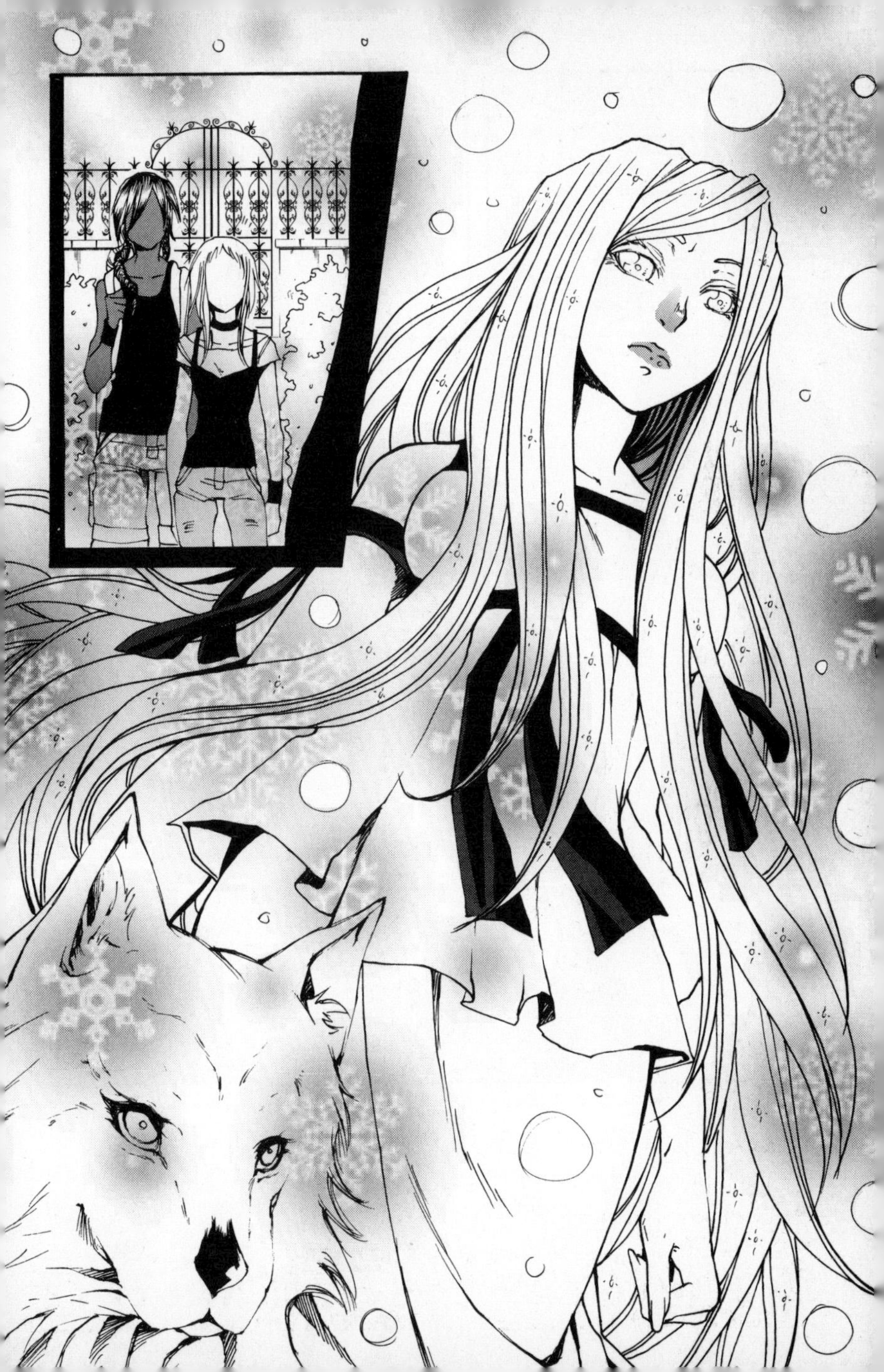

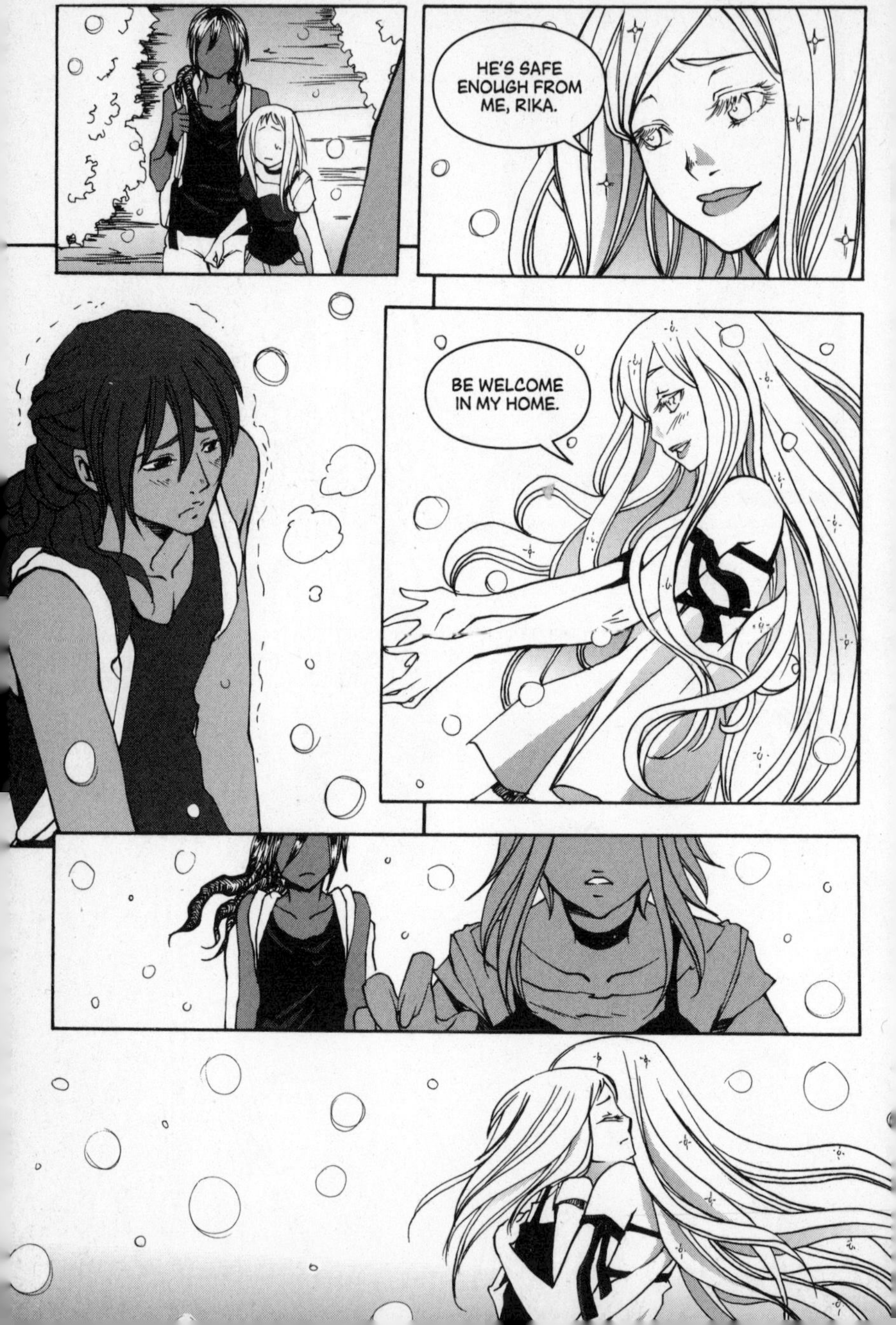
HE'S SAFE ENOUGH FROM ME, RIKA.
BE WELCOME IN MY HOME.

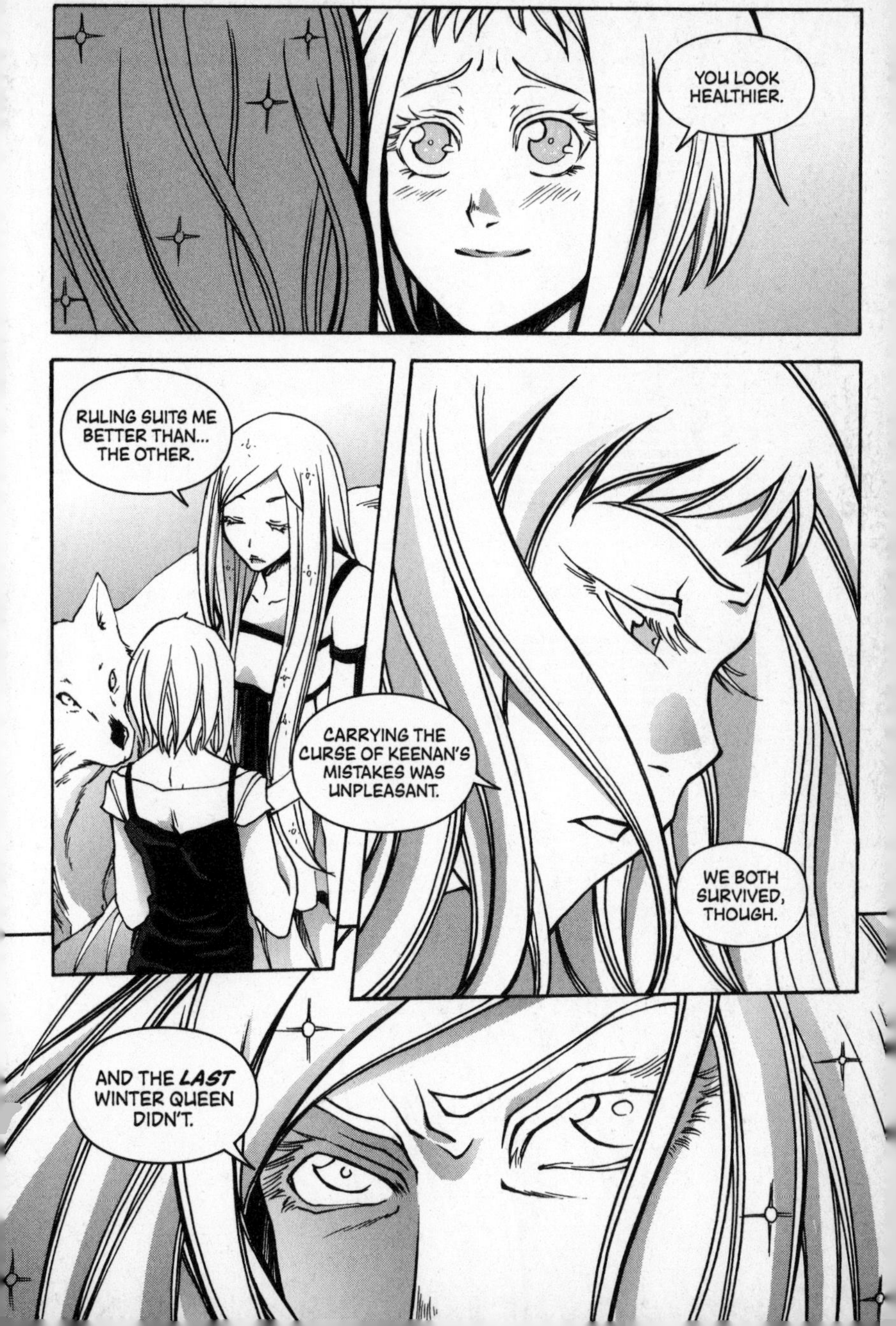
YOU LOOK HEALTHIER.
RULING SUITS ME BETTER THAN... THE OTHER.
CARRYING THE CURSE OF KEENAN'S MISTAKES WAS UNPLEASANT.
WE BOTH SURVIVED, THOUGH.
AND THE *LAST* WINTER QUEEN DIDN'T.

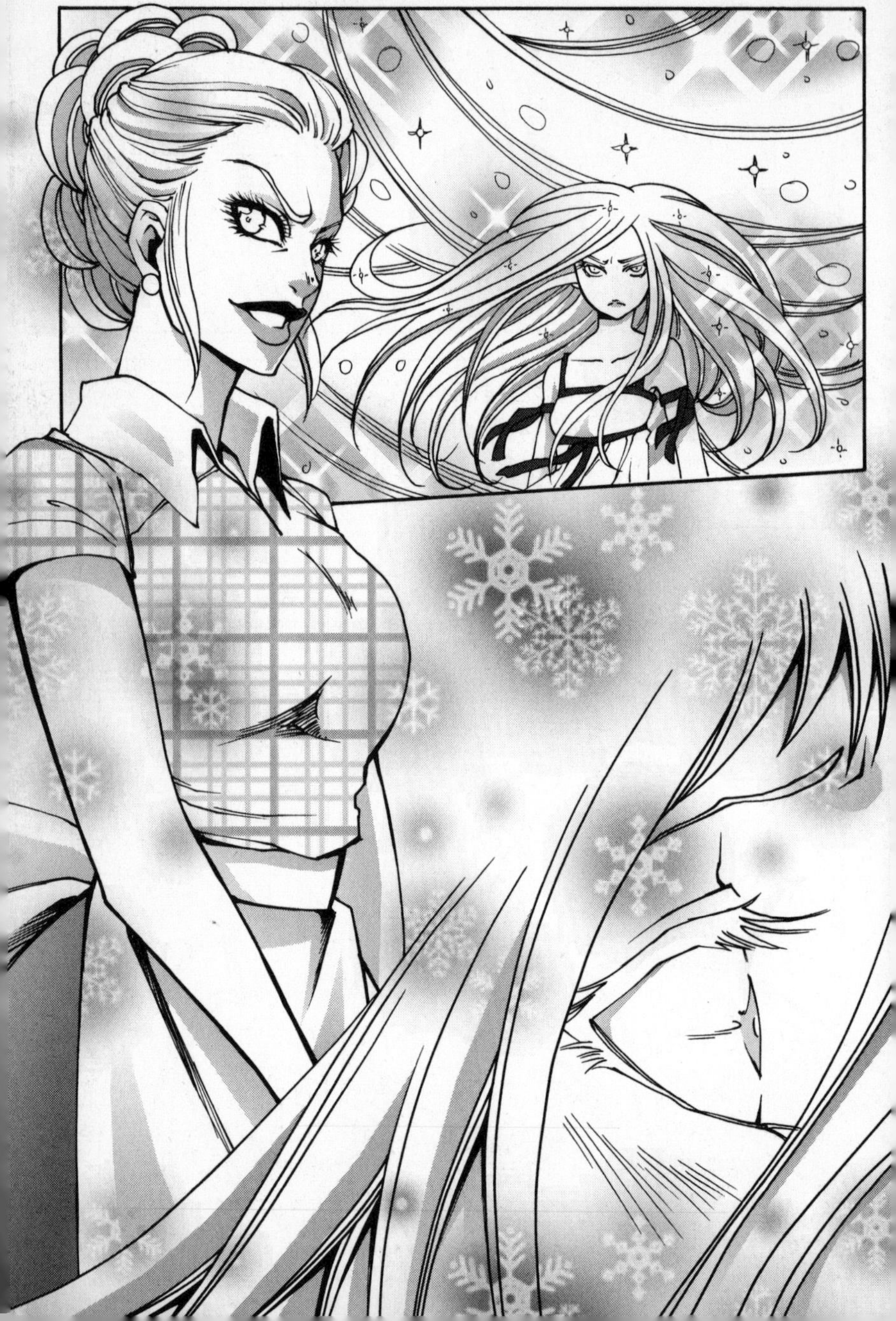

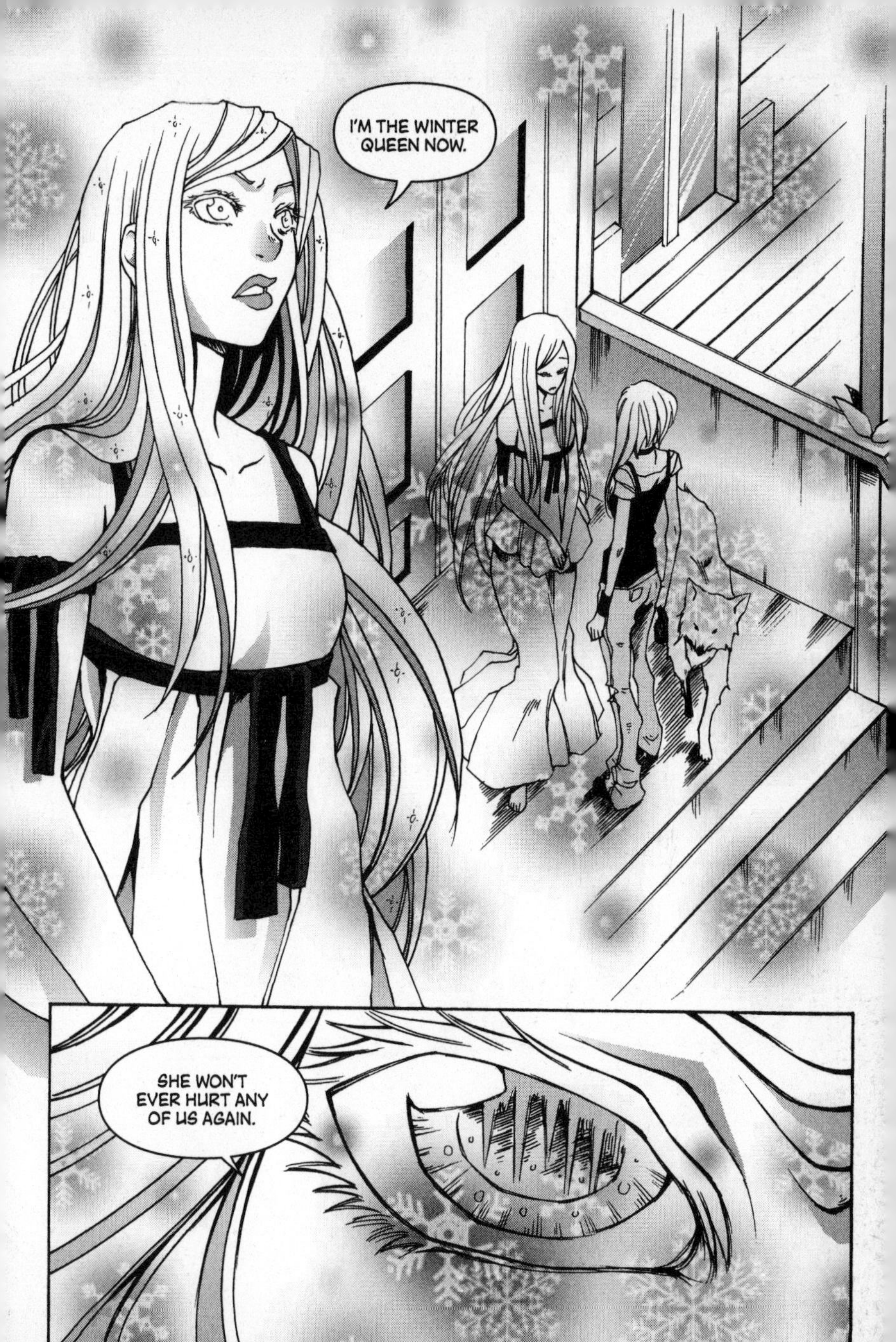
I'M THE WINTER QUEEN NOW.
SHE WON'T EVER HURT ANY OF US AGAIN.

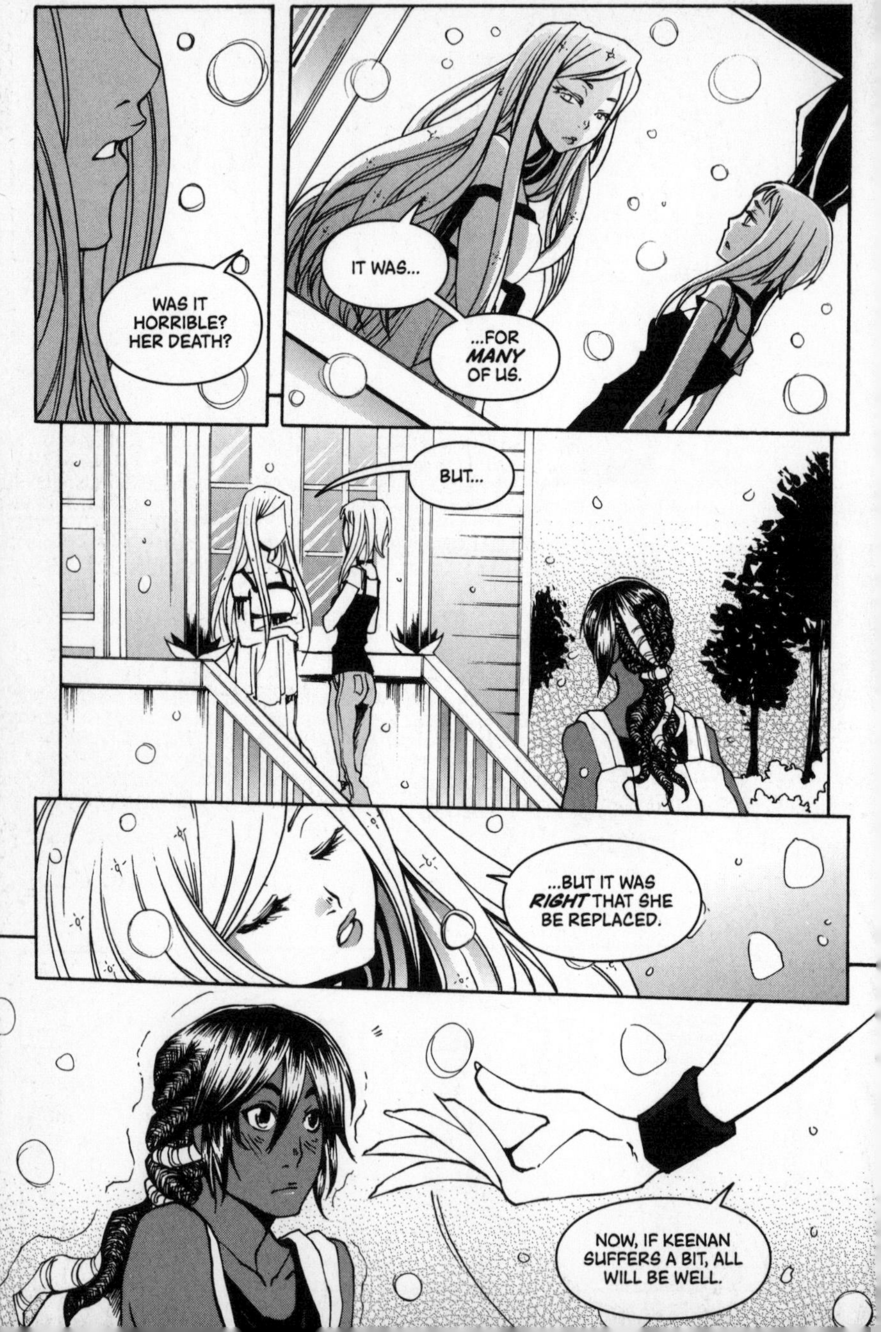
WAS IT HORRIBLE? HER DEATH?
IT WAS...
...FOR MANY OF US.
BUT...
...BUT IT WAS RIGHT THAT SHE BE REPLACED.
NOW, IF KEENAN SUFFERS A BIT, ALL WILL BE WELL.

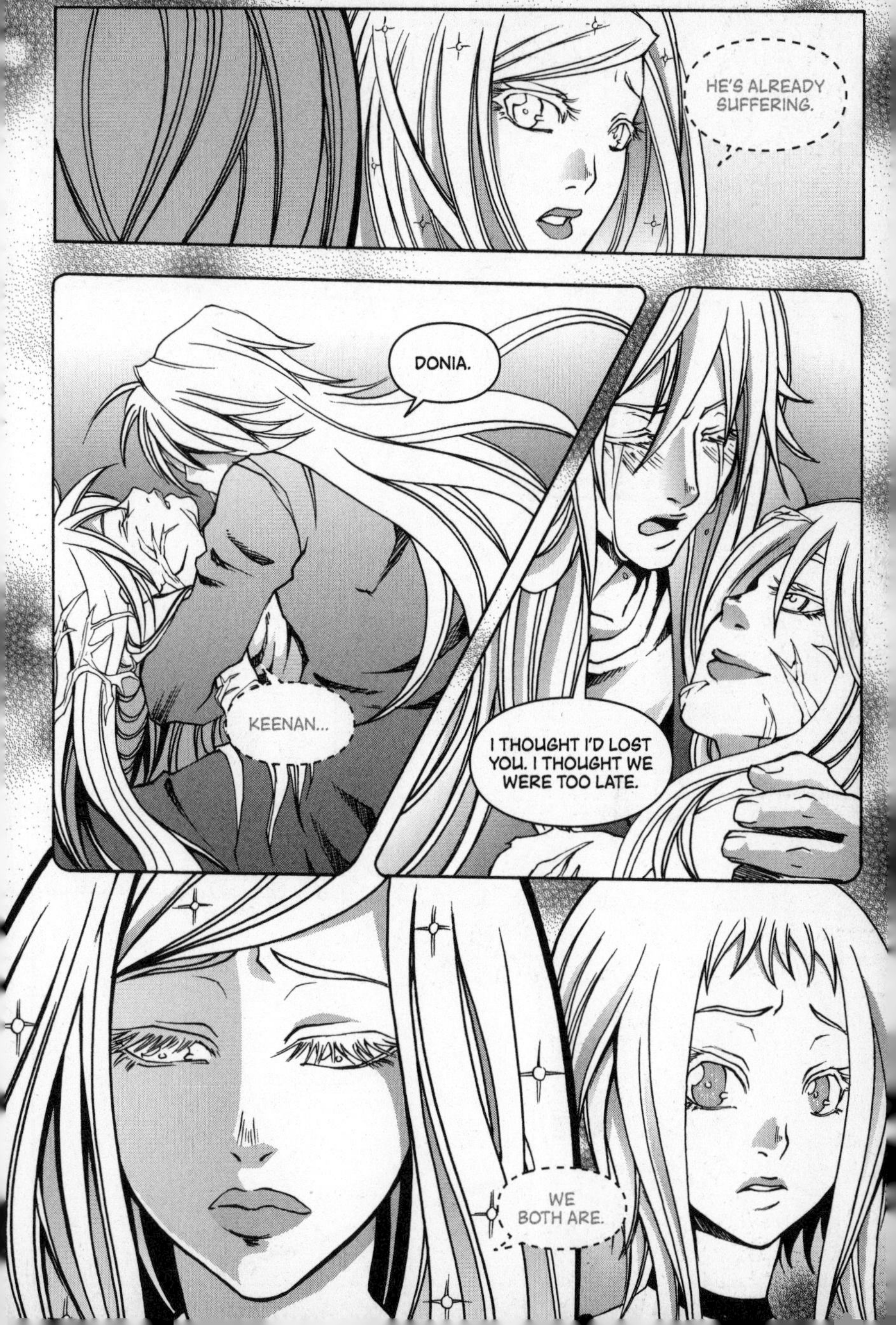
HE'S ALREADY SUFFERING.
DONIA.
KEENAN...
I THOUGHT I'D LOST YOU. I THOUGHT WE WERE TOO LATE.
WE BOTH ARE.

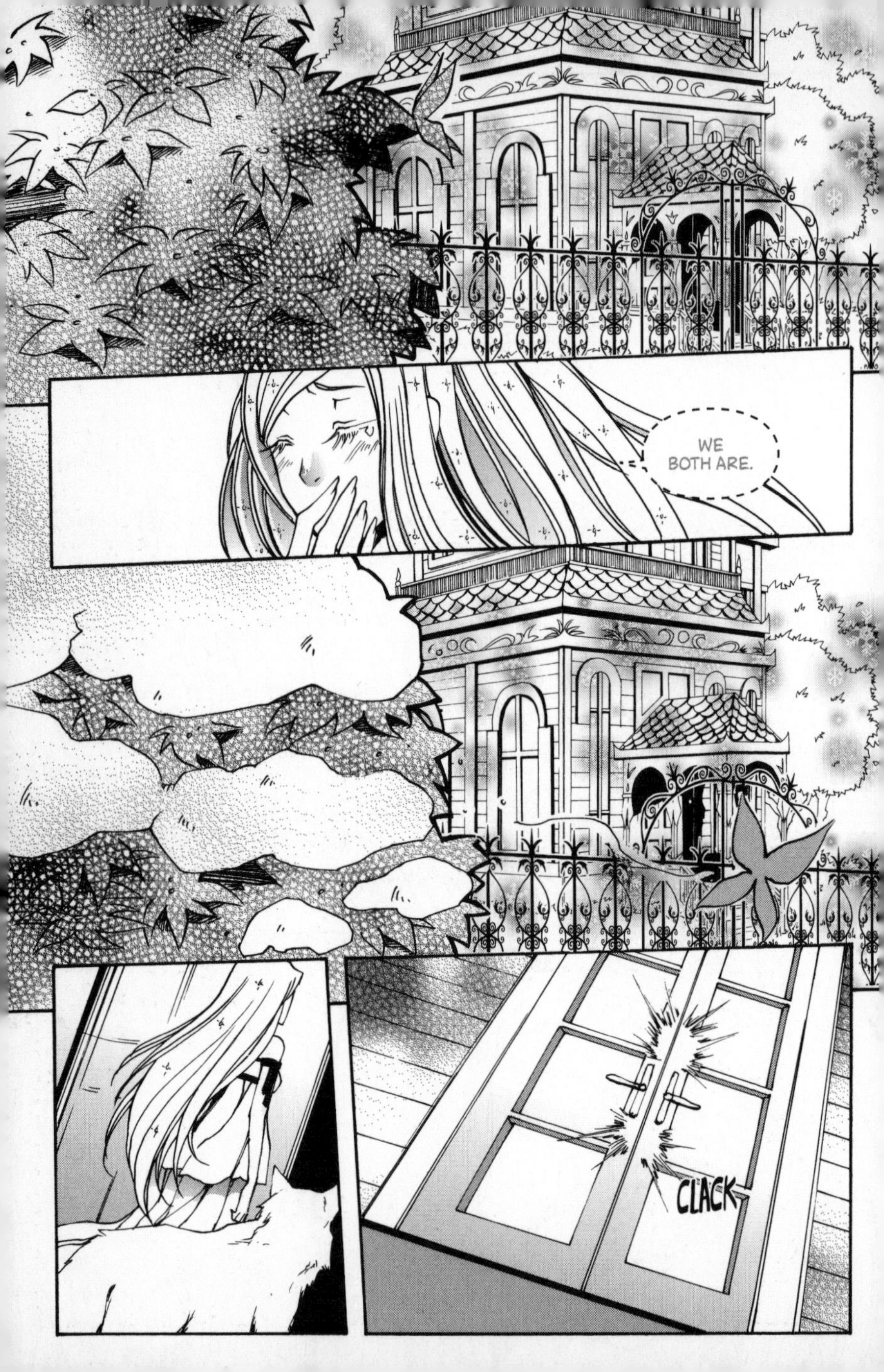
WE BOTH ARE.
CLACK

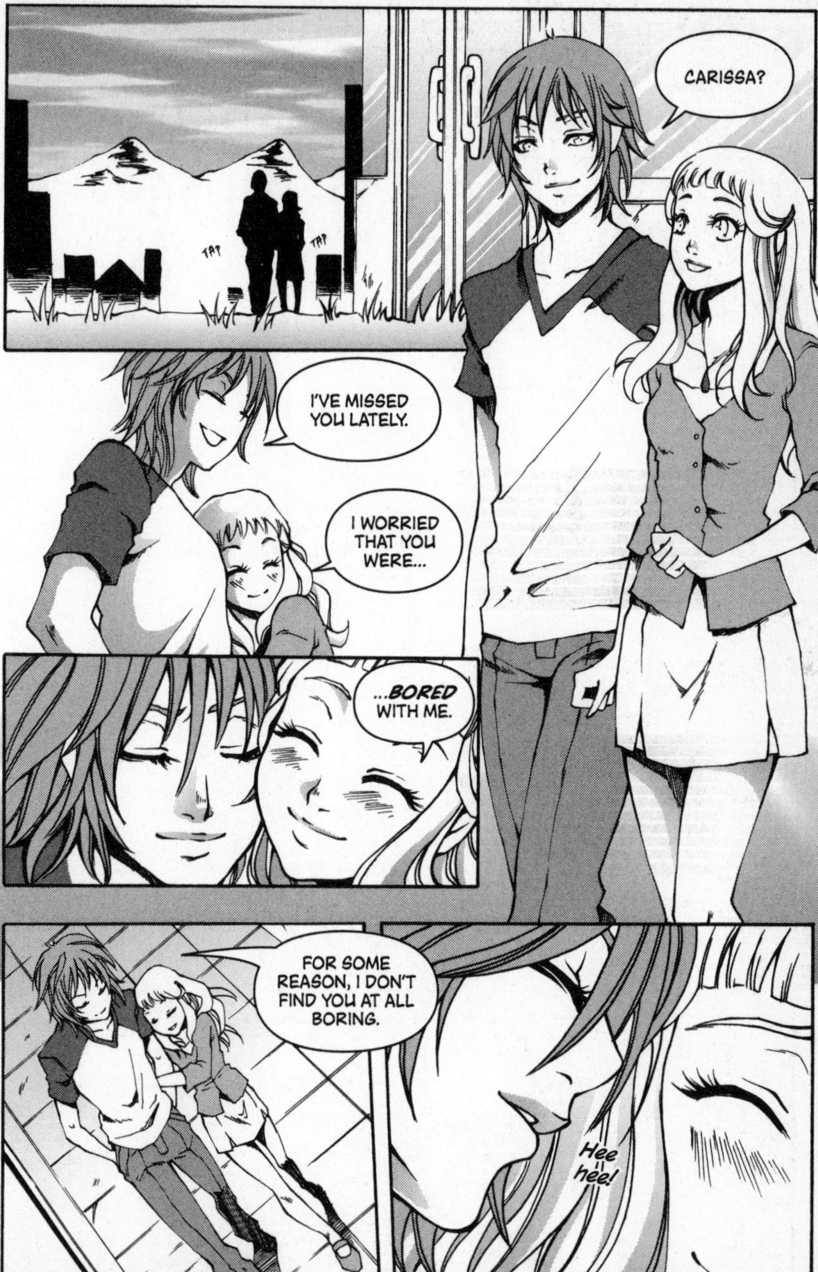
TAP
TAP
CARISSA?
I'VE MISSED YOU LATELY.
I WORRIED THAT YOU WERE...
...BORED WITH ME.
FOR SOME REASON, I DON'T FIND YOU AT ALL BORING.
Hee hee!

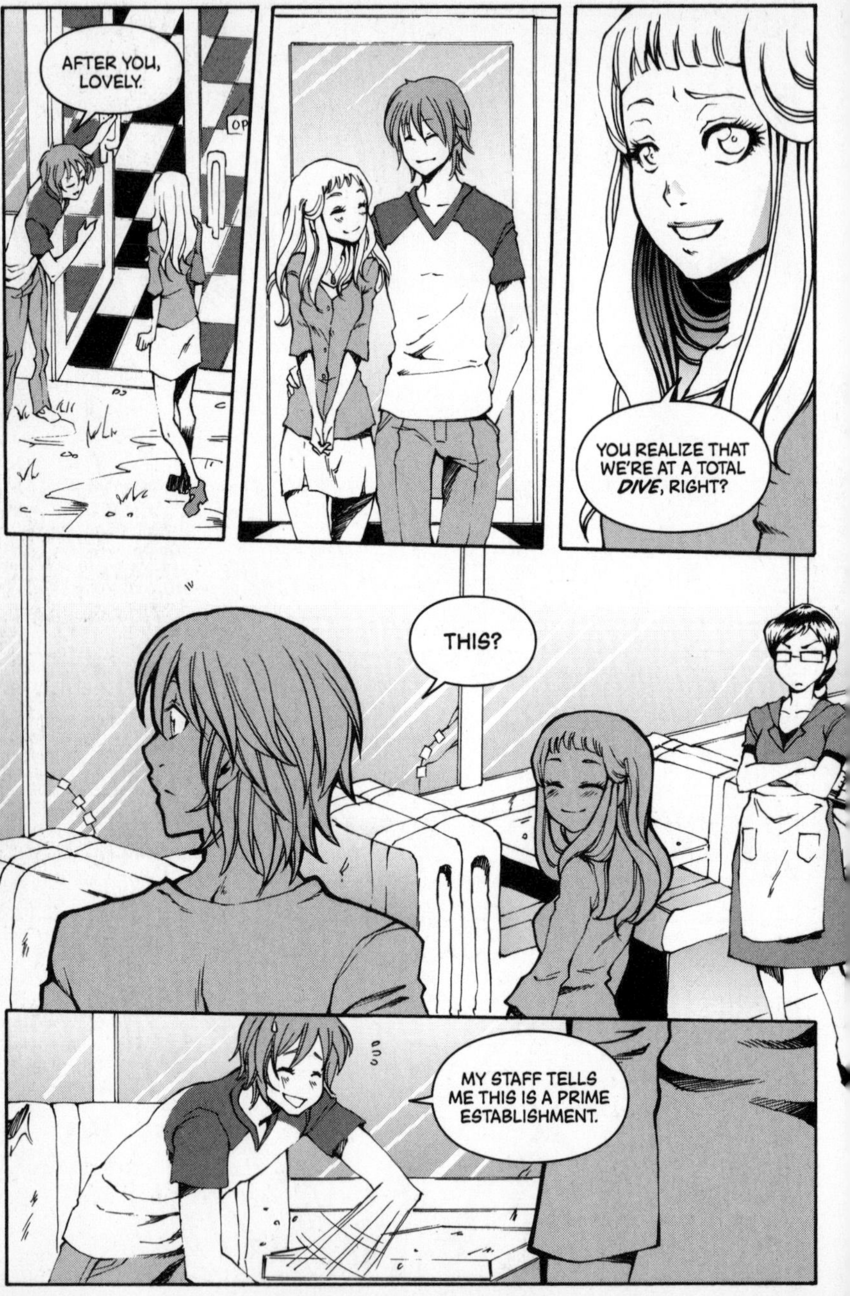
AFTER YOU, LOVELY.
YOU REALIZE THAT WE'RE AT A TOTAL *DIVE*, RIGHT?
THIS?
MY STAFF TELLS ME THIS IS A PRIME ESTABLISHMENT.

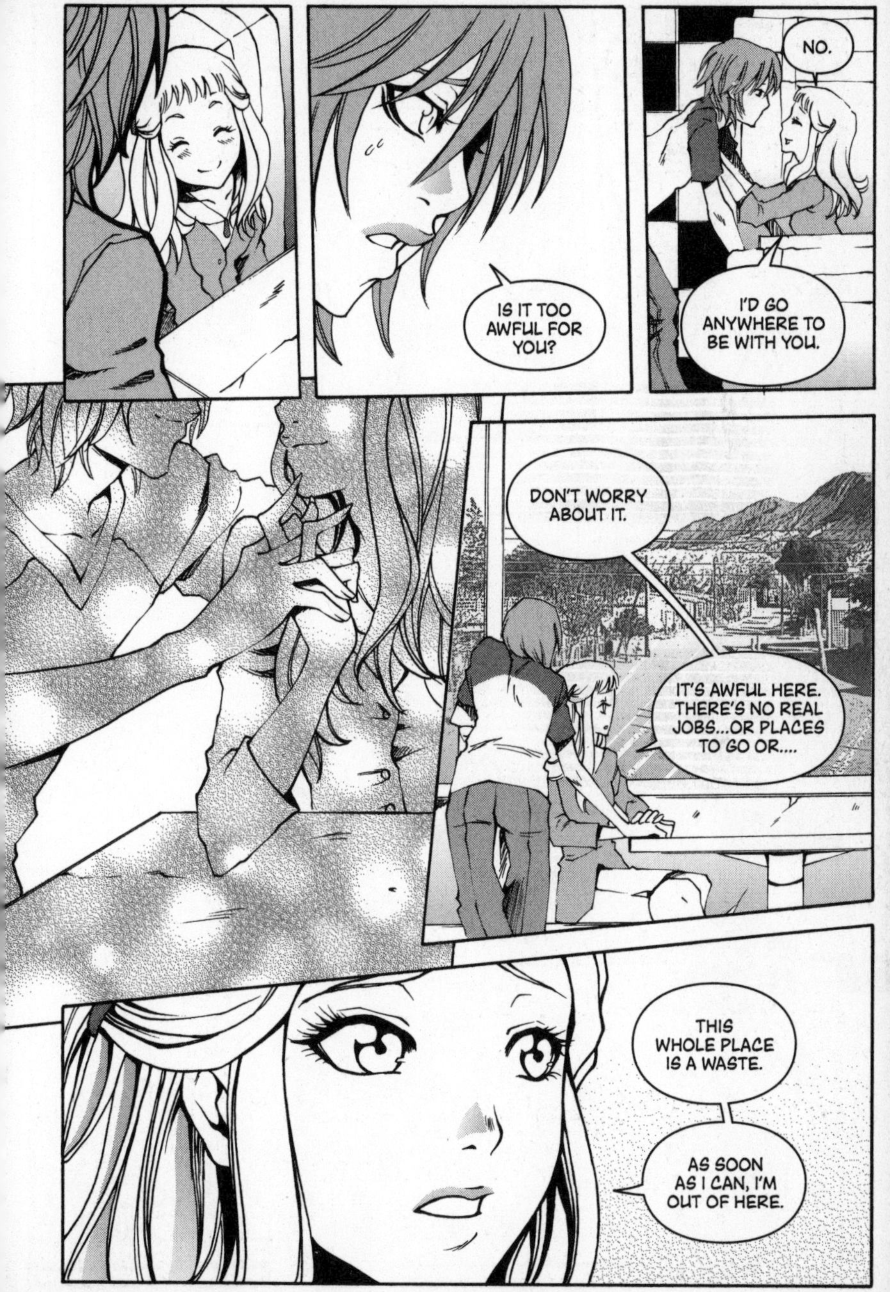
IS IT TOO AWFUL FOR YOU?
NO.
I'D GO ANYWHERE TO BE WITH YOU.
DON'T WORRY ABOUT IT.
IT'S AWFUL HERE. THERE'S NO REAL JOBS...OR PLACES TO GO OR....
THIS WHOLE PLACE IS A WASTE.
AS SOON AS I CAN, I'M OUT OF HERE.

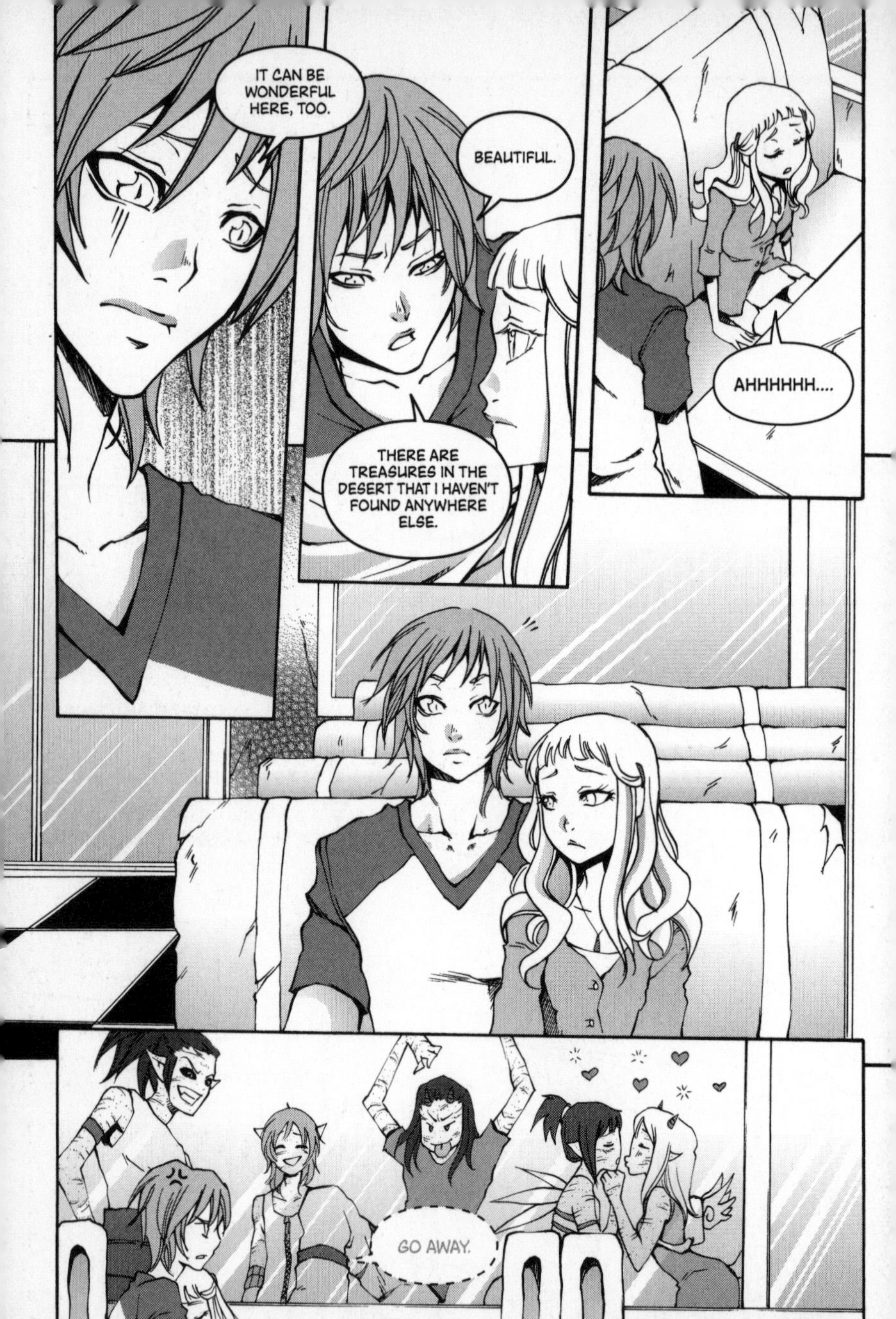
IT CAN BE WONDERFUL HERE, TOO.
BEAUTIFUL.
THERE ARE TREASURES IN THE DESERT THAT I HAVEN'T FOUND ANYWHERE ELSE.
AHHHHHH....
GO AWAY.

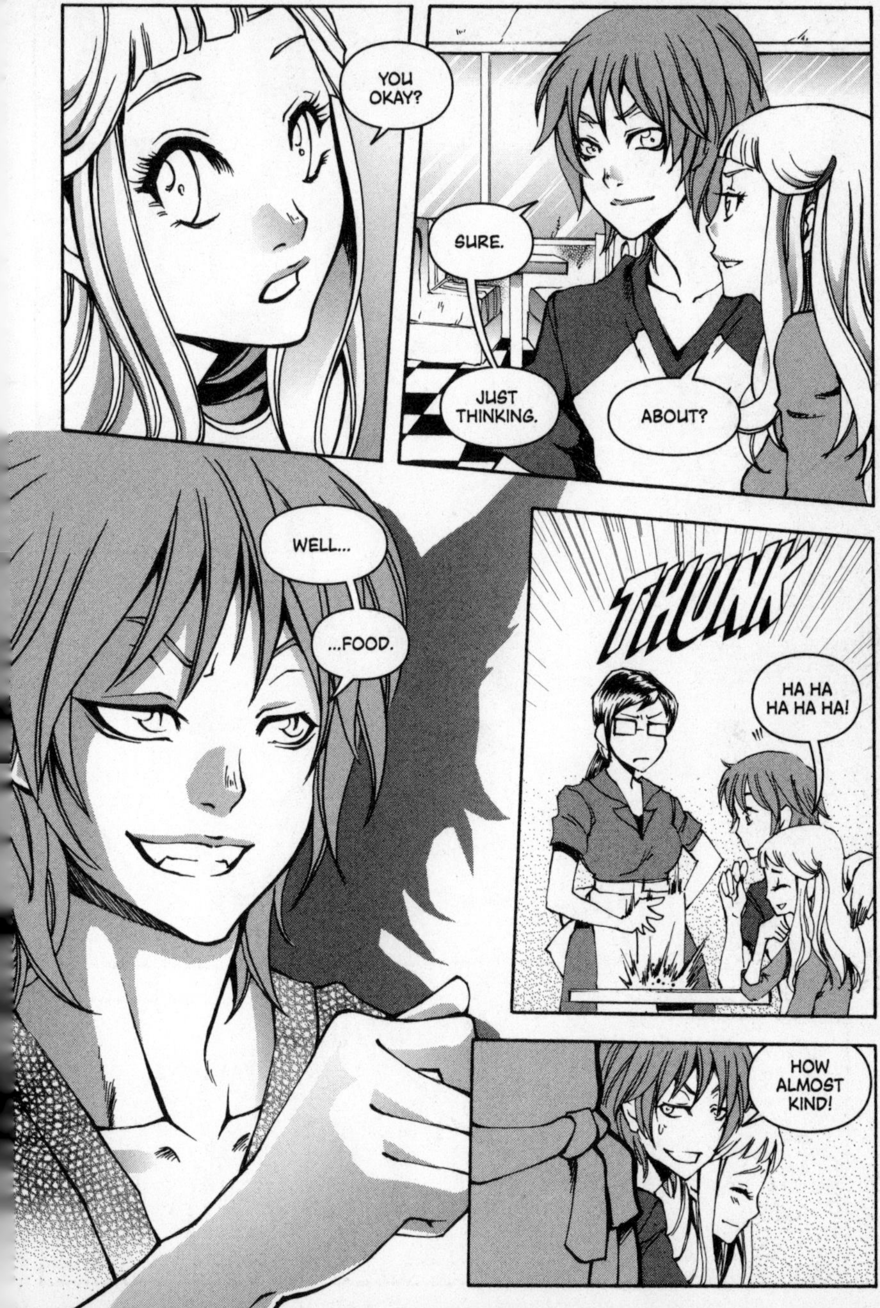
YOU OKAY?
SURE.
JUST THINKING.
ABOUT?
WELL...
...FOOD.
THUNK
HA HA HA HA HA!
HOW ALMOST KIND!

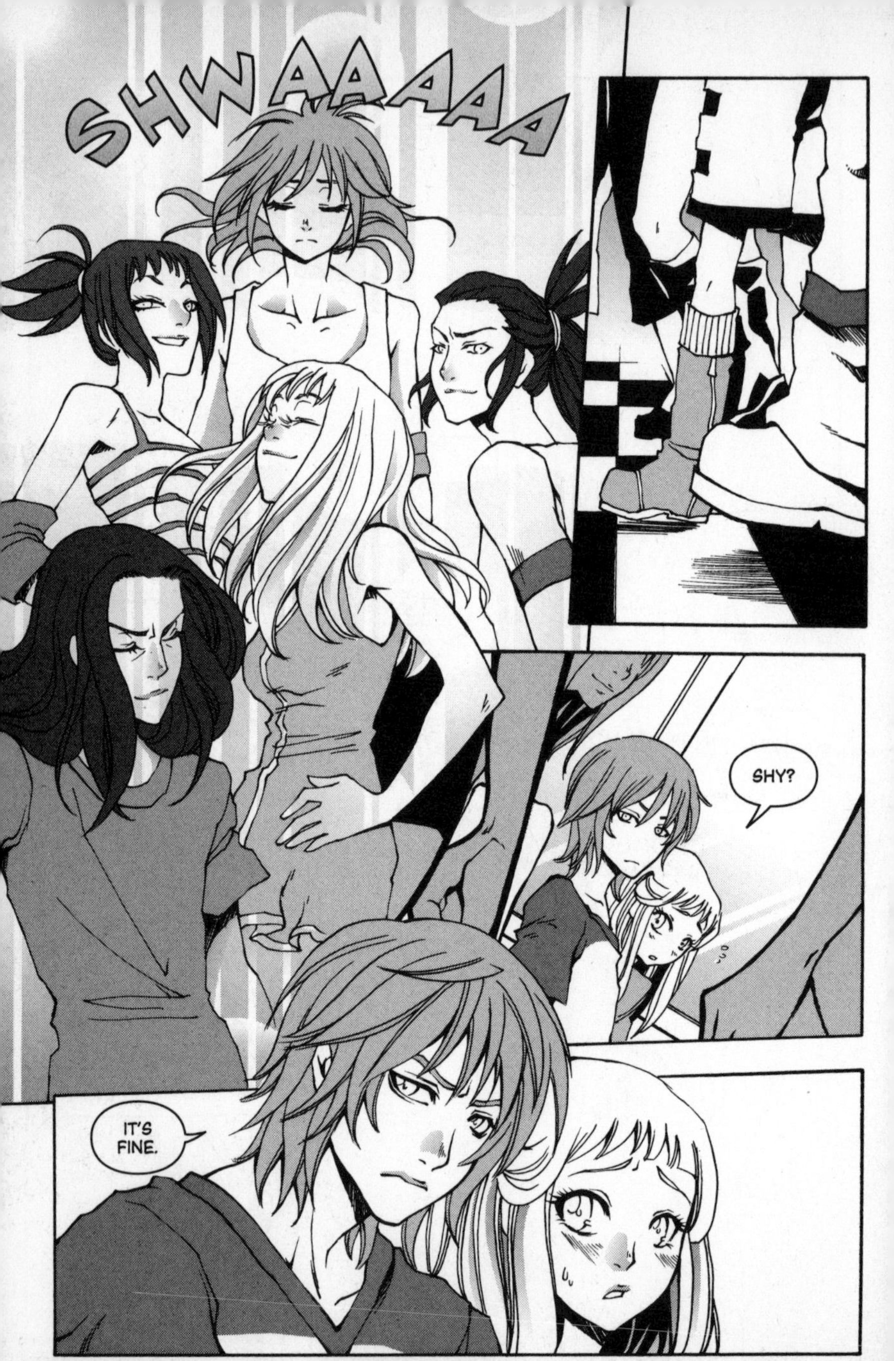
SHWAAAAA
SHY?
IT'S FINE.

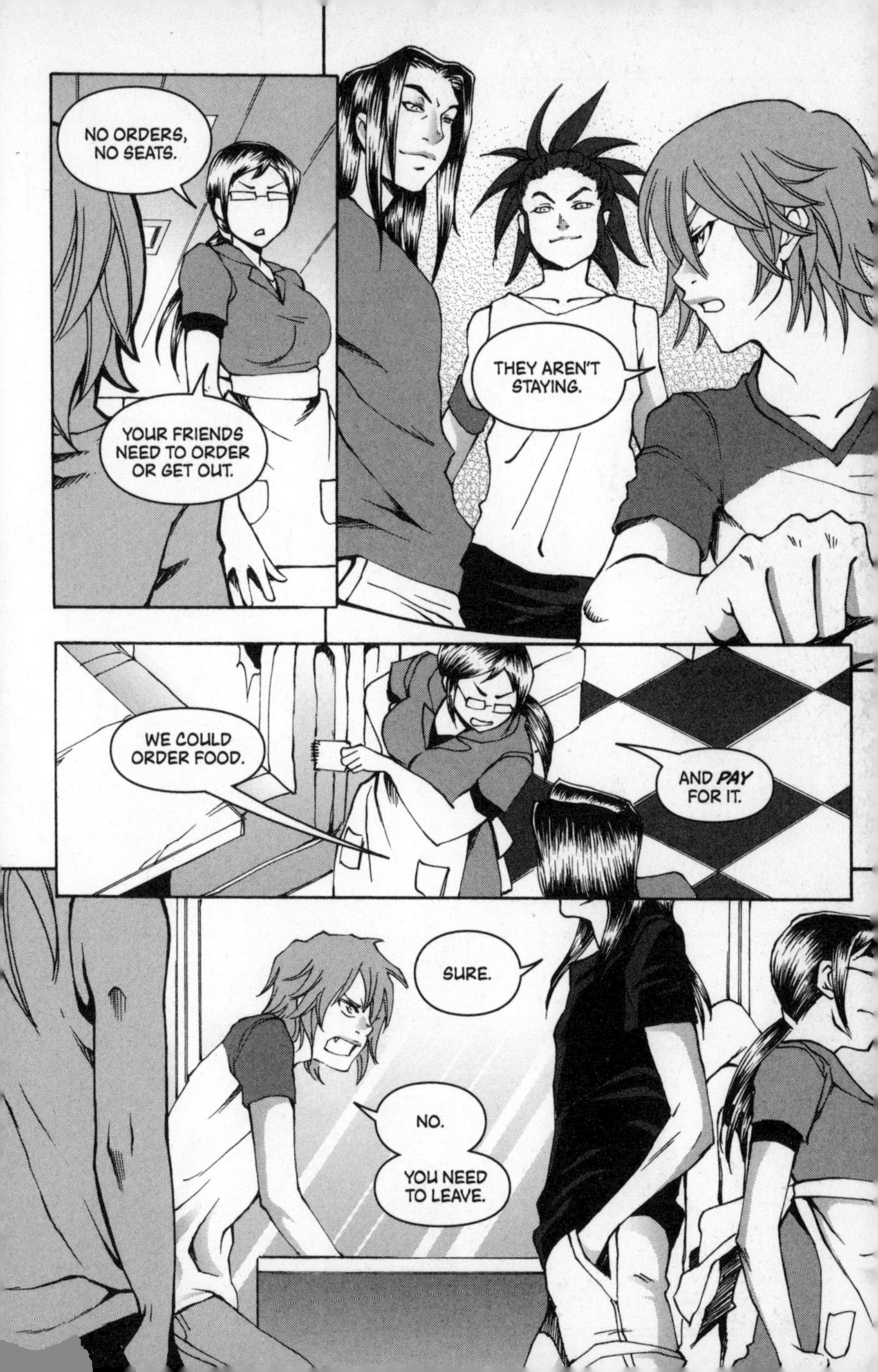
NO ORDERS, NO SEATS.
YOUR FRIENDS NEED TO ORDER OR GET OUT.
THEY AREN'T STAYING.
WE COULD ORDER FOOD.
AND *PAY* FOR IT.
SURE.
NO.
YOU NEED TO LEAVE.

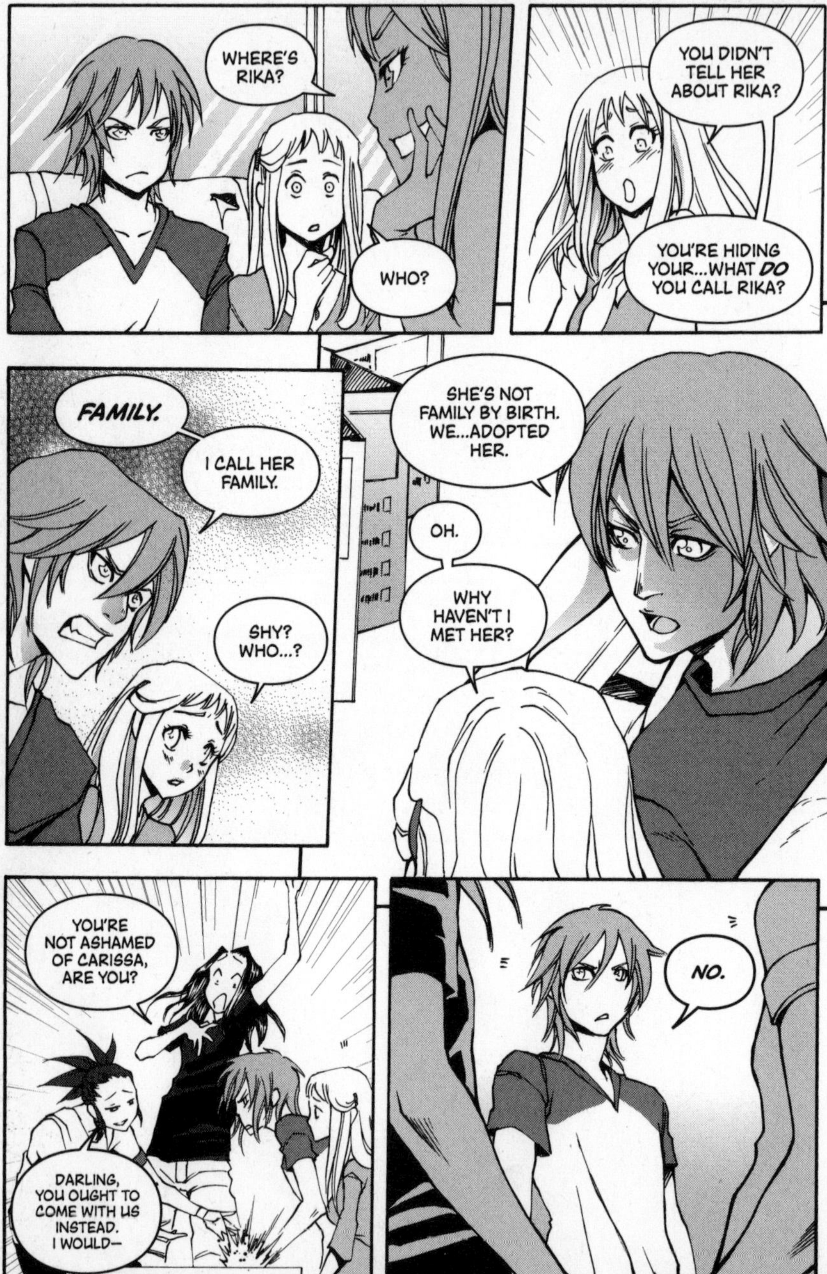
WHERE'S RIKA?
WHO?
YOU DIDN'T TELL HER ABOUT RIKA?
YOU'RE HIDING YOUR...WHAT *DO* YOU CALL RIKA?
FAMILY.
I CALL HER FAMILY.
SHY? WHO...?
SHE'S NOT FAMILY BY BIRTH. WE...ADOPTED HER.
OH.
WHY HAVEN'T I MET HER?
YOU'RE NOT ASHAMED OF CARISSA, ARE YOU?
DARLING, YOU OUGHT TO COME WITH US INSTEAD. I WOULD—
NO.

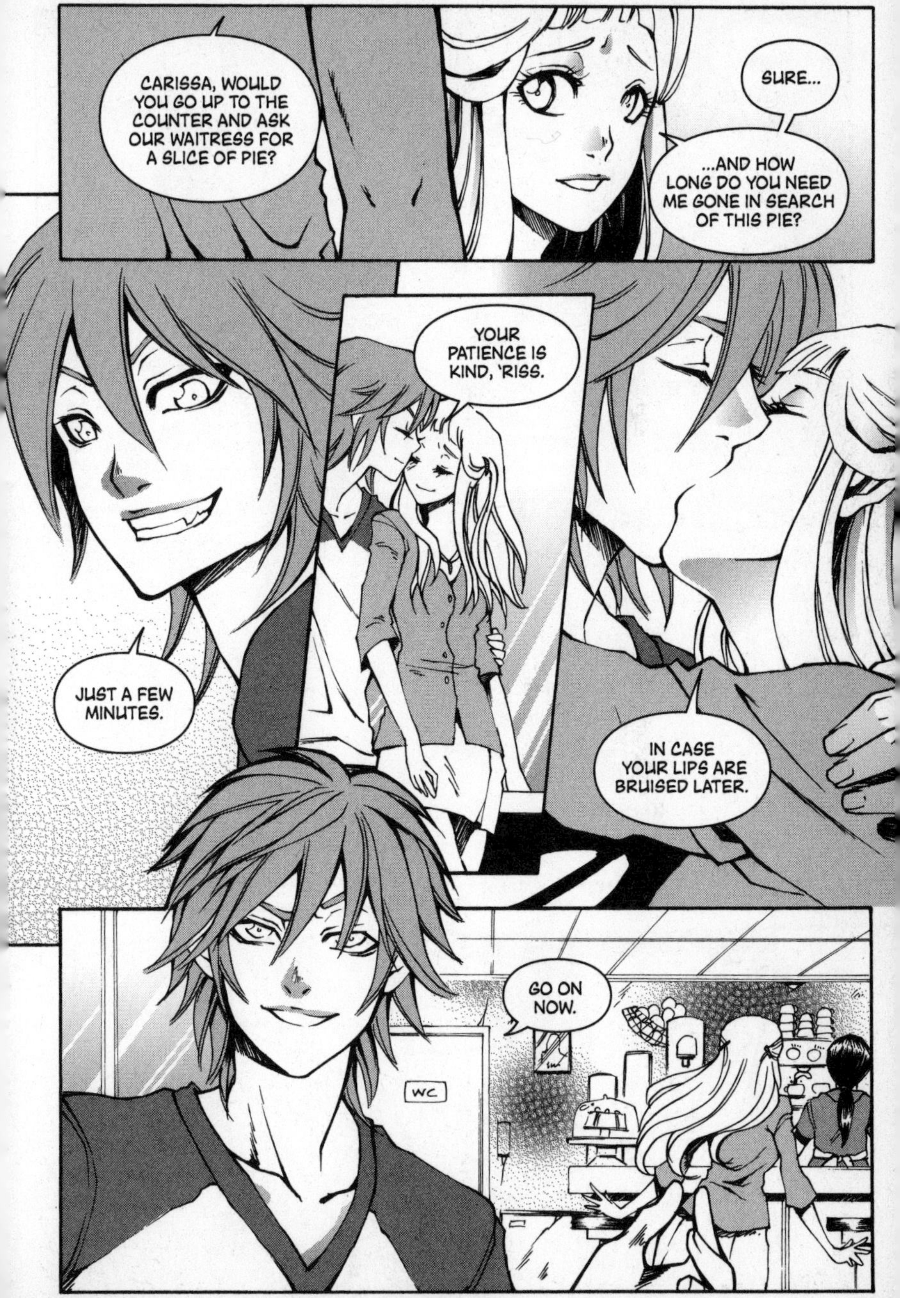
CARISSA, WOULD YOU GO UP TO THE COUNTER AND ASK OUR WAITRESS FOR A SLICE OF PIE?
SURE...
...AND HOW LONG DO YOU NEED ME GONE IN SEARCH OF THIS PIE?
JUST A FEW MINUTES.
YOUR PATIENCE IS KIND, 'RISS.
IN CASE YOUR LIPS ARE BRUISED LATER.
GO ON NOW.
WC

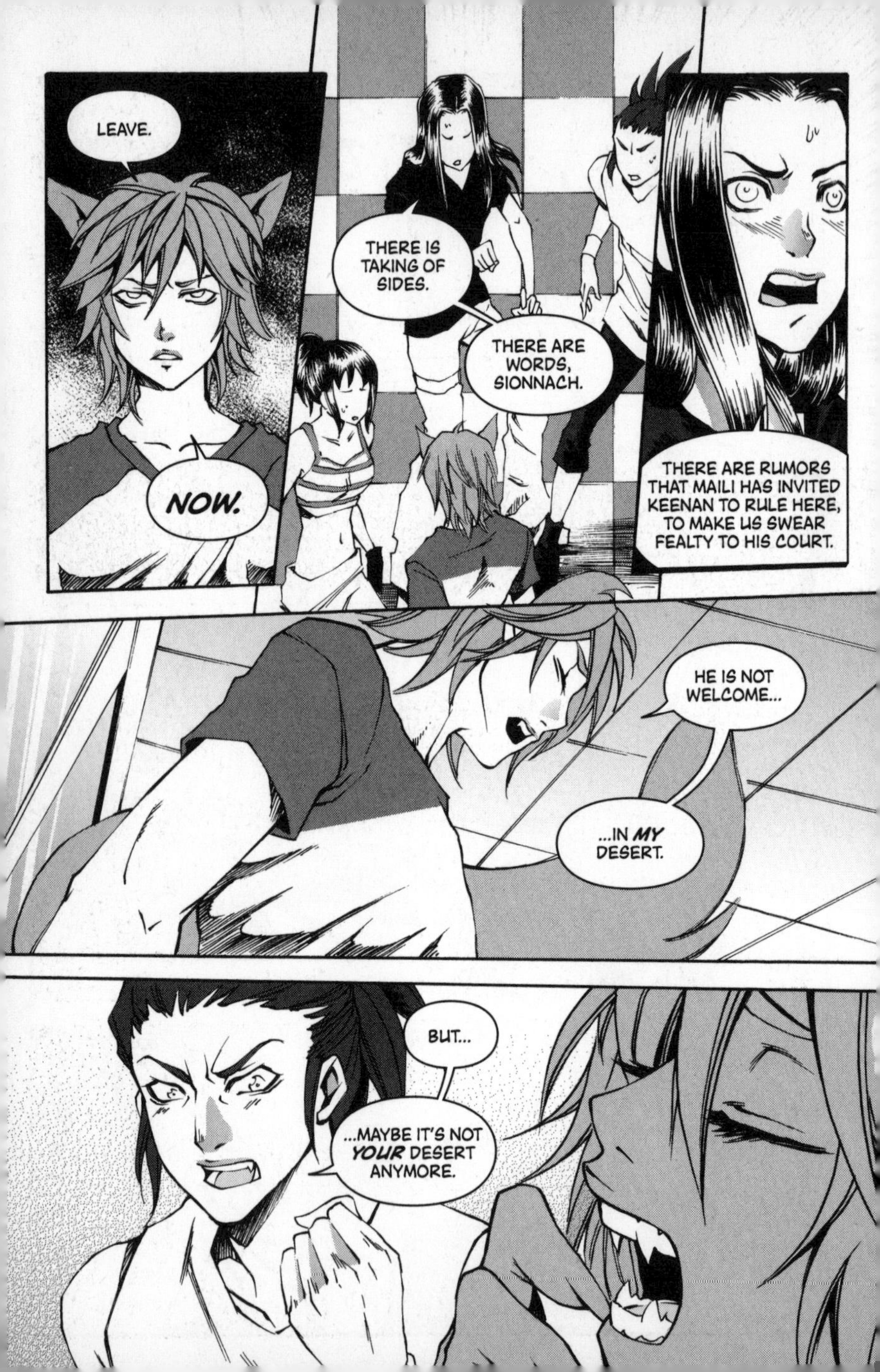
LEAVE.
NOW.
THERE IS TAKING OF SIDES.
THERE ARE WORDS, SIONNACH.
THERE ARE RUMORS THAT MAILI HAS INVITED KEENAN TO RULE HERE, TO MAKE US SWEAR FEALTY TO HIS COURT.
HE IS NOT WELCOME...
...IN *MY* DESERT.
BUT...
...MAYBE IT'S NOT *YOUR* DESERT ANYMORE.

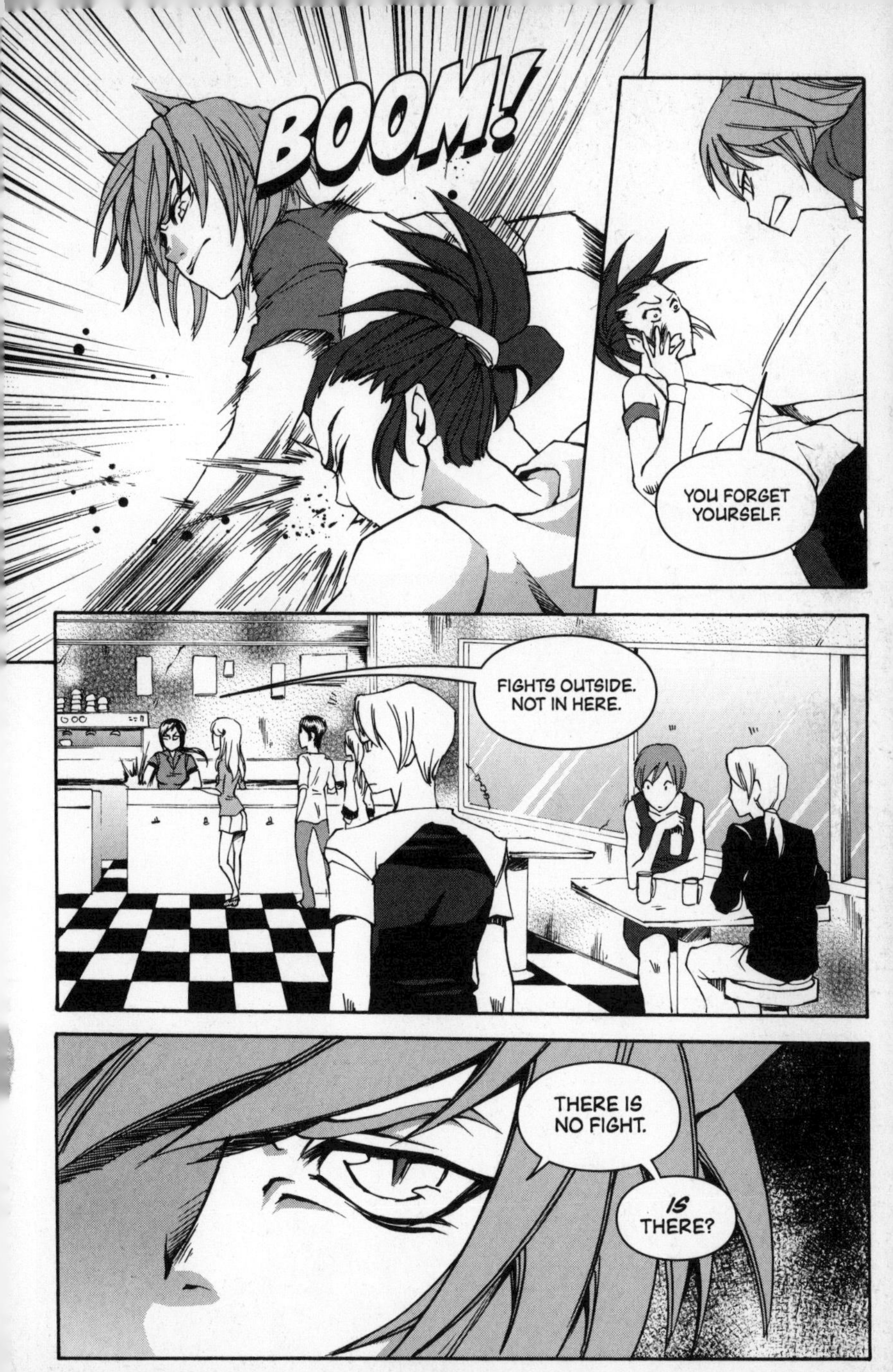
BOOM!
YOU FORGET YOURSELF.
FIGHTS OUTSIDE. NOT IN HERE.
THERE IS NO FIGHT.
IS THERE?

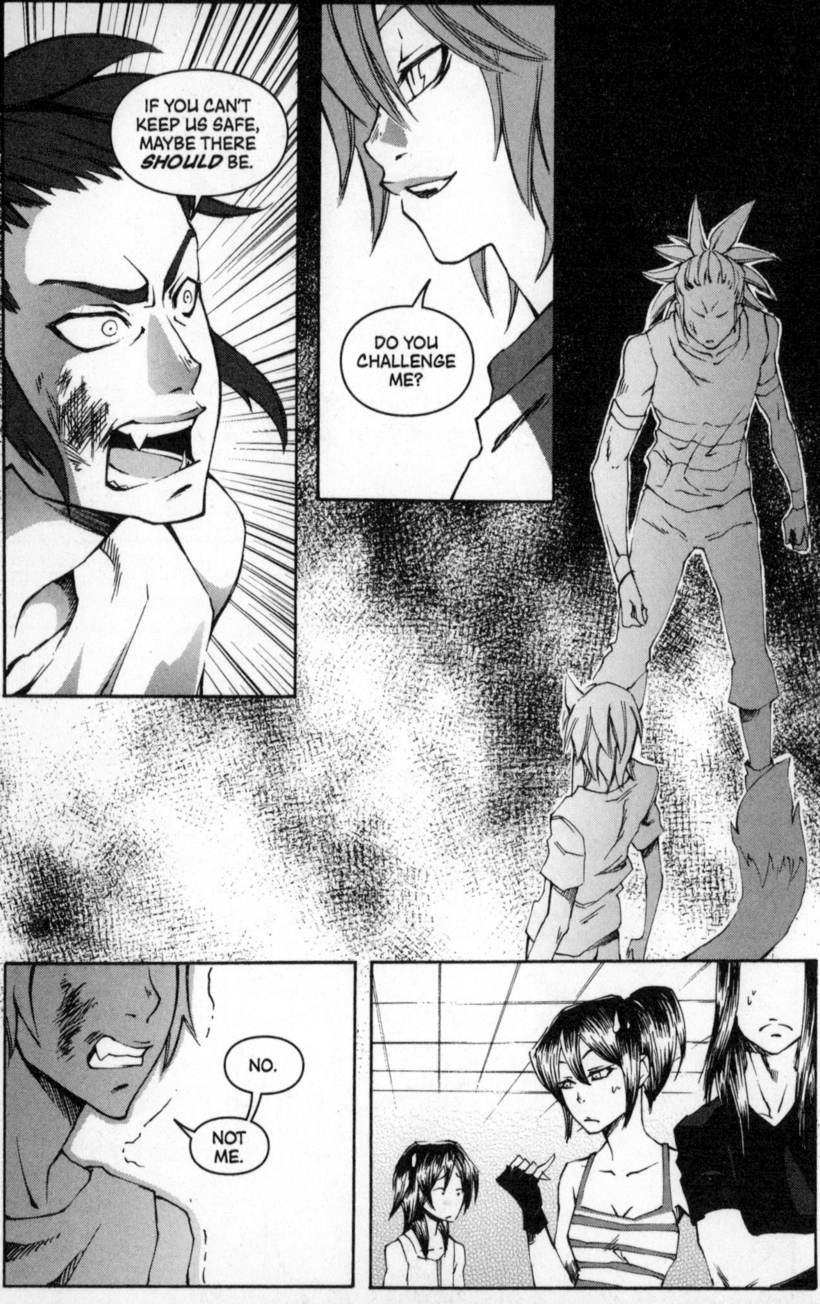
IF YOU CAN'T KEEP US SAFE, MAYBE THERE *SHOULD* BE.
DO YOU CHALLENGE ME?
NO.
NOT ME.

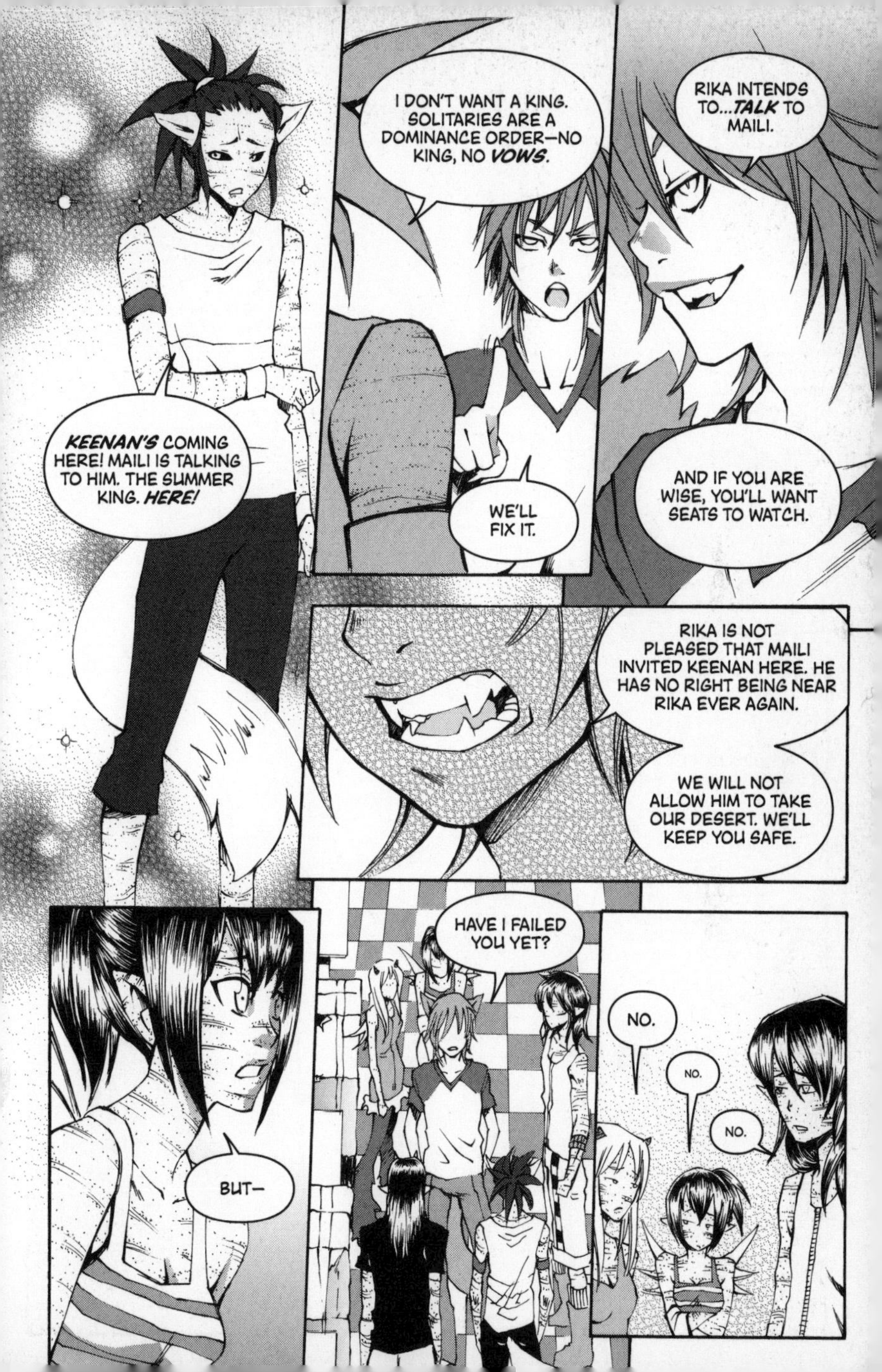
KEENAN'S COMING HERE! MAILI IS TALKING TO HIM. THE SUMMER KING. HERE!
I DON'T WANT A KING. SOLITARIES ARE A DOMINANCE ORDER—NO KING, NO VOWS.
WE'LL FIX IT.
RIKA INTENDS TO...TALK TO MAILI.
AND IF YOU ARE WISE, YOU'LL WANT SEATS TO WATCH.
RIKA IS NOT PLEASED THAT MAILI INVITED KEENAN HERE. HE HAS NO RIGHT BEING NEAR RIKA EVER AGAIN.
WE WILL NOT ALLOW HIM TO TAKE OUR DESERT. WE'LL KEEP YOU SAFE.
BUT—
HAVE I FAILED YOU YET?
NO.
NO.
NO.

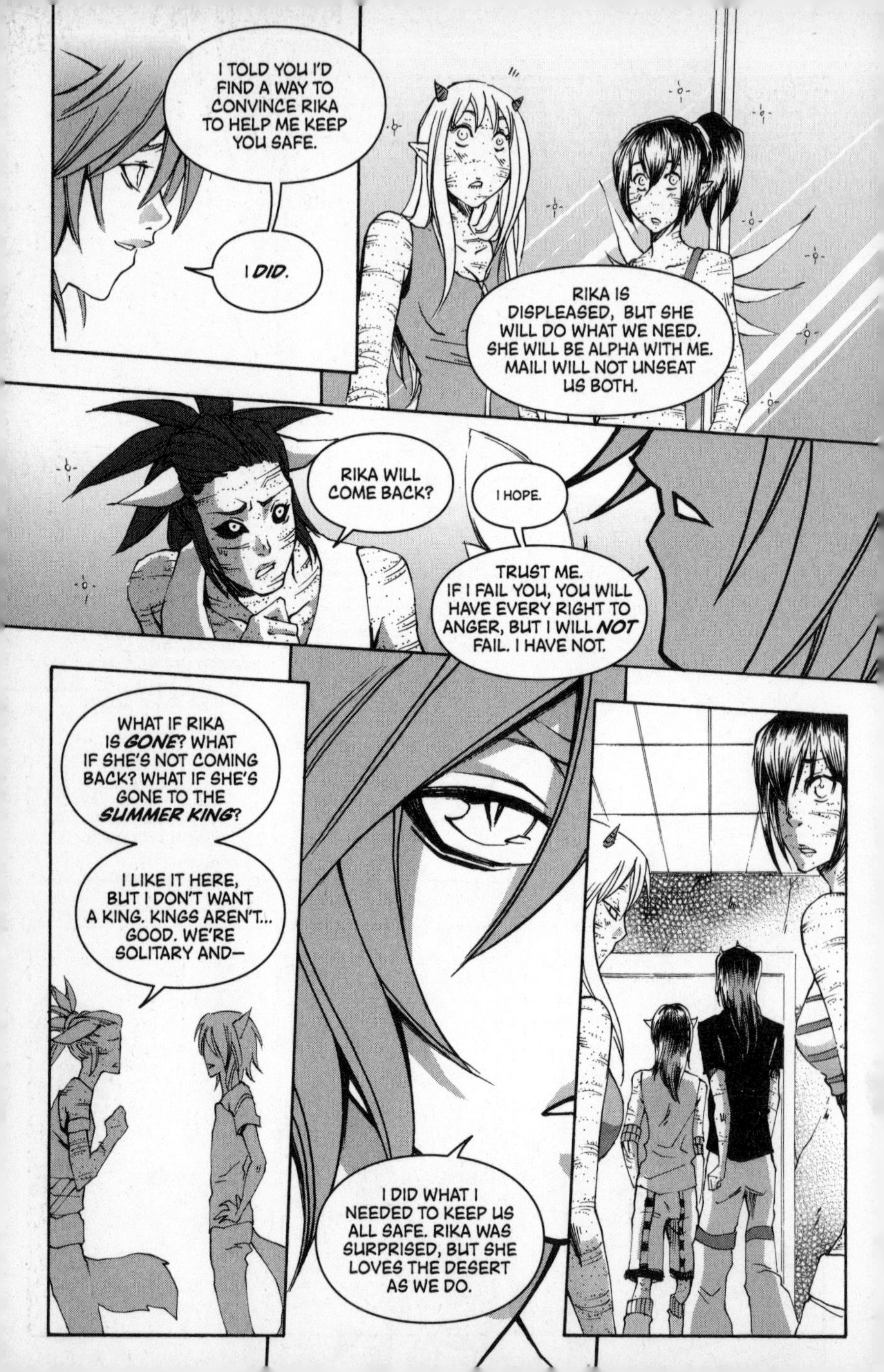

I TOLD YOU I'D FIND A WAY TO CONVINCE RIKA TO HELP ME KEEP YOU SAFE.
I *DID*.
RIKA IS DISPLEASED, BUT SHE WILL DO WHAT WE NEED. SHE WILL BE ALPHA WITH ME. MAILI WILL NOT UNSEAT US BOTH.
RIKA WILL COME BACK?
I HOPE.
TRUST ME. IF I FAIL YOU, YOU WILL HAVE EVERY RIGHT TO ANGER, BUT I WILL *NOT* FAIL. I HAVE NOT.
WHAT IF RIKA IS *GONE*? WHAT IF SHE'S NOT COMING BACK? WHAT IF SHE'S GONE TO THE *SUMMER KING*?
I LIKE IT HERE, BUT I DON'T WANT A KING. KINGS AREN'T... GOOD. WE'RE SOLITARY AND—
I DID WHAT I NEEDED TO KEEP US ALL SAFE. RIKA WAS SURPRISED, BUT SHE LOVES THE DESERT AS WE DO.

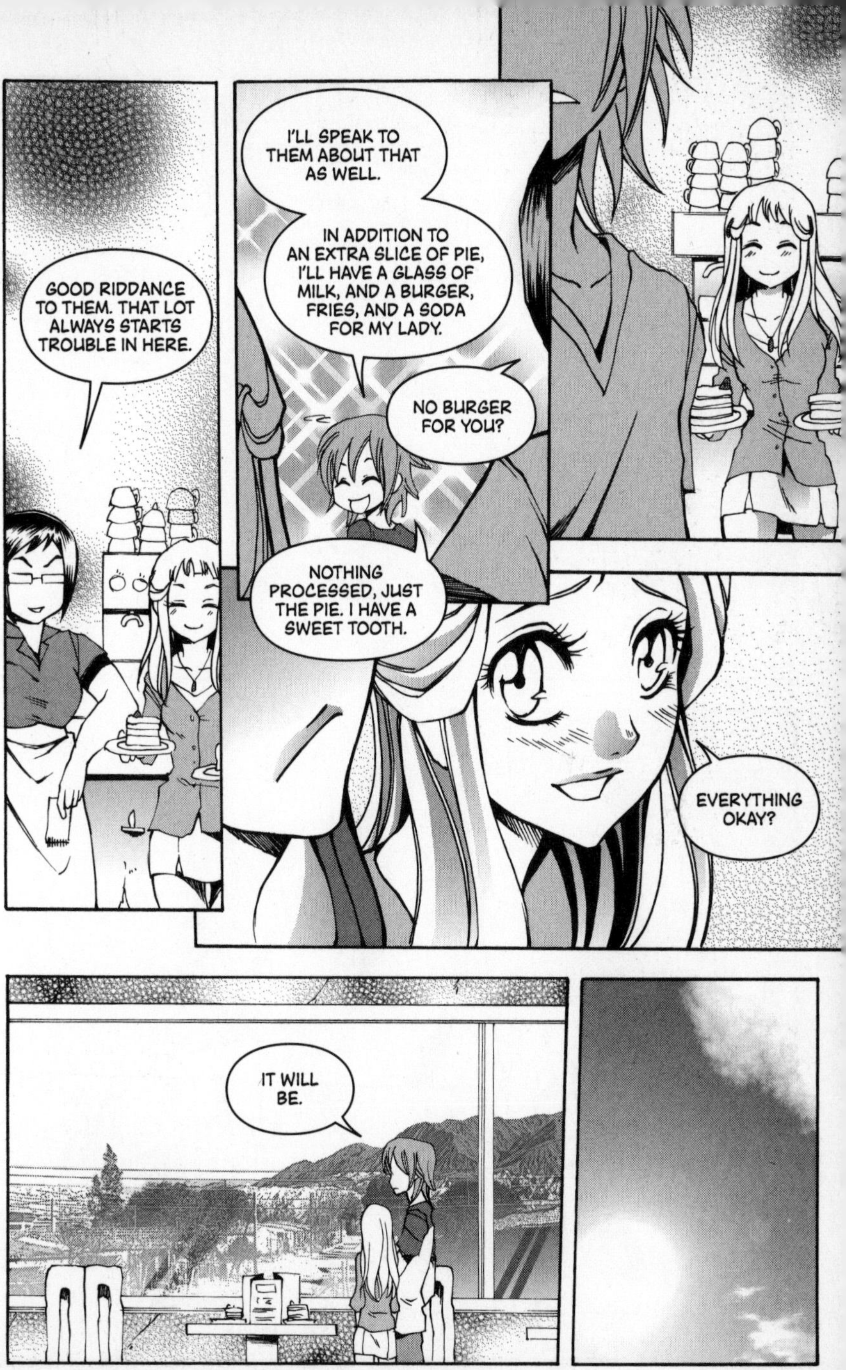
GOOD RIDDANCE TO THEM. THAT LOT ALWAYS STARTS TROUBLE IN HERE.
I'LL SPEAK TO THEM ABOUT THAT AS WELL.
IN ADDITION TO AN EXTRA SLICE OF PIE, I'LL HAVE A GLASS OF MILK, AND A BURGER, FRIES, AND A SODA FOR MY LADY.
NO BURGER FOR YOU?
NOTHING PROCESSED, JUST THE PIE. I HAVE A SWEET TOOTH.
EVERYTHING OKAY?
IT WILL BE.

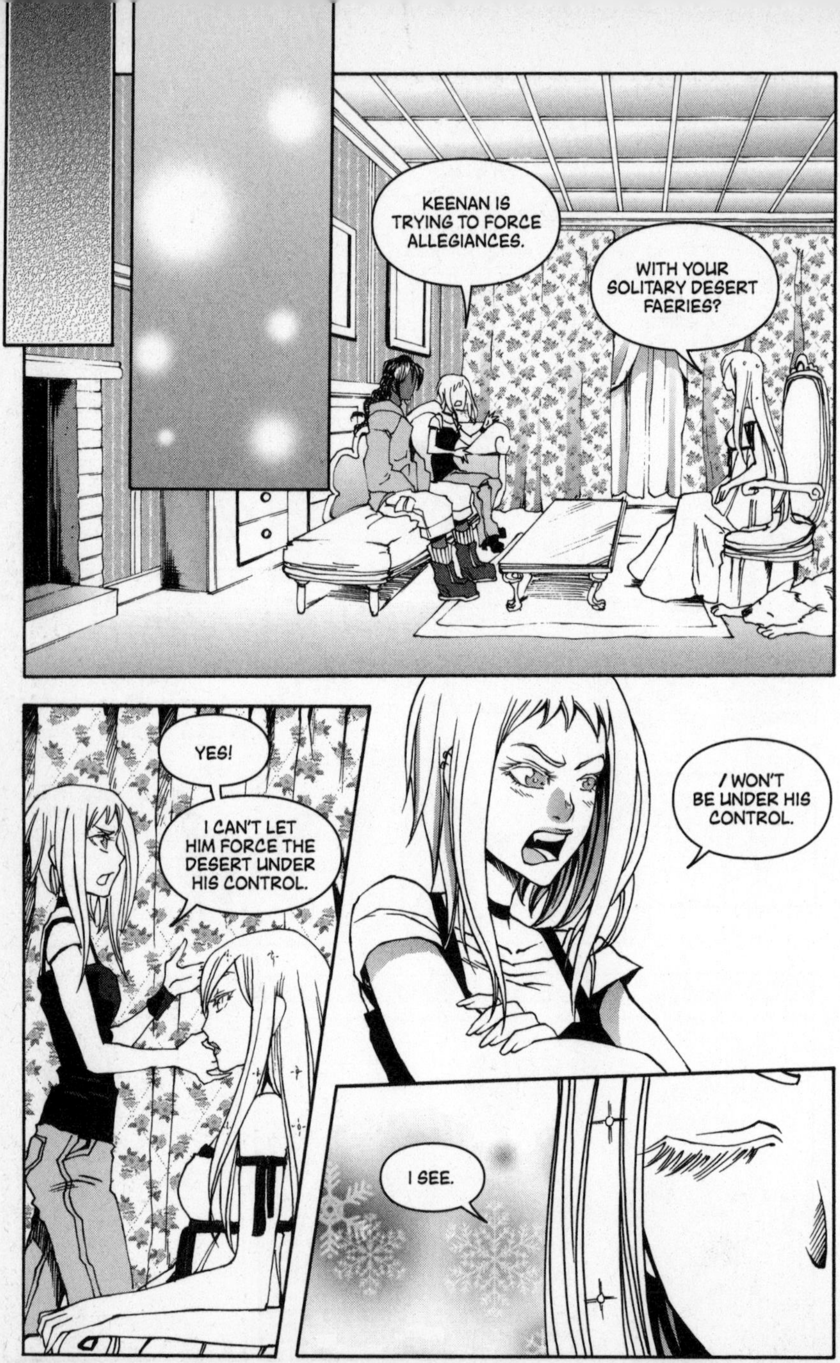
KEENAN IS TRYING TO FORCE ALLEGIANCES.
WITH YOUR SOLITARY DESERT FAERIES?
YES!
I CAN'T LET HIM FORCE THE DESERT UNDER HIS CONTROL.
I WON'T BE UNDER HIS CONTROL.
I SEE.

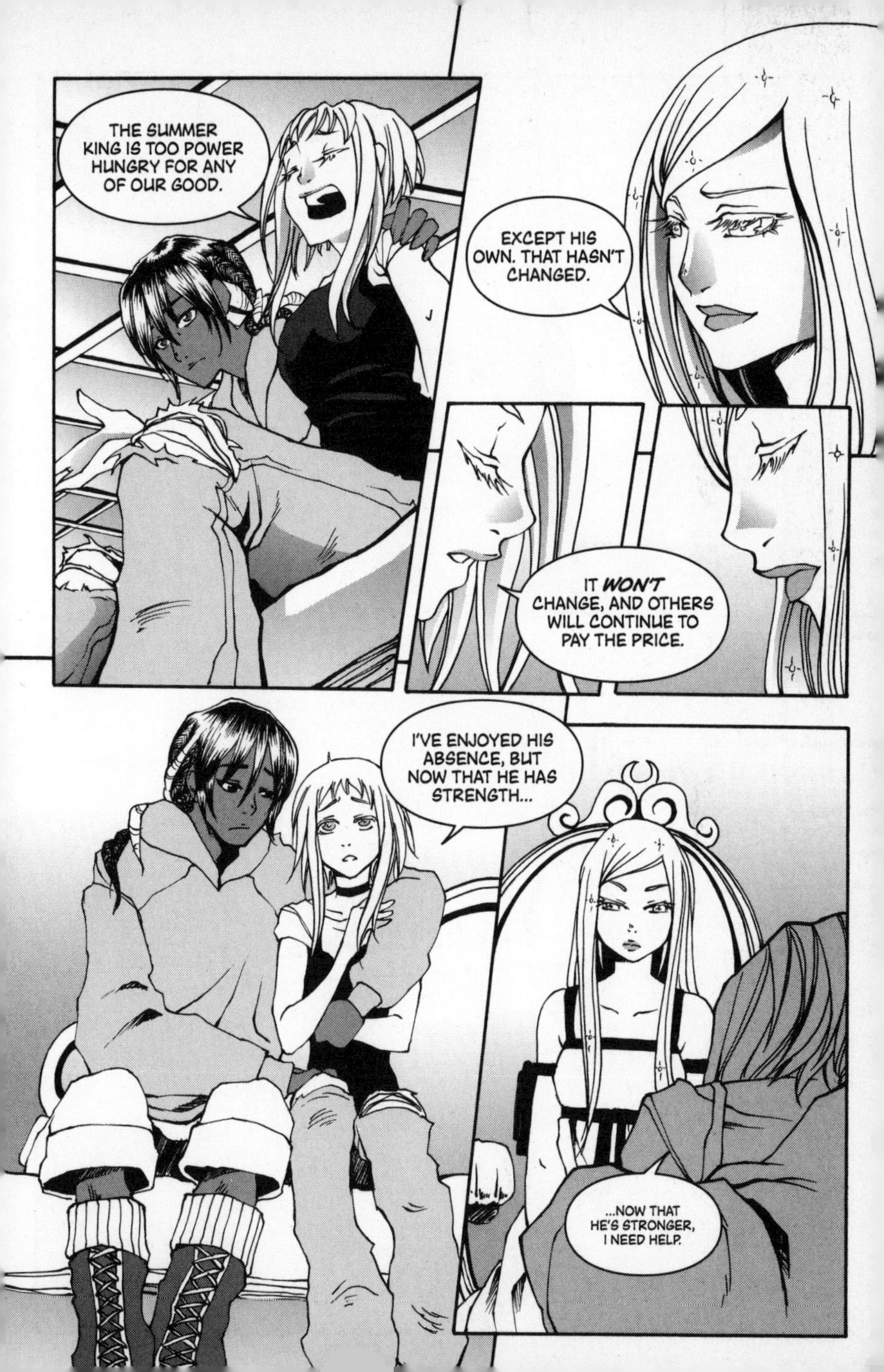
THE SUMMER KING IS TOO POWER HUNGRY FOR ANY OF OUR GOOD.
EXCEPT HIS OWN. THAT HASN'T CHANGED.
IT *WON'T* CHANGE, AND OTHERS WILL CONTINUE TO PAY THE PRICE.
I'VE ENJOYED HIS ABSENCE, BUT NOW THAT HE HAS STRENGTH...
...NOW THAT HE'S STRONGER, I NEED HELP.

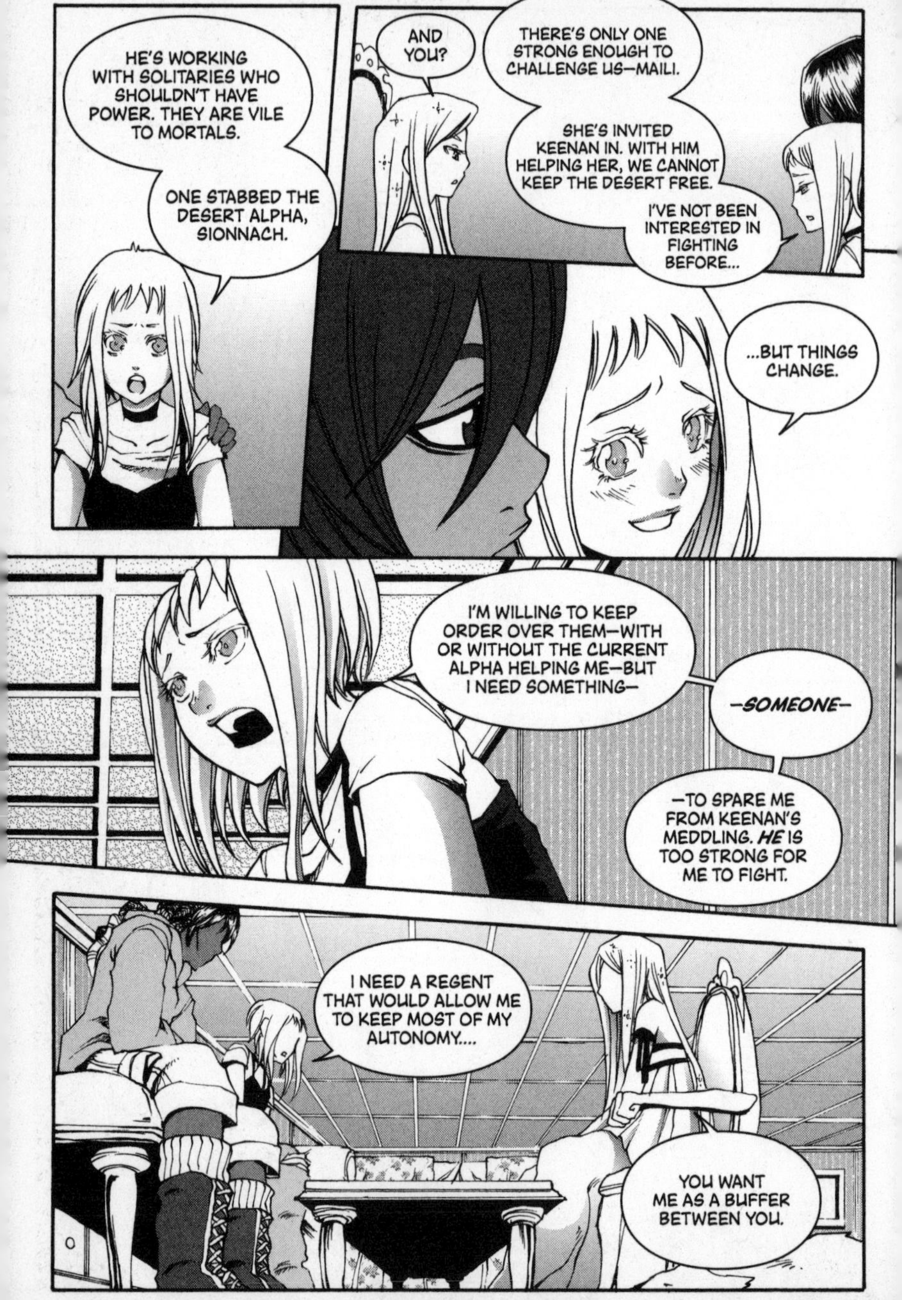
HE'S WORKING WITH SOLITARIES WHO SHOULDN'T HAVE POWER. THEY ARE VILE TO MORTALS.
ONE STABBED THE DESERT ALPHA, SIONNACH.
AND YOU?
THERE'S ONLY ONE STRONG ENOUGH TO CHALLENGE US—MAILI.
SHE'S INVITED KEENAN IN. WITH HIM HELPING HER, WE CANNOT KEEP THE DESERT FREE.
I'VE NOT BEEN INTERESTED IN FIGHTING BEFORE...
...BUT THINGS CHANGE.
I'M WILLING TO KEEP ORDER OVER THEM—WITH OR WITHOUT THE CURRENT ALPHA HELPING ME—BUT I NEED SOMETHING—
—SOMEONE—
—TO SPARE ME FROM KEENAN'S MEDDLING. HE IS TOO STRONG FOR ME TO FIGHT.
I NEED A REGENT THAT WOULD ALLOW ME TO KEEP MOST OF MY AUTONOMY....
YOU WANT ME AS A BUFFER BETWEEN YOU.

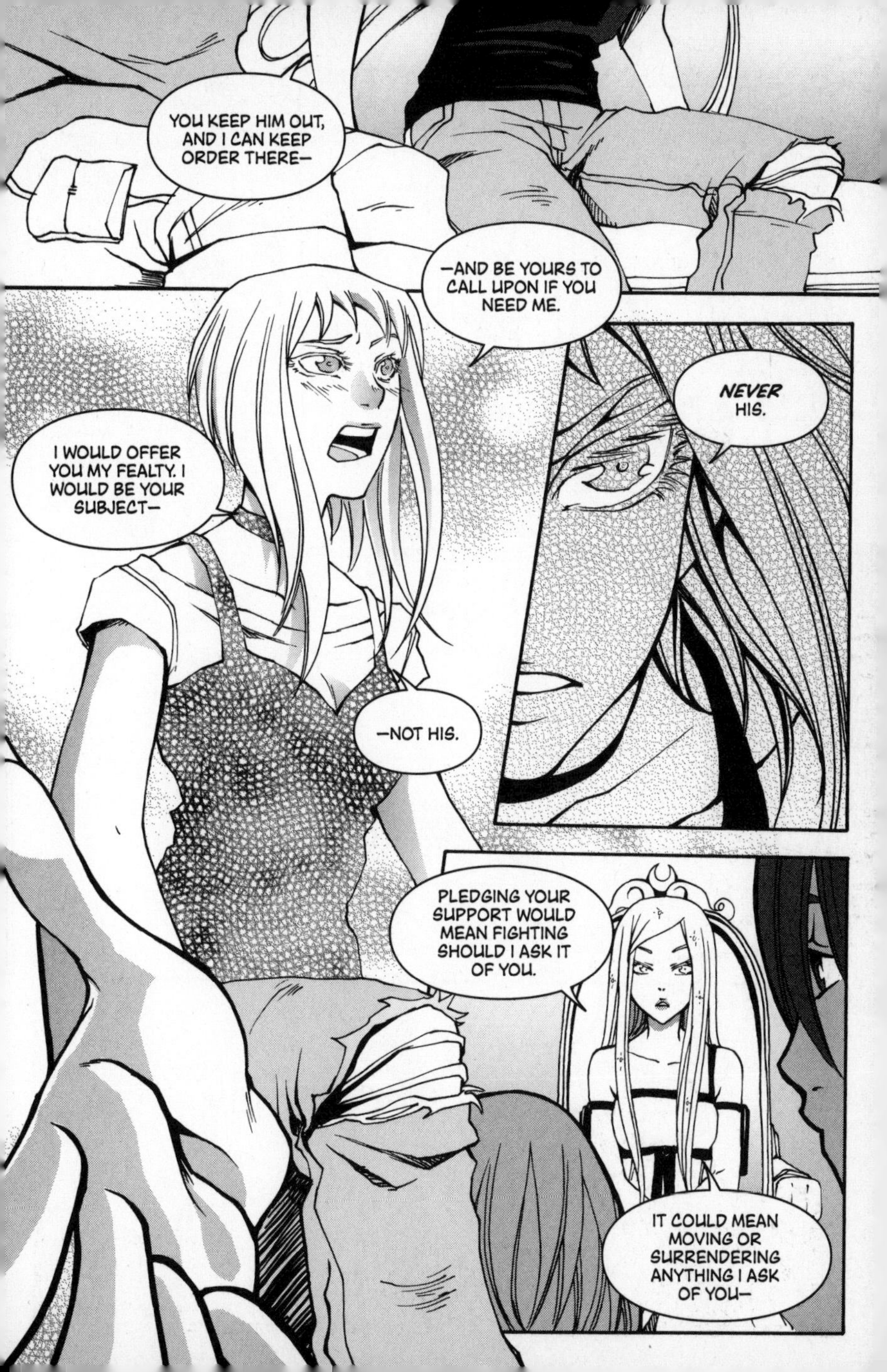
YOU KEEP HIM OUT, AND I CAN KEEP ORDER THERE—
—AND BE YOURS TO CALL UPON IF YOU NEED ME.
I WOULD OFFER YOU MY FEALTY. I WOULD BE YOUR SUBJECT—
—NOT HIS.
NEVER HIS.
PLEDGING YOUR SUPPORT WOULD MEAN FIGHTING SHOULD I ASK IT OF YOU.
IT COULD MEAN MOVING OR SURRENDERING ANYTHING I ASK OF YOU—

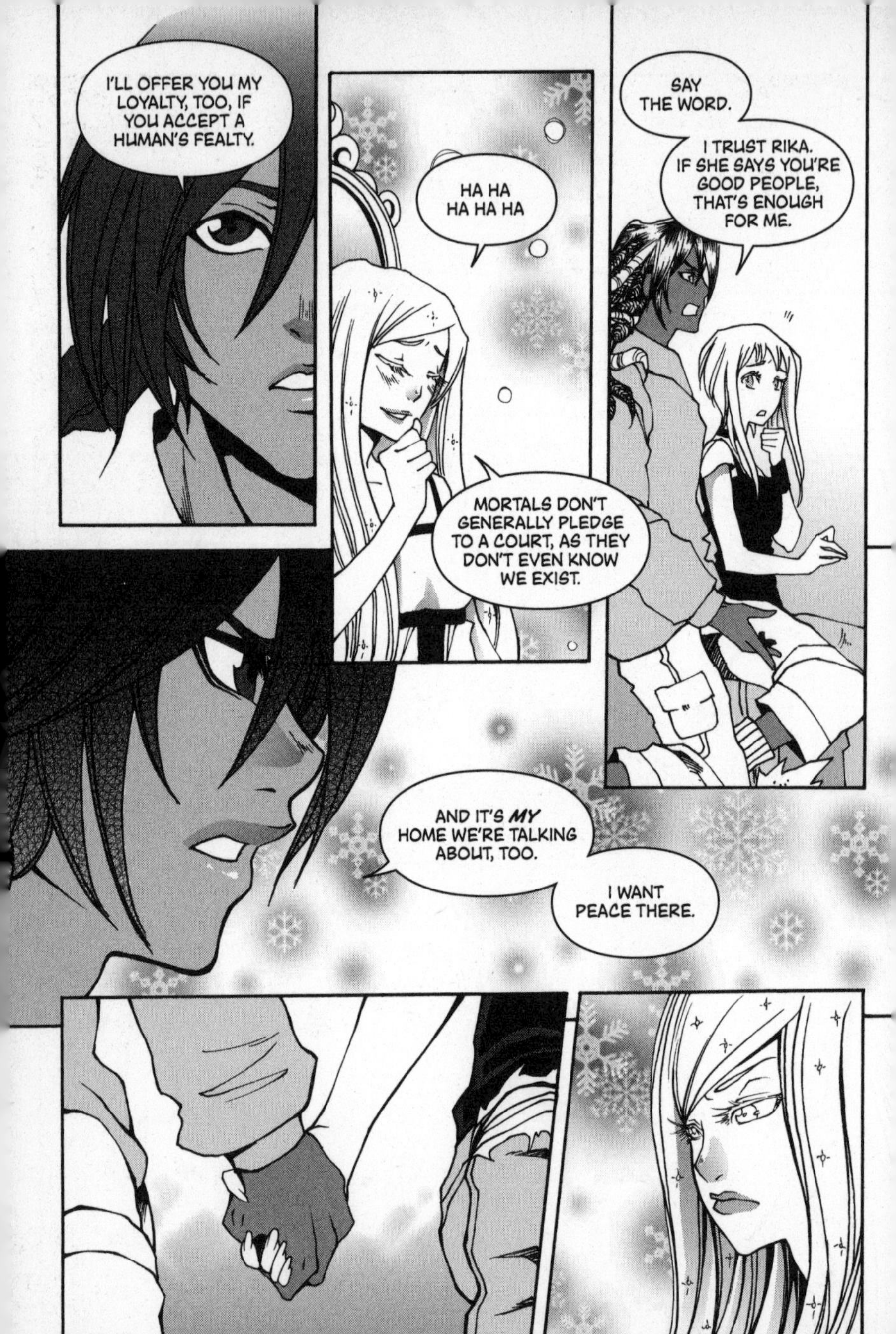
I'LL OFFER YOU MY LOYALTY, TOO, IF YOU ACCEPT A HUMAN'S FEALTY.
HA HA HA HA HA
MORTALS DON'T GENERALLY PLEDGE TO A COURT, AS THEY DON'T EVEN KNOW WE EXIST.
SAY THE WORD.
I TRUST RIKA. IF SHE SAYS YOU'RE GOOD PEOPLE, THAT'S ENOUGH FOR ME.
AND IT'S *MY* HOME WE'RE TALKING ABOUT, TOO.
I WANT PEACE THERE.

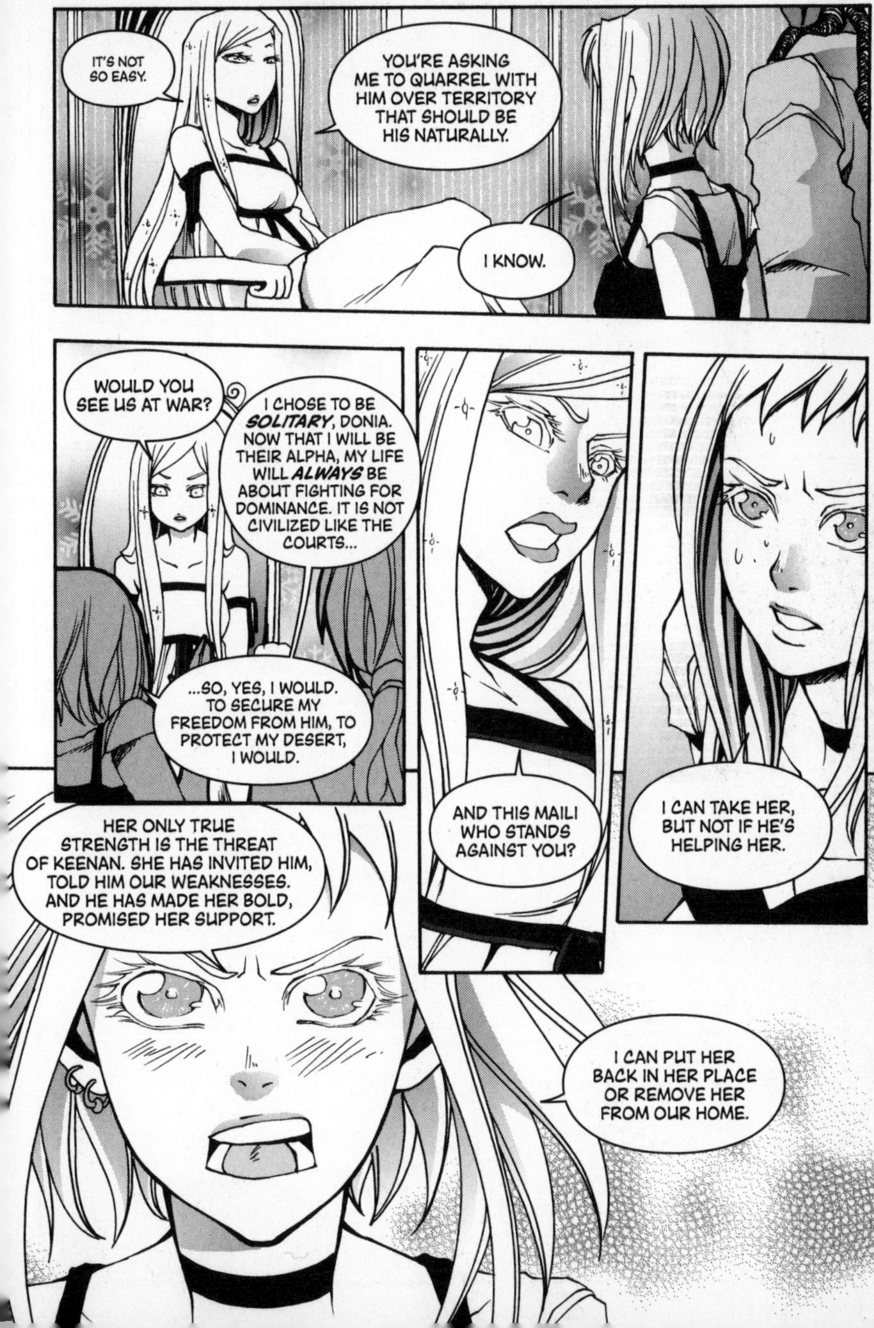
IT'S NOT SO EASY.
YOU'RE ASKING ME TO QUARREL WITH HIM OVER TERRITORY THAT SHOULD BE HIS NATURALLY.
I KNOW.
WOULD YOU SEE US AT WAR?
I CHOSE TO BE *SOLITARY*, DONIA. NOW THAT I WILL BE THEIR ALPHA, MY LIFE WILL *ALWAYS* BE ABOUT FIGHTING FOR DOMINANCE. IT IS NOT CIVILIZED LIKE THE COURTS...
...SO, YES, I WOULD. TO SECURE MY FREEDOM FROM HIM, TO PROTECT MY DESERT, I WOULD.
AND THIS MAILI WHO STANDS AGAINST YOU?
I CAN TAKE HER, BUT NOT IF HE'S HELPING HER.
HER ONLY TRUE STRENGTH IS THE THREAT OF KEENAN. SHE HAS INVITED HIM, TOLD HIM OUR WEAKNESSES. AND HE HAS MADE HER BOLD, PROMISED HER SUPPORT.
I CAN PUT HER BACK IN HER PLACE OR REMOVE HER FROM OUR HOME.

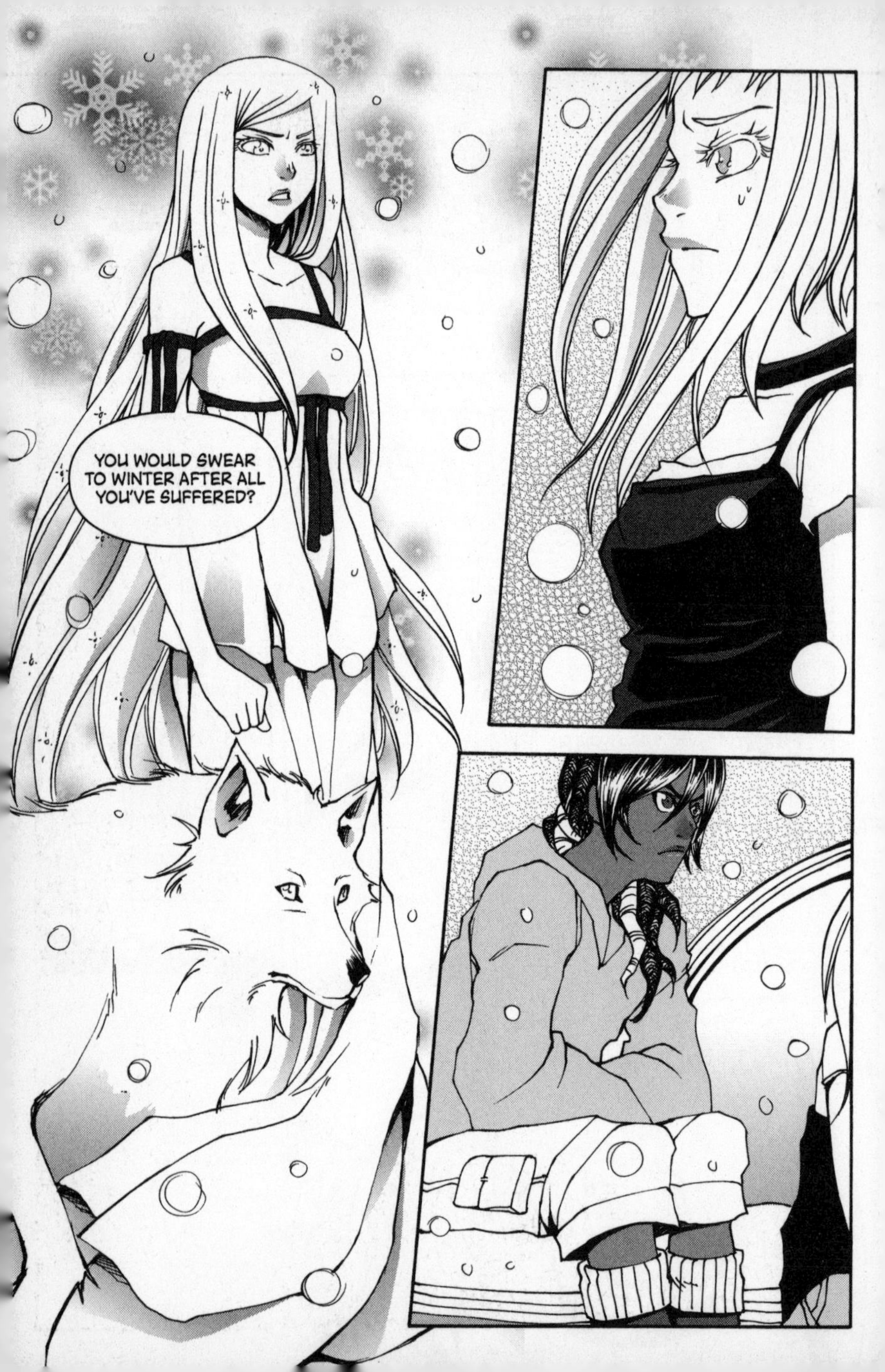
YOU WOULD SWEAR TO WINTER AFTER ALL YOU'VE SUFFERED?

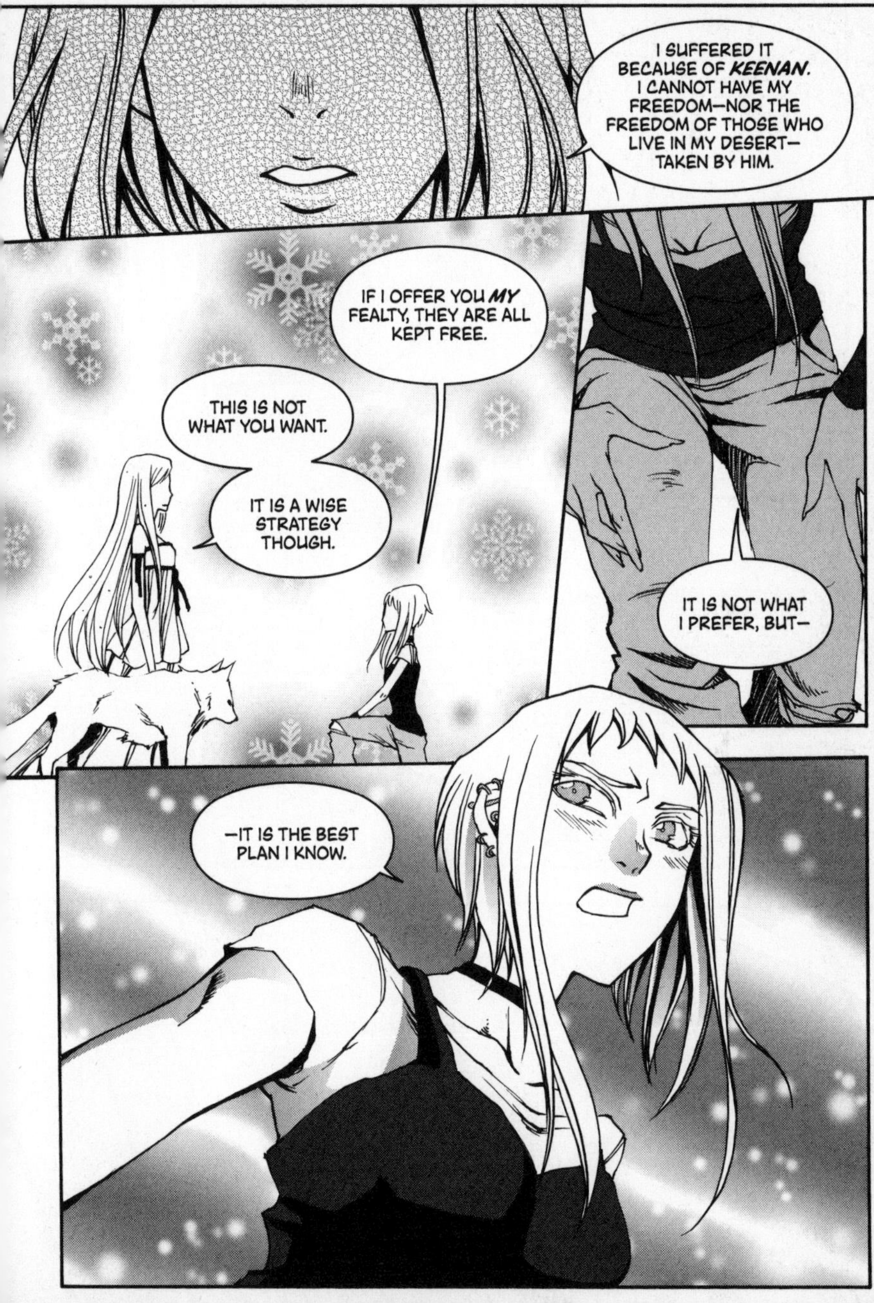
I SUFFERED IT BECAUSE OF ***KEENAN.*** I CANNOT HAVE MY FREEDOM—NOR THE FREEDOM OF THOSE WHO LIVE IN MY DESERT—TAKEN BY HIM.
IF I OFFER YOU ***MY*** FEALTY, THEY ARE ALL KEPT FREE.
THIS IS NOT WHAT YOU WANT.
IT IS A WISE STRATEGY THOUGH.
IT IS NOT WHAT I PREFER, BUT—
—IT IS THE BEST PLAN I KNOW.

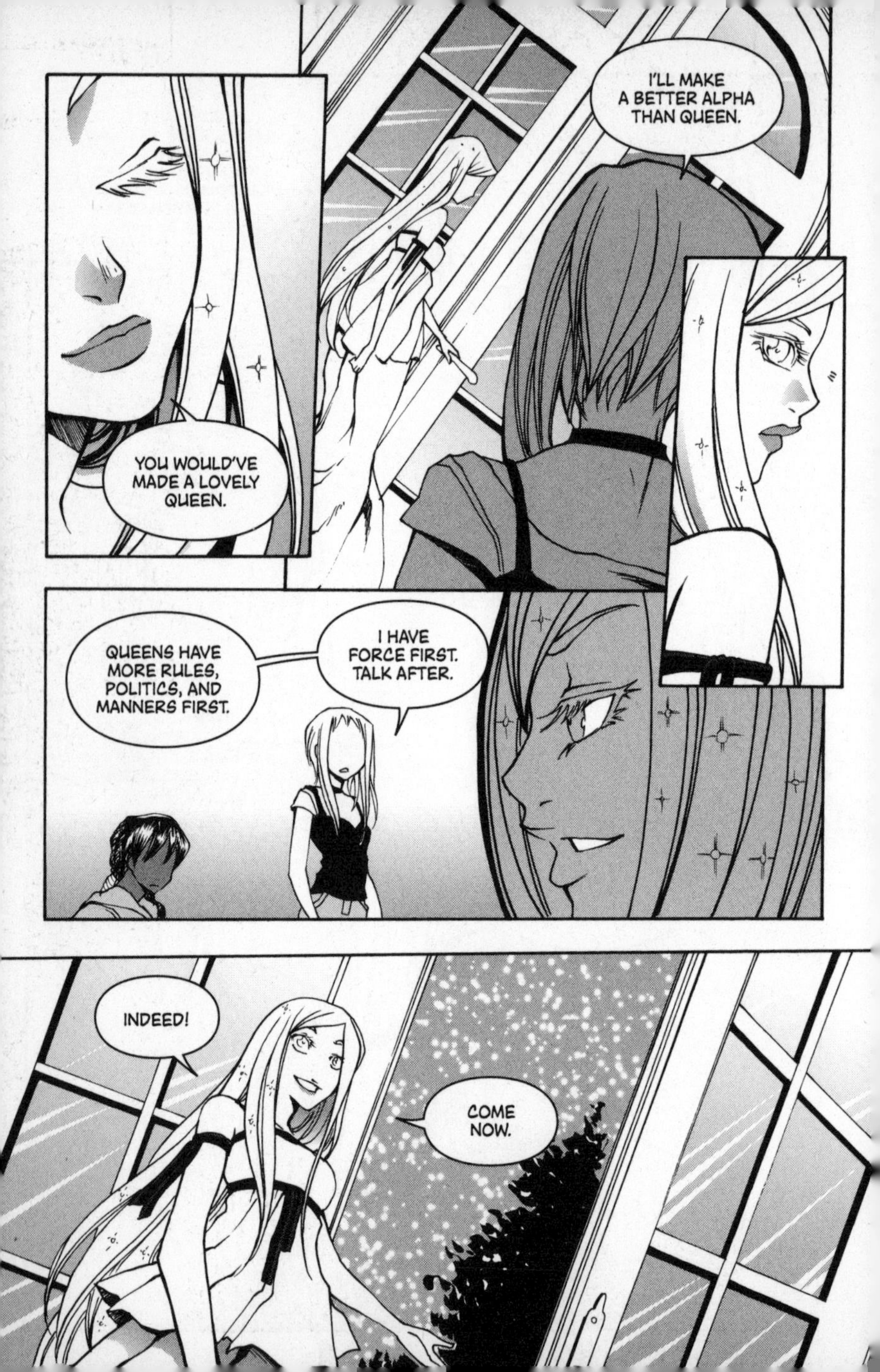
YOU WOULD'VE MADE A LOVELY QUEEN.
I'LL MAKE A BETTER ALPHA THAN QUEEN.
I HAVE FORCE FIRST. TALK AFTER.
QUEENS HAVE MORE RULES, POLITICS, AND MANNERS FIRST.
INDEED!
COME NOW.

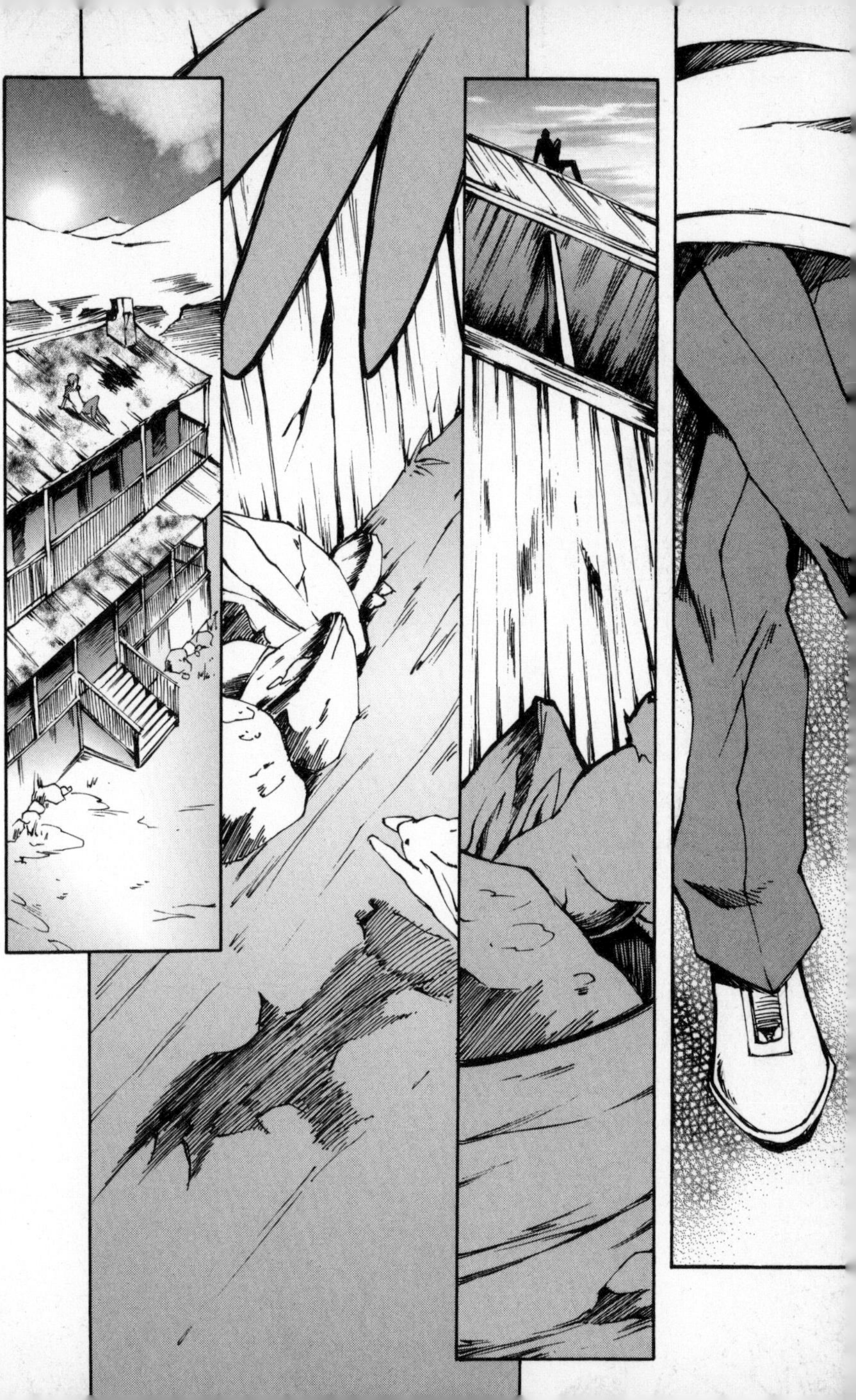

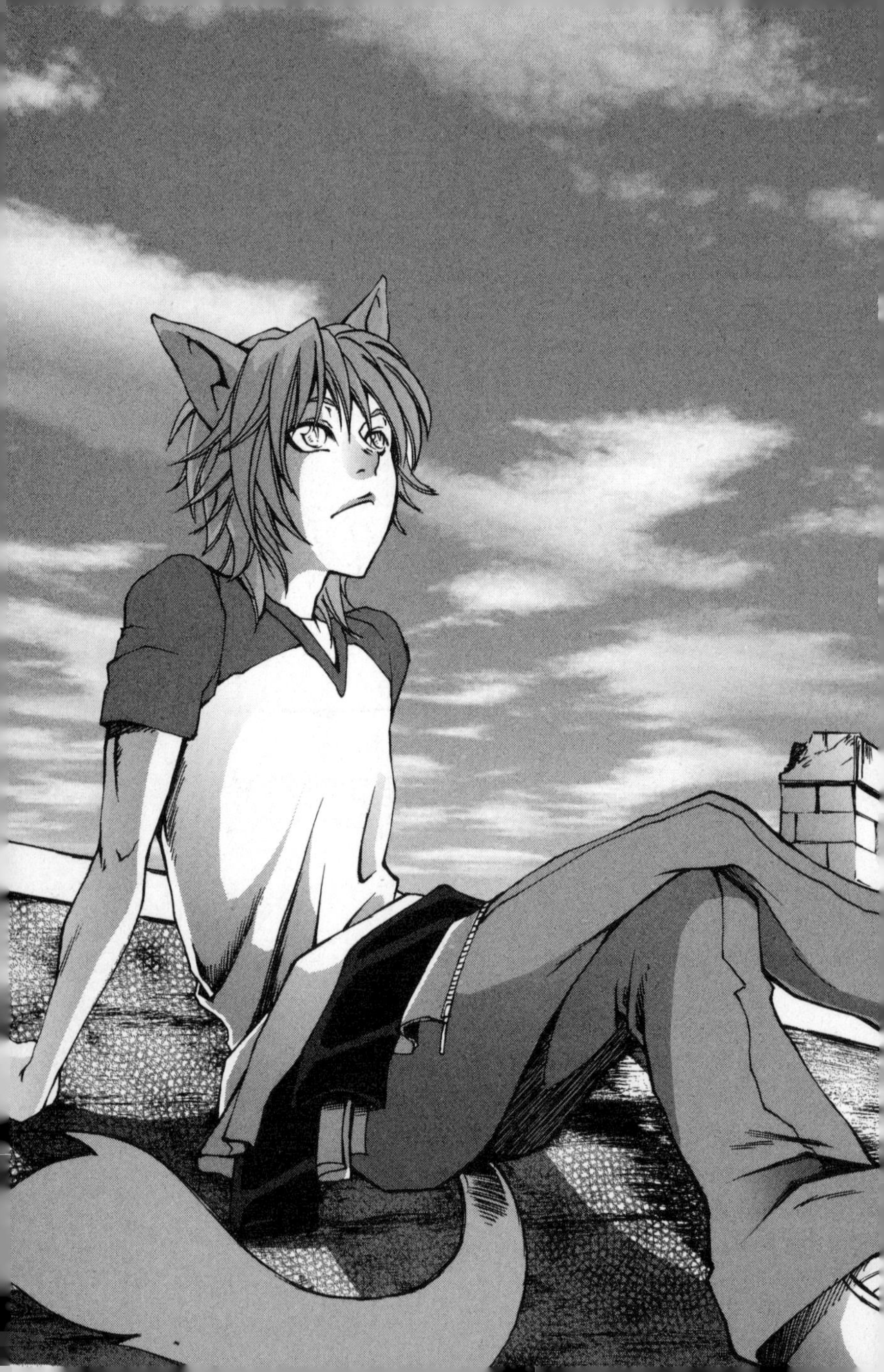

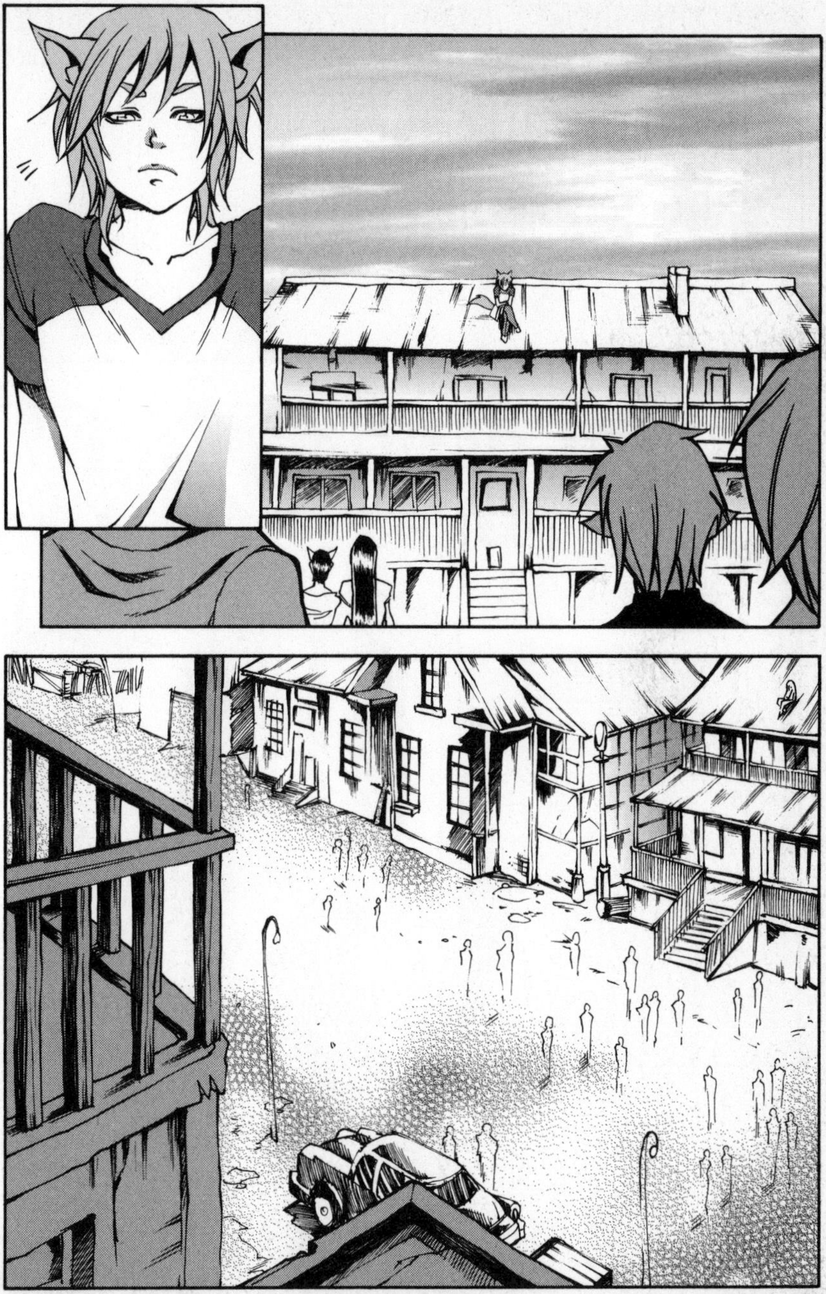

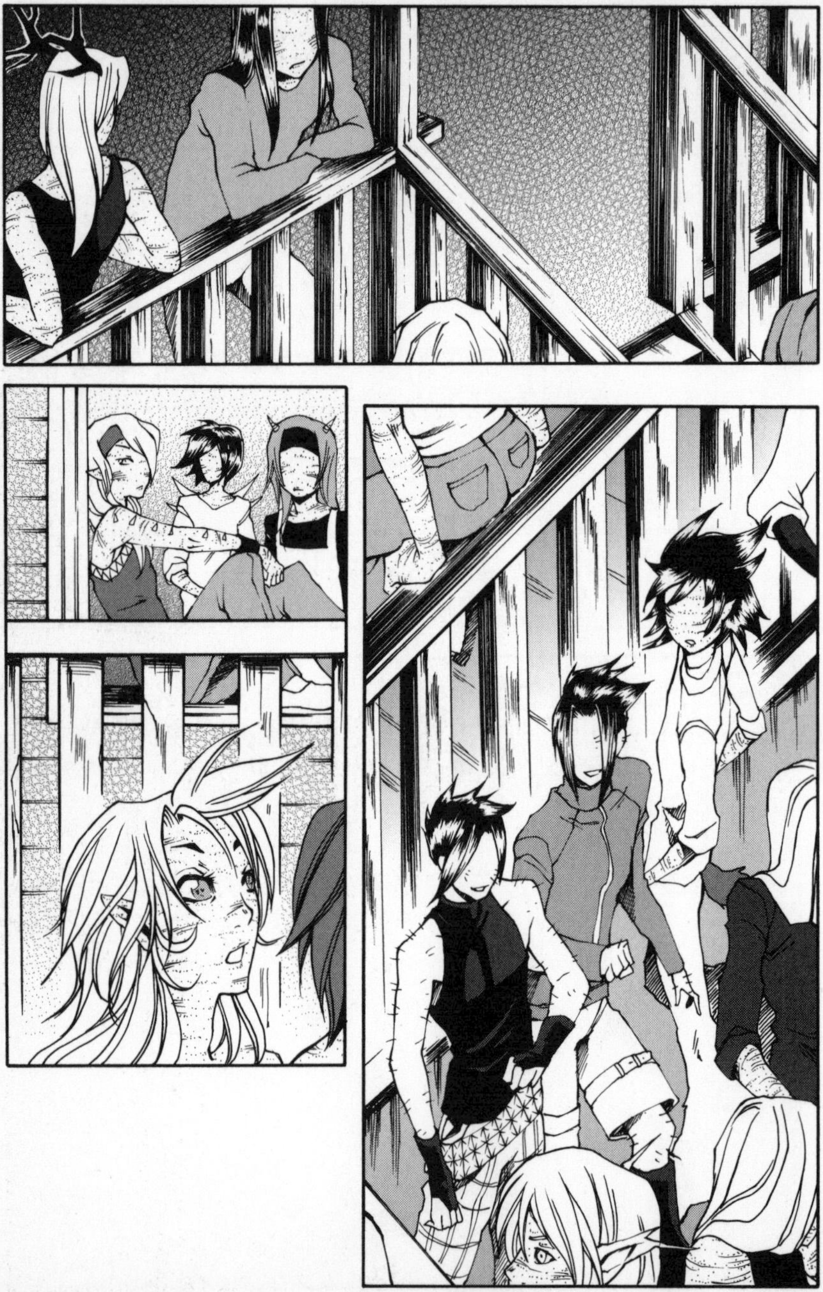

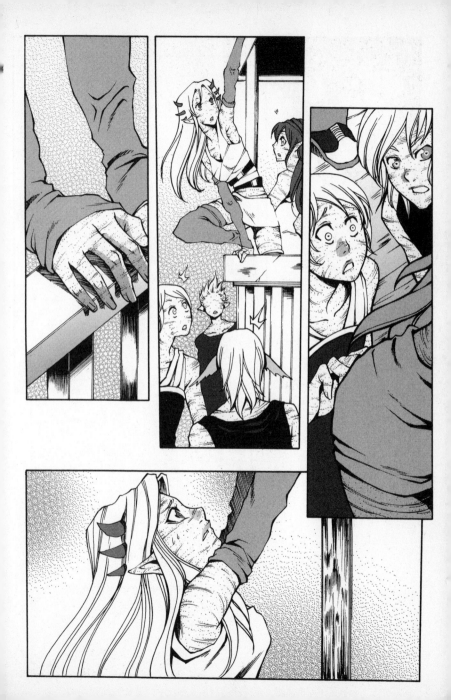

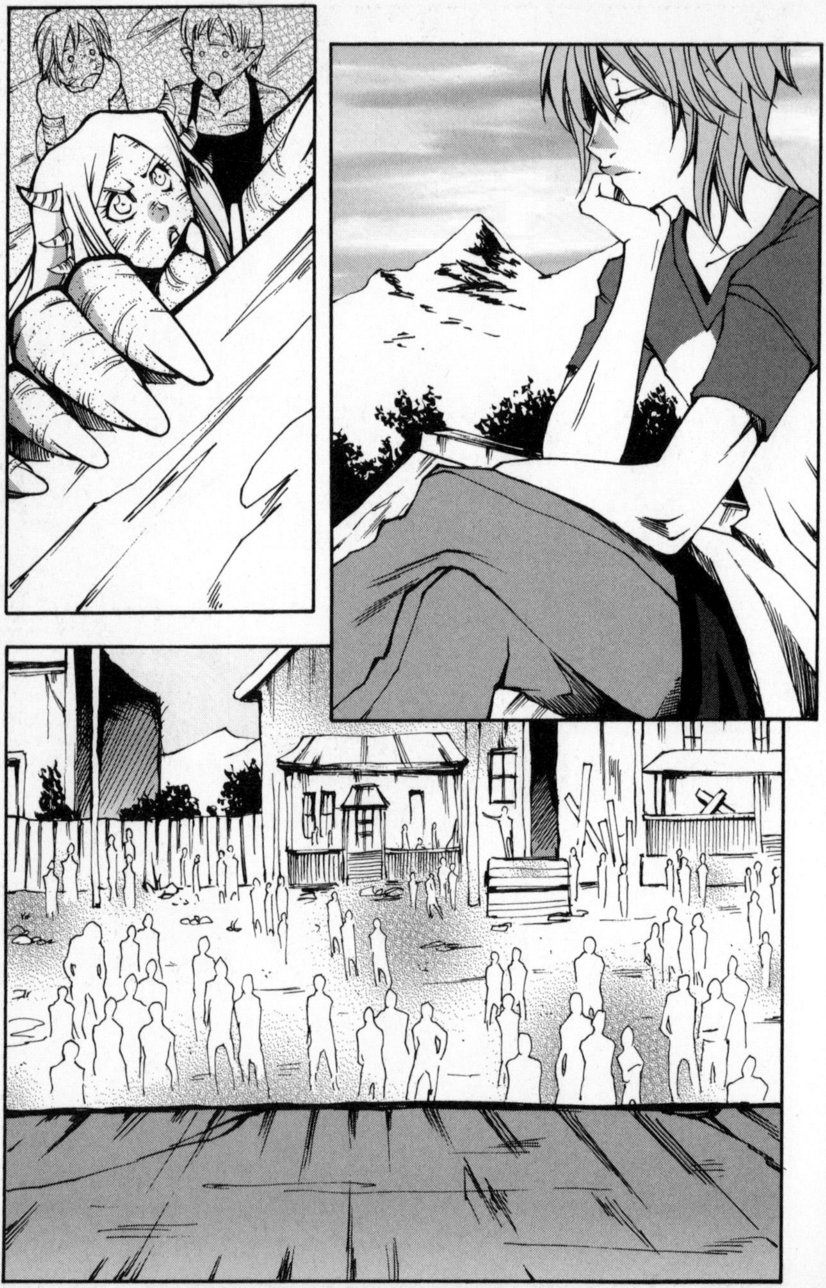

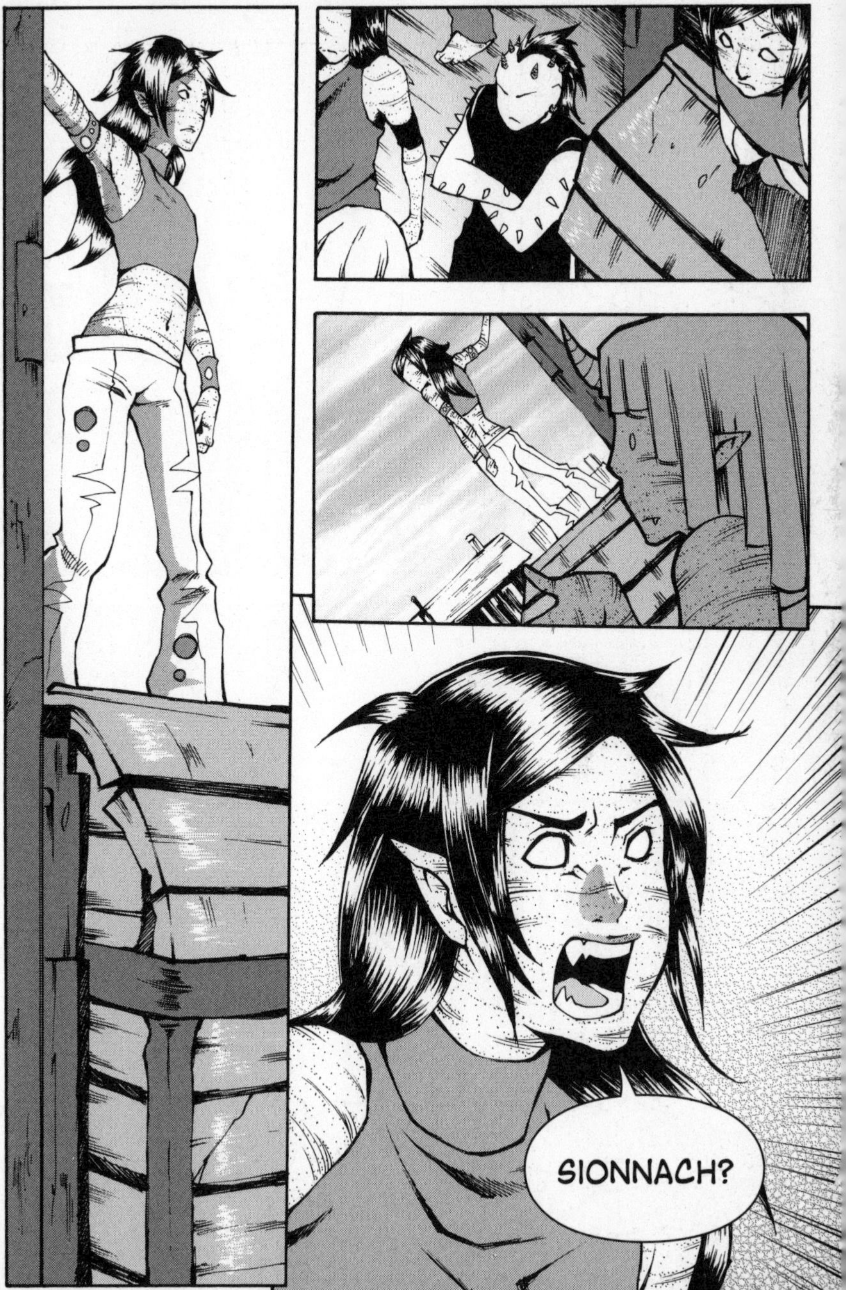
SIONNACH?

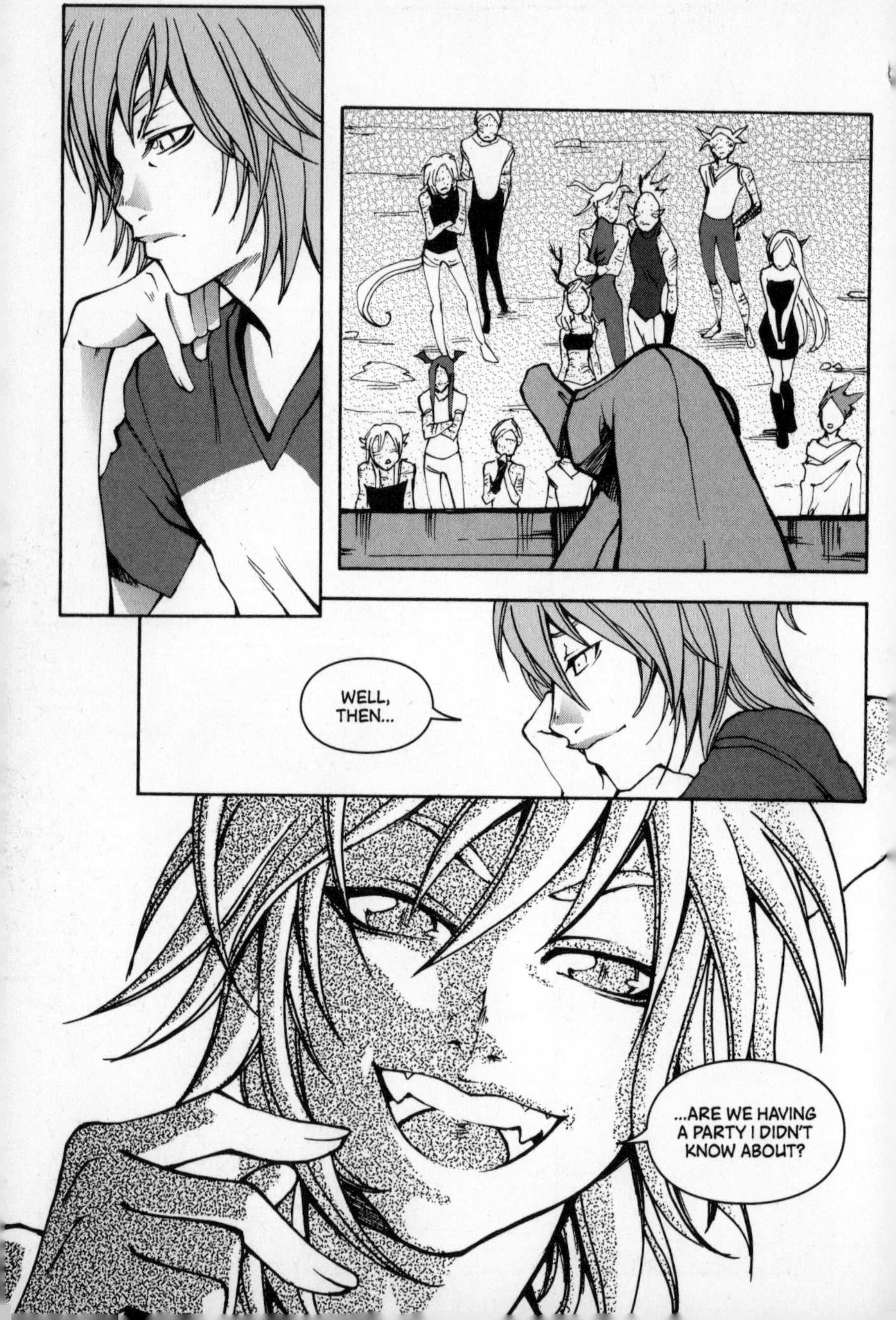
WELL, THEN...
...ARE WE HAVING A PARTY I DIDN'T KNOW ABOUT?

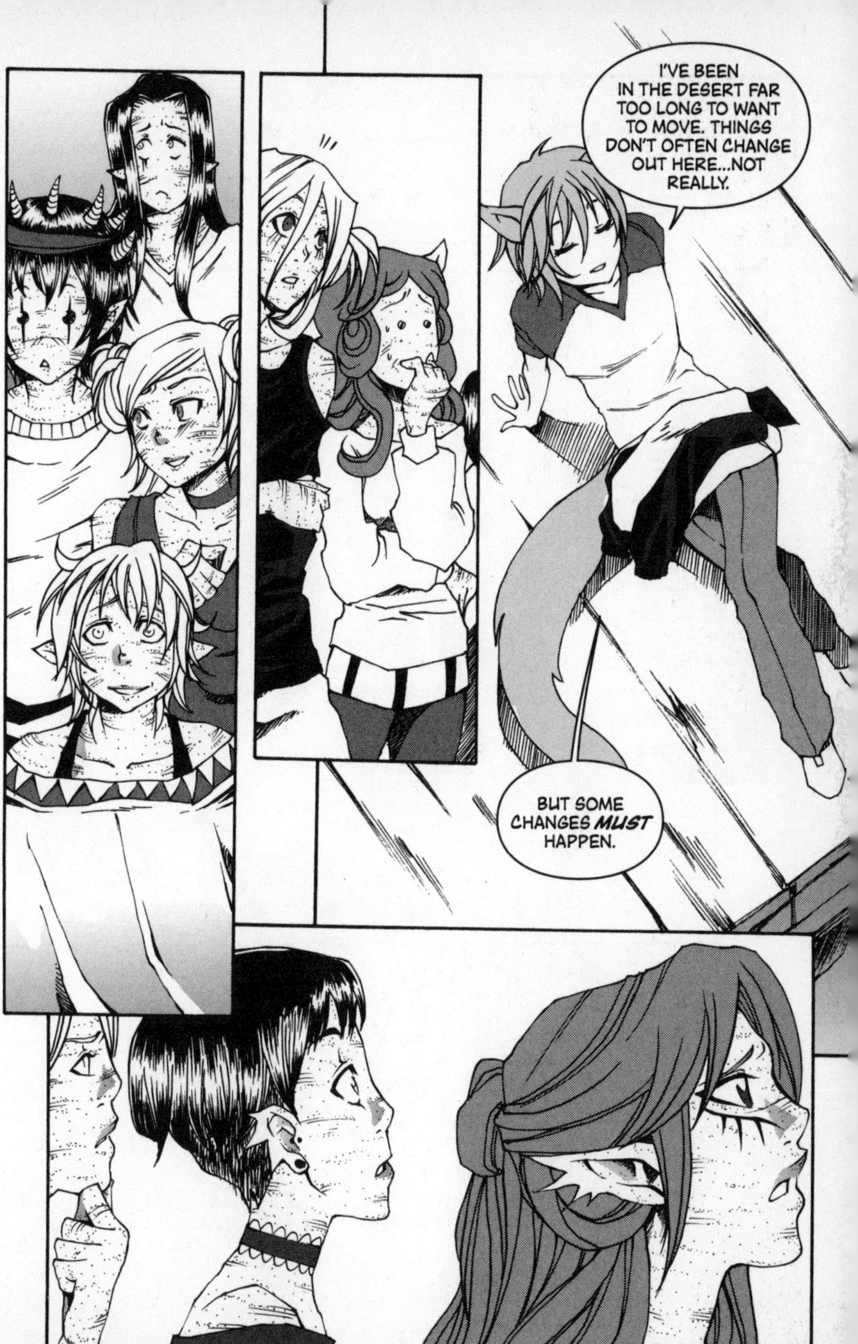
I'VE BEEN IN THE DESERT FAR TOO LONG TO WANT TO MOVE. THINGS DON'T OFTEN CHANGE OUT HERE...NOT REALLY.
BUT SOME CHANGES *MUST* HAPPEN.

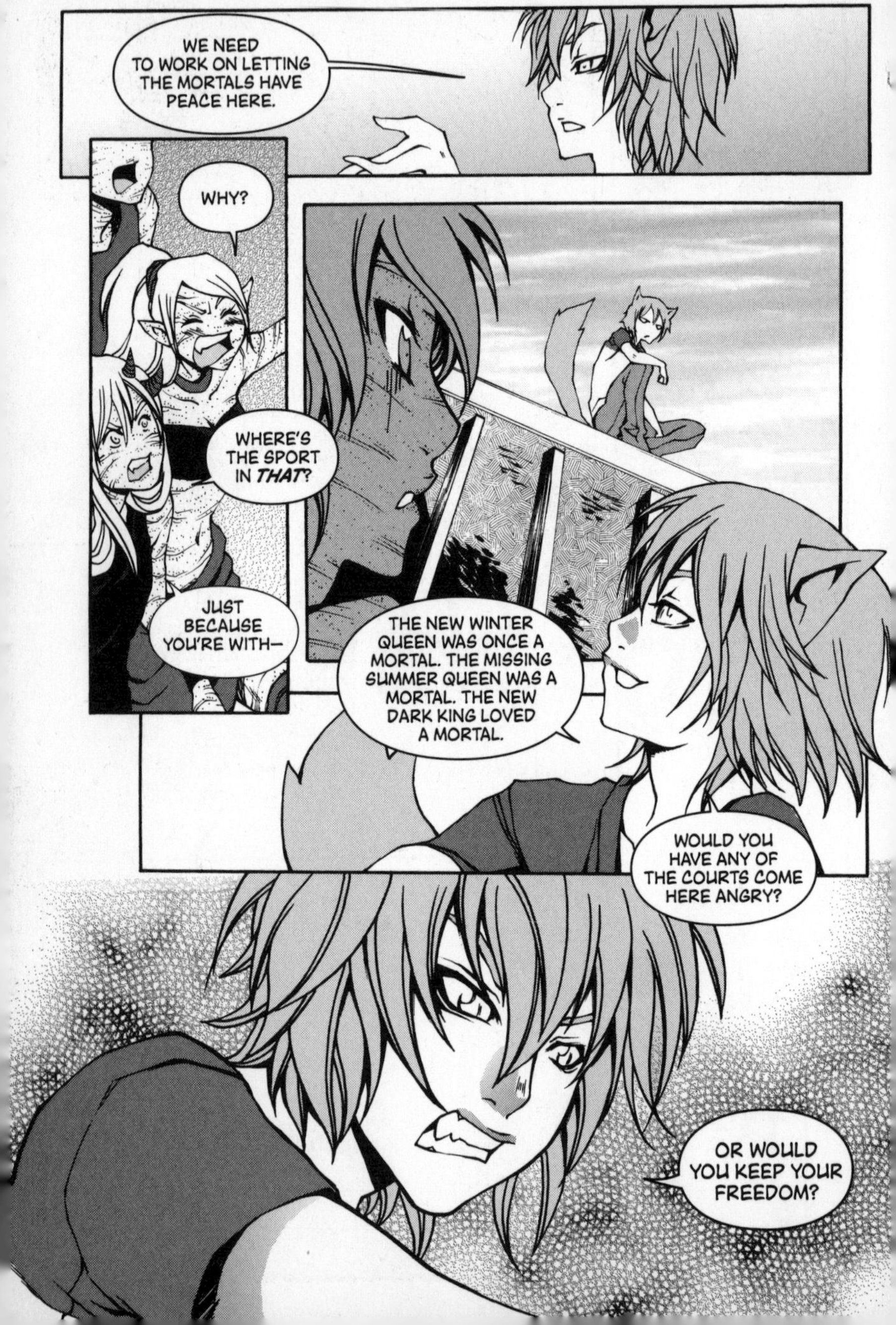
WE NEED TO WORK ON LETTING THE MORTALS HAVE PEACE HERE.
WHY?
WHERE'S THE SPORT IN *THAT*?
JUST BECAUSE YOU'RE WITH—
THE NEW WINTER QUEEN WAS ONCE A MORTAL. THE MISSING SUMMER QUEEN WAS A MORTAL. THE NEW DARK KING LOVED A MORTAL.
WOULD YOU HAVE ANY OF THE COURTS COME HERE ANGRY?
OR WOULD YOU KEEP YOUR FREEDOM?

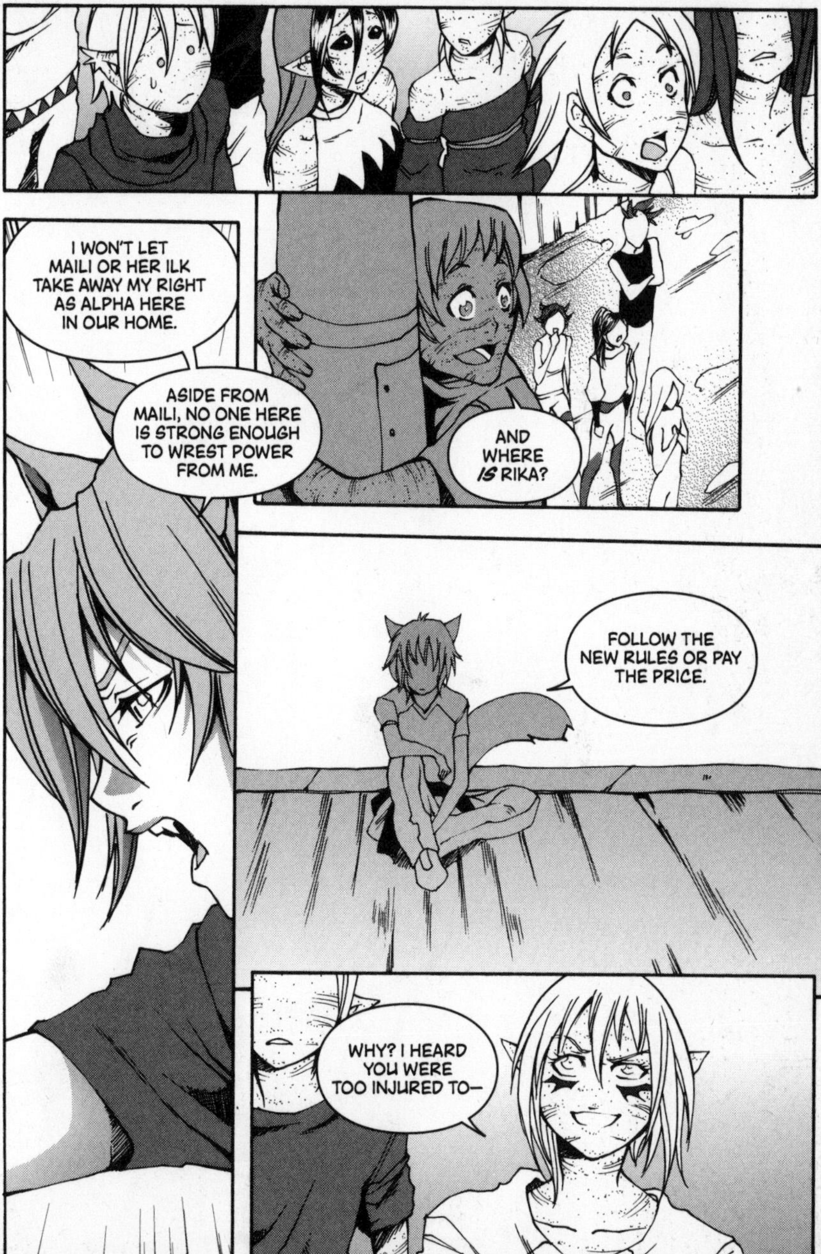
I WON'T LET MAILI OR HER ILK TAKE AWAY MY RIGHT AS ALPHA HERE IN OUR HOME.
ASIDE FROM MAILI, NO ONE HERE IS STRONG ENOUGH TO WREST POWER FROM ME.
AND WHERE *IS* RIKA?
FOLLOW THE NEW RULES OR PAY THE PRICE.
WHY? I HEARD YOU WERE TOO INJURED TO—

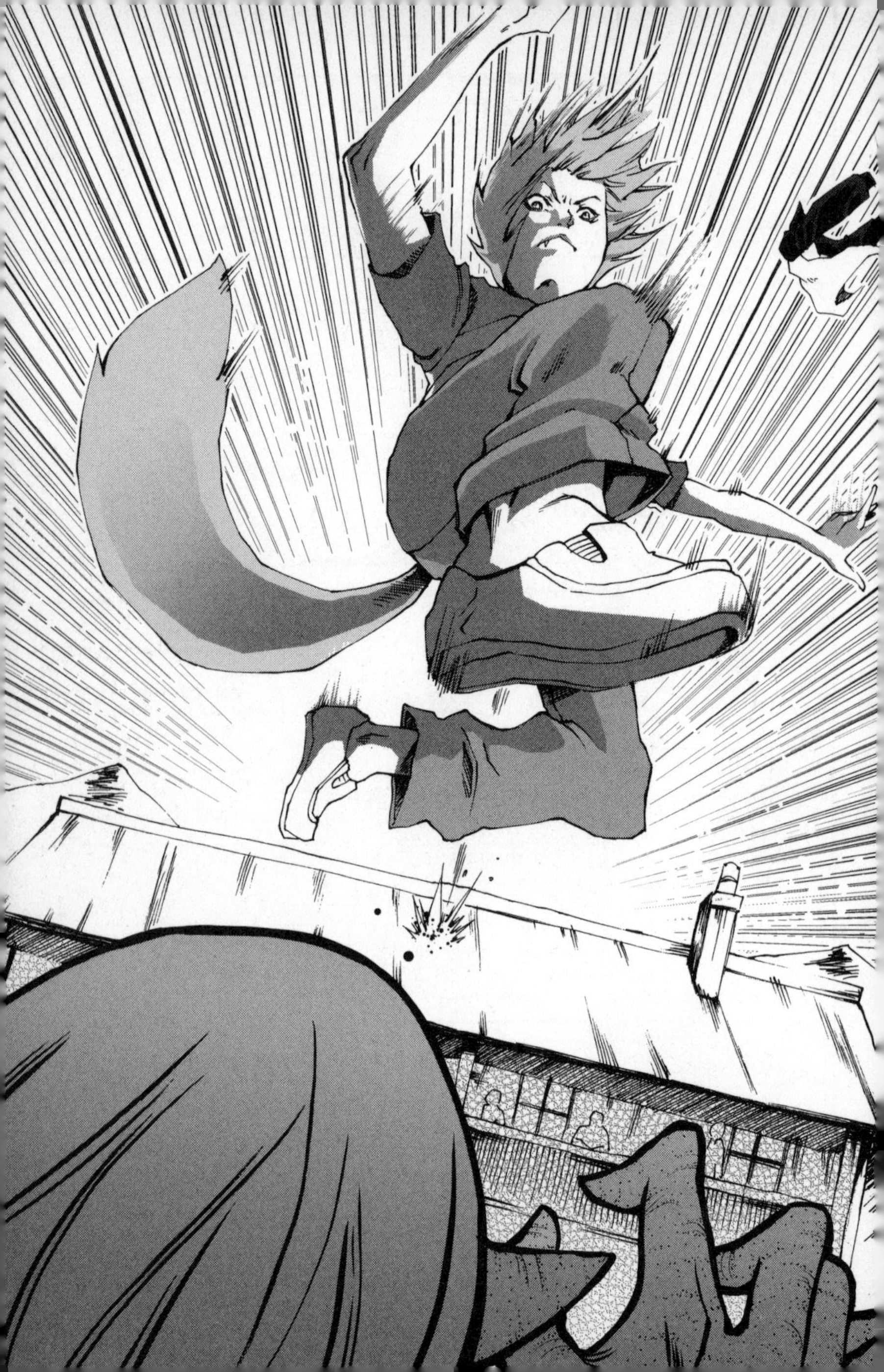

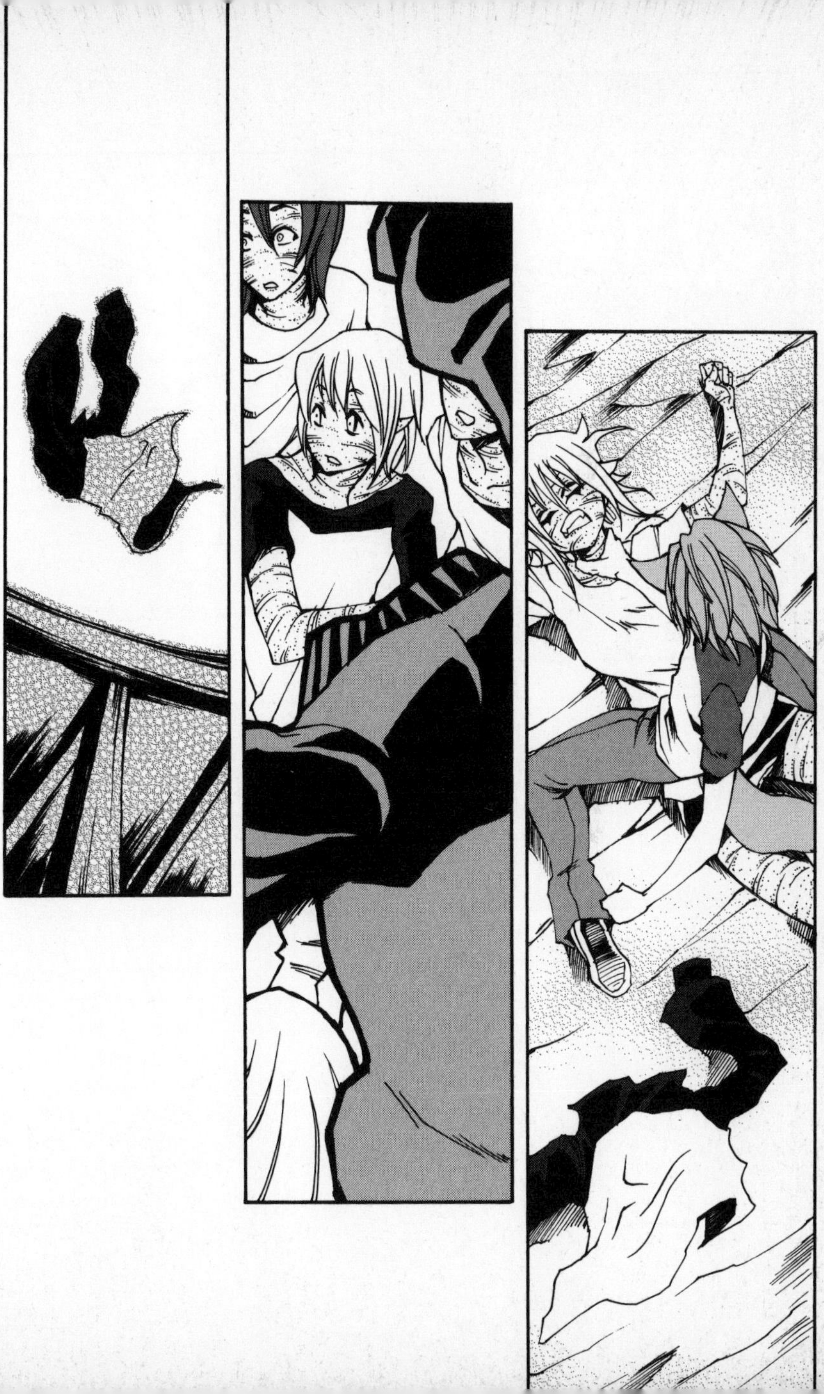

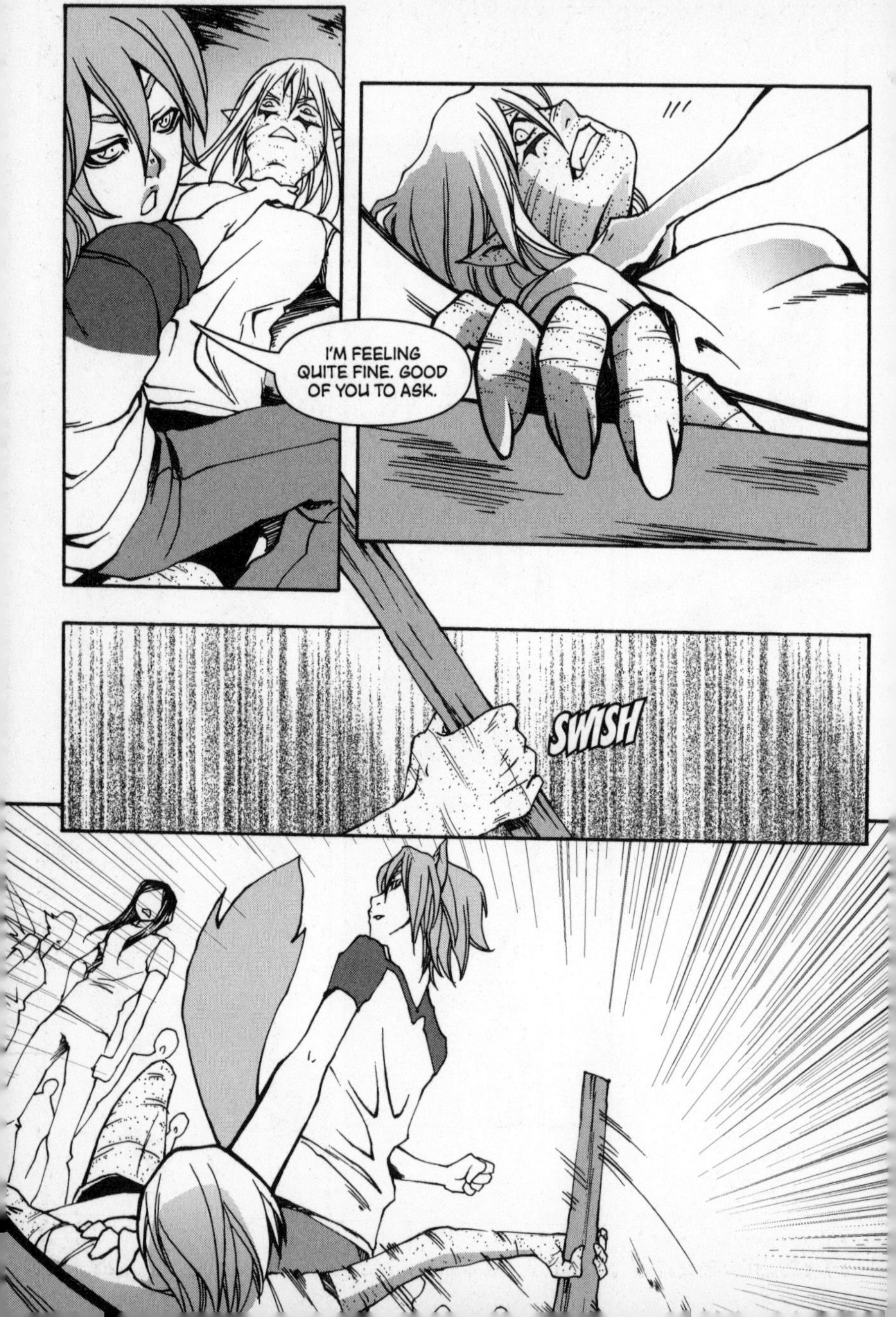
I'M FEELING QUITE FINE. GOOD OF YOU TO ASK.
SWISH

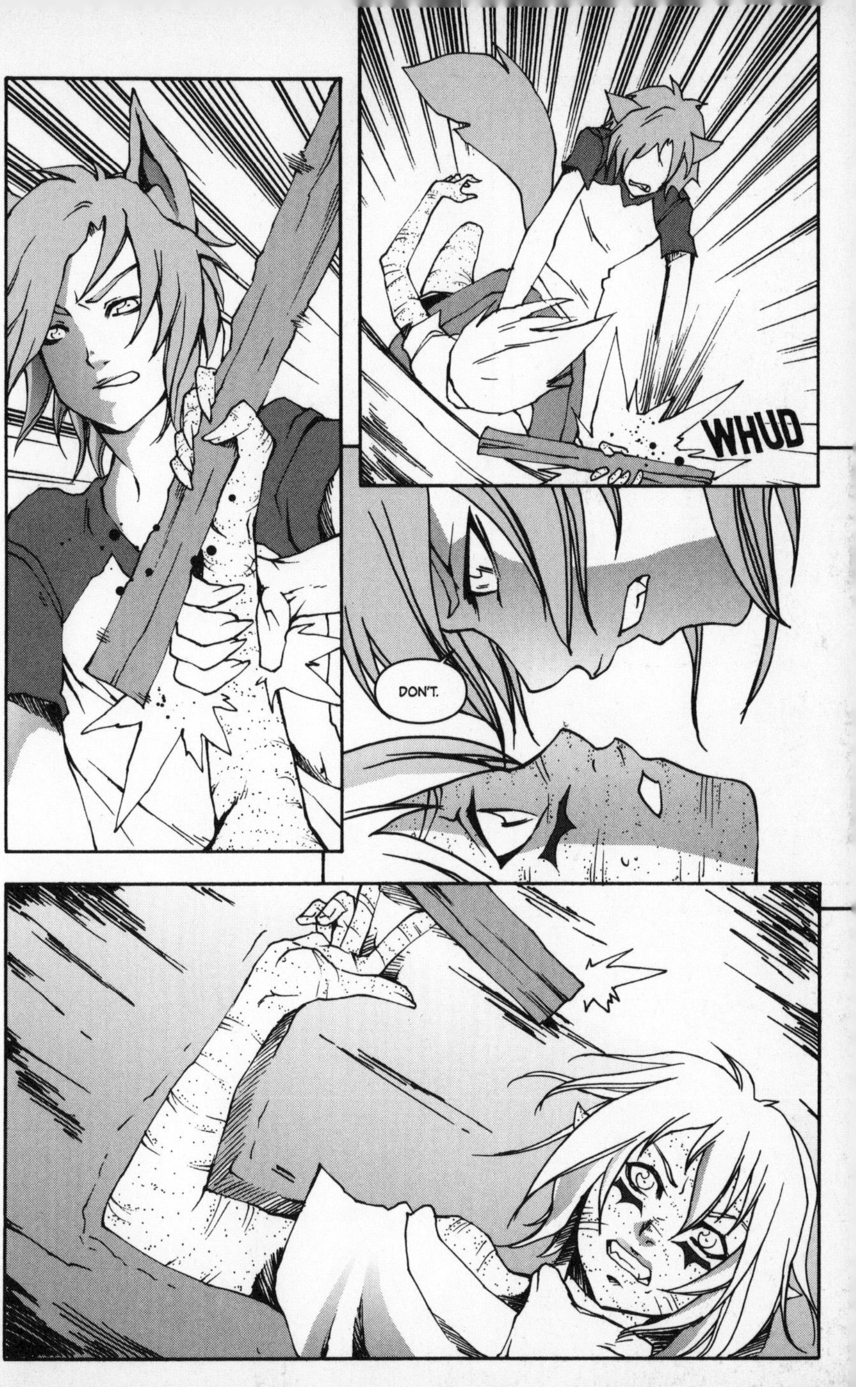
WHUD
DON'T.

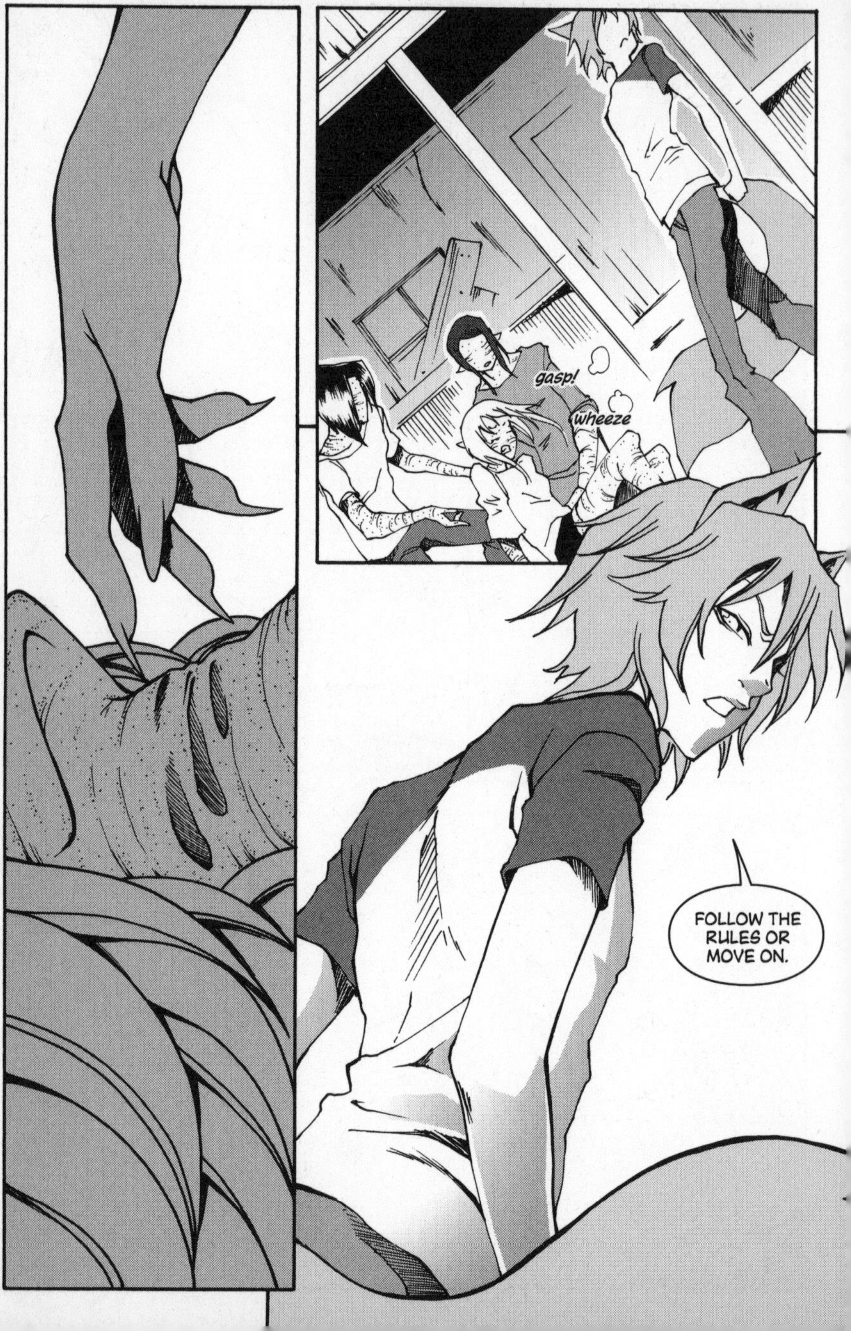
gasp!
wheeze
FOLLOW THE RULES OR MOVE ON.

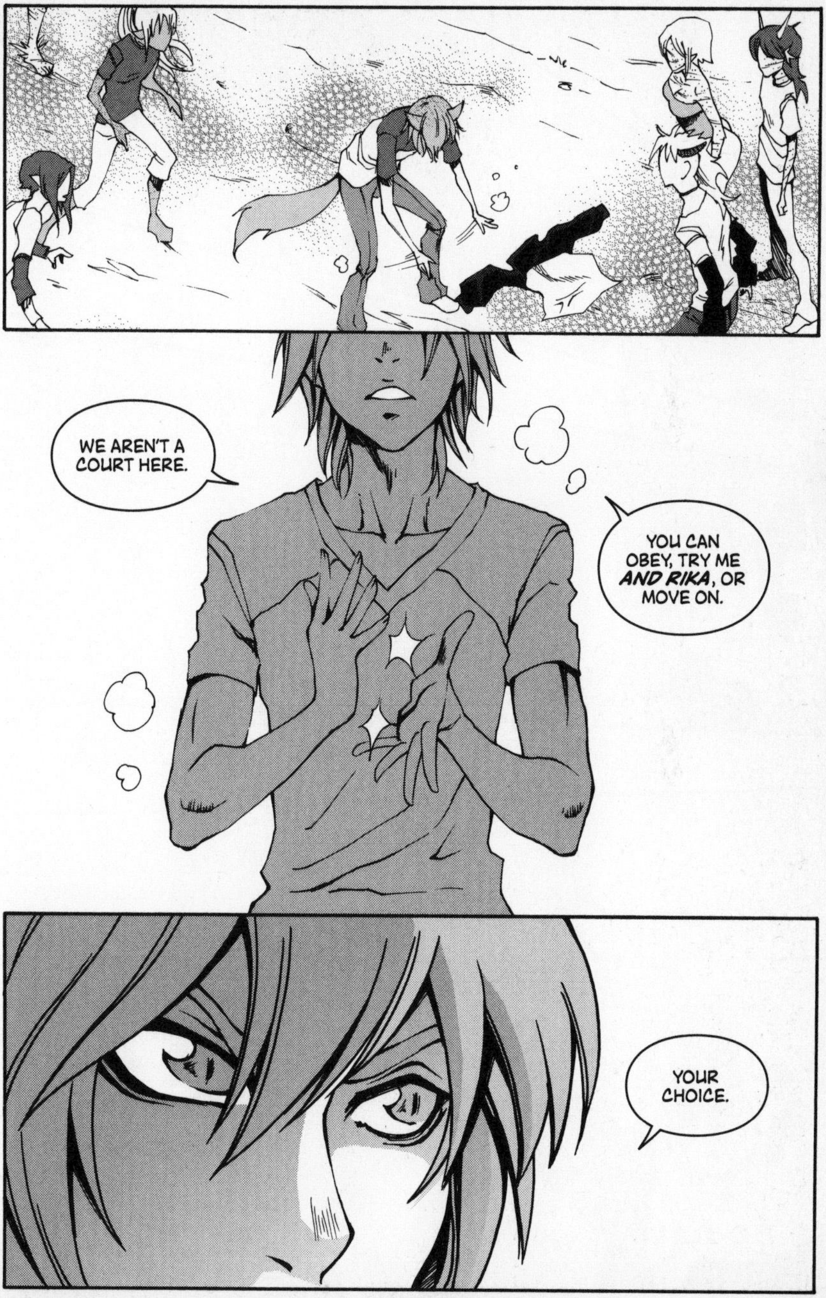
WE AREN'T A COURT HERE.
YOU CAN OBEY, TRY ME AND RIKA, OR MOVE ON.
YOUR CHOICE.

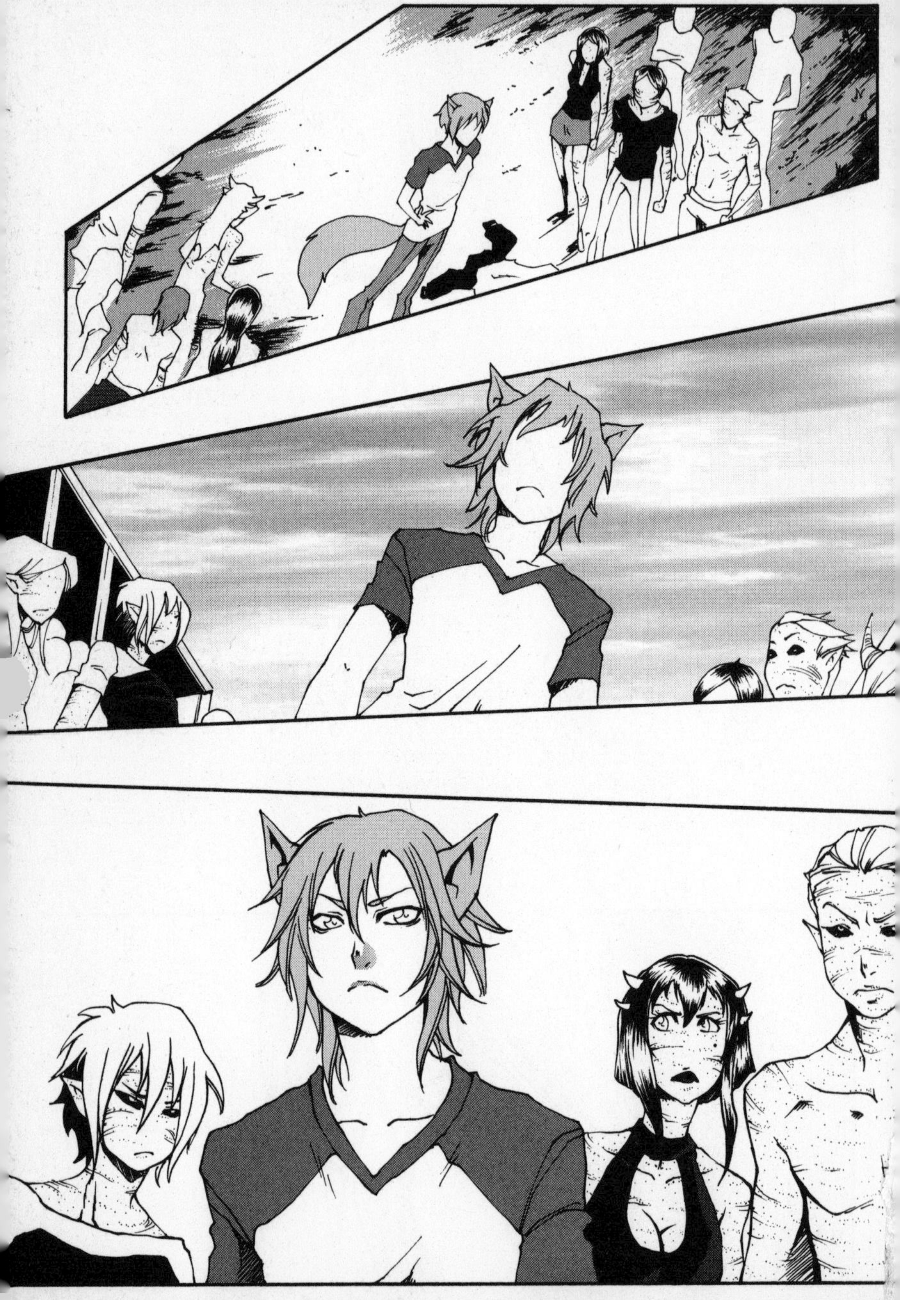

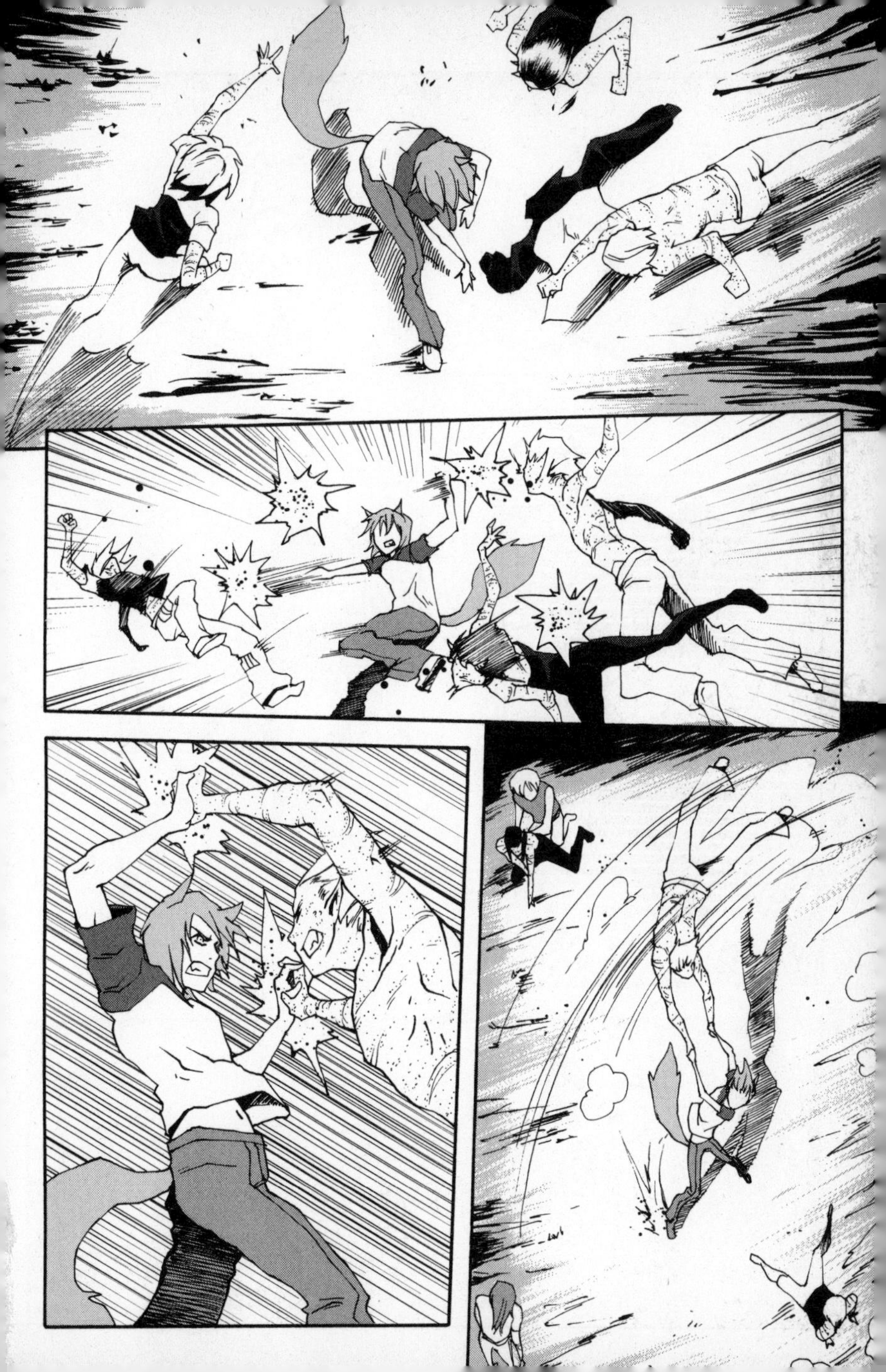

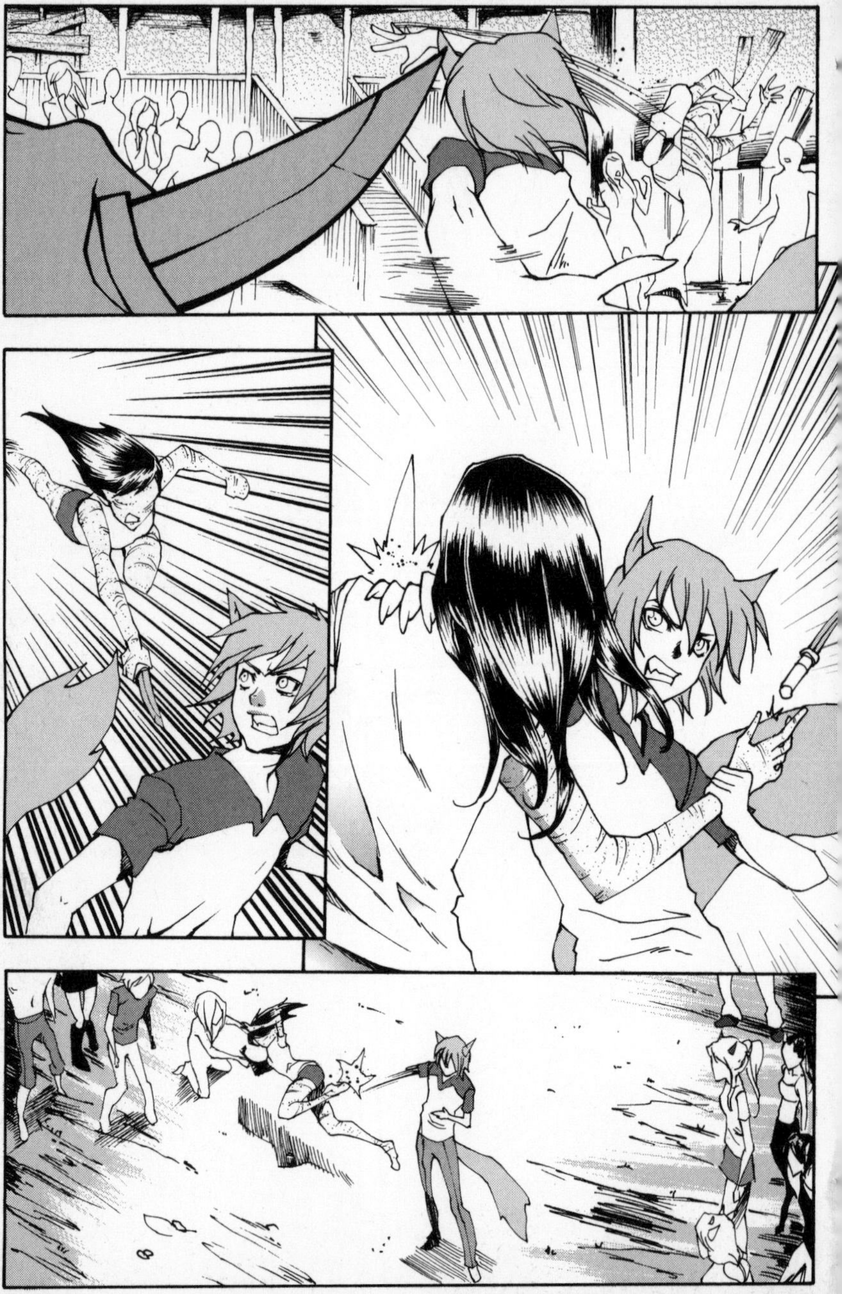

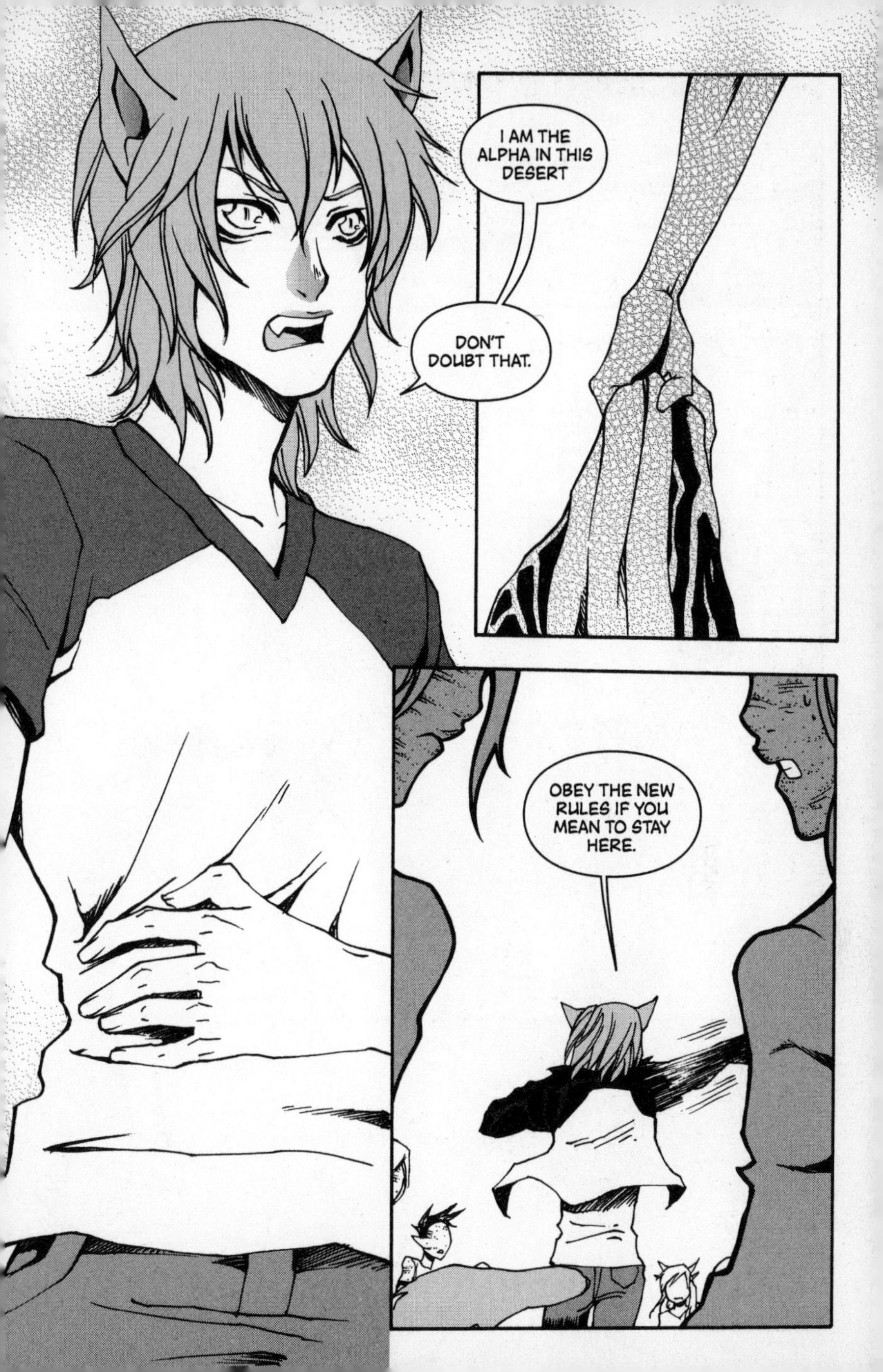
I AM THE ALPHA IN THIS DESERT
DON'T DOUBT THAT.
OBEY THE NEW RULES IF YOU MEAN TO STAY HERE.

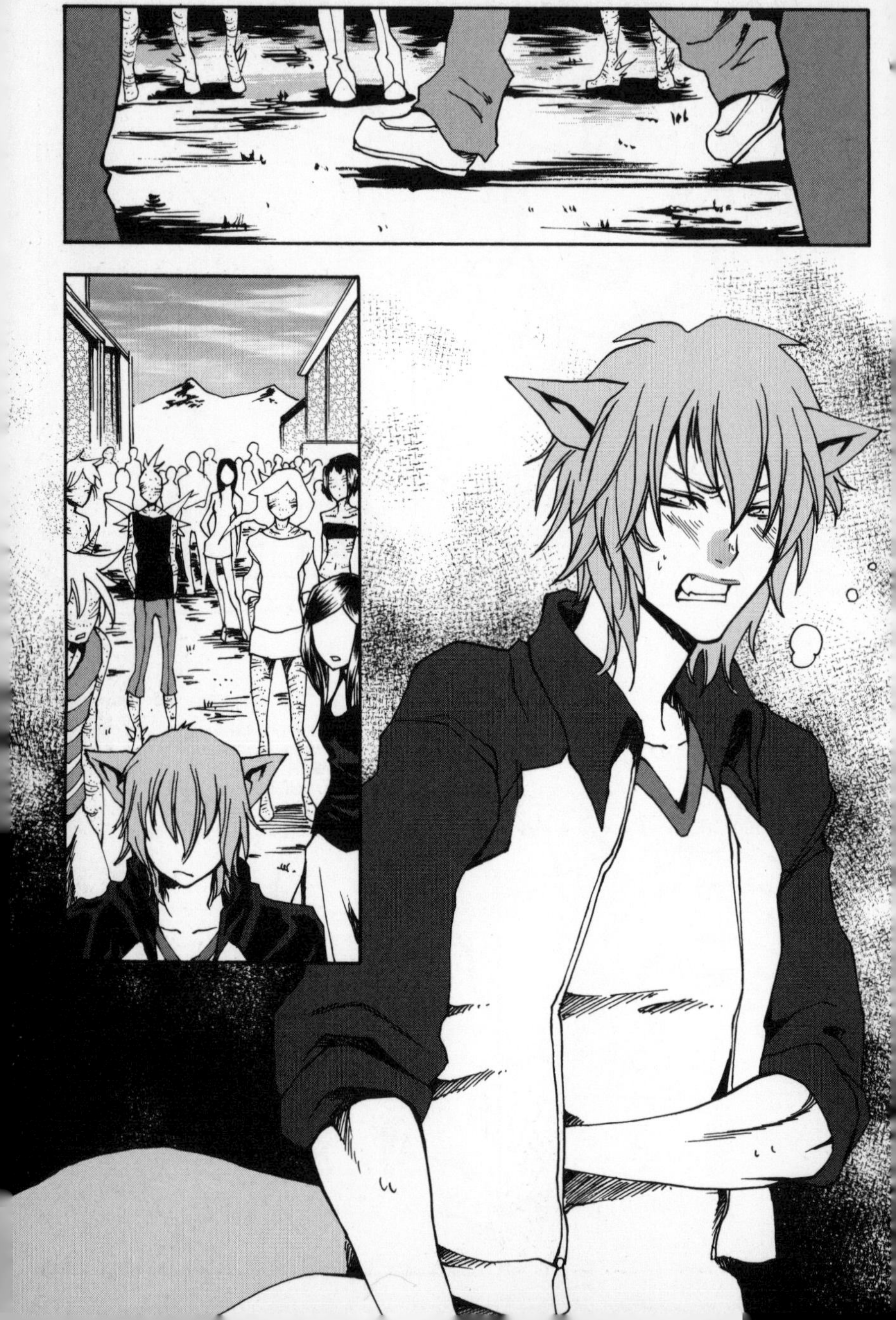

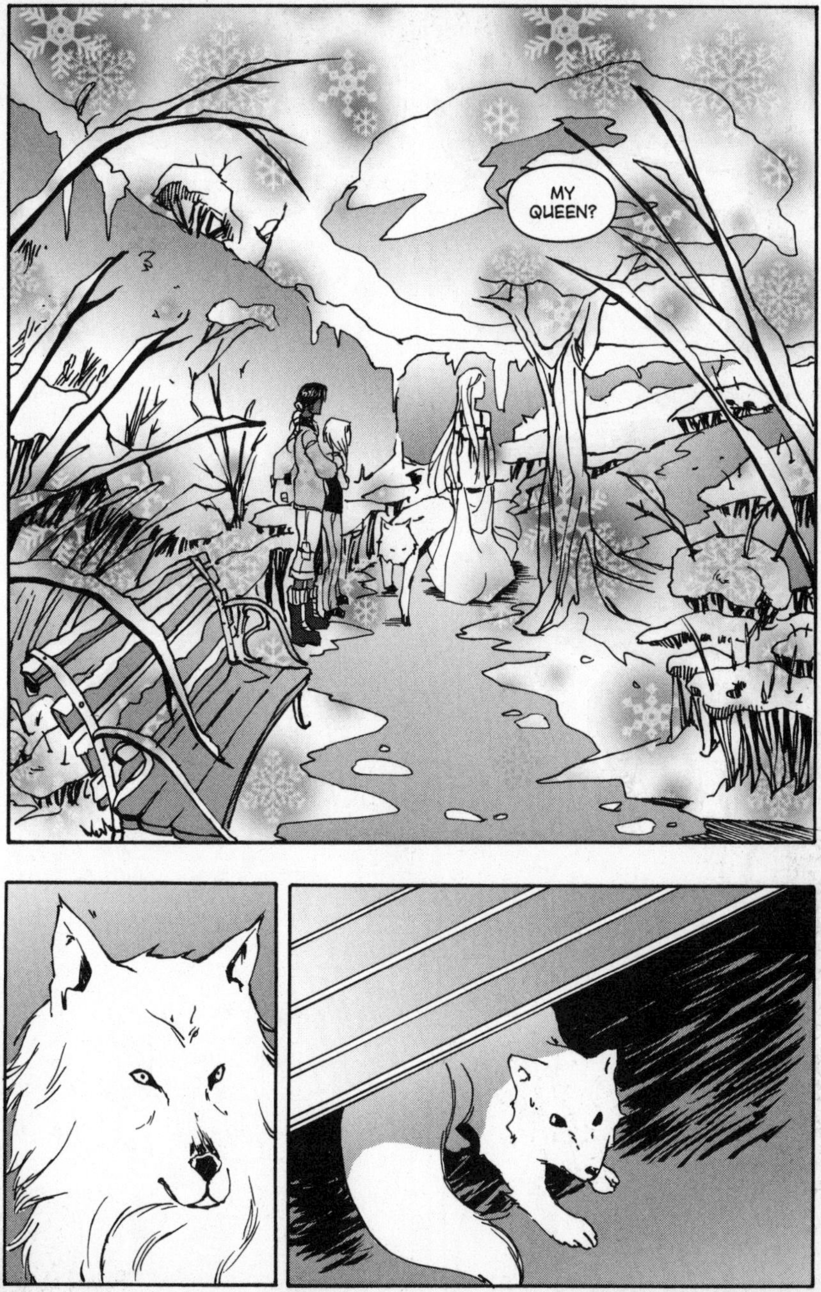
MY QUEEN?

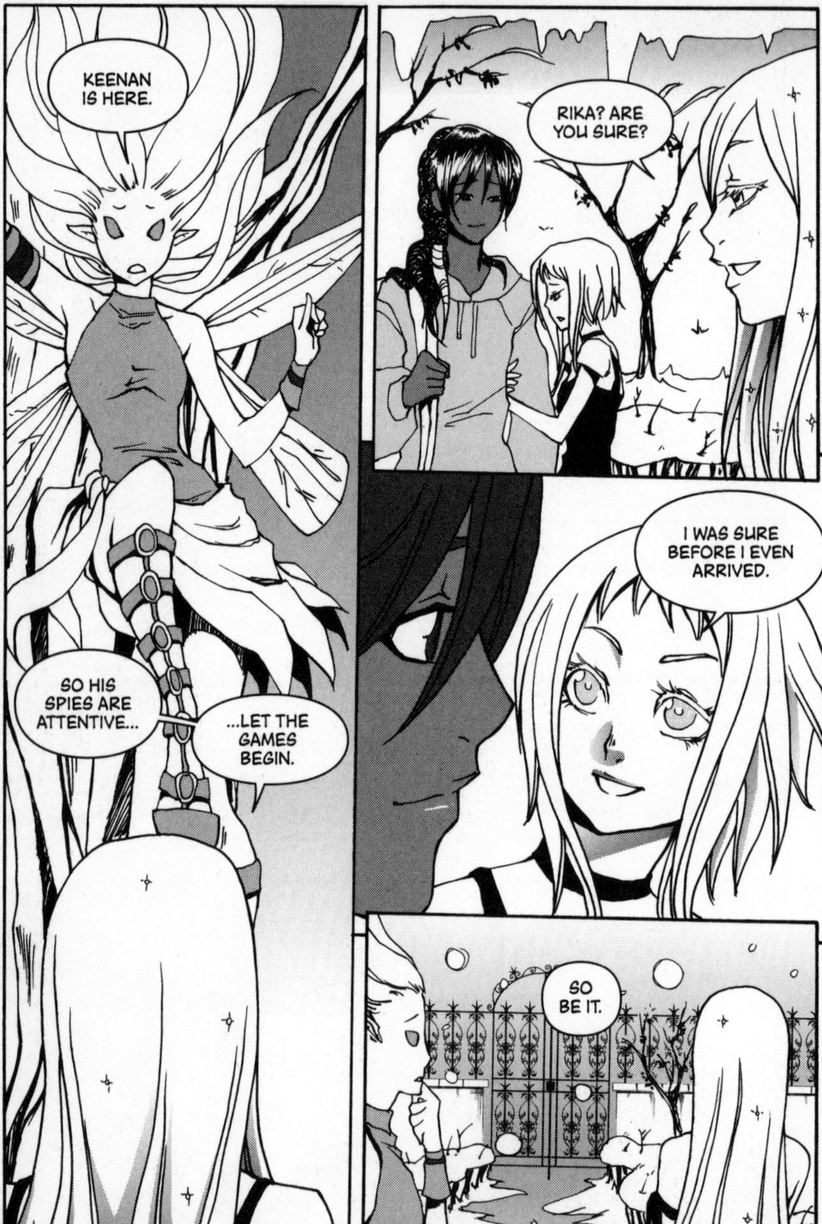
KEENAN IS HERE.
SO HIS SPIES ARE ATTENTIVE...
...LET THE GAMES BEGIN.
RIKA? ARE YOU SURE?
I WAS SURE BEFORE I EVEN ARRIVED.
SO BE IT.

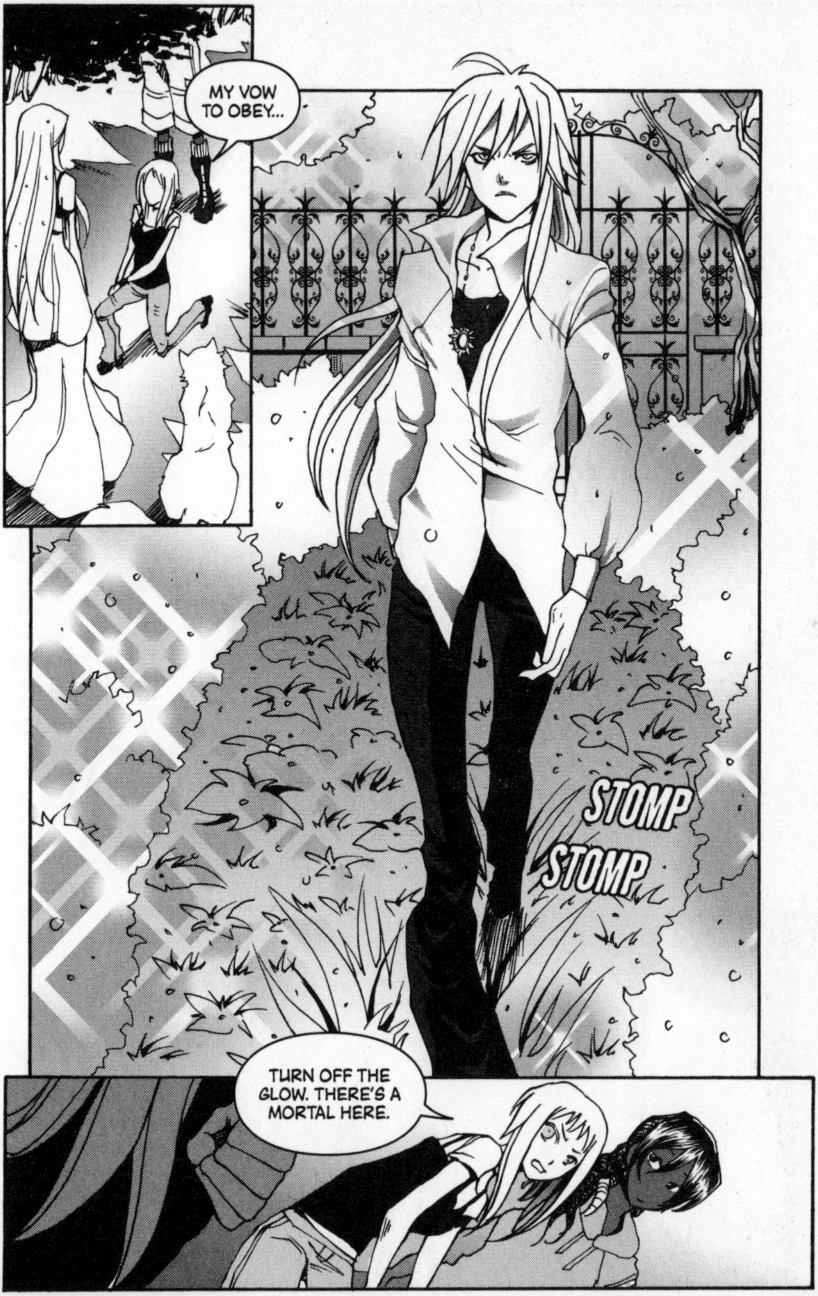
MY VOW TO OBEY...
STOMP
STOMP
TURN OFF THE GLOW. THERE'S A MORTAL HERE.

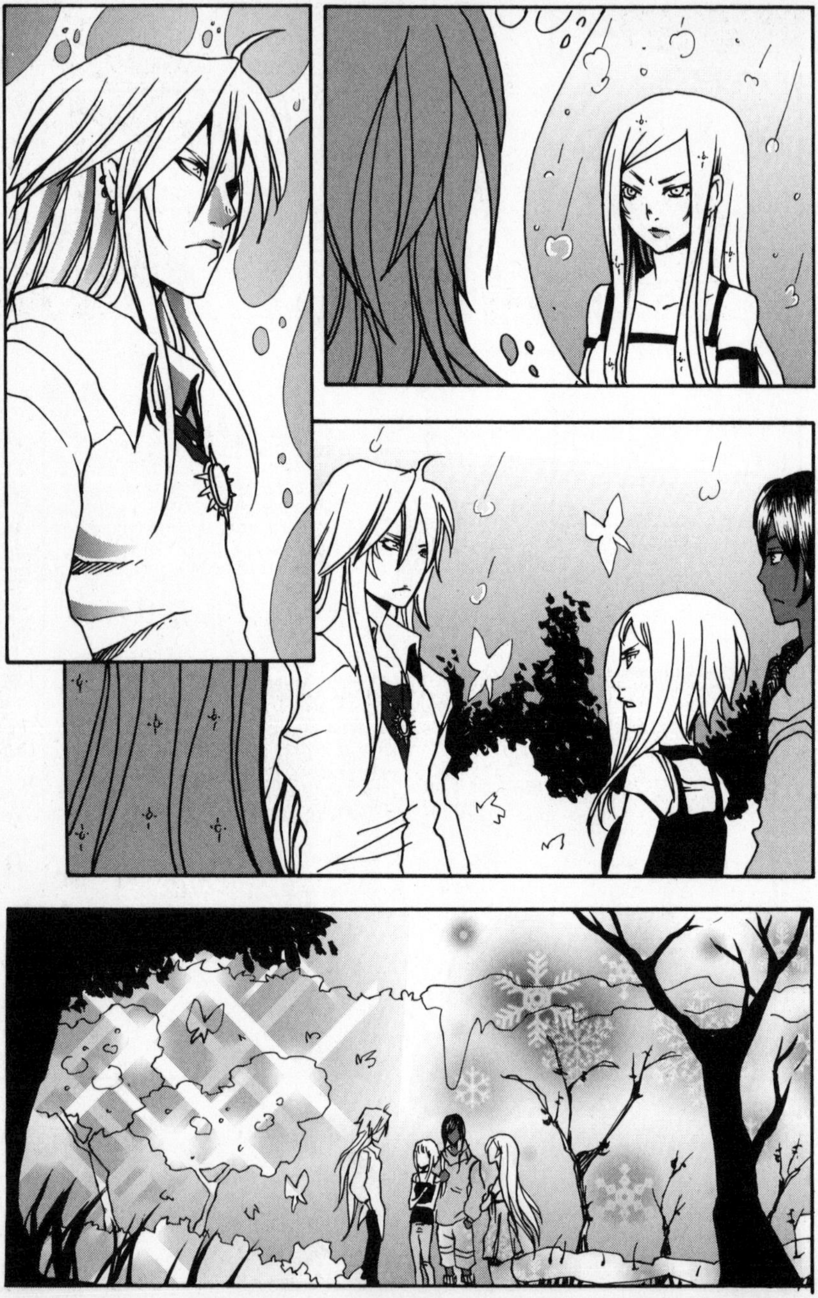

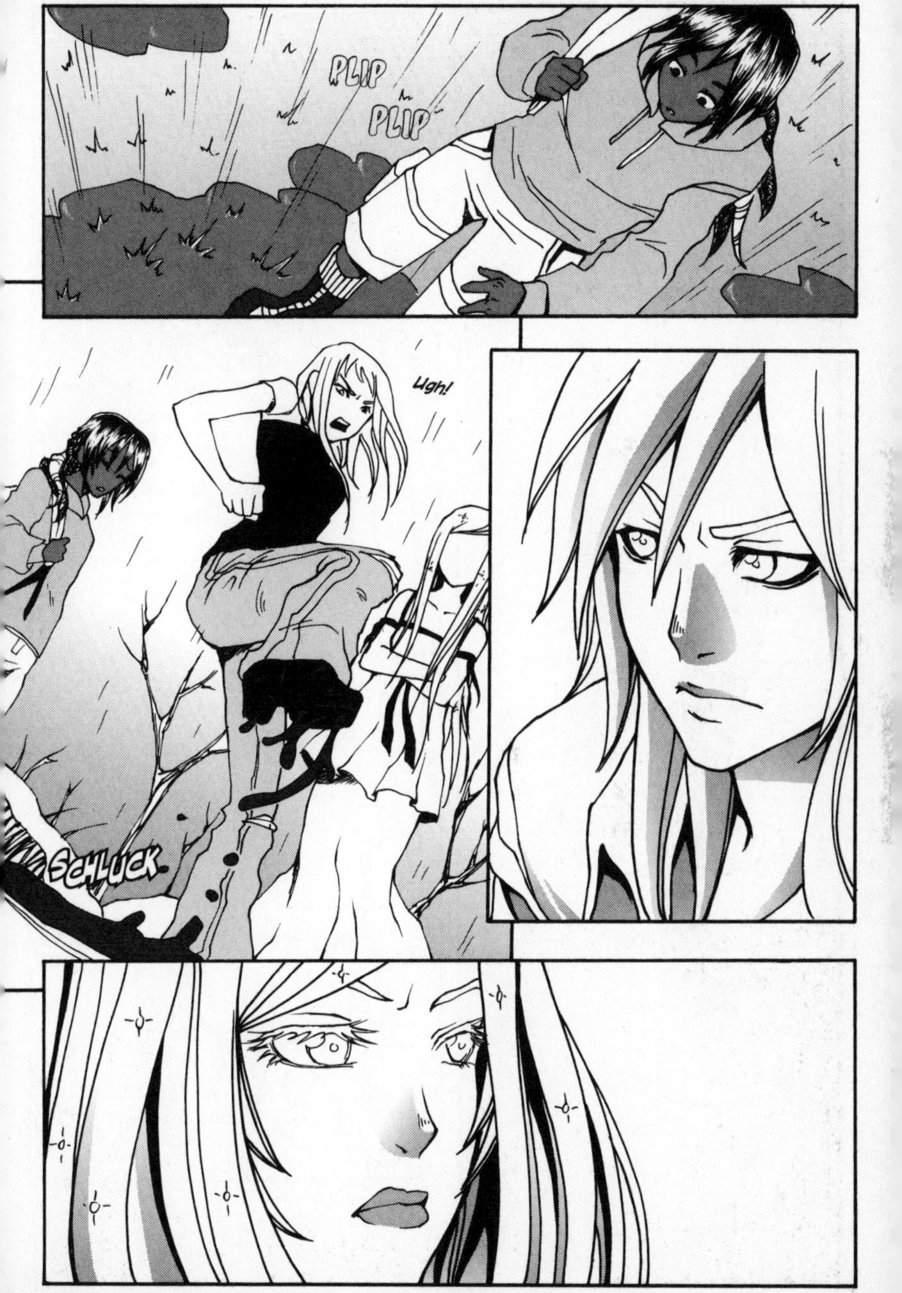
PLIP
PLIP
Ugh!
SCHLUCK

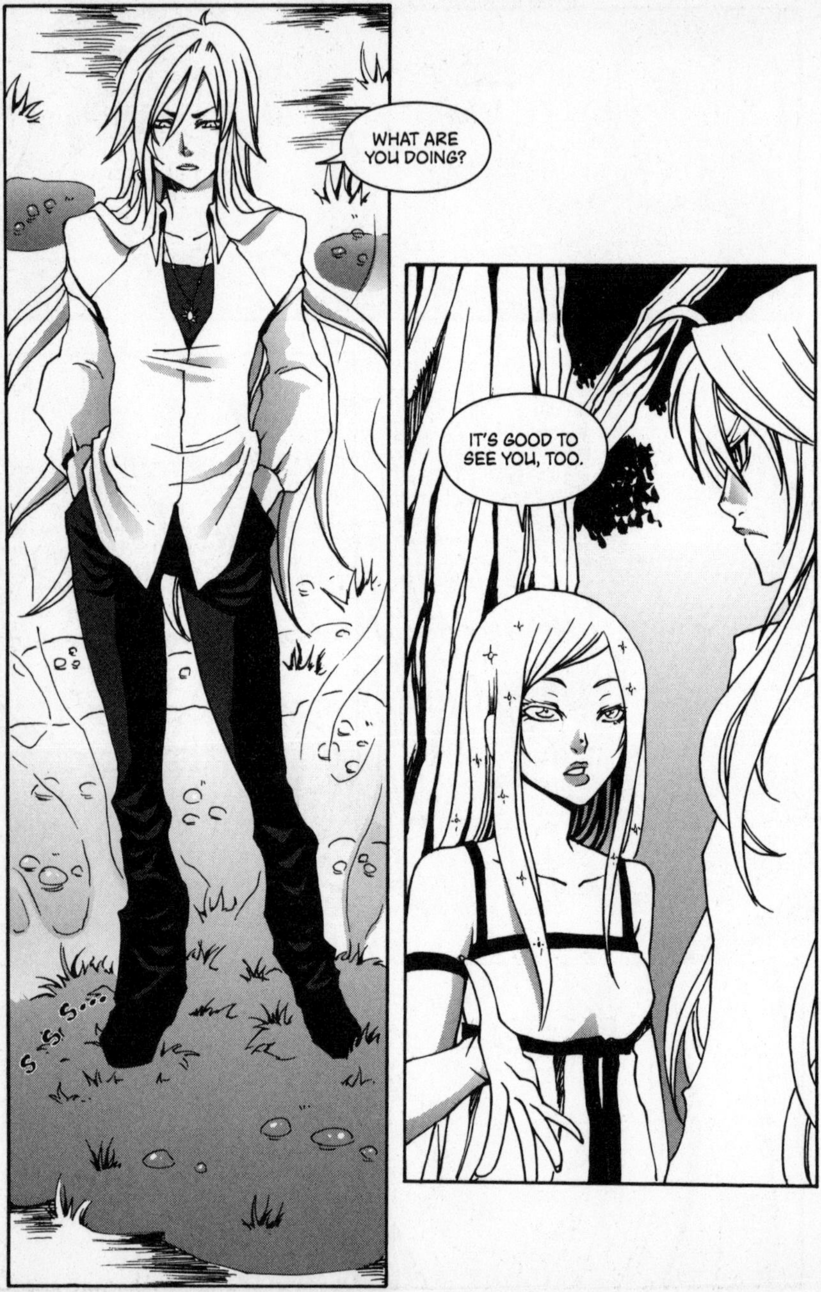
WHAT ARE YOU DOING?
IT'S GOOD TO SEE YOU, TOO.

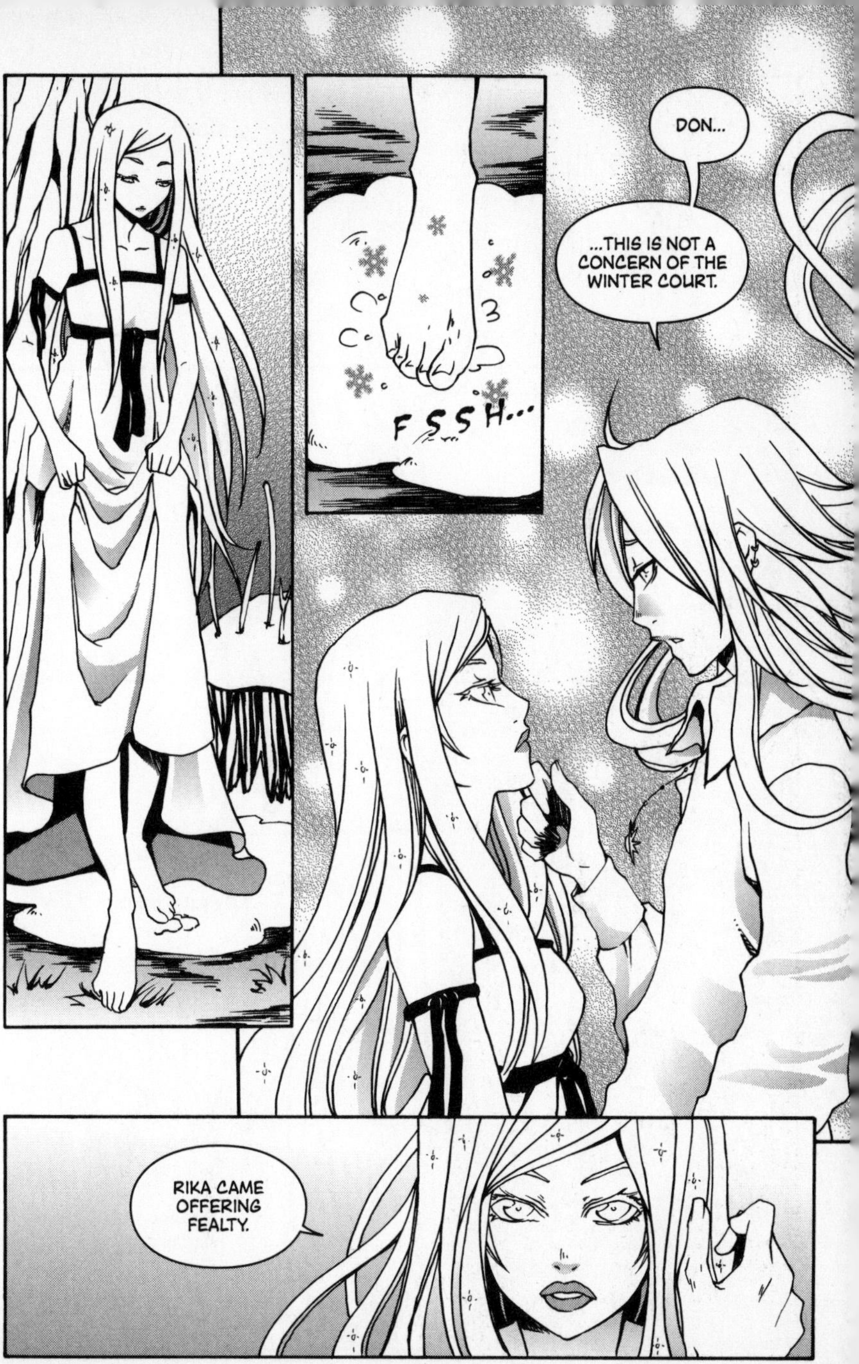
FSSH...
DON...
...THIS IS NOT A CONCERN OF THE WINTER COURT.
RIKA CAME OFFERING FEALTY.

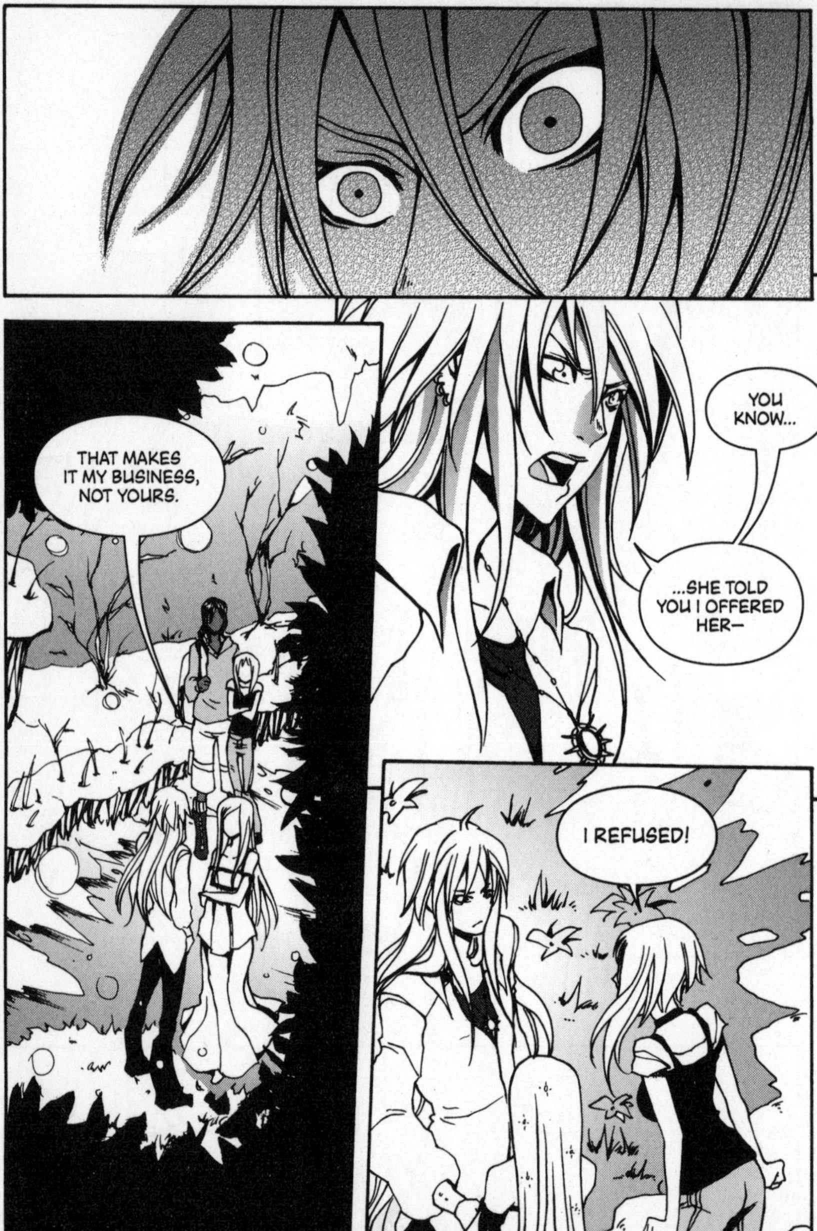
THAT MAKES IT MY BUSINESS, NOT YOURS.
YOU KNOW...
...SHE TOLD YOU I OFFERED HER—
I REFUSED!

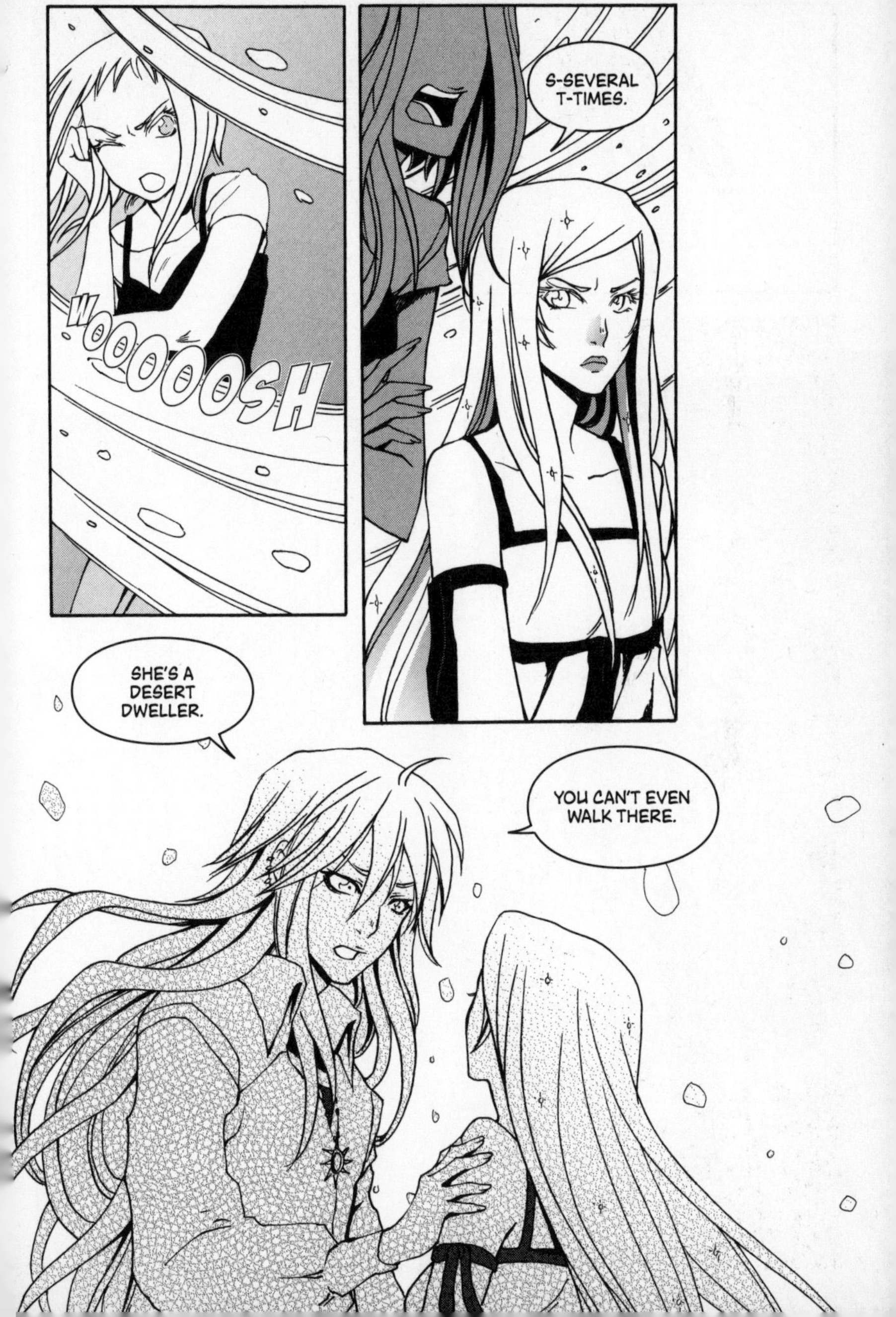
WOOOOOSH
S-SEVERAL T-TIMES.
SHE'S A DESERT DWELLER.
YOU CAN'T EVEN WALK THERE.

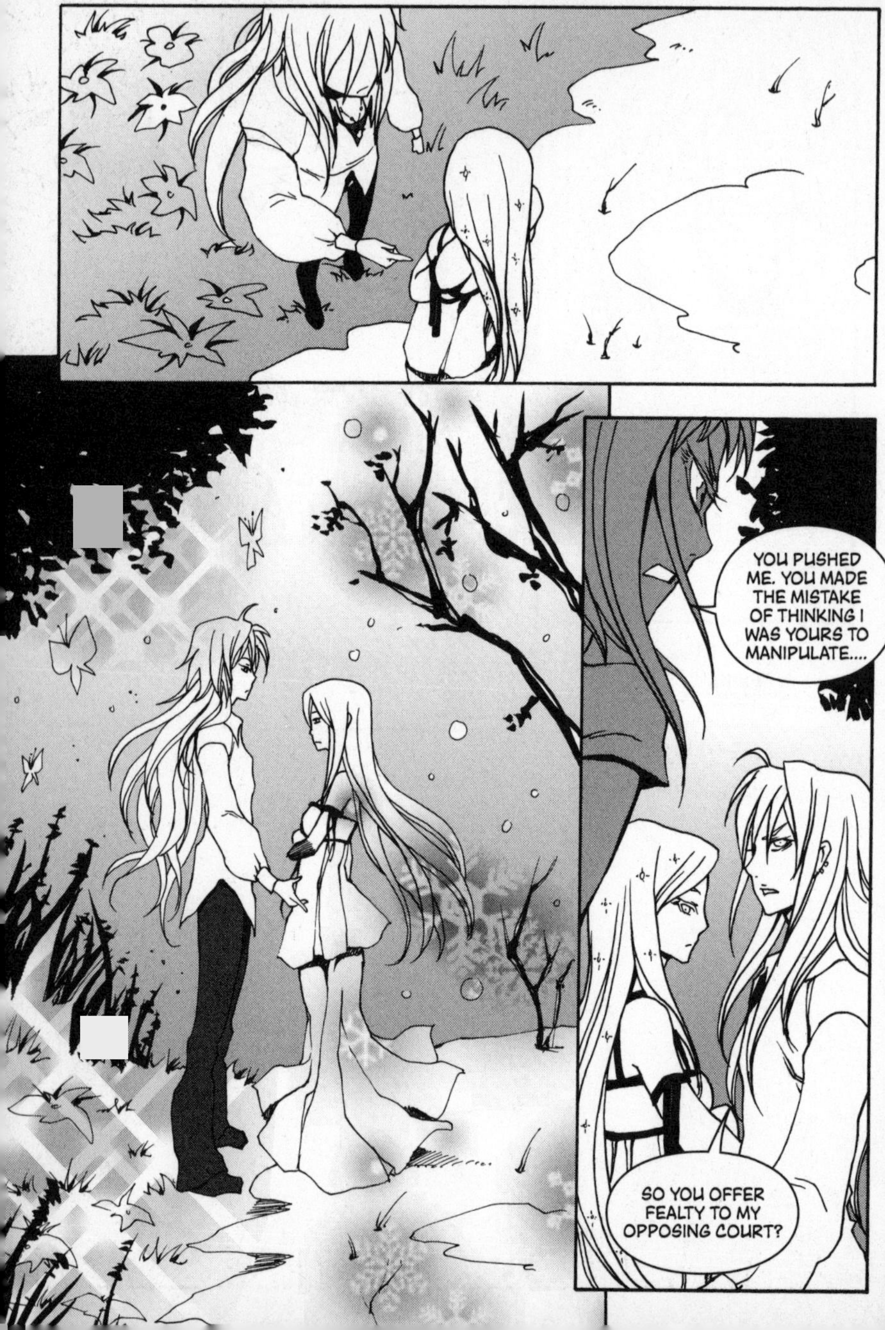
YOU PUSHED ME. YOU MADE THE MISTAKE OF THINKING I WAS YOURS TO MANIPULATE....
SO YOU OFFER FEALTY TO MY OPPOSING COURT?

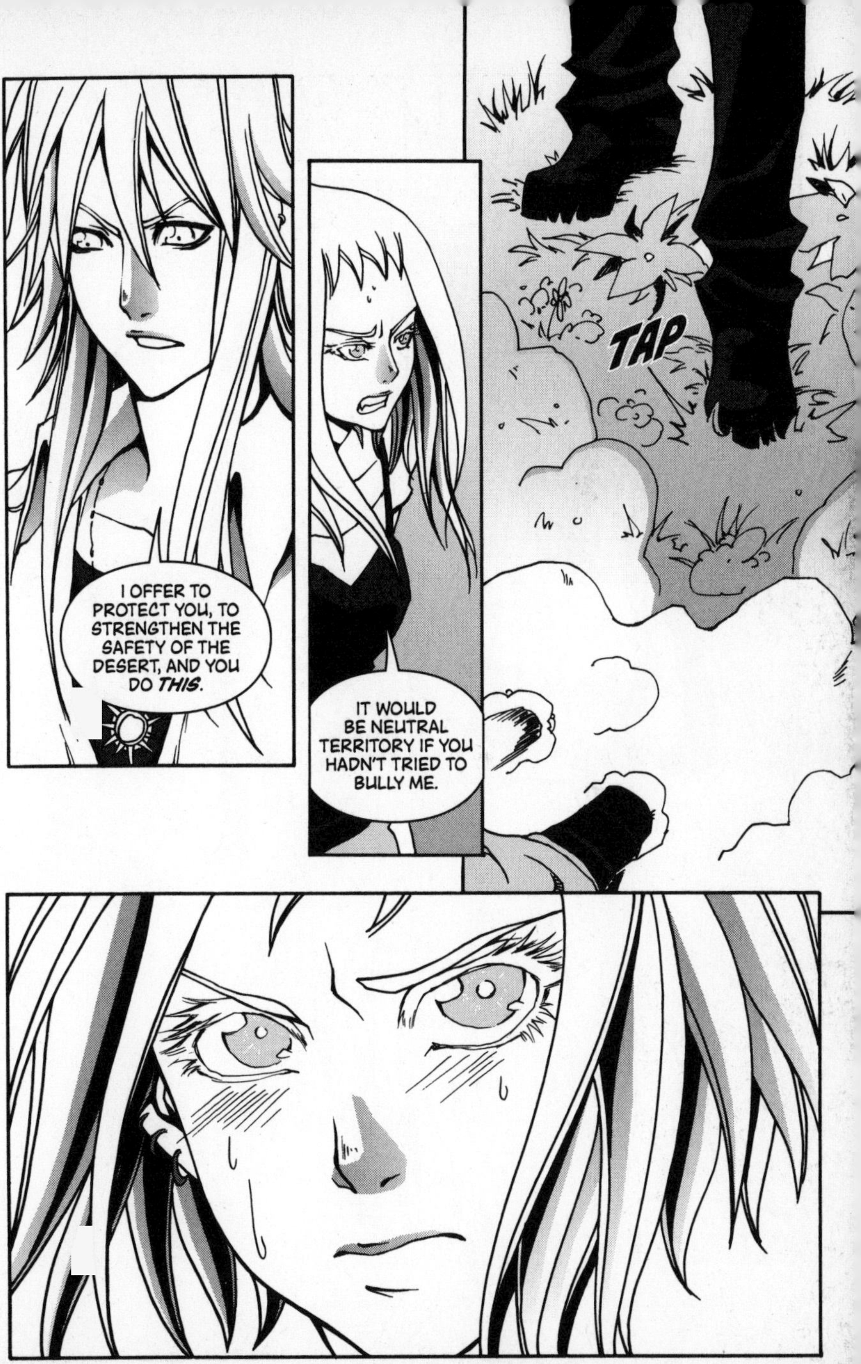
I OFFER TO PROTECT YOU, TO STRENGTHEN THE SAFETY OF THE DESERT, AND YOU DO *THIS*.
IT WOULD BE NEUTRAL TERRITORY IF YOU HADN'T TRIED TO BULLY ME.
TAP

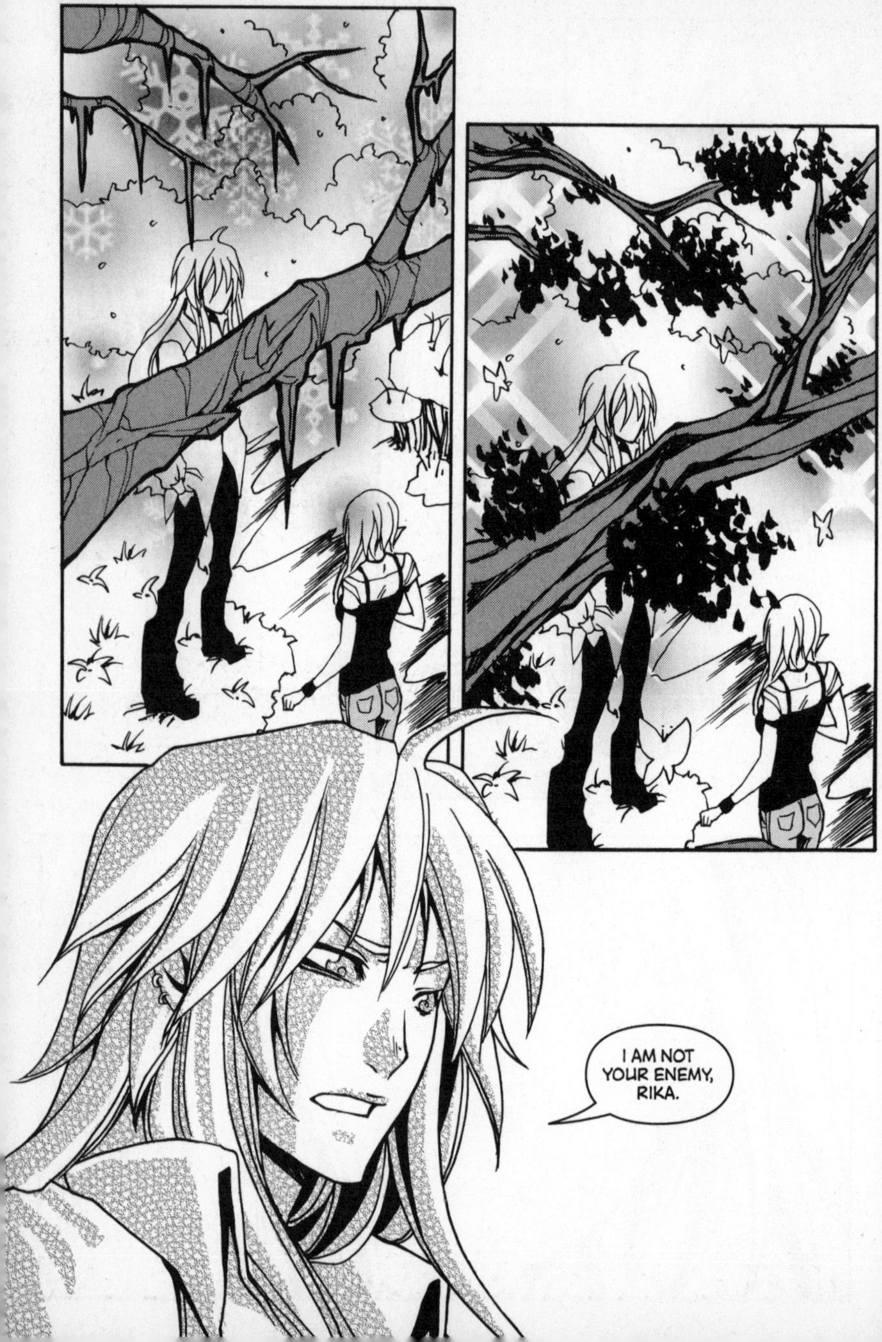
I AM NOT YOUR ENEMY, RIKA.

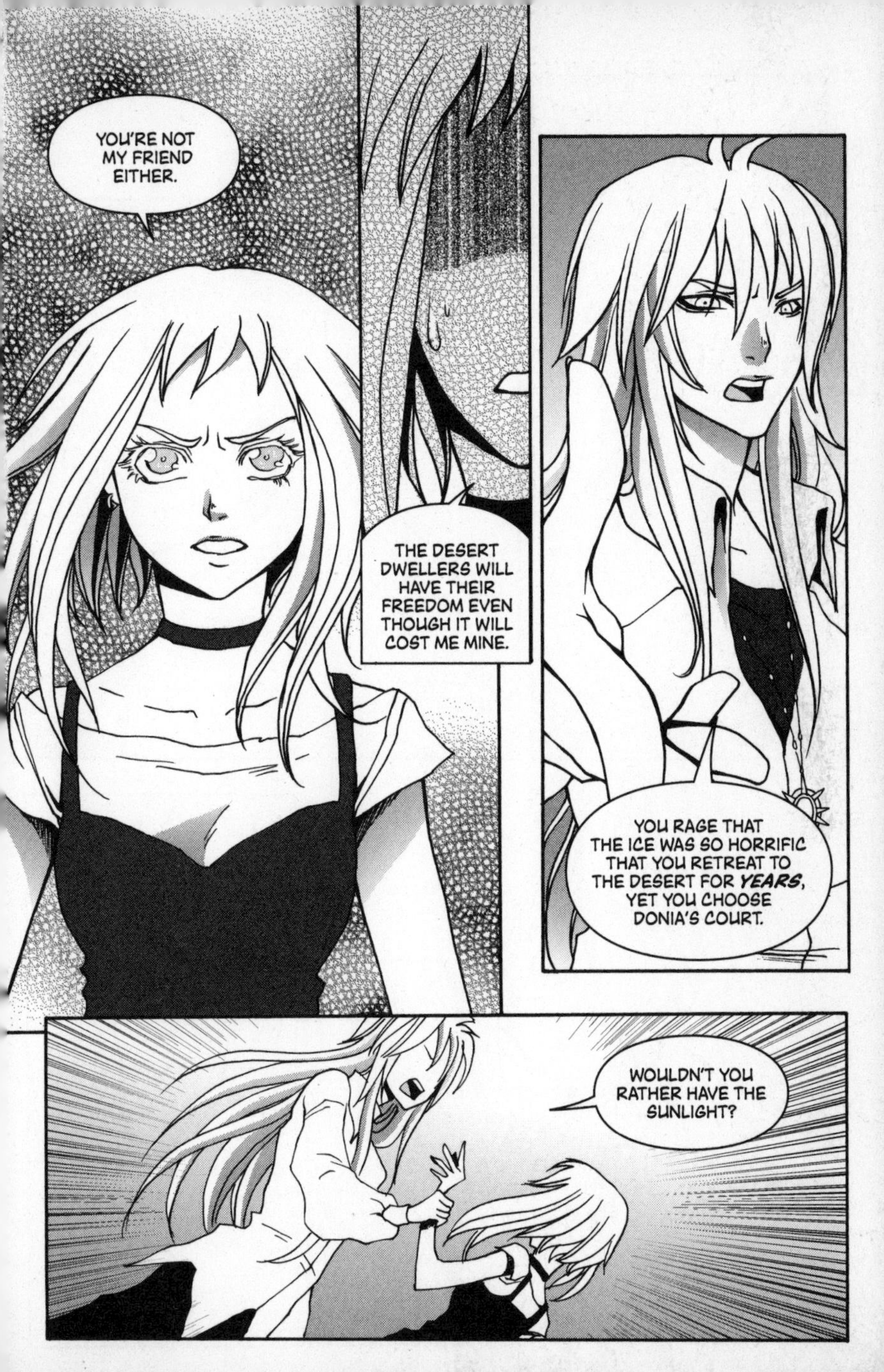

YOU'RE NOT MY FRIEND EITHER.
THE DESERT DWELLERS WILL HAVE THEIR FREEDOM EVEN THOUGH IT WILL COST ME MINE.
YOU RAGE THAT THE ICE WAS SO HORRIFIC THAT YOU RETREAT TO THE DESERT FOR *YEARS*, YET YOU CHOOSE DONIA'S COURT.
WOULDN'T YOU RATHER HAVE THE SUNLIGHT?

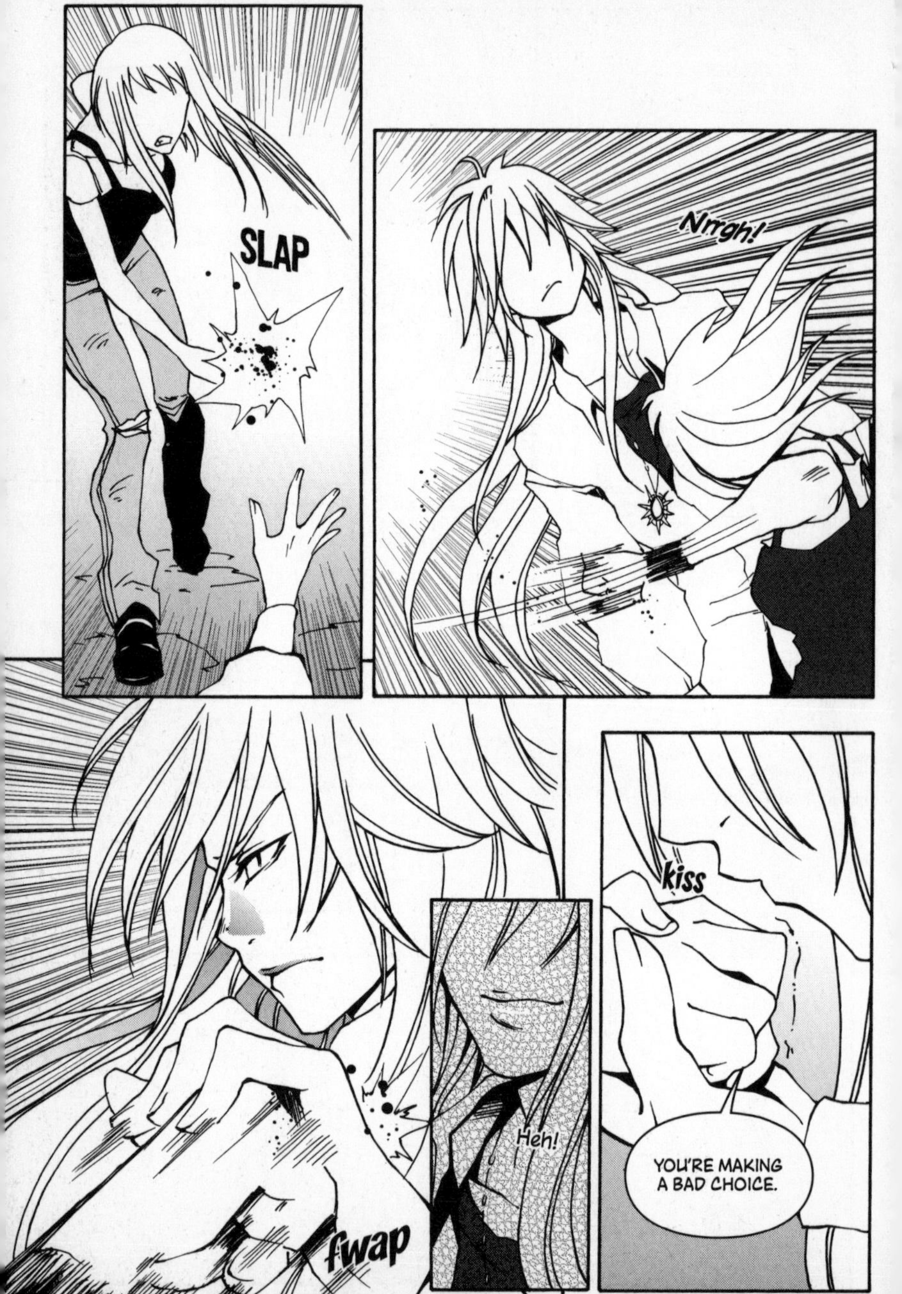
SLAP
Nrrgh!
fwap
Heh!
kiss
YOU'RE MAKING A BAD CHOICE.

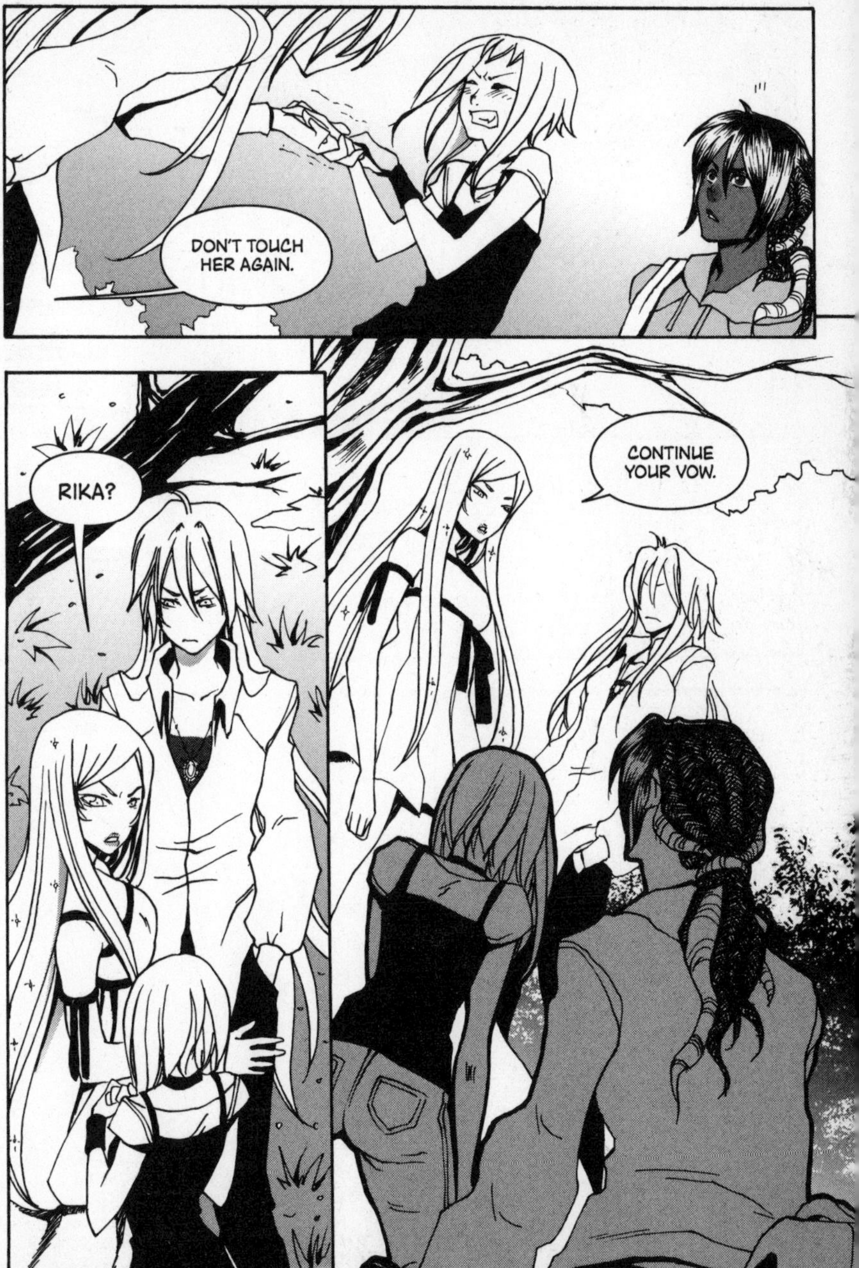
DON'T TOUCH HER AGAIN.
RIKA?
CONTINUE YOUR VOW.

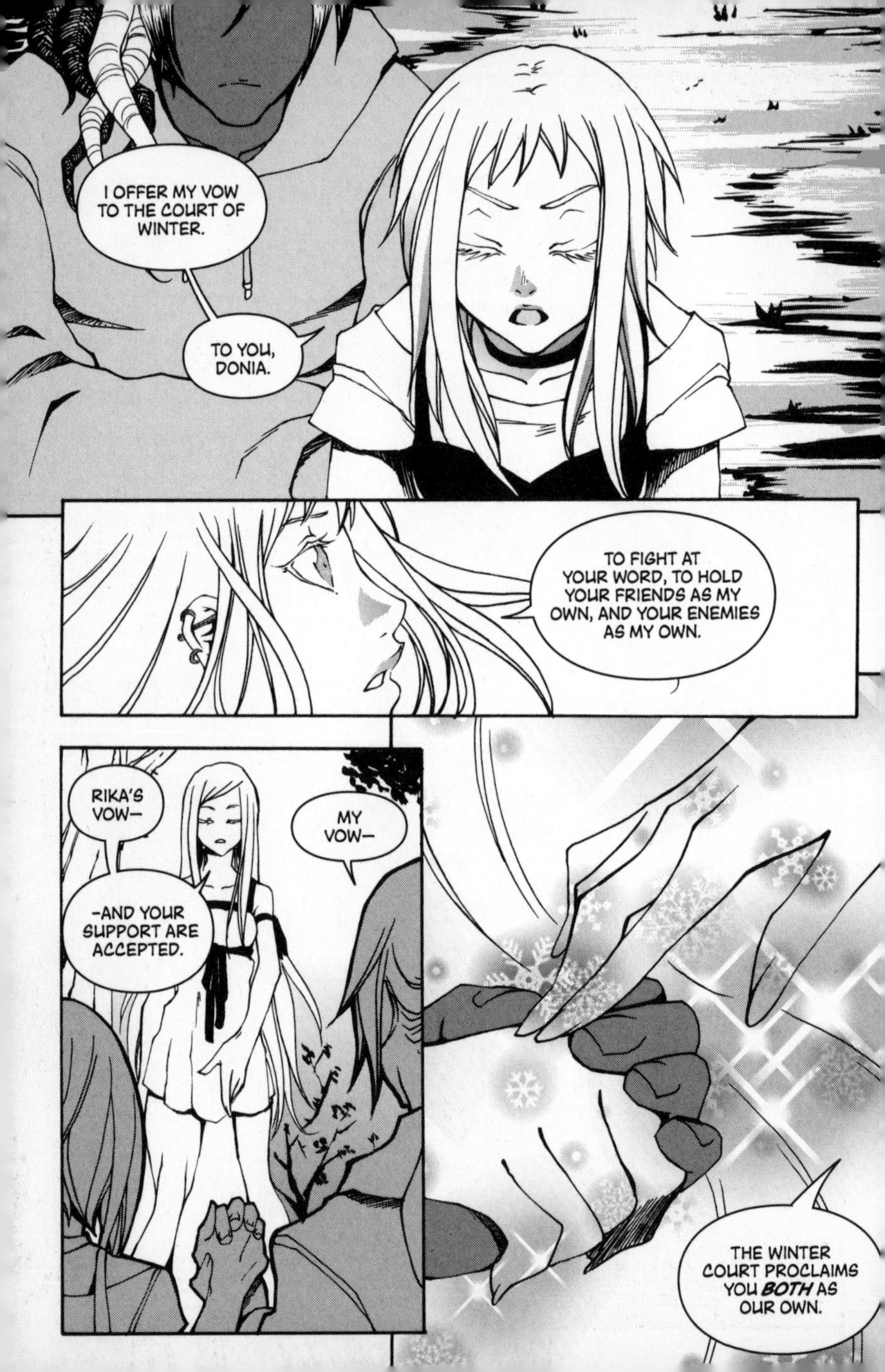
I OFFER MY VOW TO THE COURT OF WINTER.
TO YOU, DONIA.
TO FIGHT AT YOUR WORD, TO HOLD YOUR FRIENDS AS MY OWN, AND YOUR ENEMIES AS MY OWN.
RIKA'S VOW—
MY VOW—
-AND YOUR SUPPORT ARE ACCEPTED.
THE WINTER COURT PROCLAIMS YOU *BOTH* AS OUR OWN.

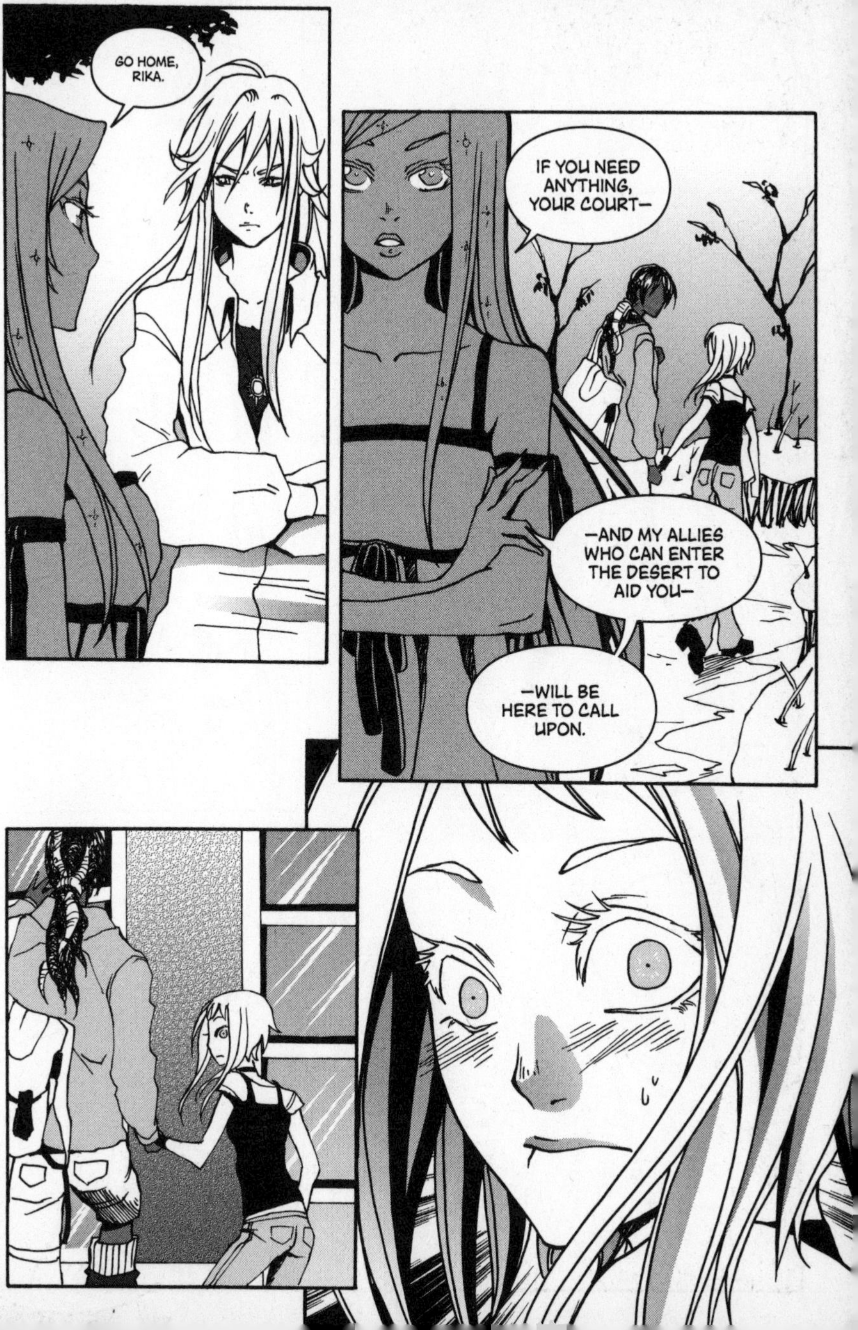
GO HOME, RIKA.
IF YOU NEED ANYTHING, YOUR COURT—
—AND MY ALLIES WHO CAN ENTER THE DESERT TO AID YOU—
—WILL BE HERE TO CALL UPON.

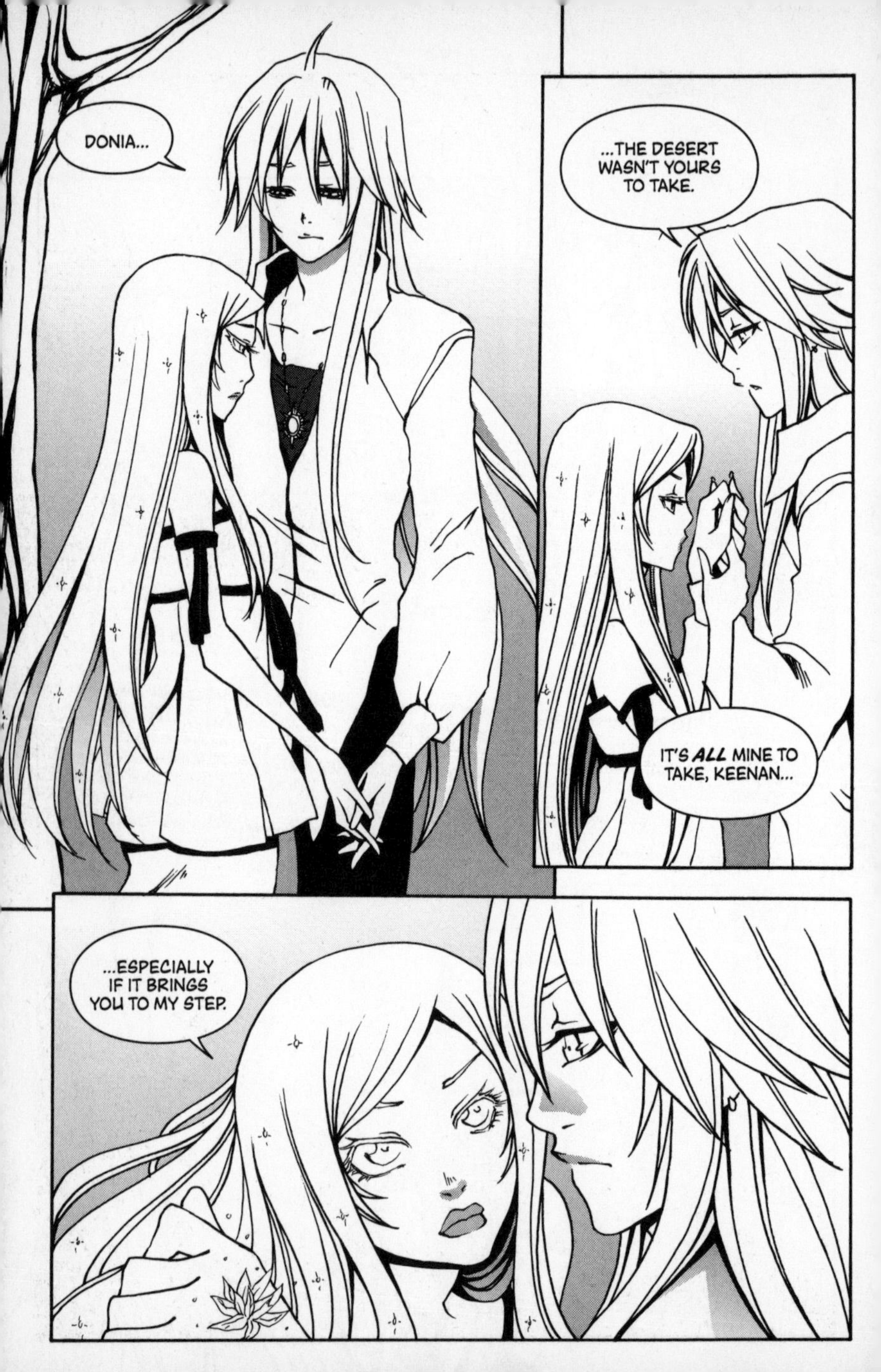
DONIA...
...THE DESERT WASN'T YOURS TO TAKE.
IT'S ALL MINE TO TAKE, KEENAN...
...ESPECIALLY IF IT BRINGS YOU TO MY STEP.

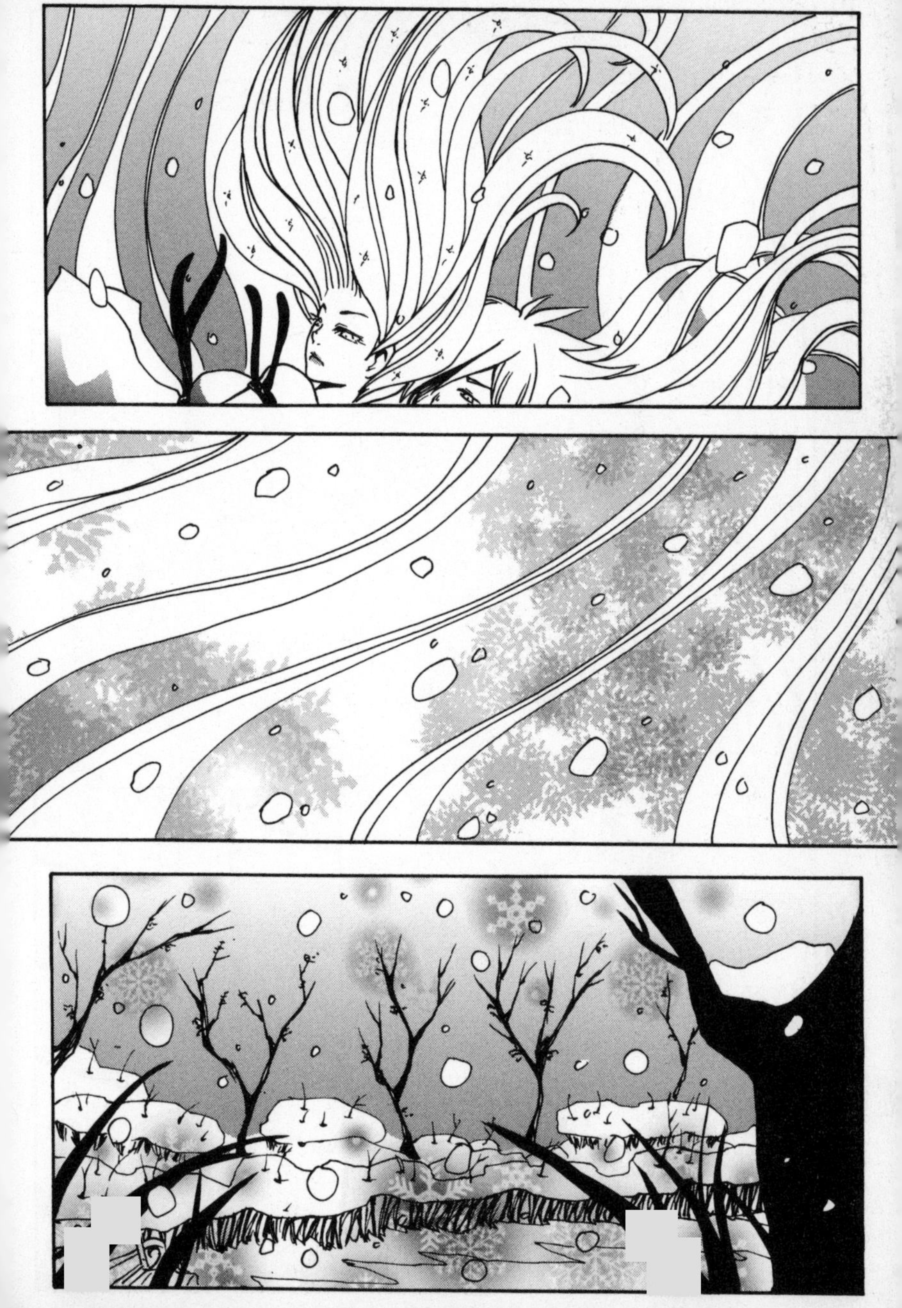

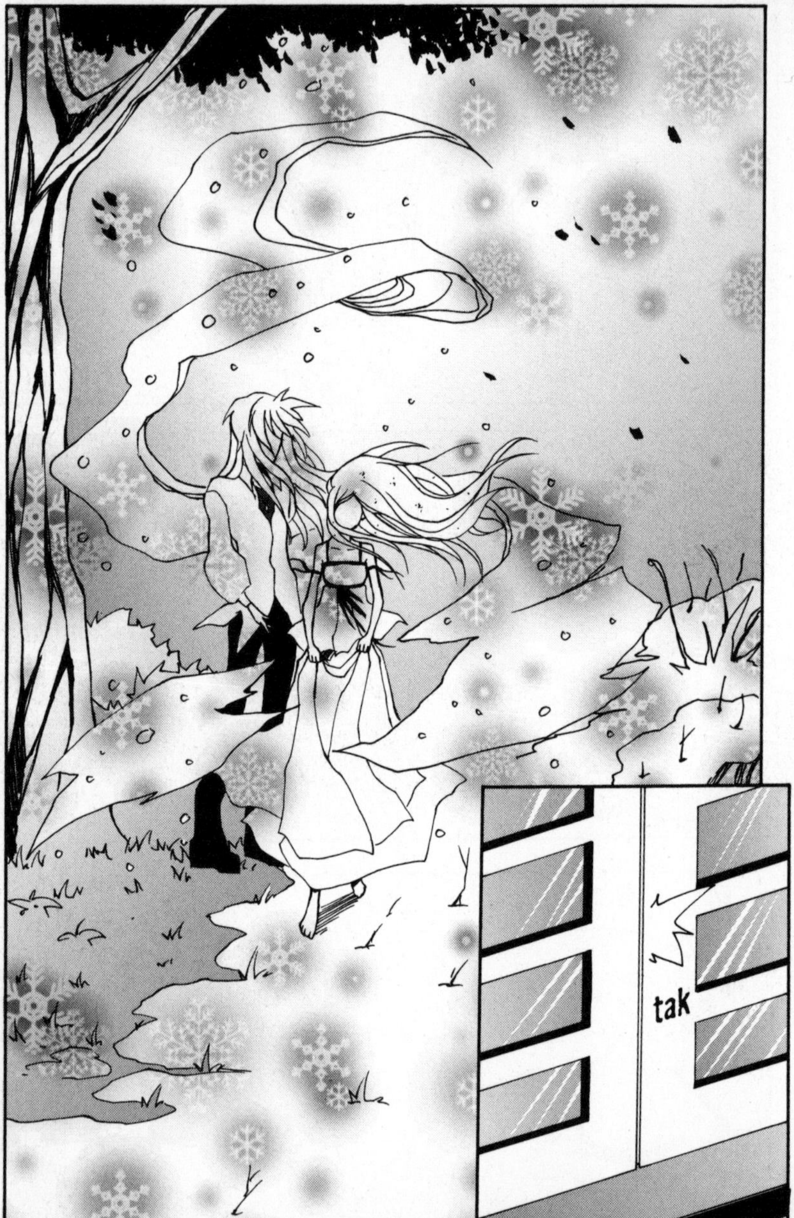
tak

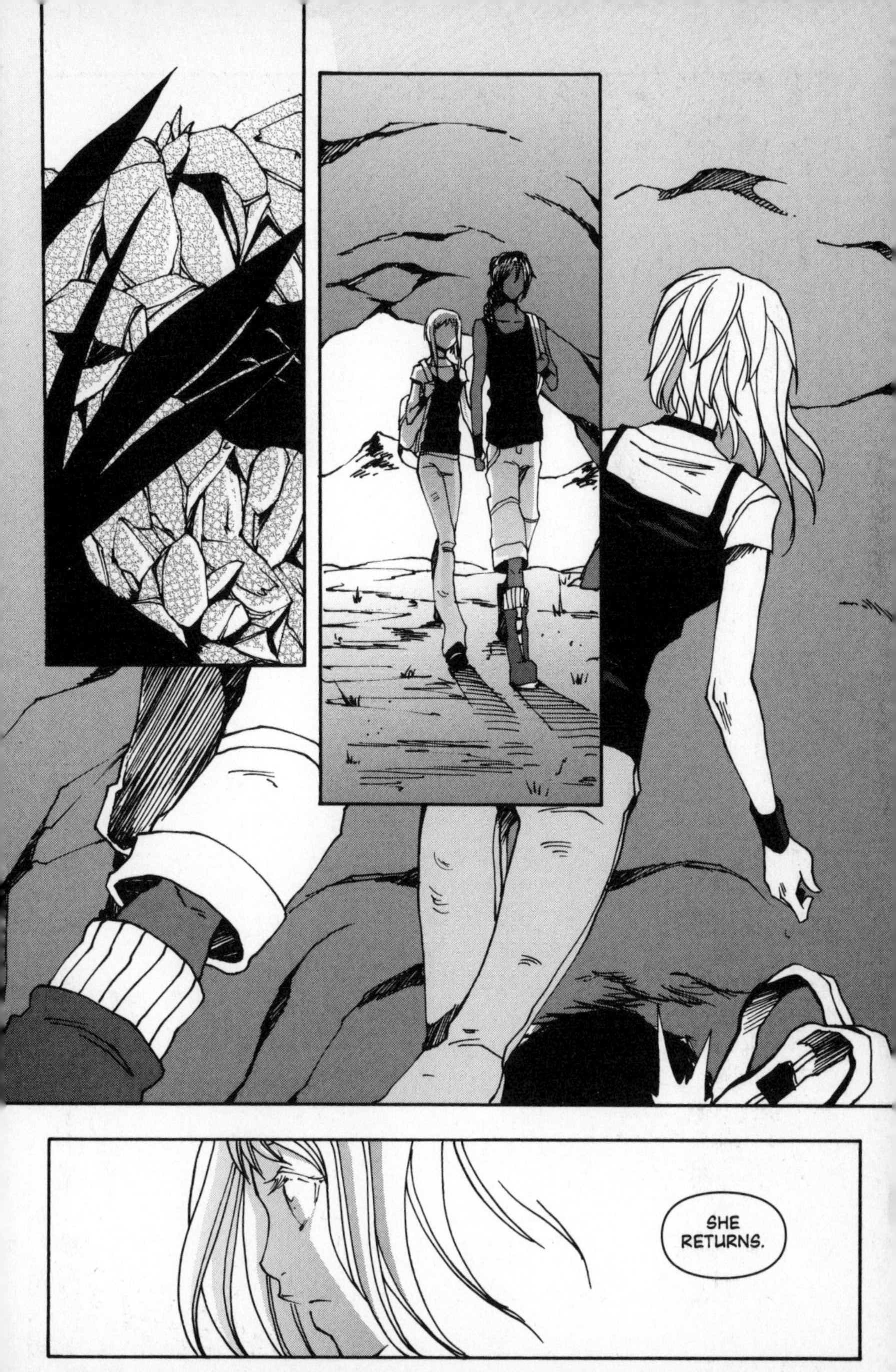
SHE RETURNS.

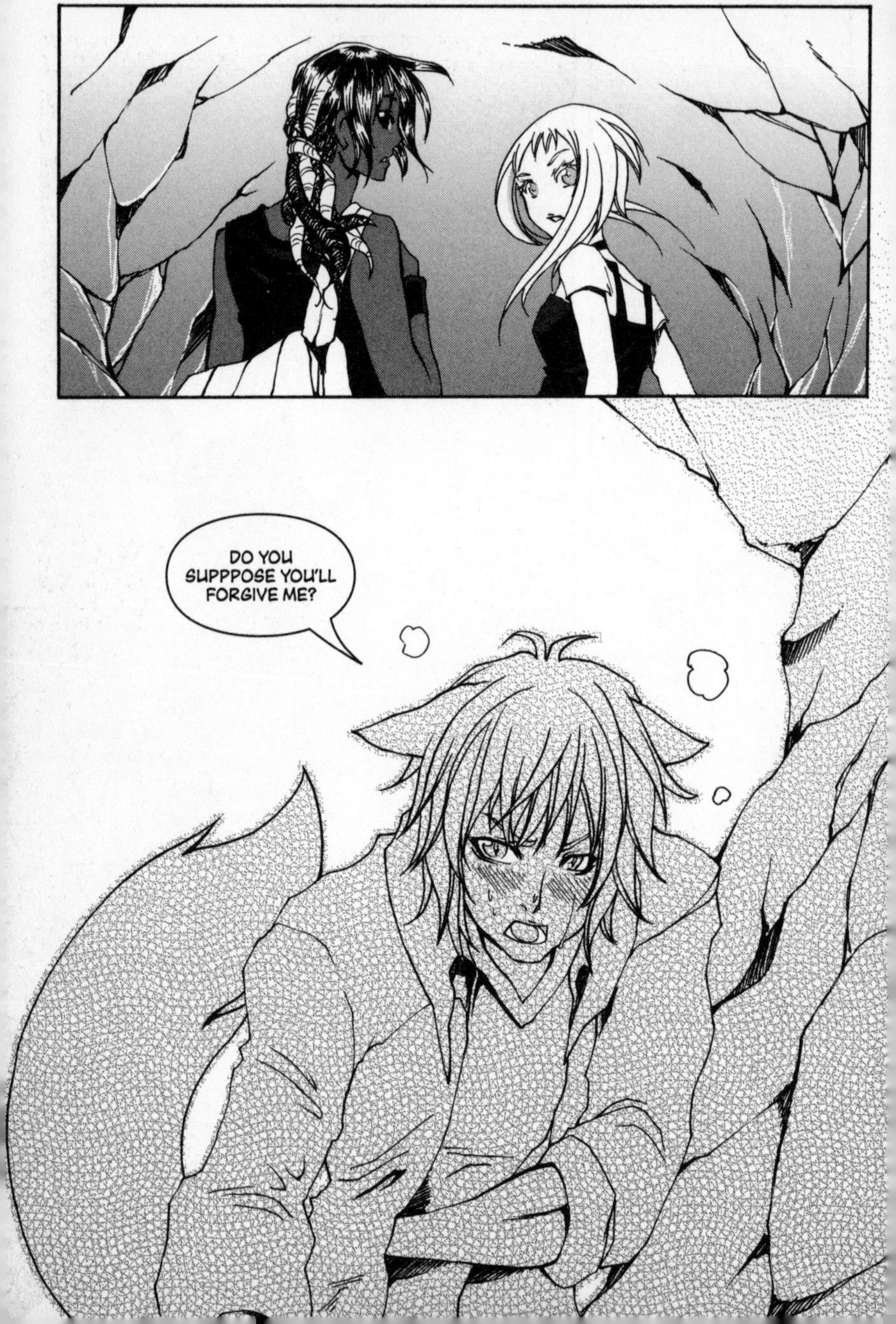
DO YOU SUPPPOSE YOU'LL FORGIVE ME?

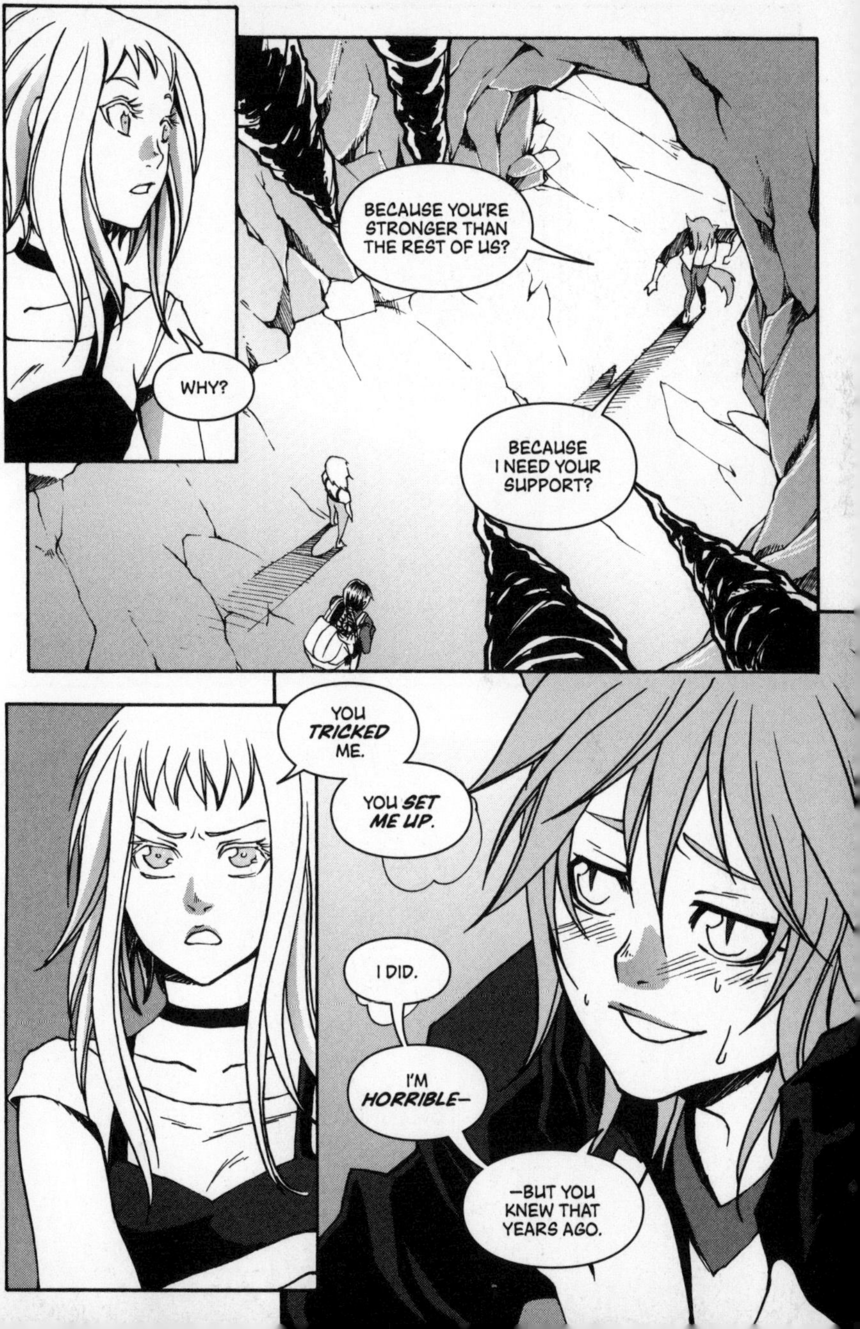
WHY?
BECAUSE YOU'RE STRONGER THAN THE REST OF US?
BECAUSE I NEED YOUR SUPPORT?
YOU *TRICKED* ME.
YOU *SET ME UP*.
I DID.
I'M *HORRIBLE*—
—BUT YOU KNEW THAT YEARS AGO.

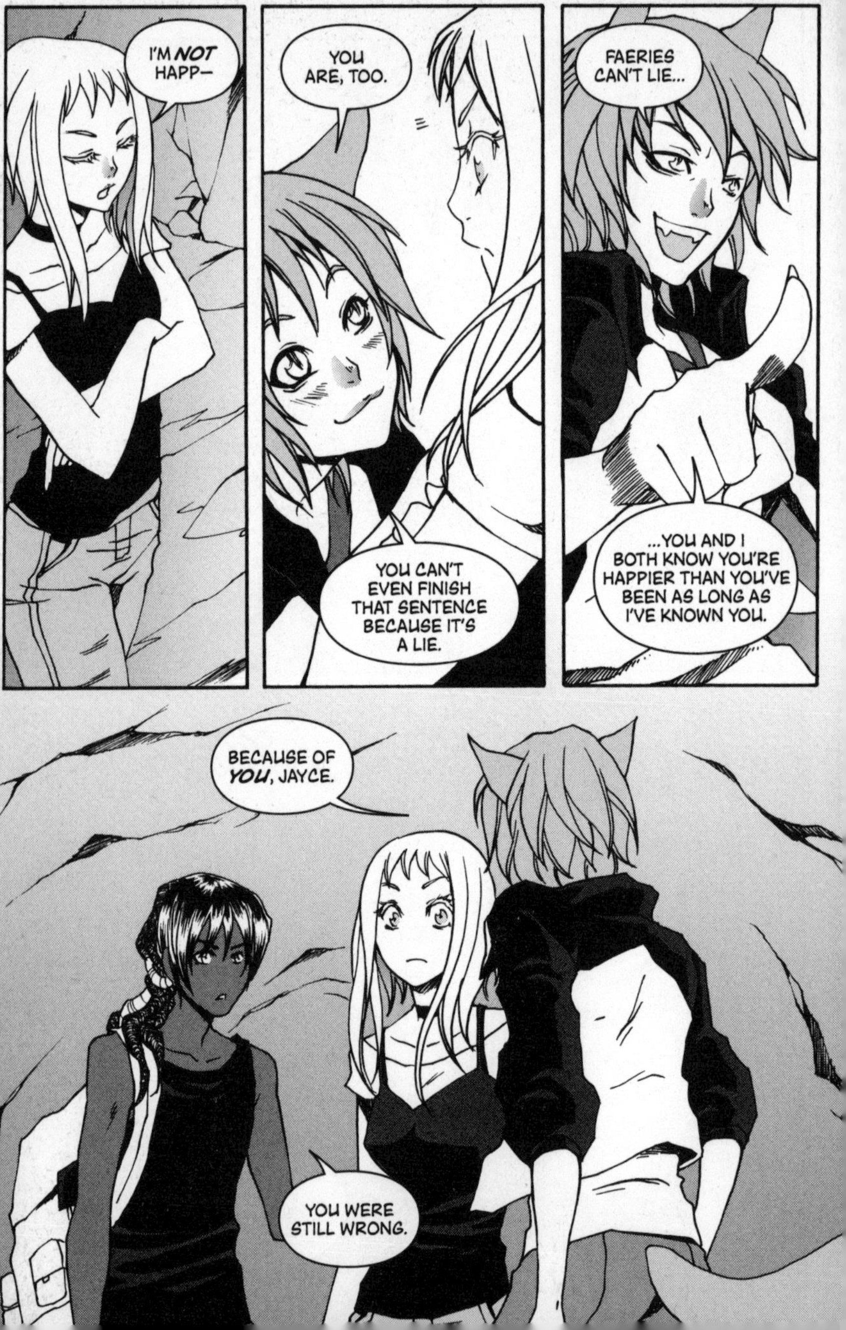
I'M **NOT** HAPP—
YOU ARE, TOO.
YOU CAN'T EVEN FINISH THAT SENTENCE BECAUSE IT'S A LIE.
FAERIES CAN'T LIE...
...YOU AND I BOTH KNOW YOU'RE HAPPIER THAN YOU'VE BEEN AS LONG AS I'VE KNOWN YOU.
BECAUSE OF **YOU**, JAYCE.
YOU WERE STILL WRONG.

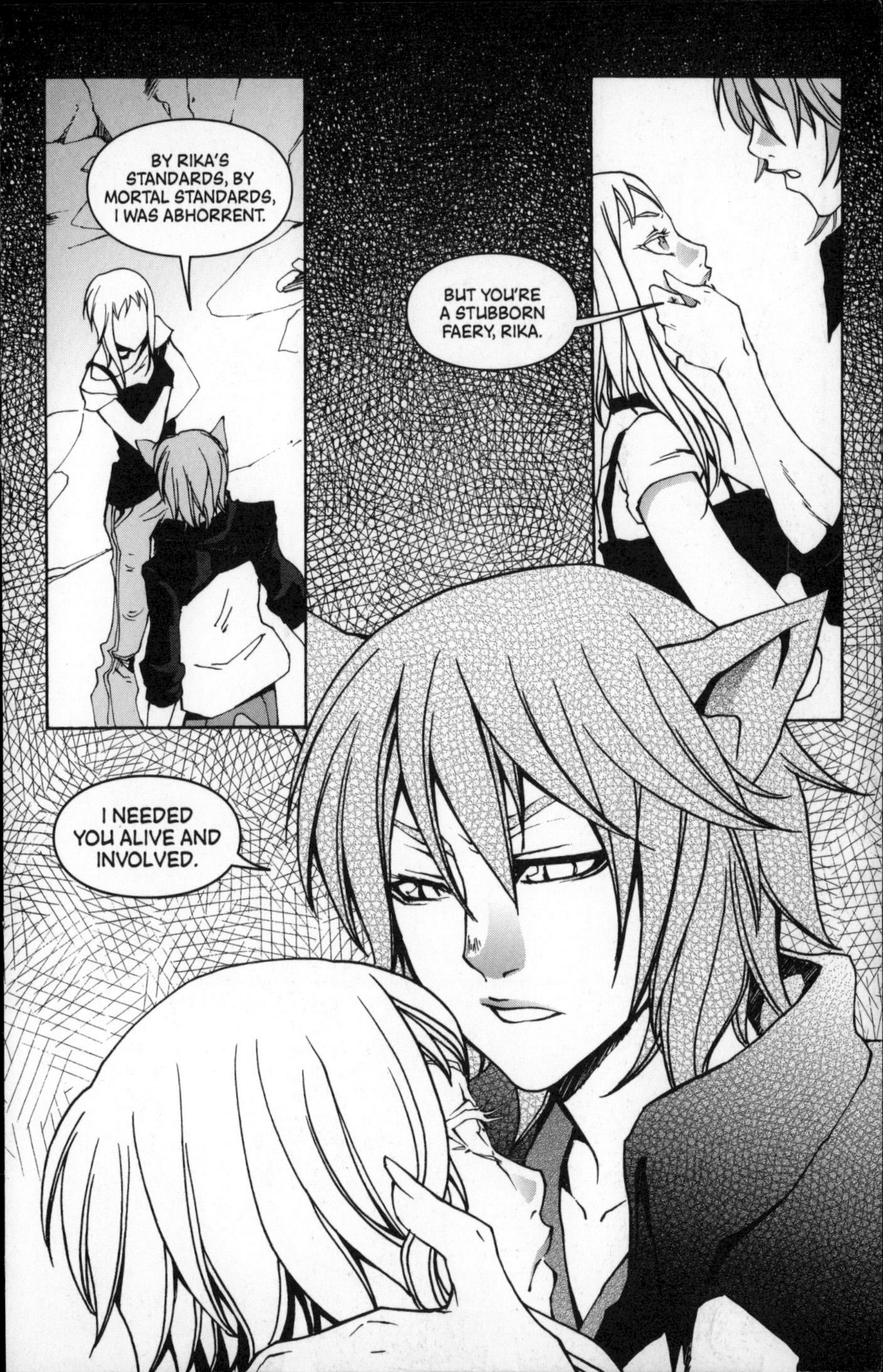
BY RIKA'S STANDARDS, BY MORTAL STANDARDS, I WAS ABHORRENT.
BUT YOU'RE A STUBBORN FAERY, RIKA.
I NEEDED YOU ALIVE AND INVOLVED.

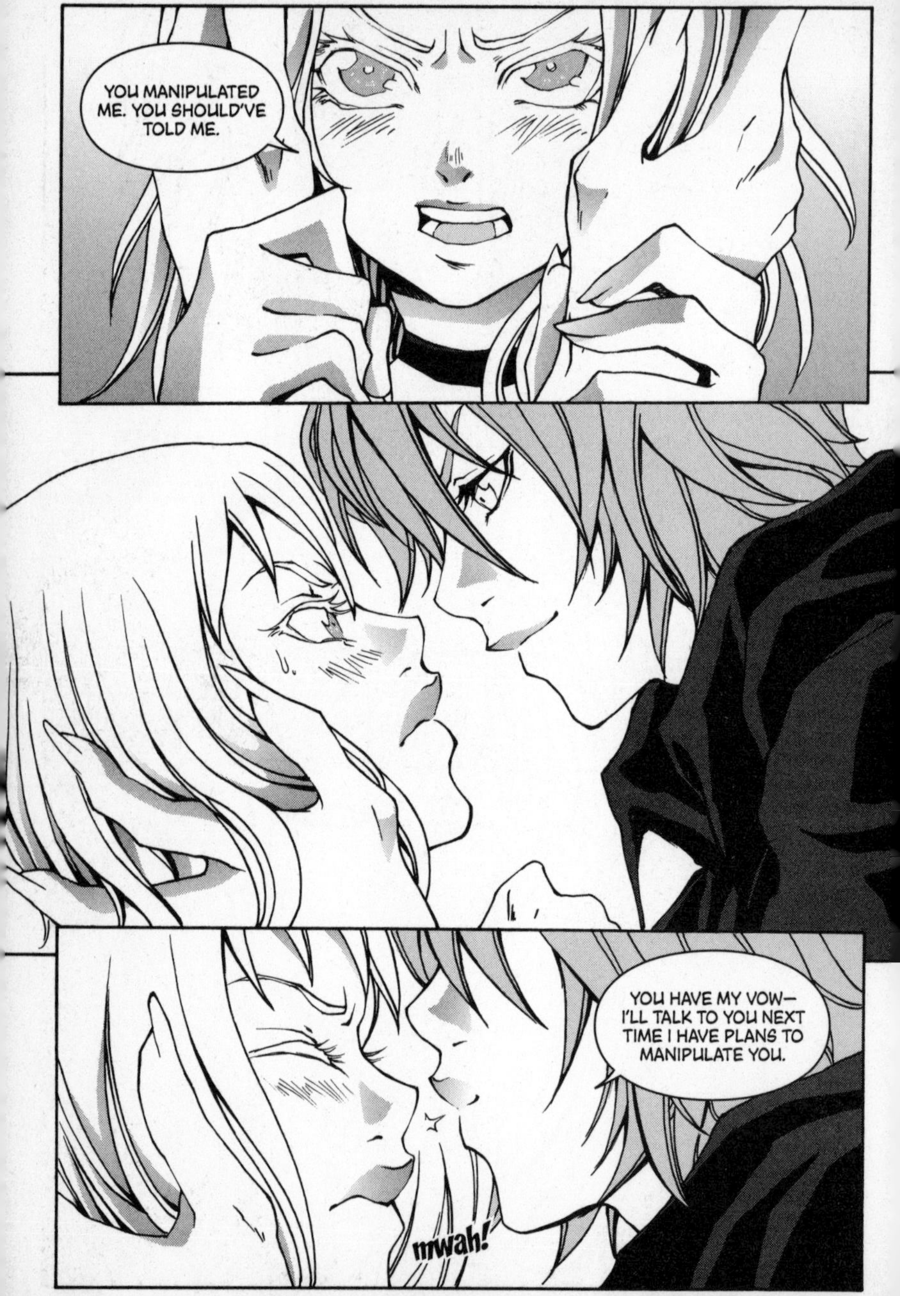
YOU MANIPULATED ME. YOU SHOULD'VE TOLD ME.
YOU HAVE MY VOW— I'LL TALK TO YOU NEXT TIME I HAVE PLANS TO MANIPULATE YOU.
mwah!

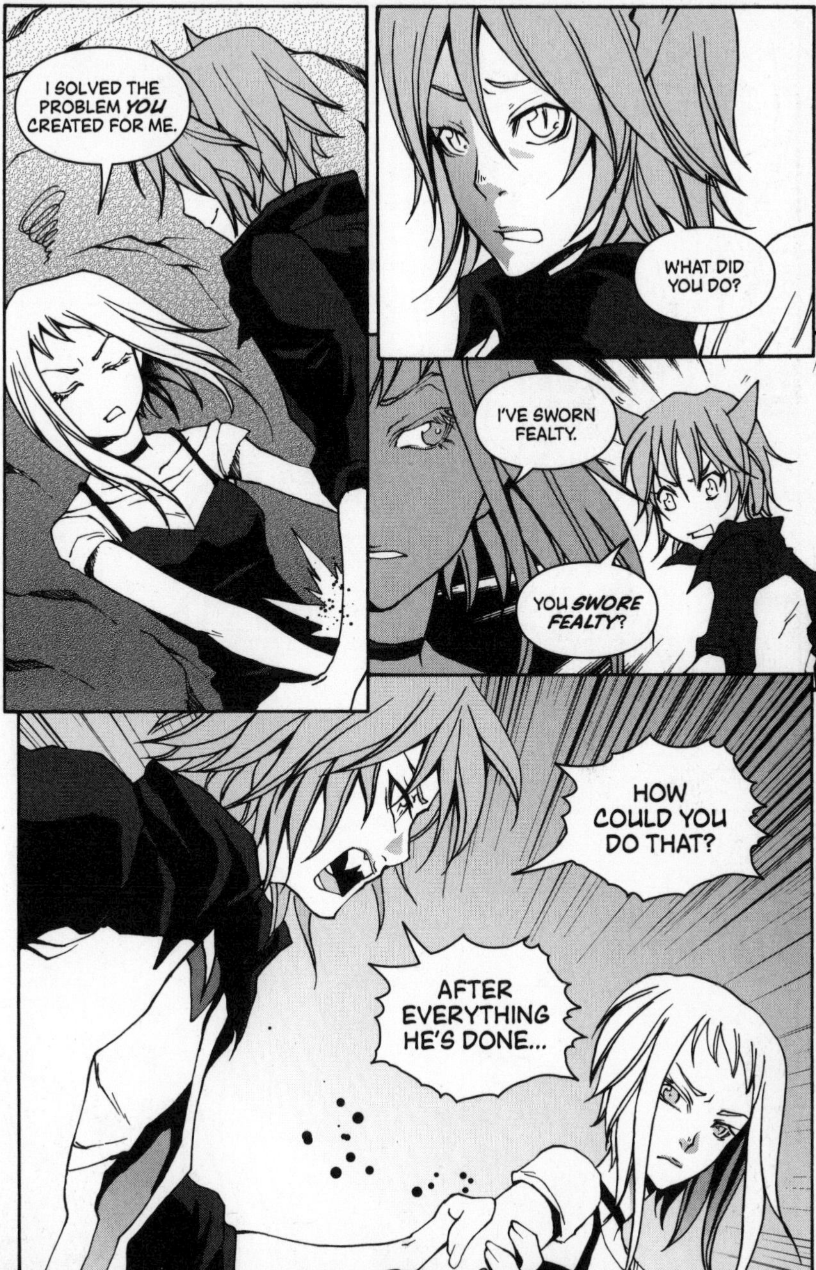
I SOLVED THE PROBLEM *YOU* CREATED FOR ME.
WHAT DID YOU DO?
I'VE SWORN FEALTY.
YOU *SWORE FEALTY*?
HOW COULD YOU DO THAT?
AFTER EVERYTHING HE'S DONE...

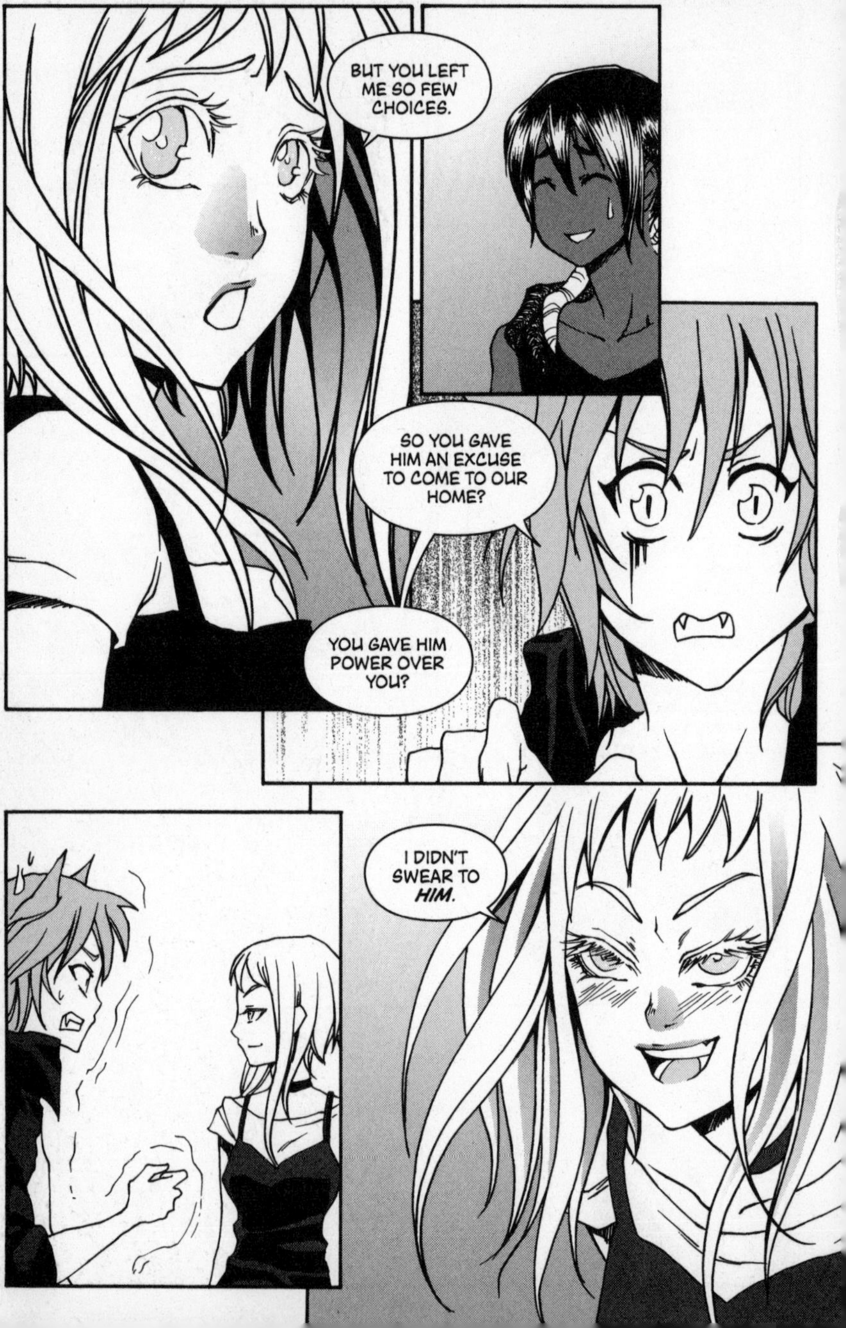
BUT YOU LEFT ME SO FEW CHOICES.
SO YOU GAVE HIM AN EXCUSE TO COME TO OUR HOME?
YOU GAVE HIM POWER OVER YOU?
I DIDN'T SWEAR TO *HIM*.

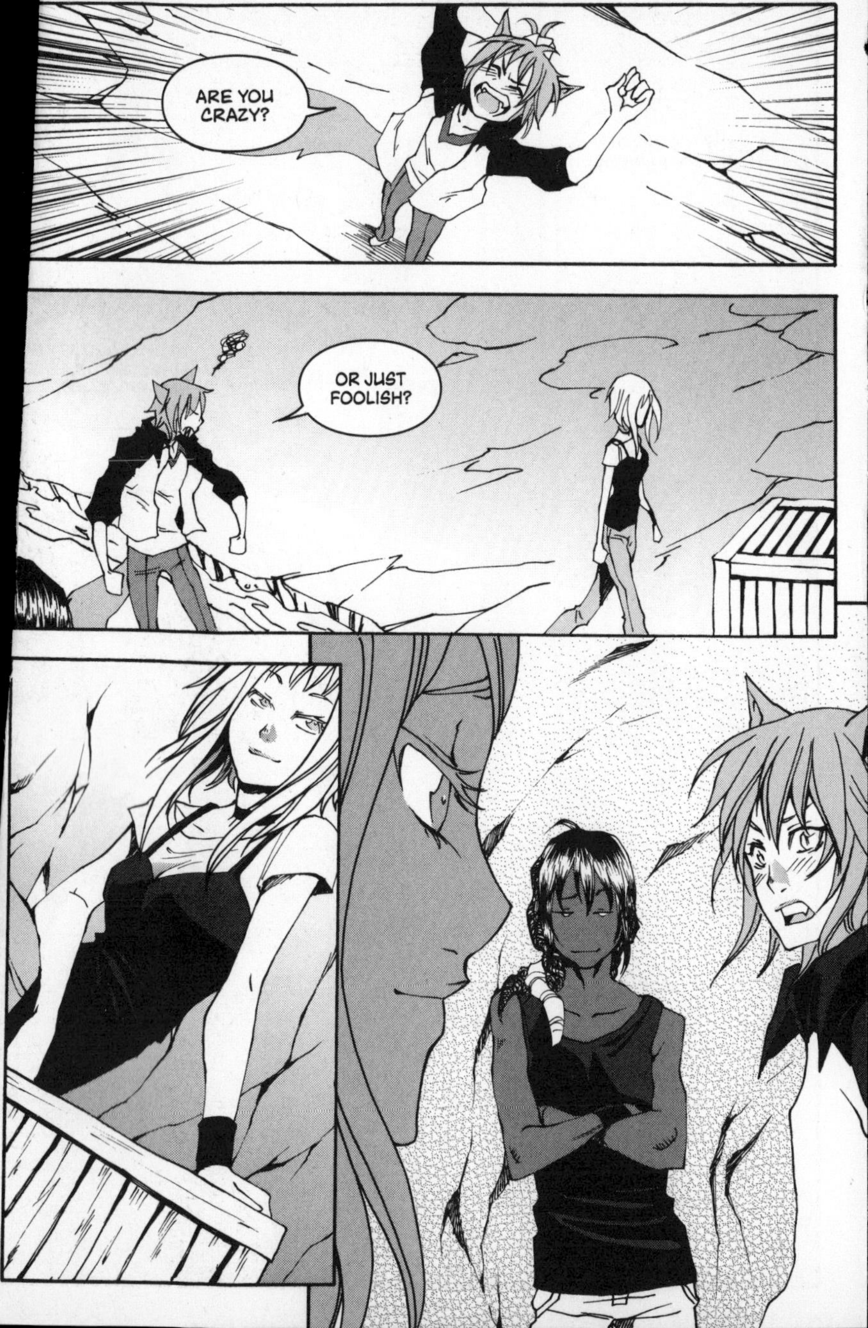
ARE YOU CRAZY?
OR JUST FOOLISH?

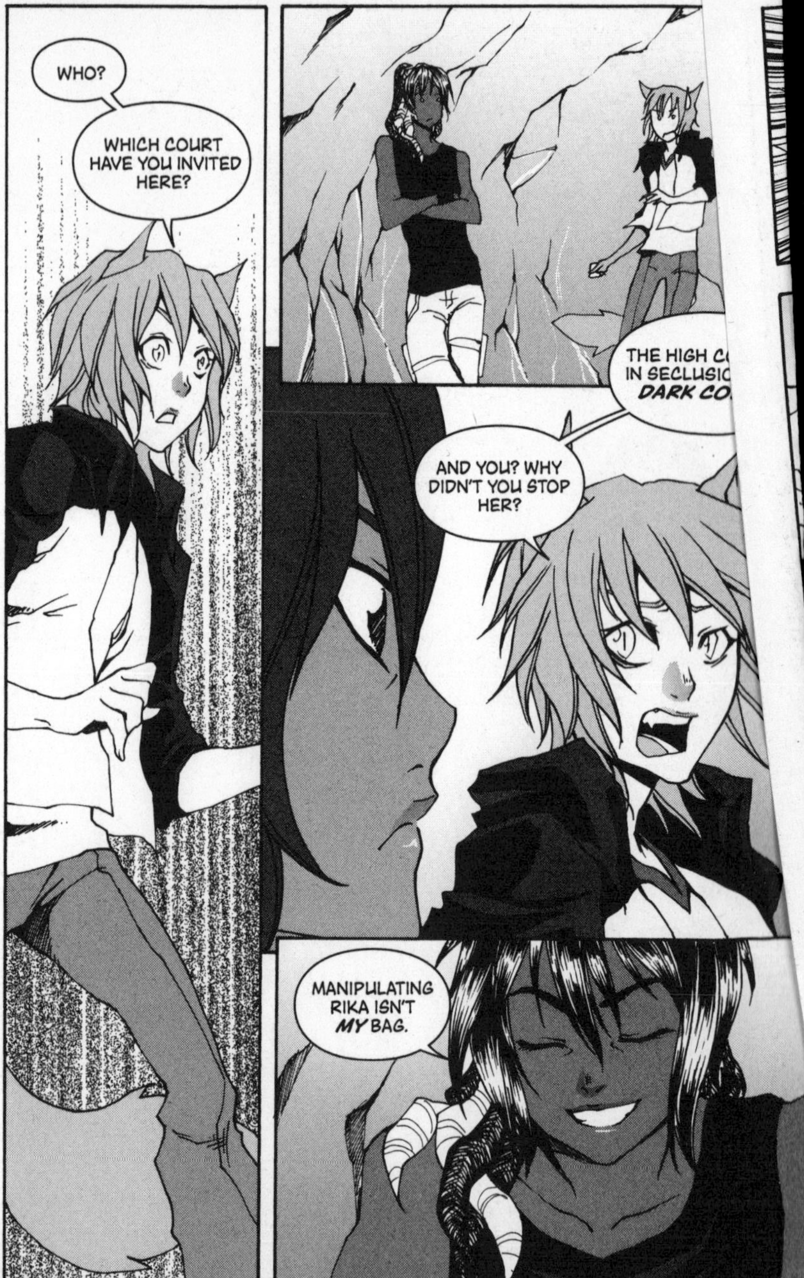
WHO?
WHICH COURT HAVE YOU INVITED HERE?
THE HIGH CO IN SECLUSIO *DARK CO*
AND YOU? WHY DIDN'T YOU STOP HER?
MANIPULATING RIKA ISN'T *MY* BAG.

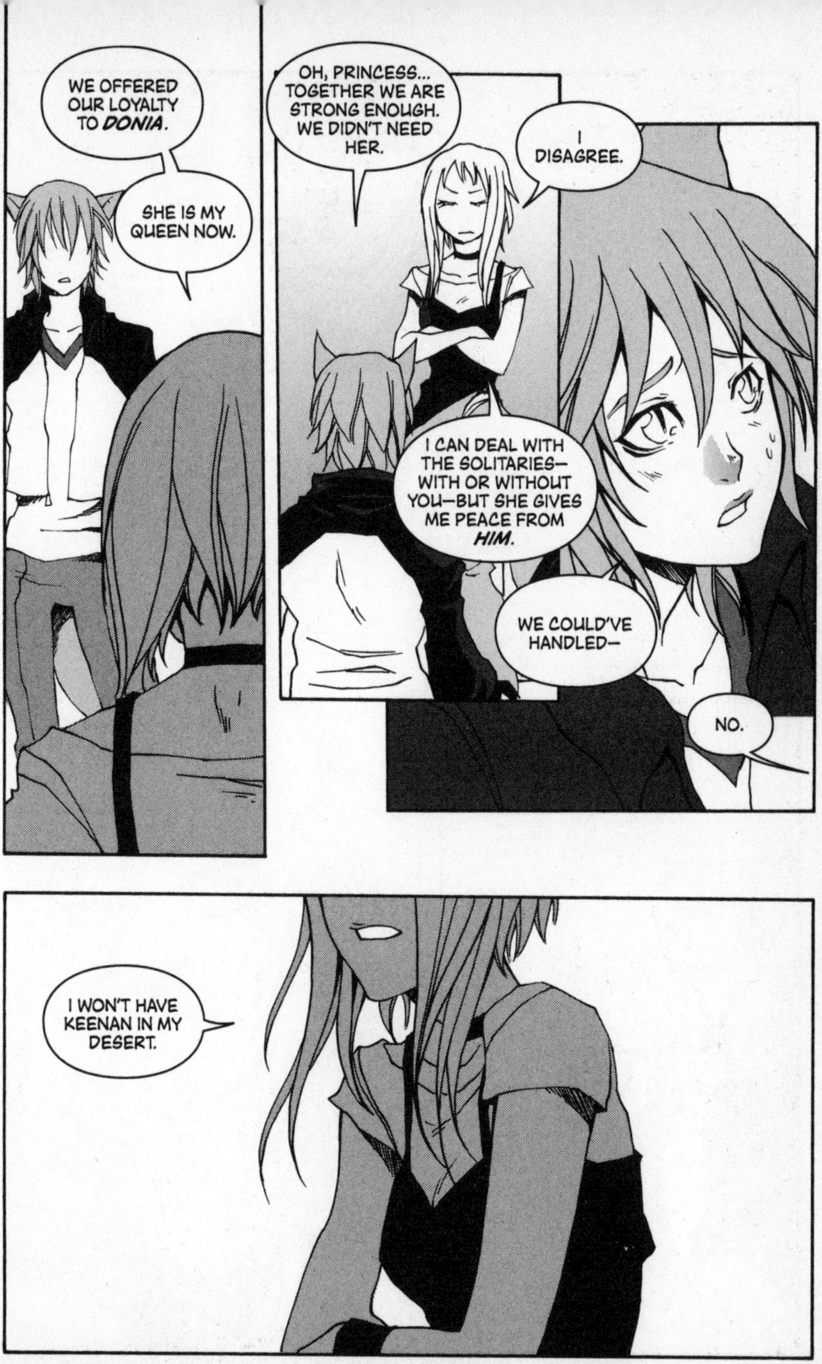
WE OFFERED OUR LOYALTY TO DONIA.
SHE IS MY QUEEN NOW.
OH, PRINCESS... TOGETHER WE ARE STRONG ENOUGH. WE DIDN'T NEED HER.
I DISAGREE.
I CAN DEAL WITH THE SOLITARIES—WITH OR WITHOUT YOU—BUT SHE GIVES ME PEACE FROM HIM.
WE COULD'VE HANDLED—
NO.
I WON'T HAVE KEENAN IN MY DESERT.

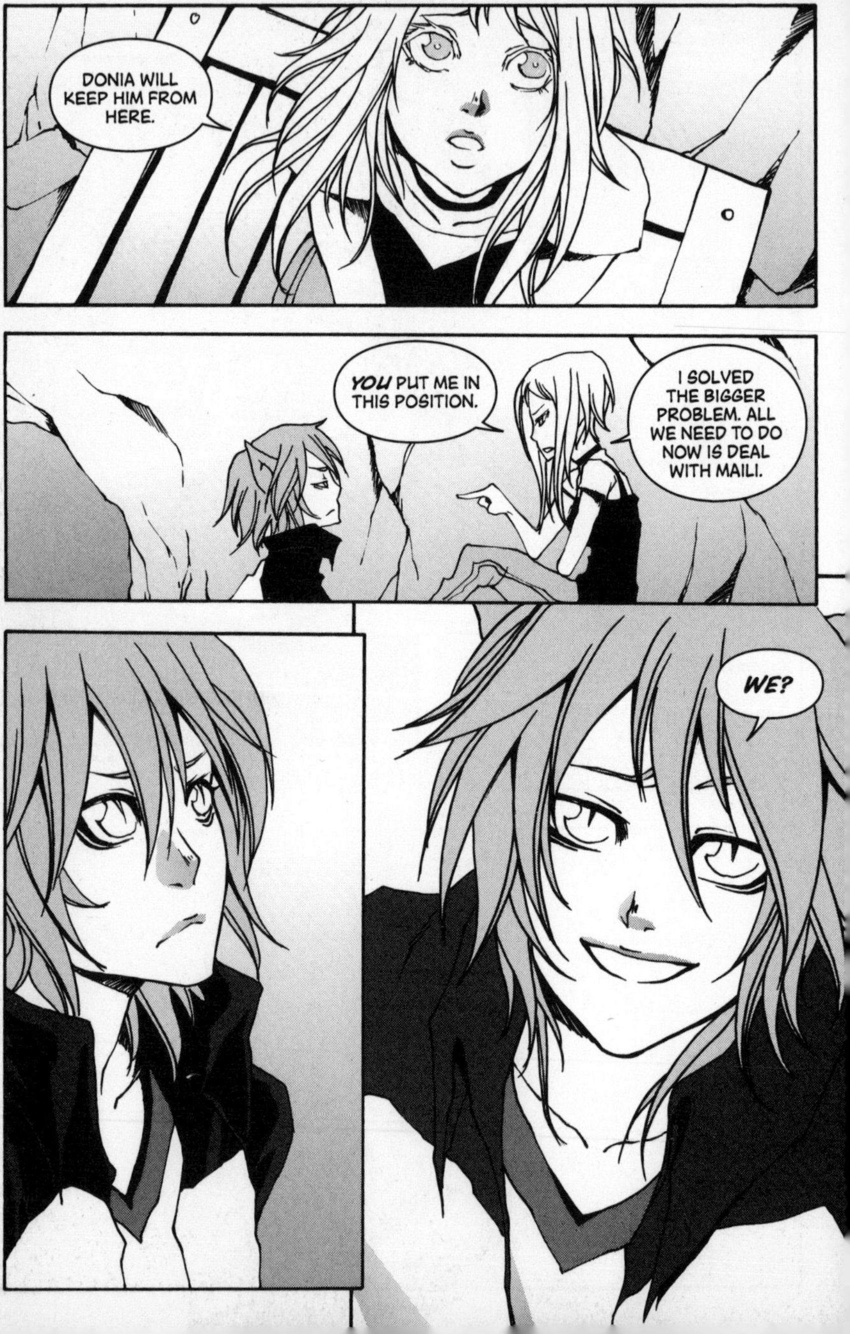
DONIA WILL KEEP HIM FROM HERE.
YOU PUT ME IN THIS POSITION.
I SOLVED THE BIGGER PROBLEM. ALL WE NEED TO DO NOW IS DEAL WITH MAILI.
WE?

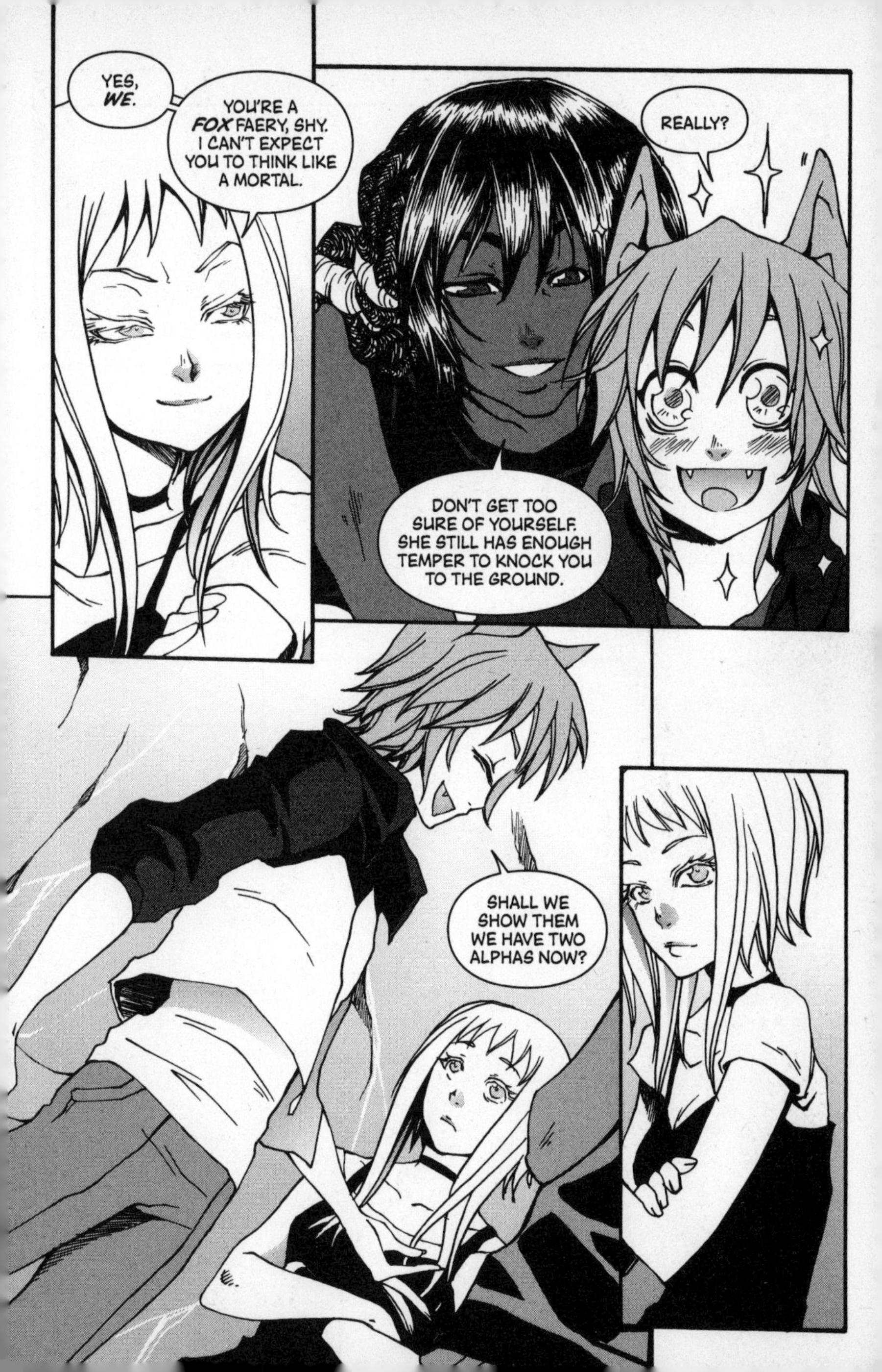
YES, *WE*.
YOU'RE A *FOX* FAERY, SHY. I CAN'T EXPECT YOU TO THINK LIKE A MORTAL.
REALLY?
DON'T GET TOO SURE OF YOURSELF. SHE STILL HAS ENOUGH TEMPER TO KNOCK YOU TO THE GROUND.
SHALL WE SHOW THEM WE HAVE TWO ALPHAS NOW?

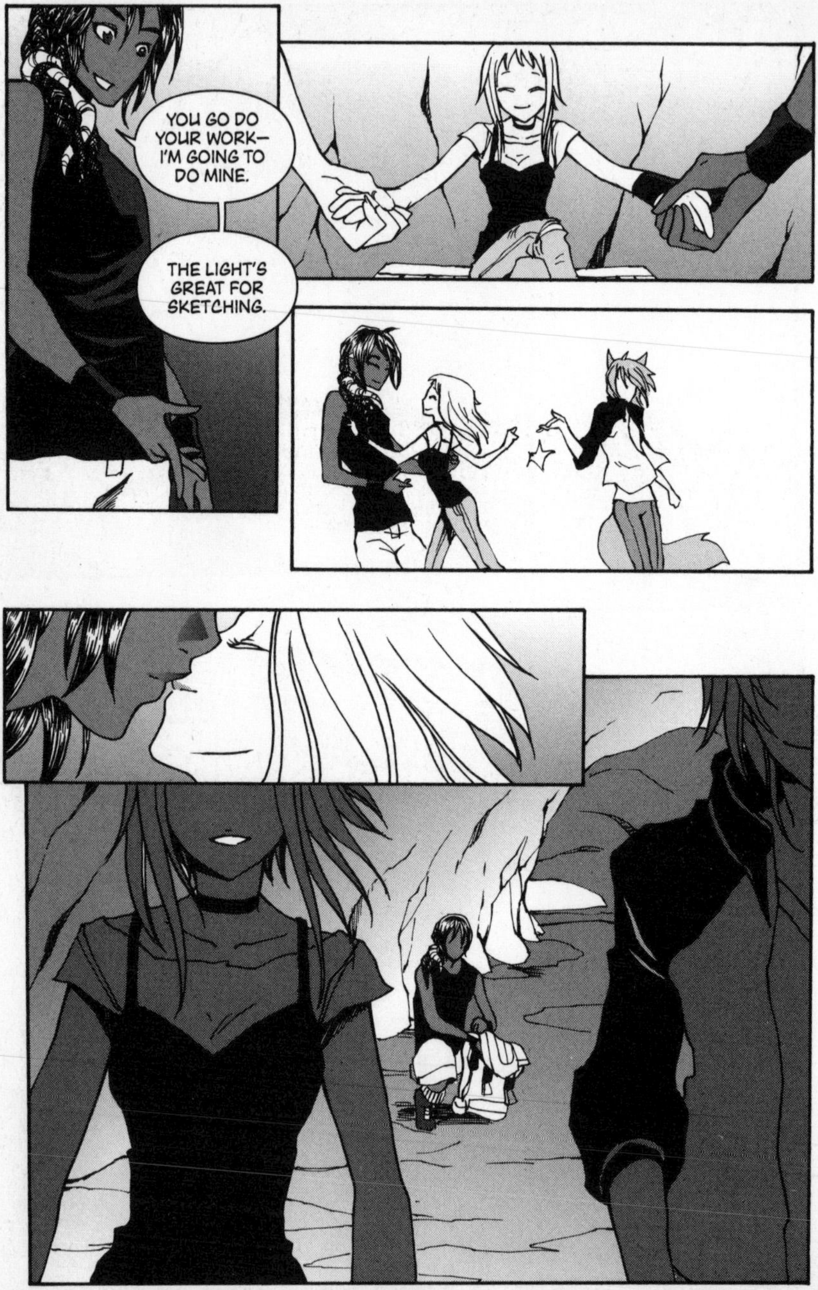
YOU GO DO YOUR WORK—I'M GOING TO DO MINE.
THE LIGHT'S GREAT FOR SKETCHING.

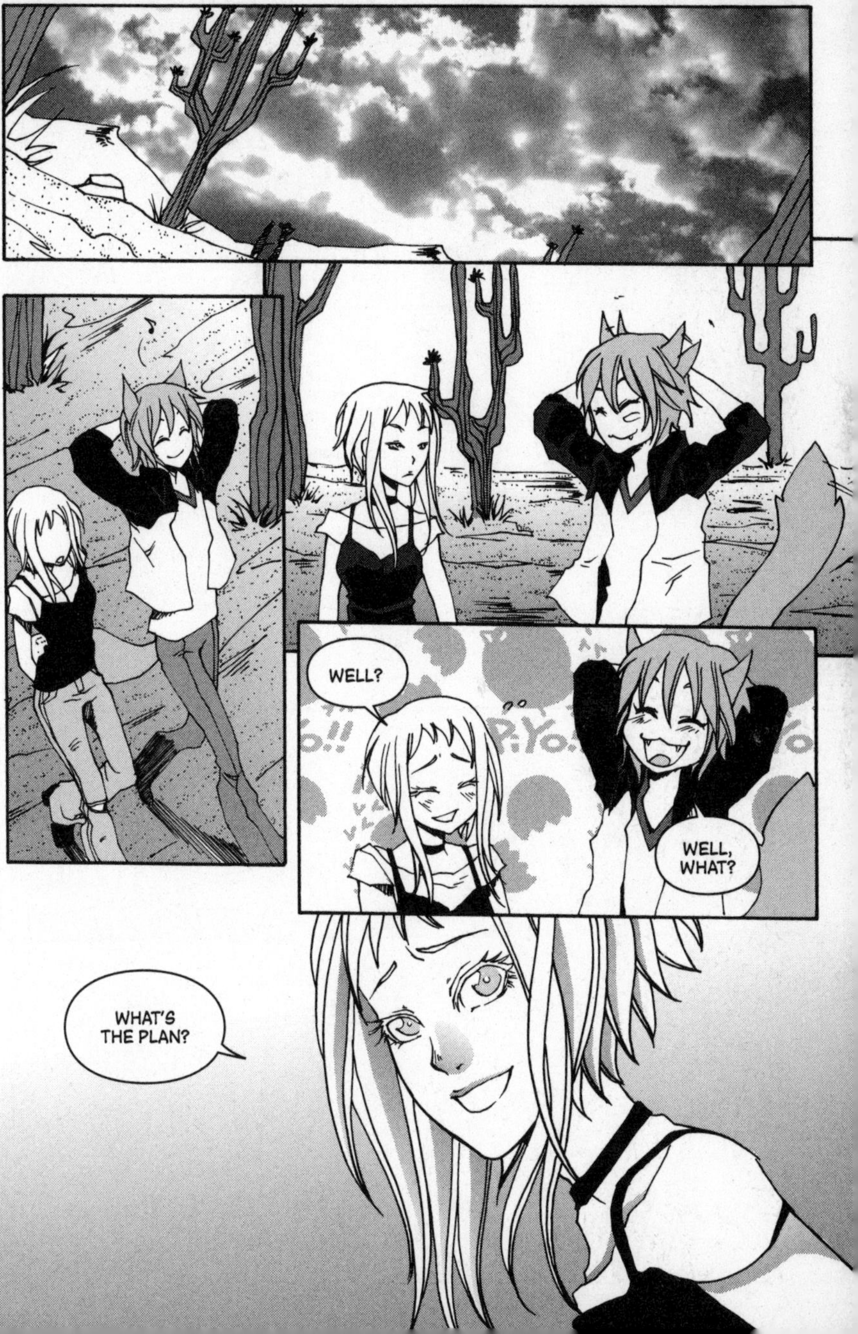
WELL?
PiYo!
WELL, WHAT?
WHAT'S THE PLAN?

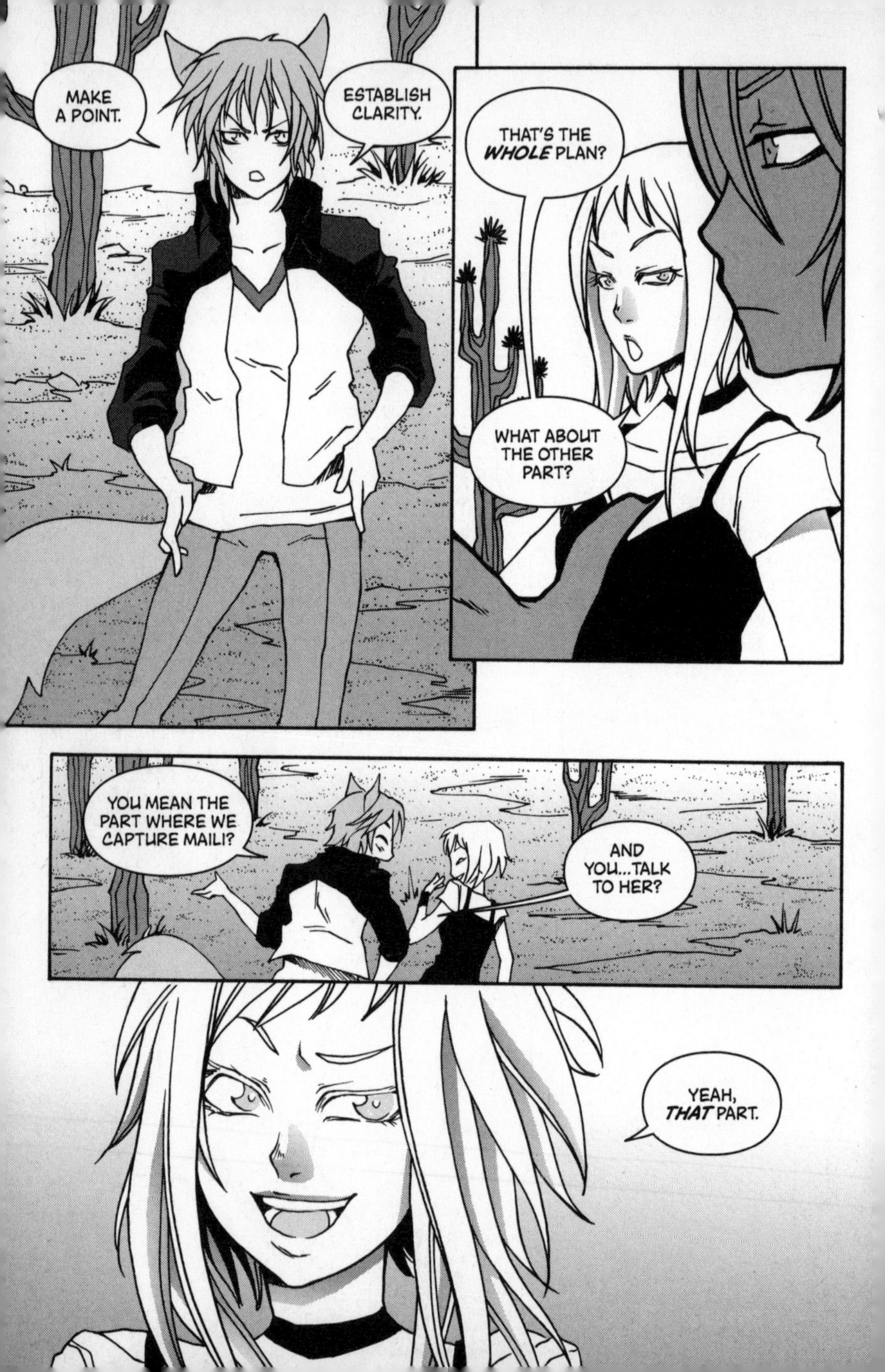
MAKE A POINT.
ESTABLISH CLARITY.
THAT'S THE *WHOLE* PLAN?
WHAT ABOUT THE OTHER PART?
YOU MEAN THE PART WHERE WE CAPTURE MAILI?
AND YOU...TALK TO HER?
YEAH, *THAT* PART.

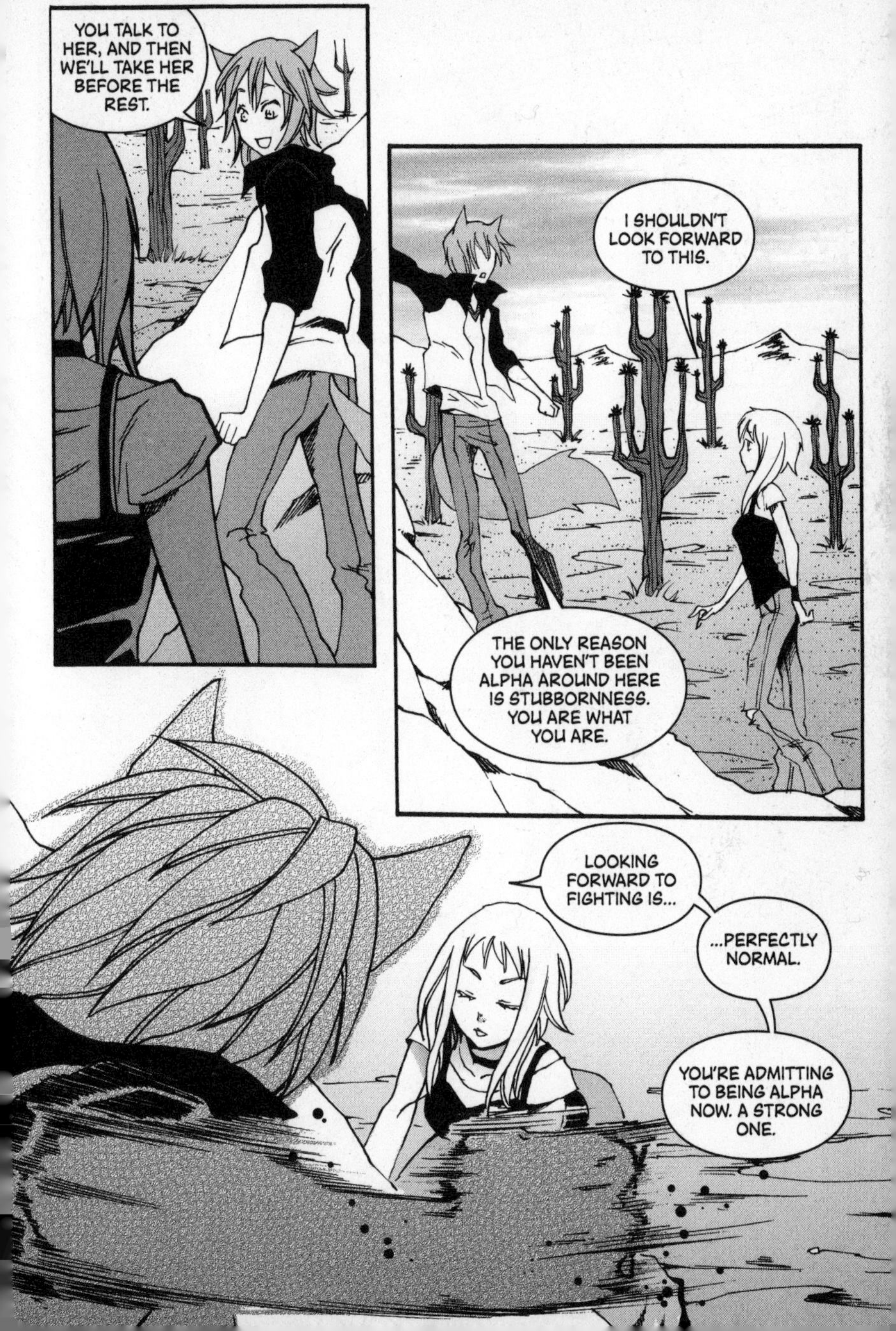
YOU TALK TO HER, AND THEN WE'LL TAKE HER BEFORE THE REST.
I SHOULDN'T LOOK FORWARD TO THIS.
THE ONLY REASON YOU HAVEN'T BEEN ALPHA AROUND HERE IS STUBBORNNESS. YOU ARE WHAT YOU ARE.
LOOKING FORWARD TO FIGHTING IS...
...PERFECTLY NORMAL.
YOU'RE ADMITTING TO BEING ALPHA NOW. A STRONG ONE.

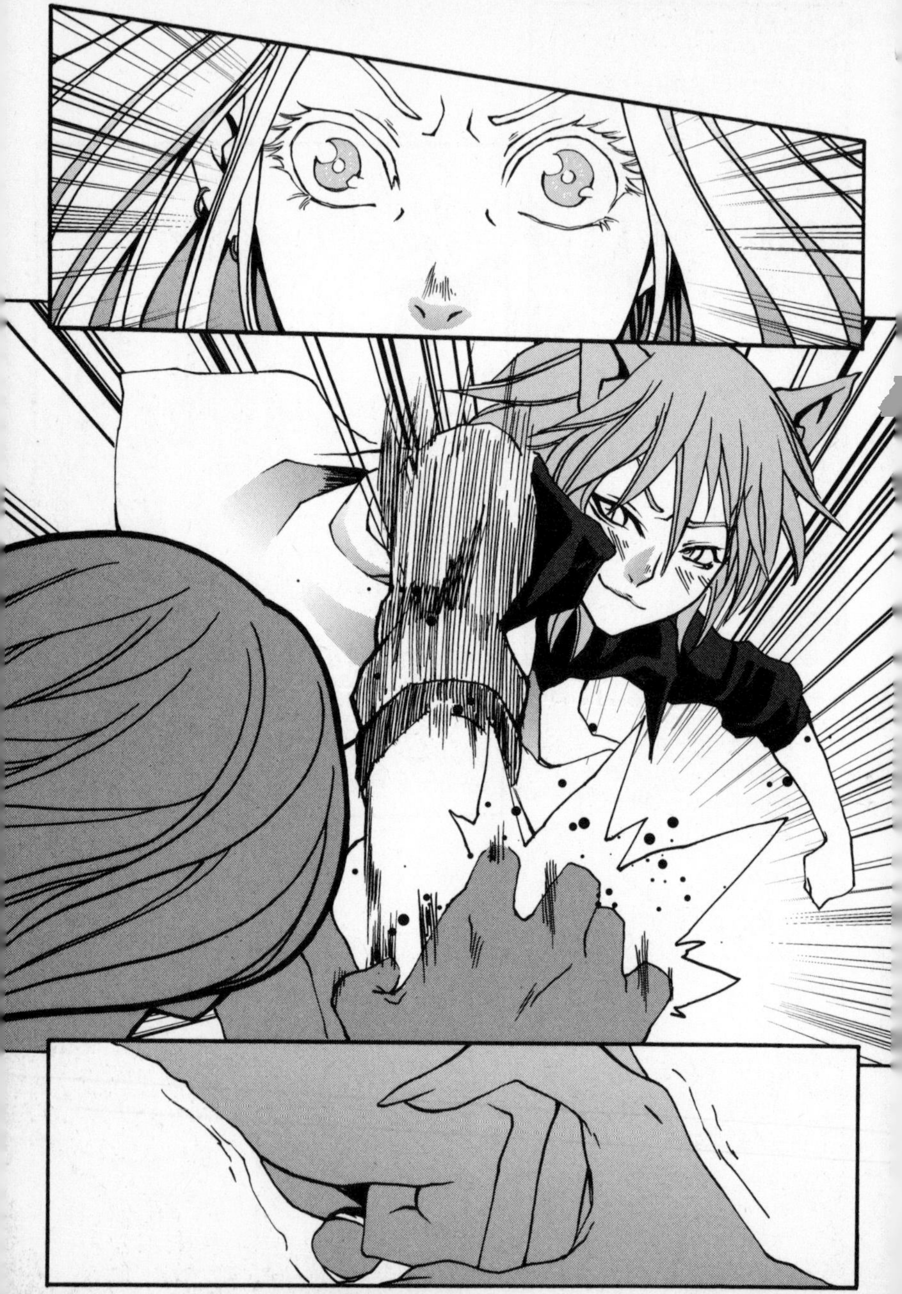

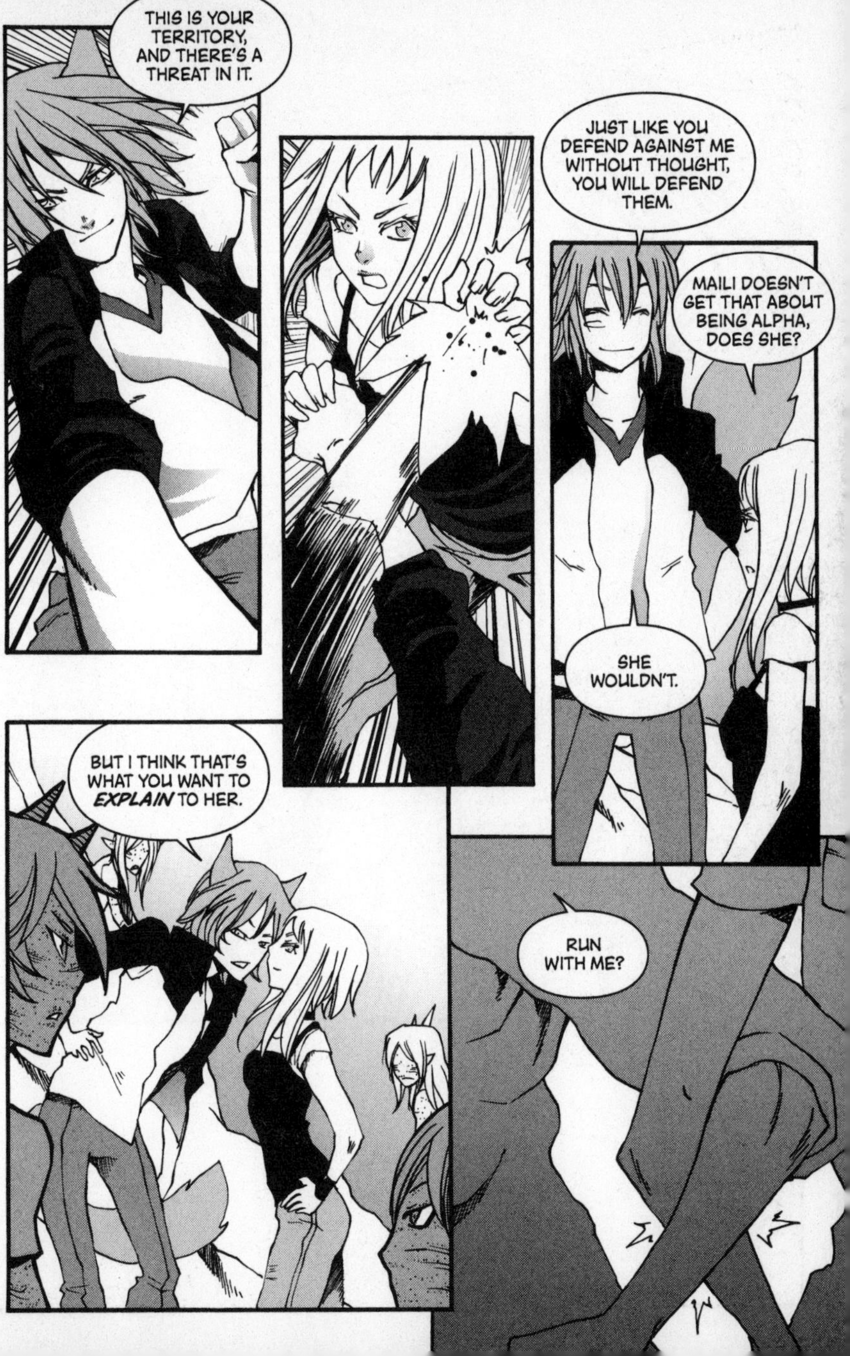
THIS IS YOUR TERRITORY, AND THERE'S A THREAT IN IT.
JUST LIKE YOU DEFEND AGAINST ME WITHOUT THOUGHT, YOU WILL DEFEND THEM.
MAILI DOESN'T GET THAT ABOUT BEING ALPHA, DOES SHE?
SHE WOULDN'T.
BUT I THINK THAT'S WHAT YOU WANT TO *EXPLAIN* TO HER.
RUN WITH ME?

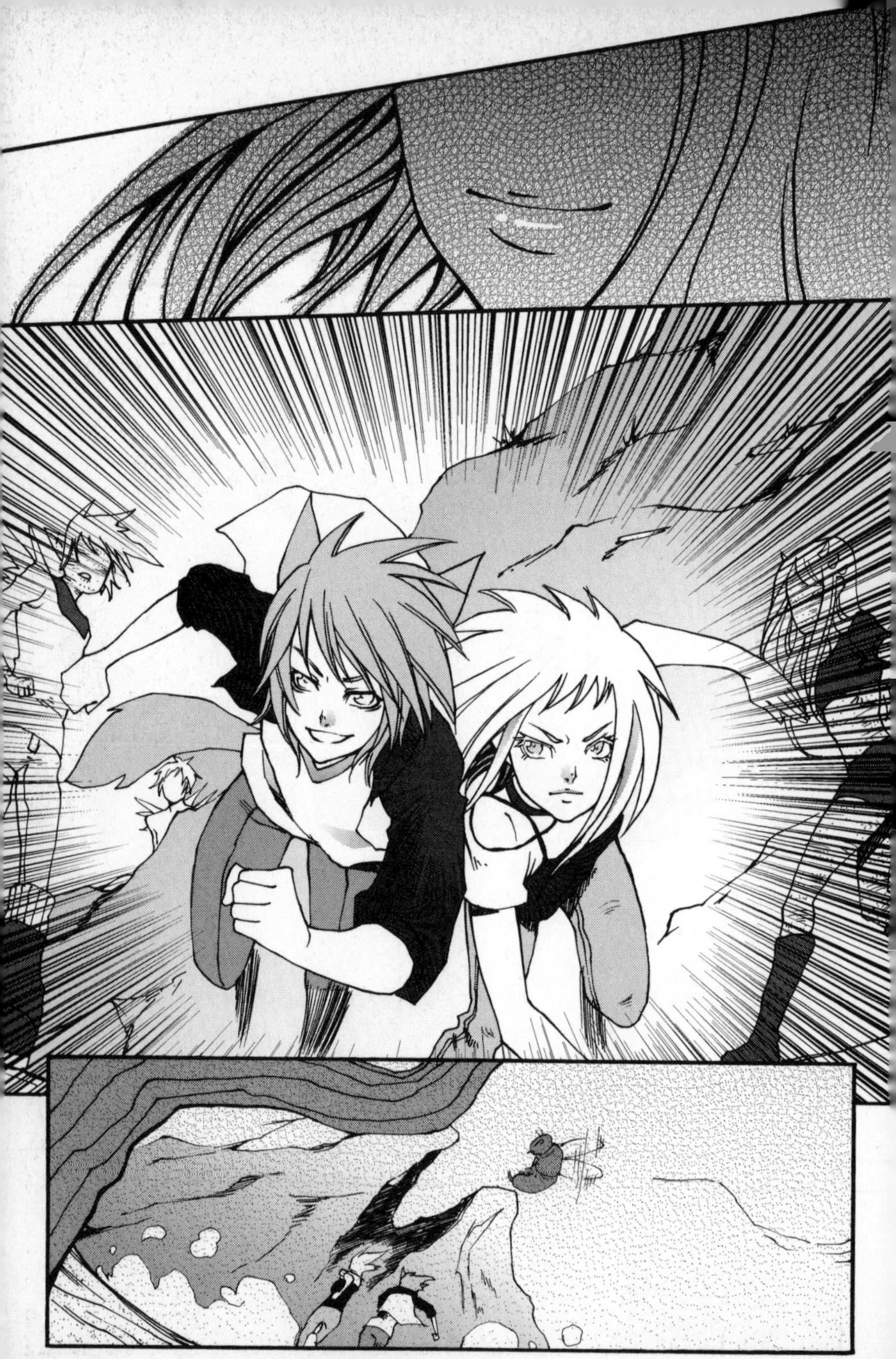

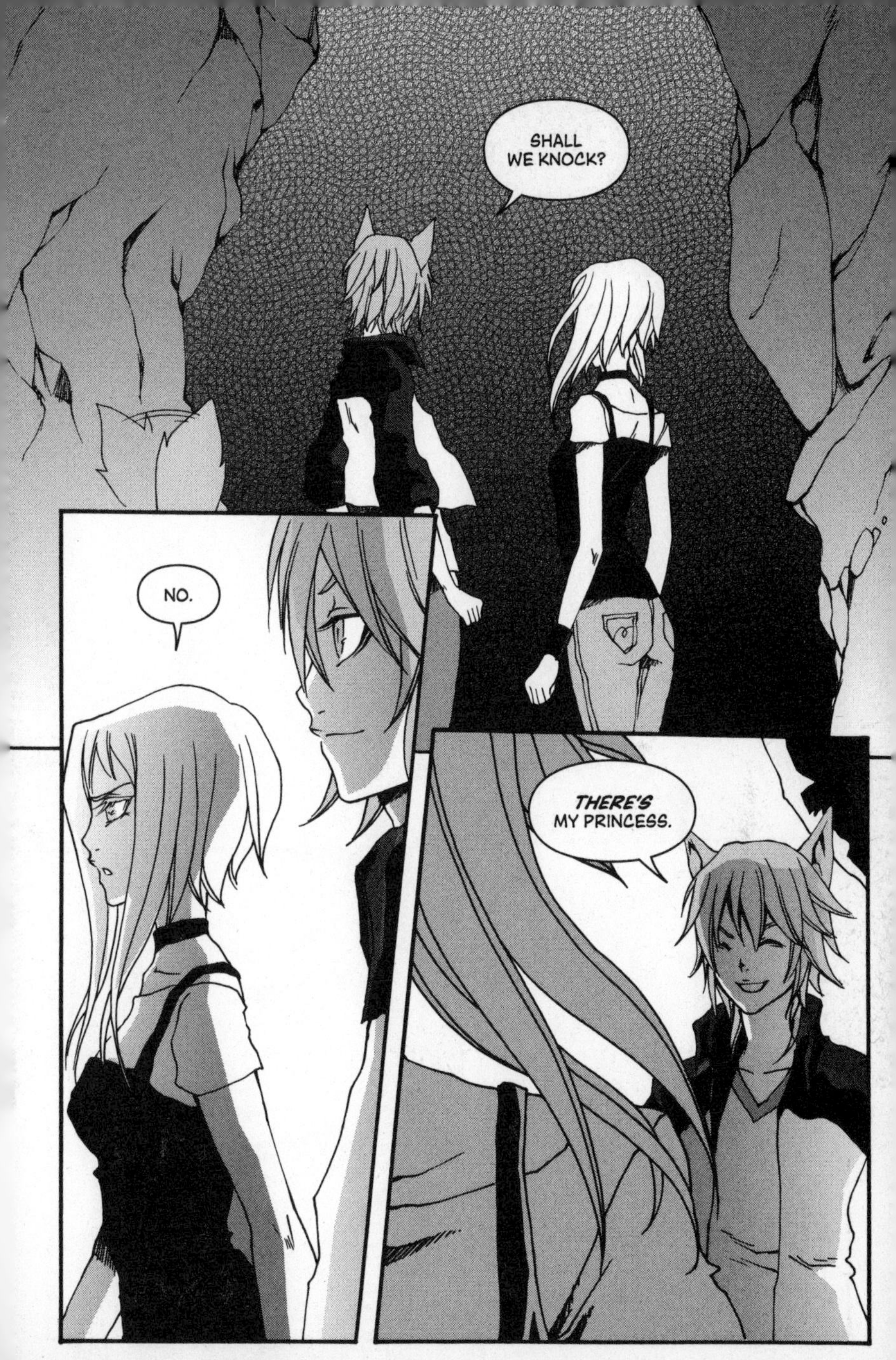
SHALL WE KNOCK?
NO.
THERE'S MY PRINCESS.

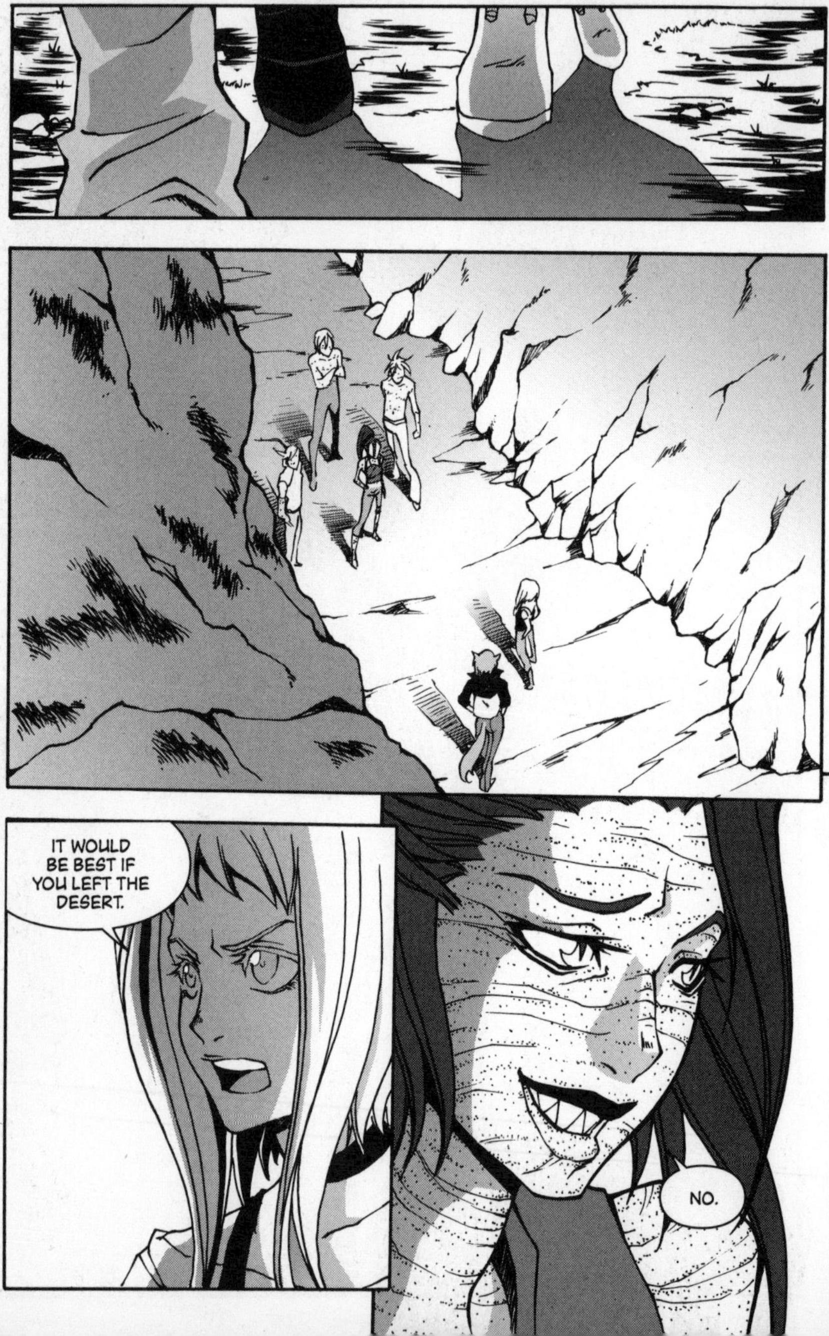
IT WOULD BE BEST IF YOU LEFT THE DESERT.
NO.

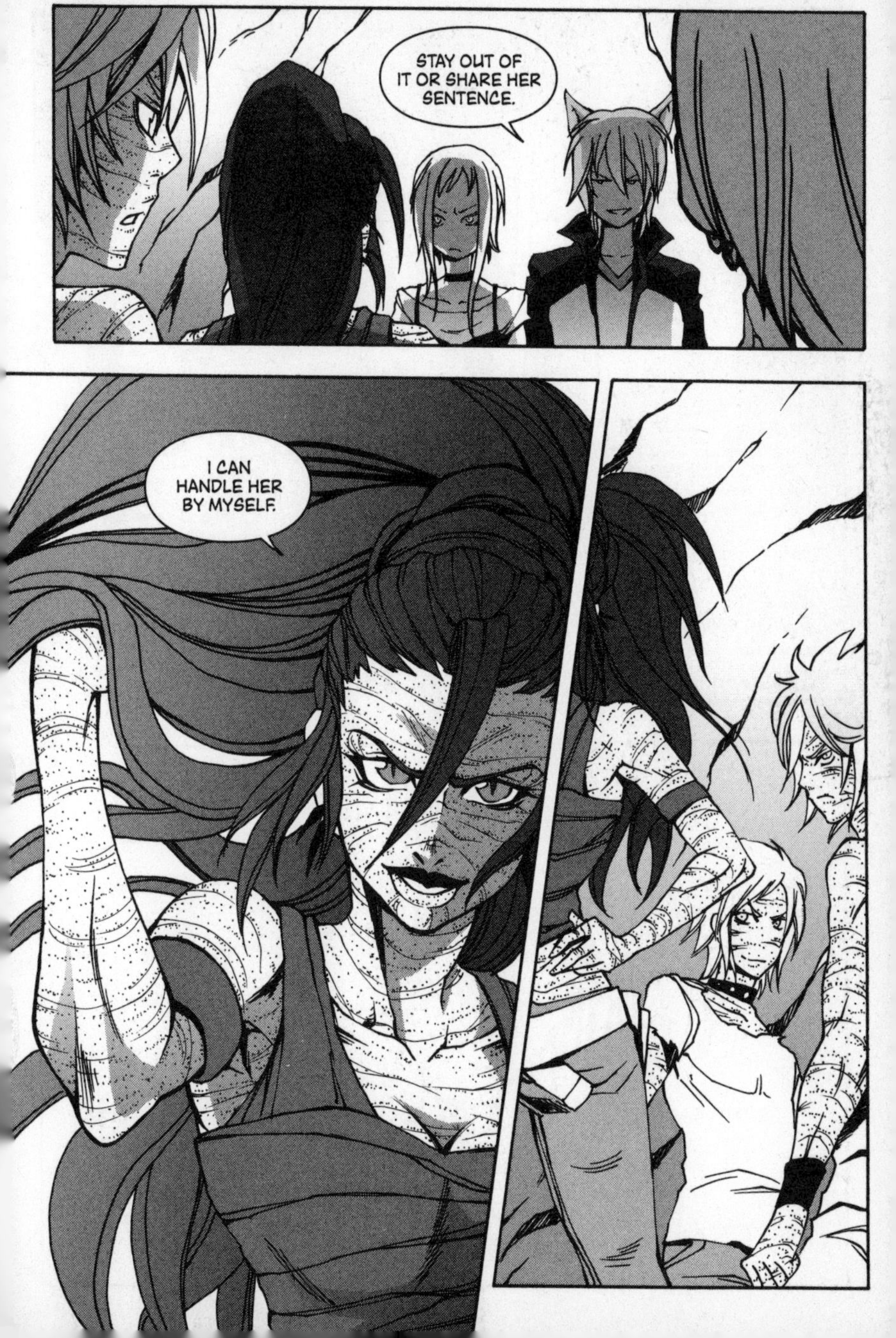
STAY OUT OF IT OR SHARE HER SENTENCE.
I CAN HANDLE HER BY MYSELF.

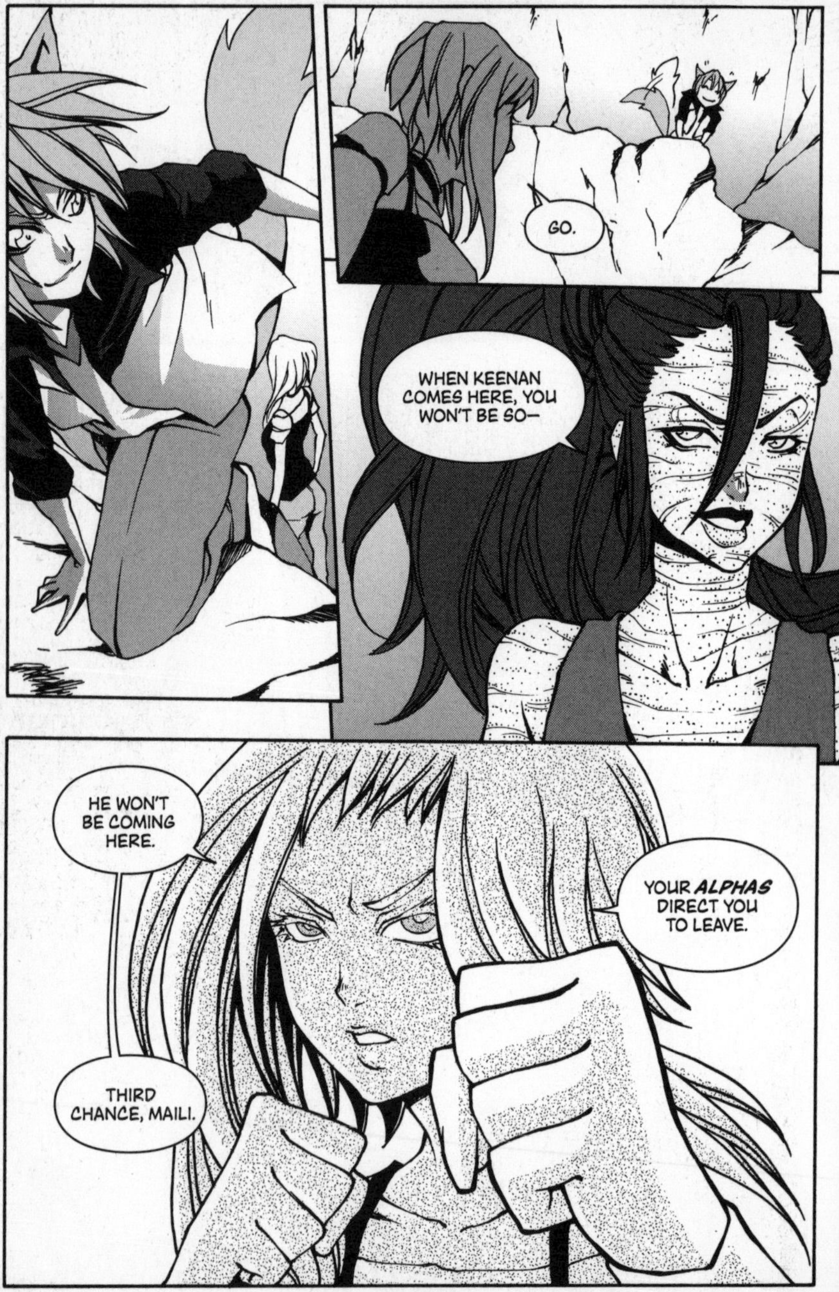
GO.
WHEN KEENAN COMES HERE, YOU WON'T BE SO—
HE WON'T BE COMING HERE.
YOUR *ALPHAS* DIRECT YOU TO LEAVE.
THIRD CHANCE, MAILI.

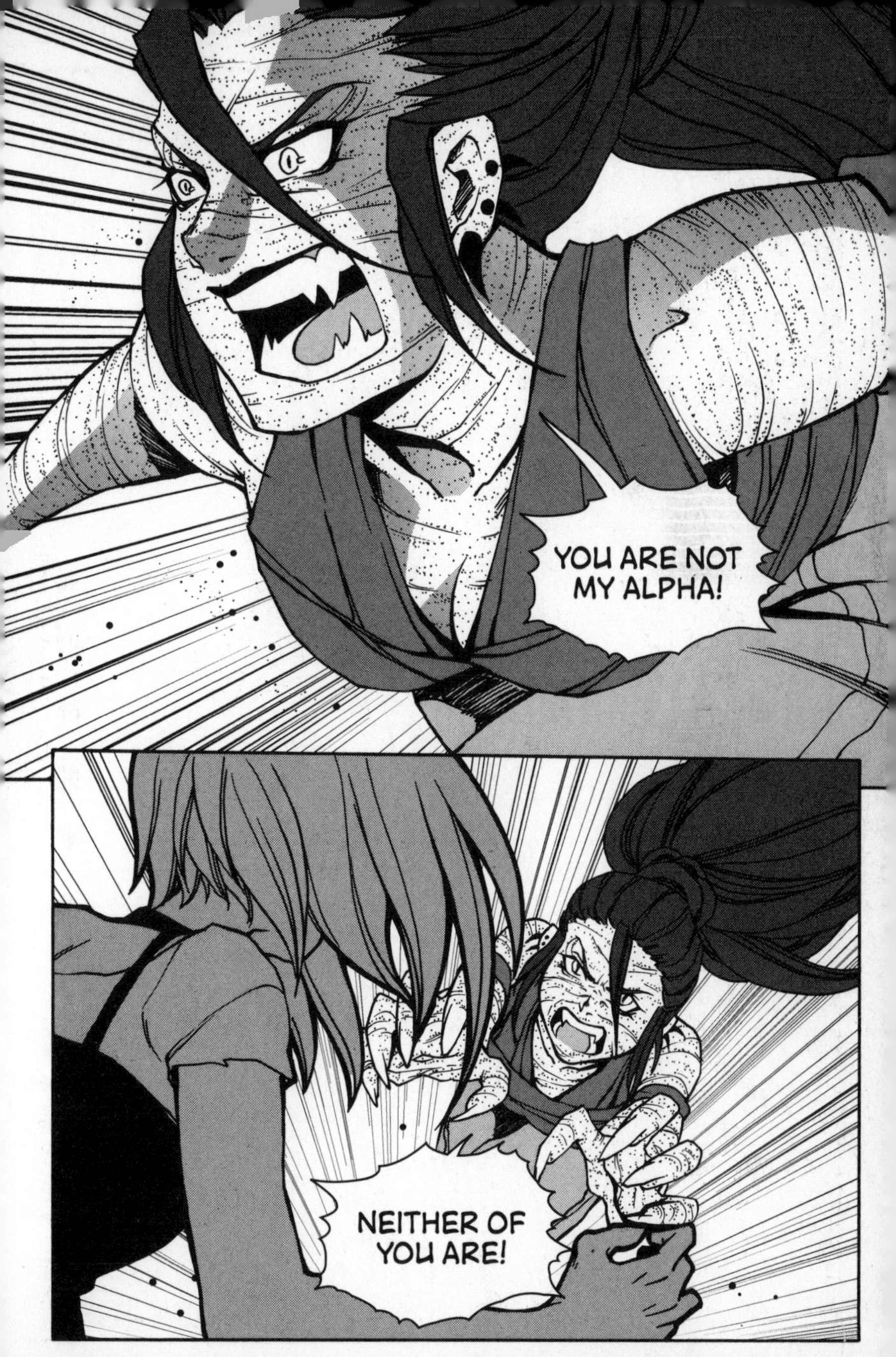
YOU ARE NOT MY ALPHA!
NEITHER OF YOU ARE!

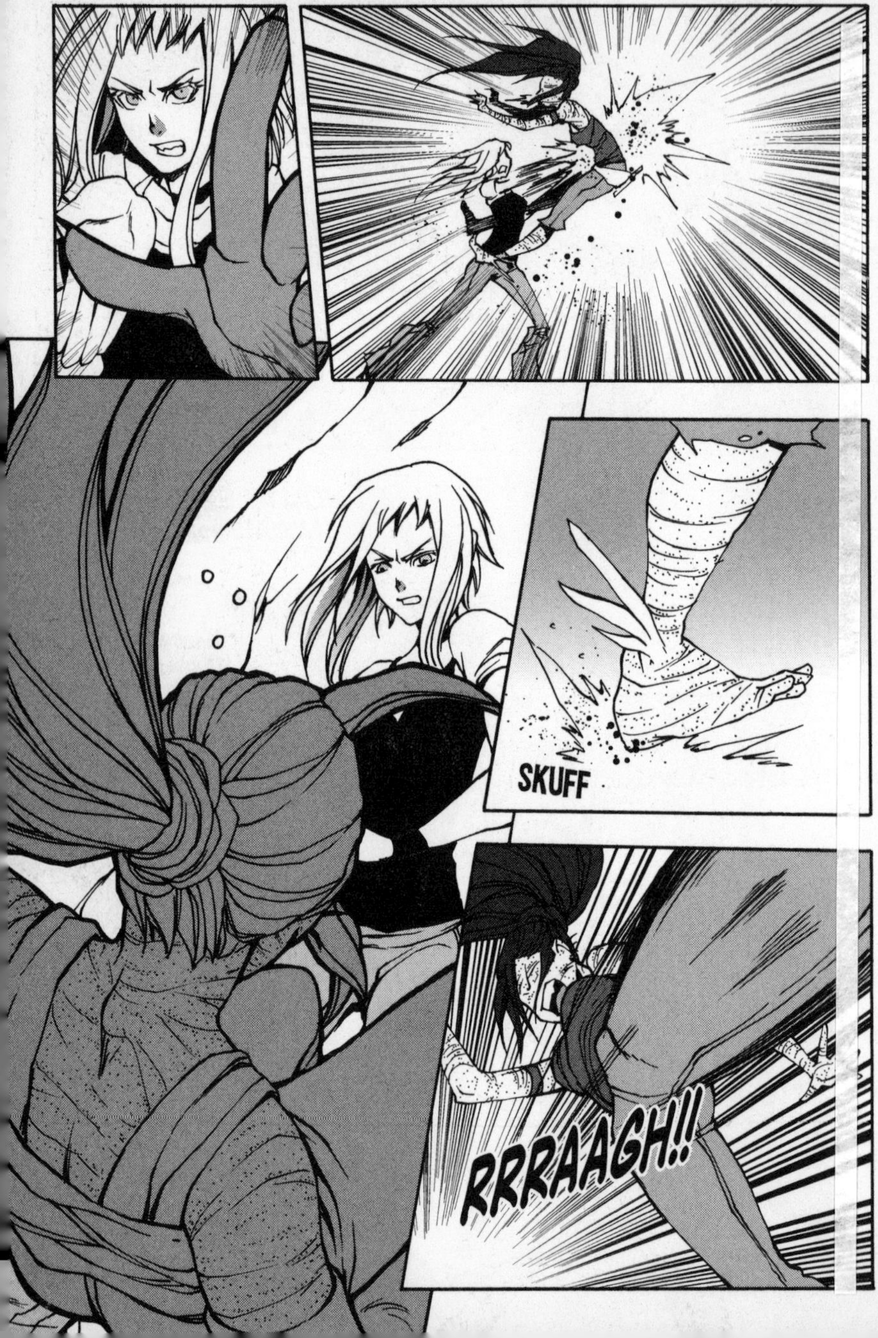
SKUFF
RRRAAGH!!

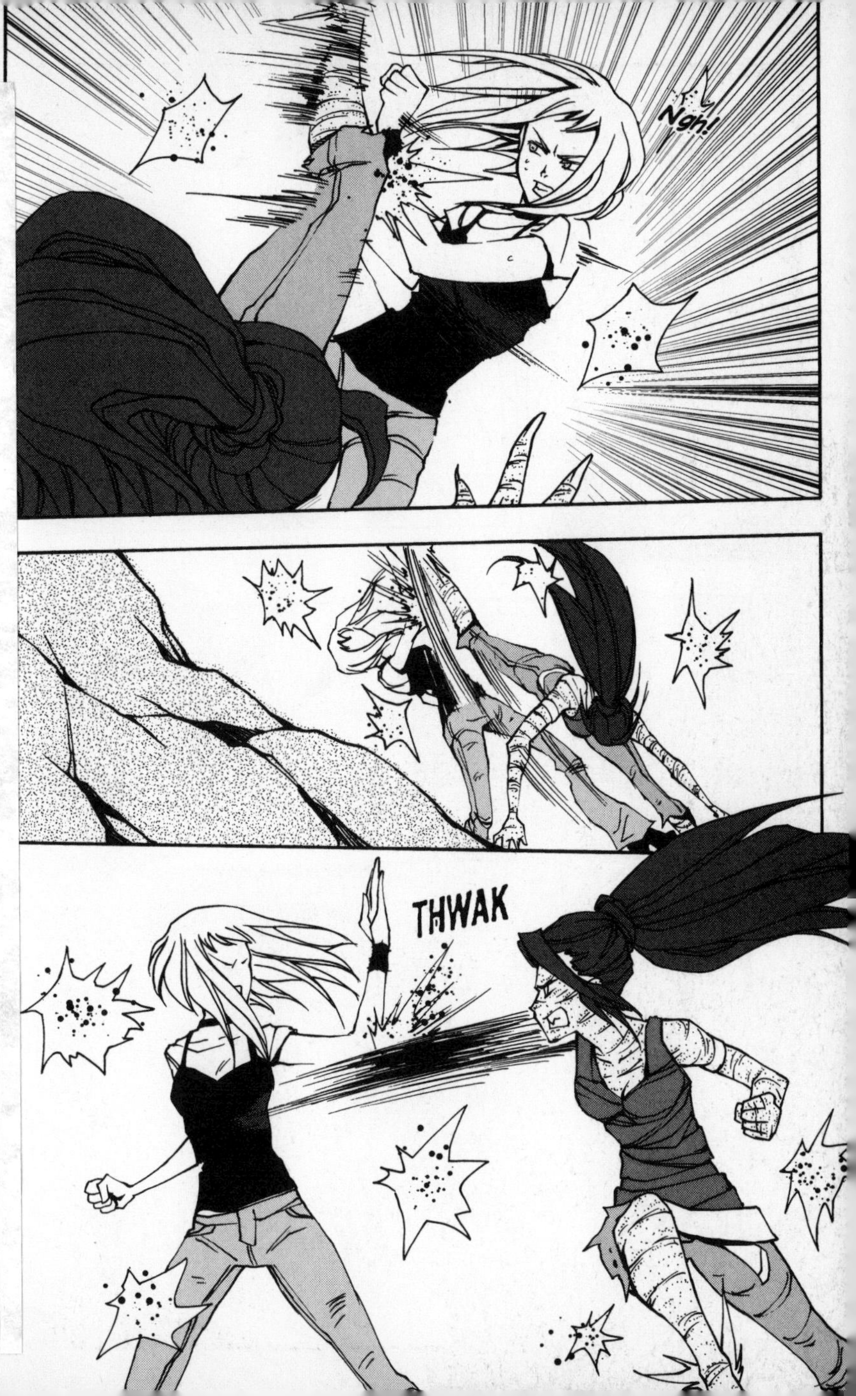
Ngh!
THWAK

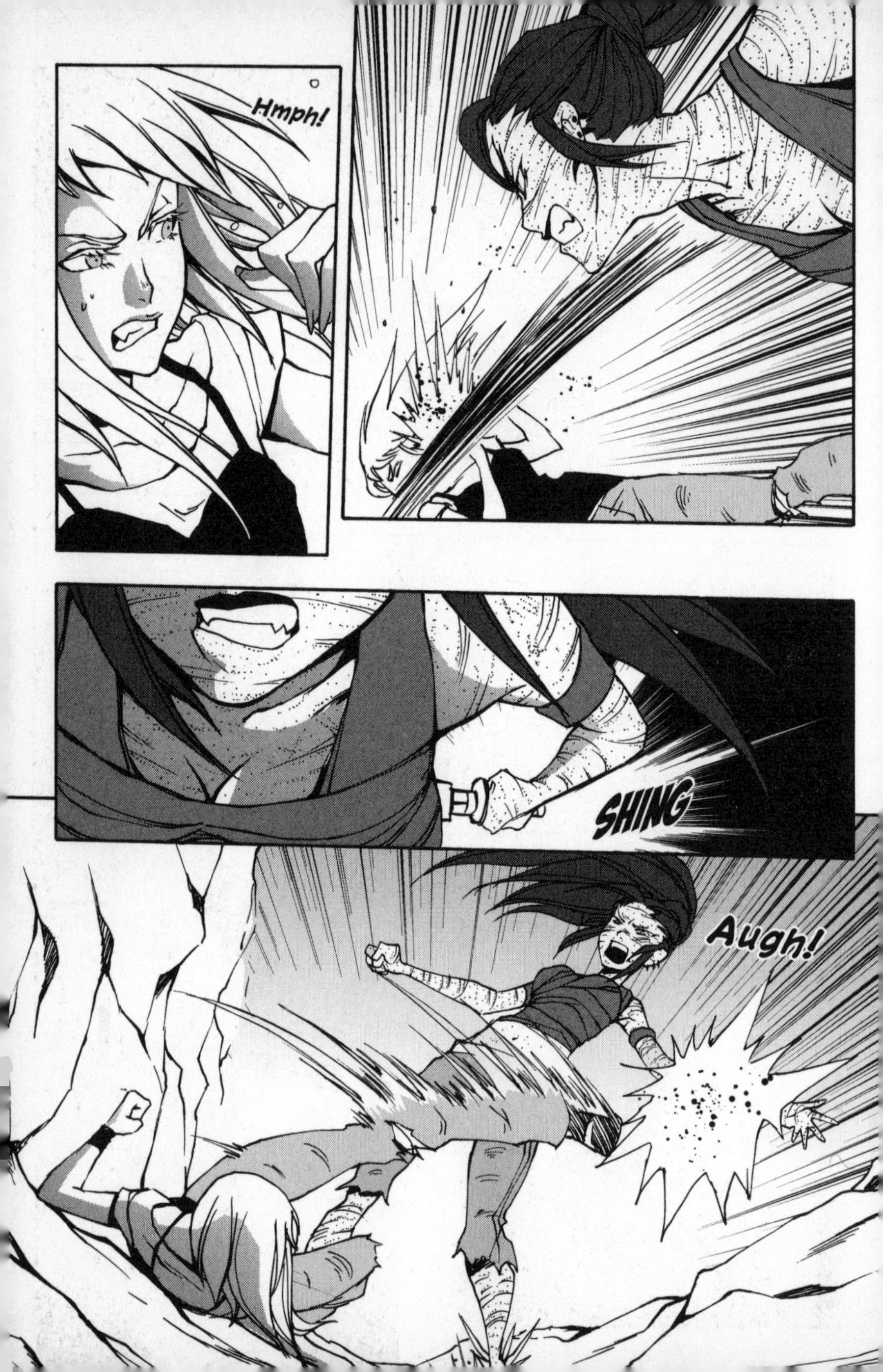
Hmph!
SHING
Augh!

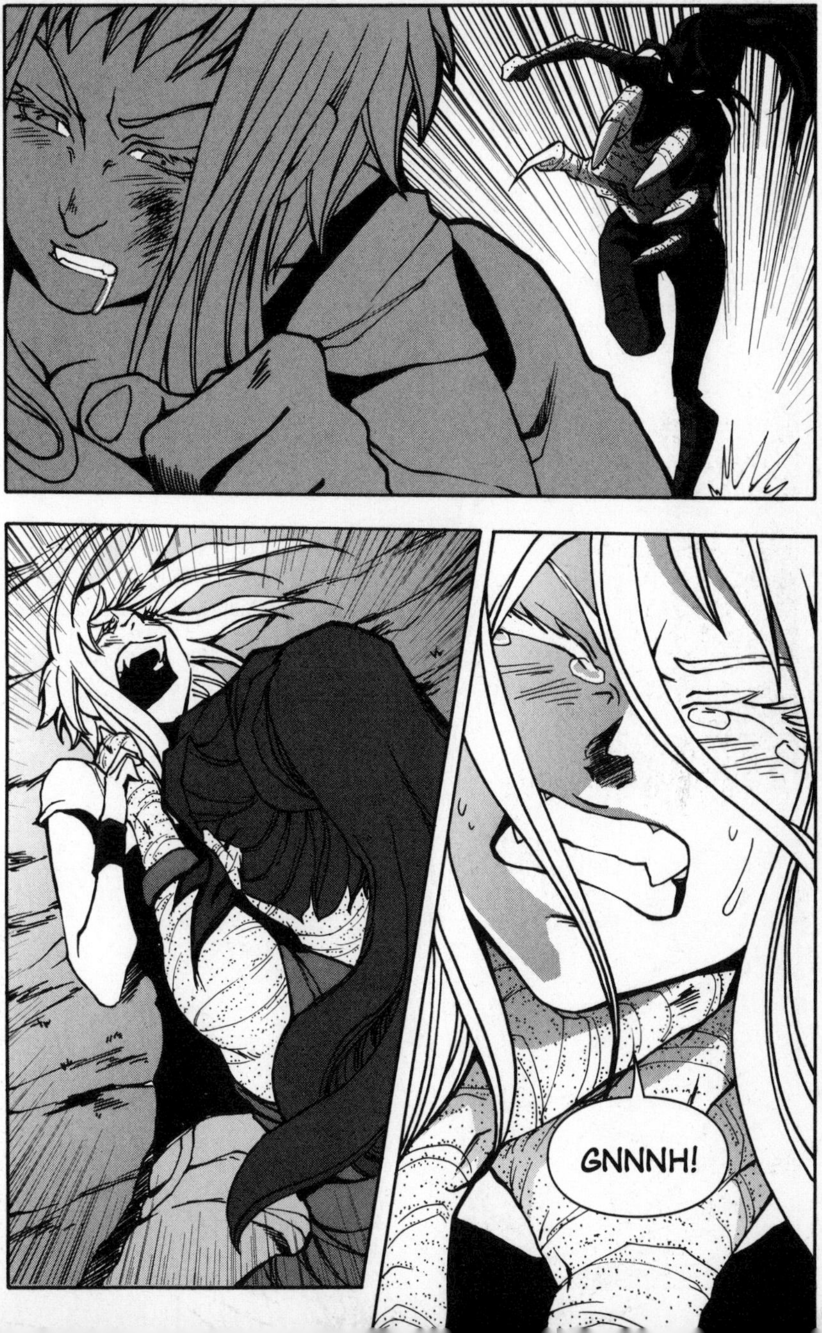
GNNNH!

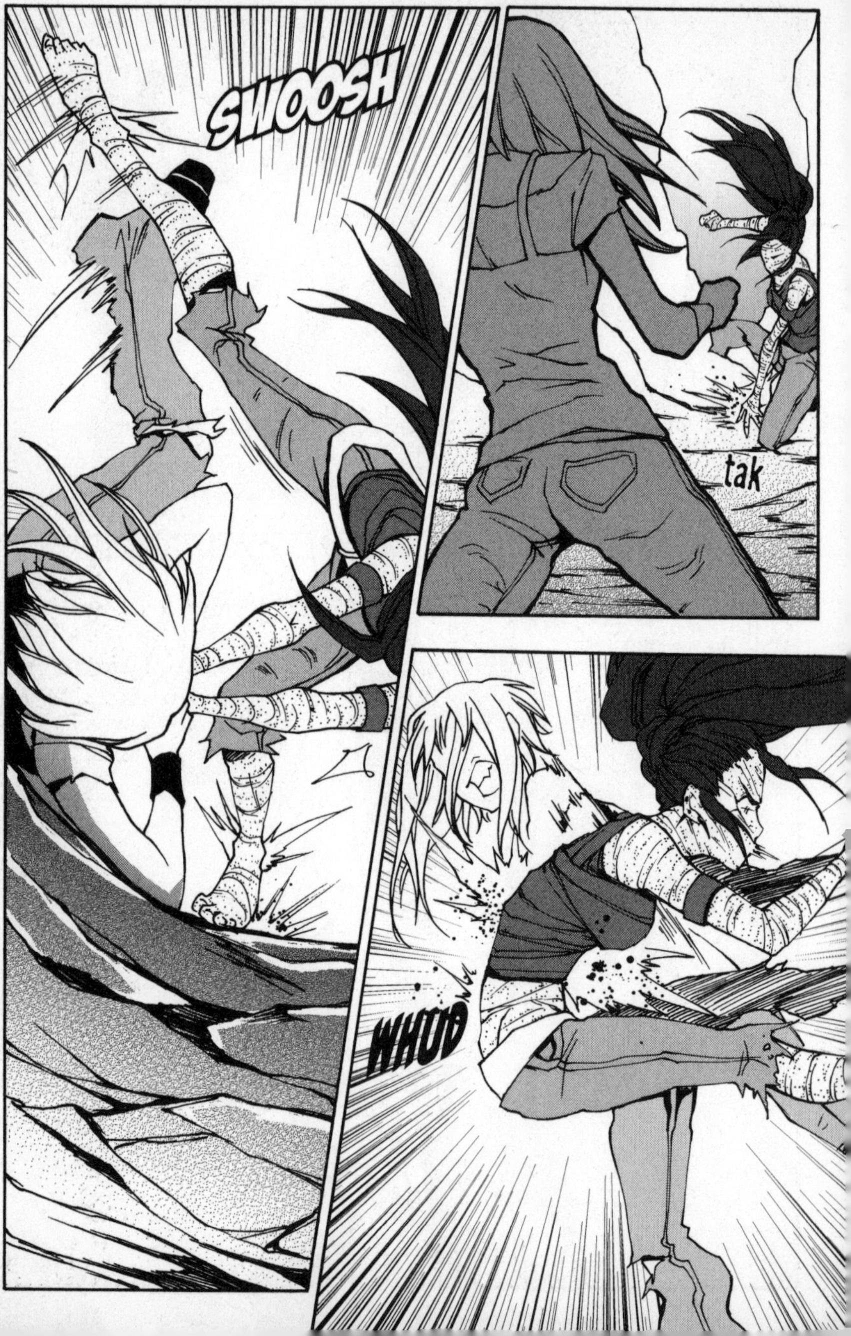
SWOOSH
tak
WHUD

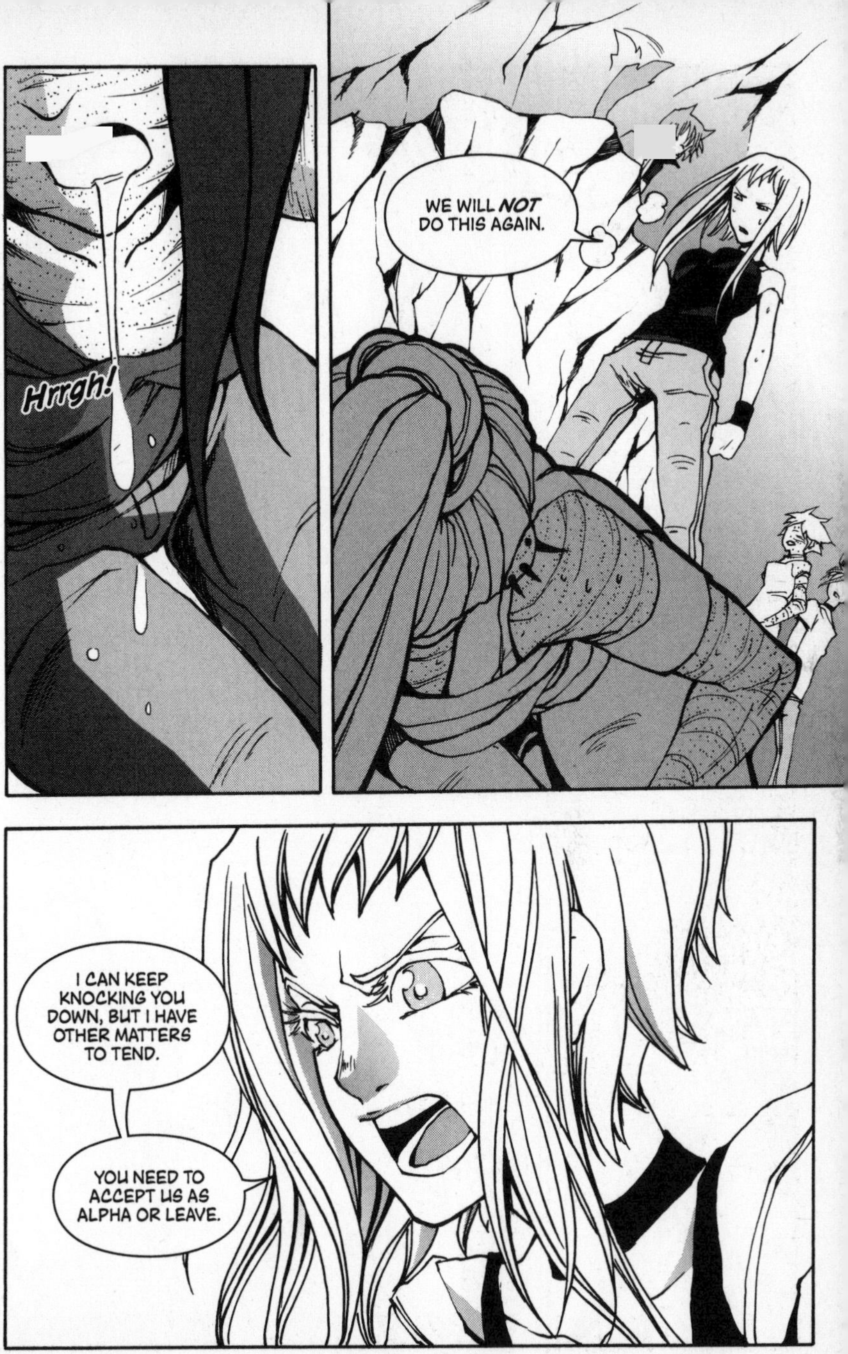
Hrrgh!
WE WILL *NOT* DO THIS AGAIN.
I CAN KEEP KNOCKING YOU DOWN, BUT I HAVE OTHER MATTERS TO TEND.
YOU NEED TO ACCEPT US AS ALPHA OR LEAVE.

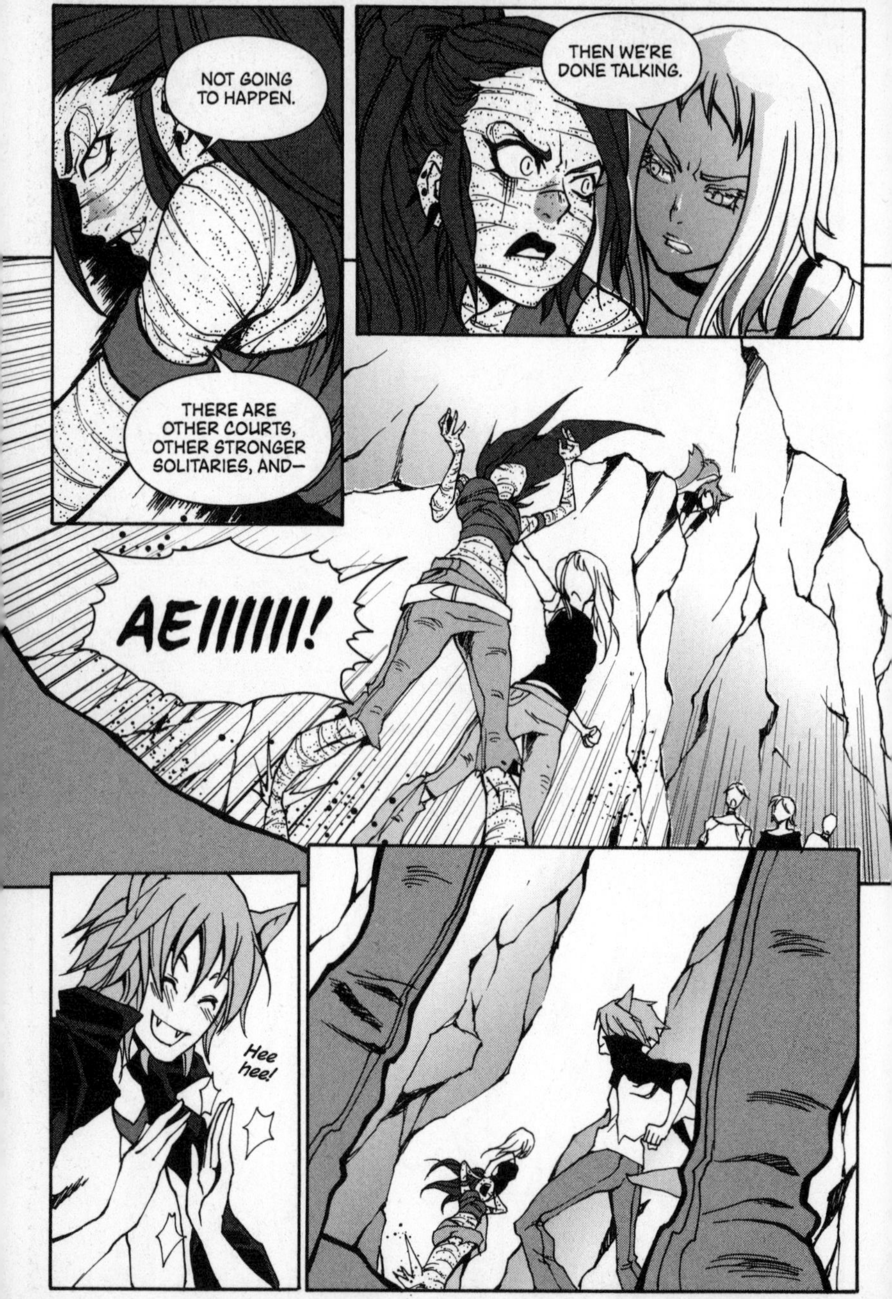
NOT GOING TO HAPPEN.
THERE ARE OTHER COURTS, OTHER STRONGER SOLITARIES, AND—
THEN WE'RE DONE TALKING.
AEIIIIIII!
Hee hee!

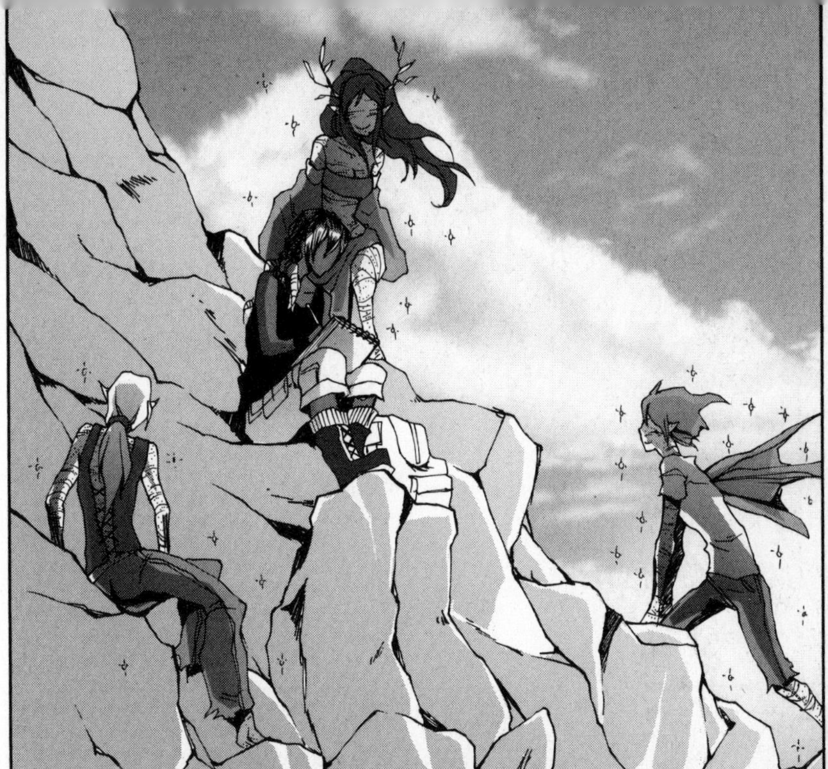
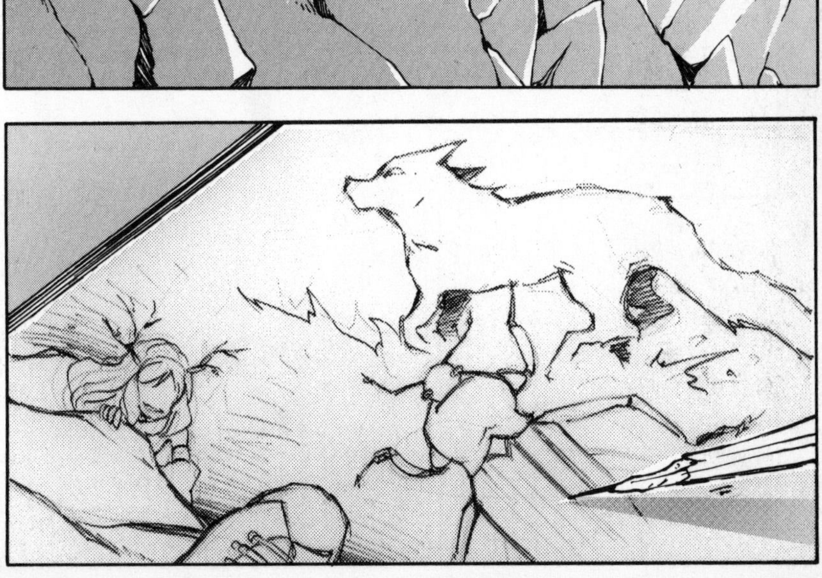

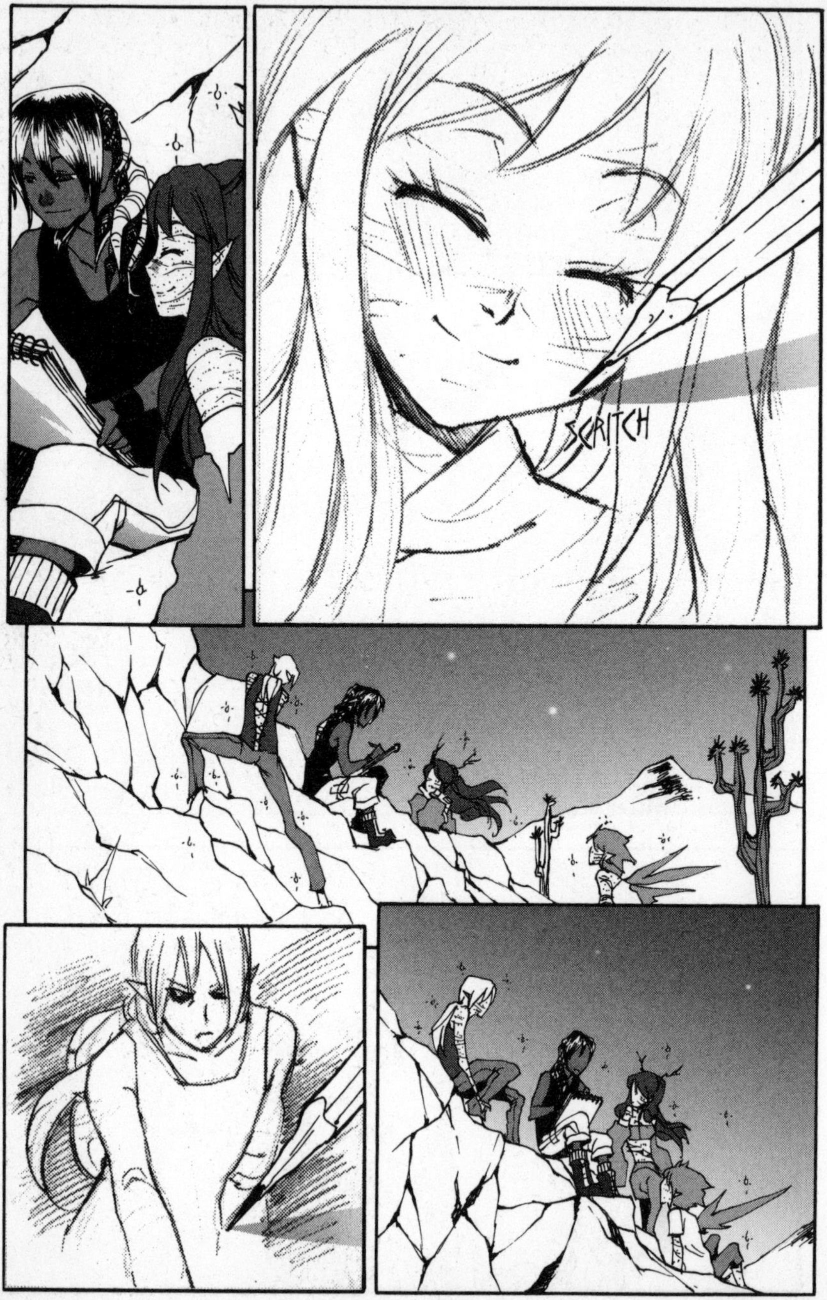
SCRITCH

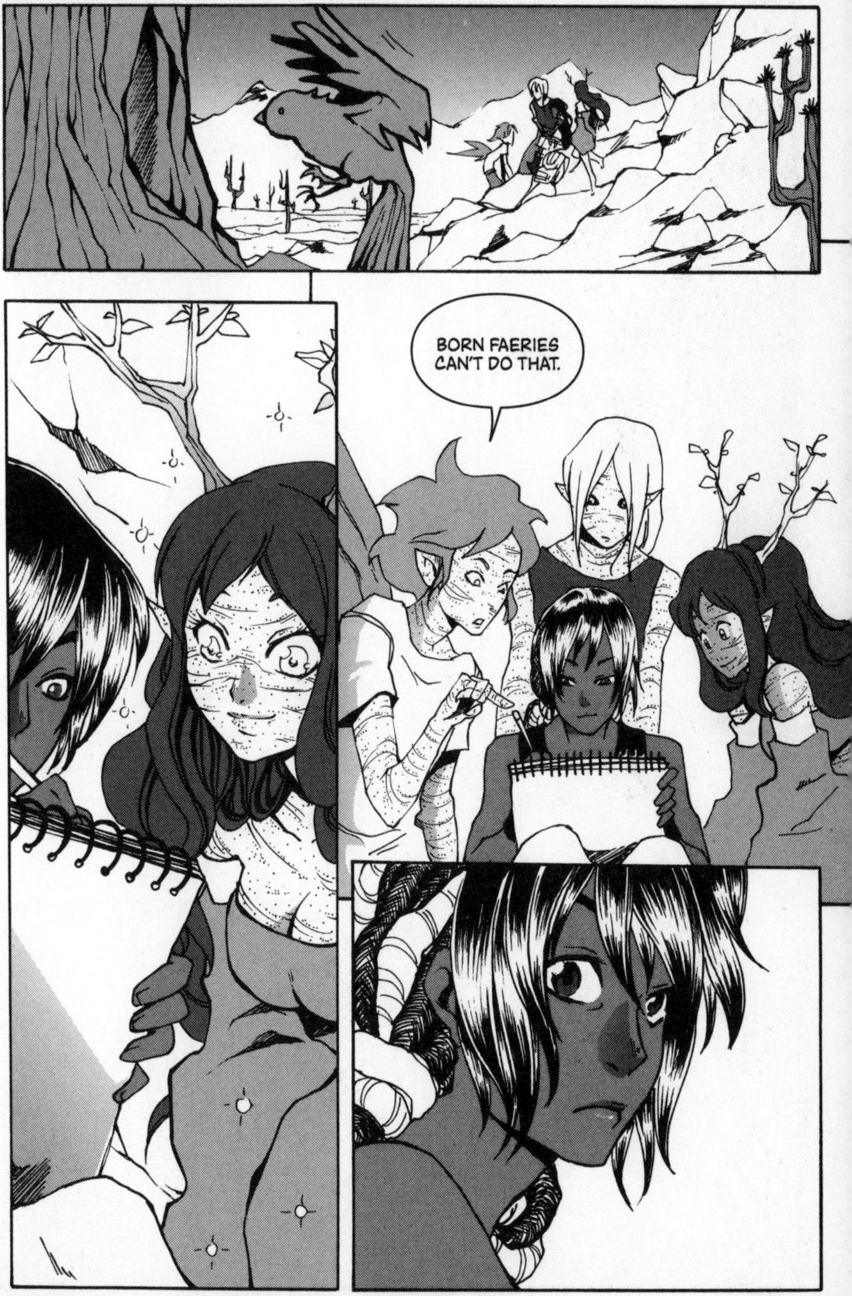
BORN FAERIES CAN'T DO THAT.

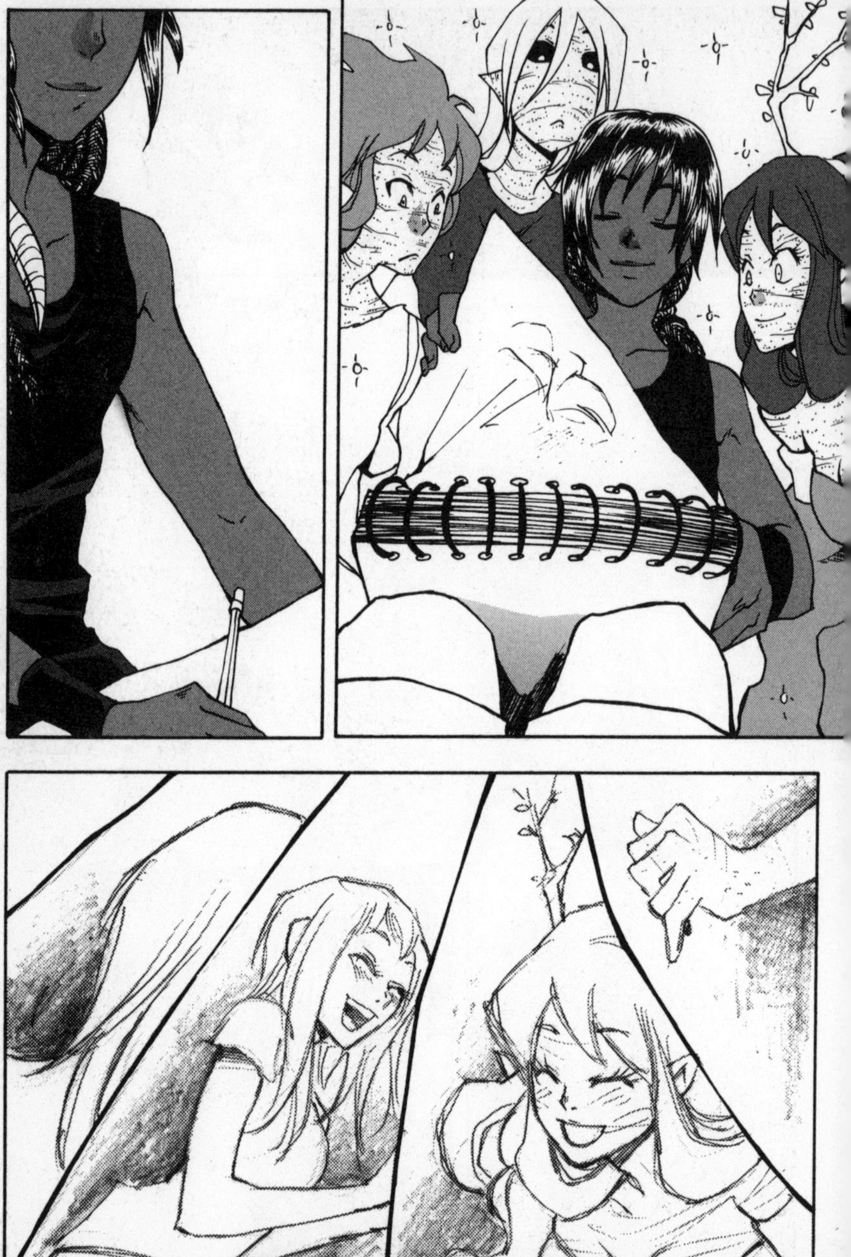

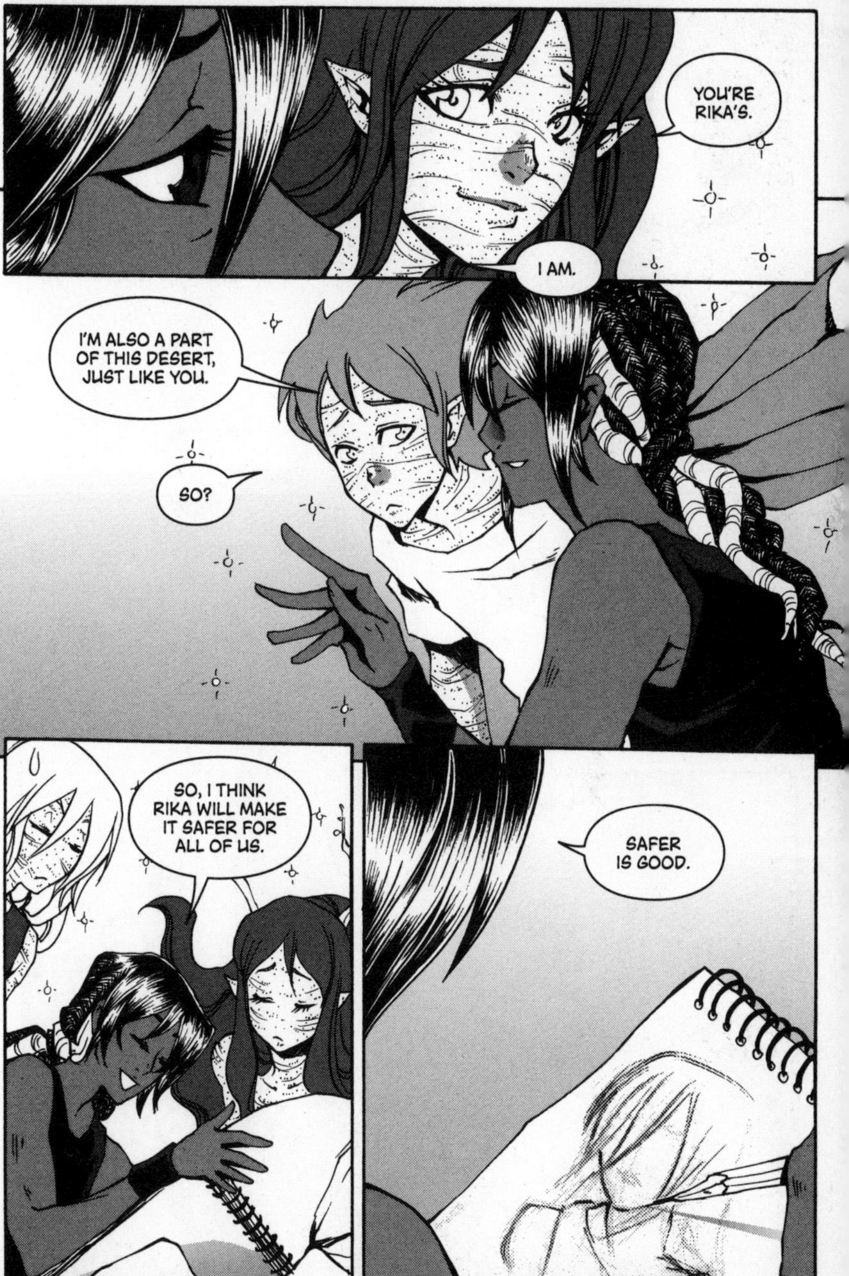
YOU'RE RIKA'S.
I AM.
I'M ALSO A PART OF THIS DESERT, JUST LIKE YOU.
SO?
SO, I THINK RIKA WILL MAKE IT SAFER FOR ALL OF US.
SAFER IS GOOD.

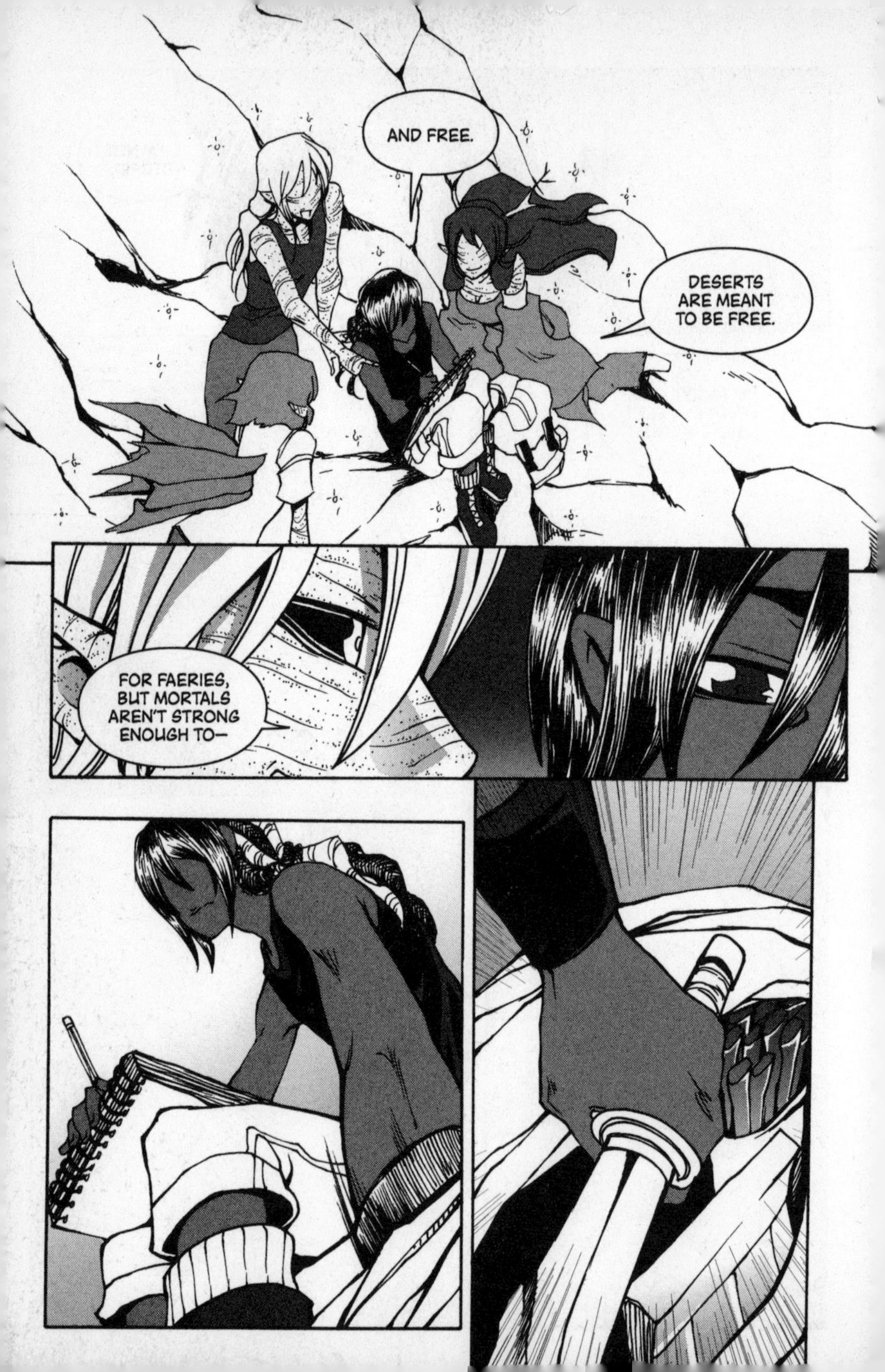
AND FREE.
DESERTS ARE MEANT TO BE FREE.
FOR FAERIES, BUT MORTALS AREN'T STRONG ENOUGH TO—

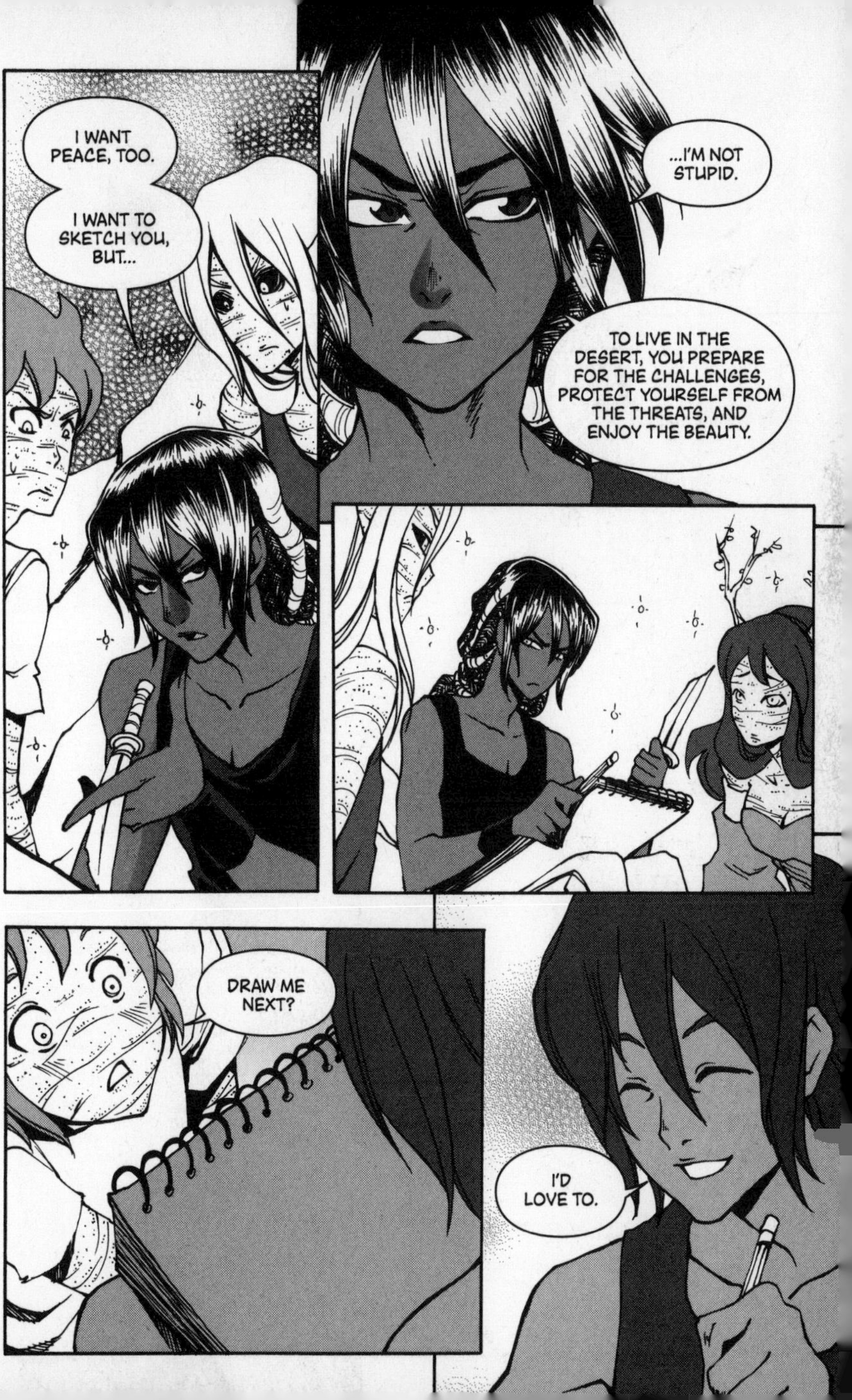
I WANT PEACE, TOO.
I WANT TO SKETCH YOU, BUT...
...I'M NOT STUPID.
TO LIVE IN THE DESERT, YOU PREPARE FOR THE CHALLENGES, PROTECT YOURSELF FROM THE THREATS, AND ENJOY THE BEAUTY.
DRAW ME NEXT?
I'D LOVE TO.

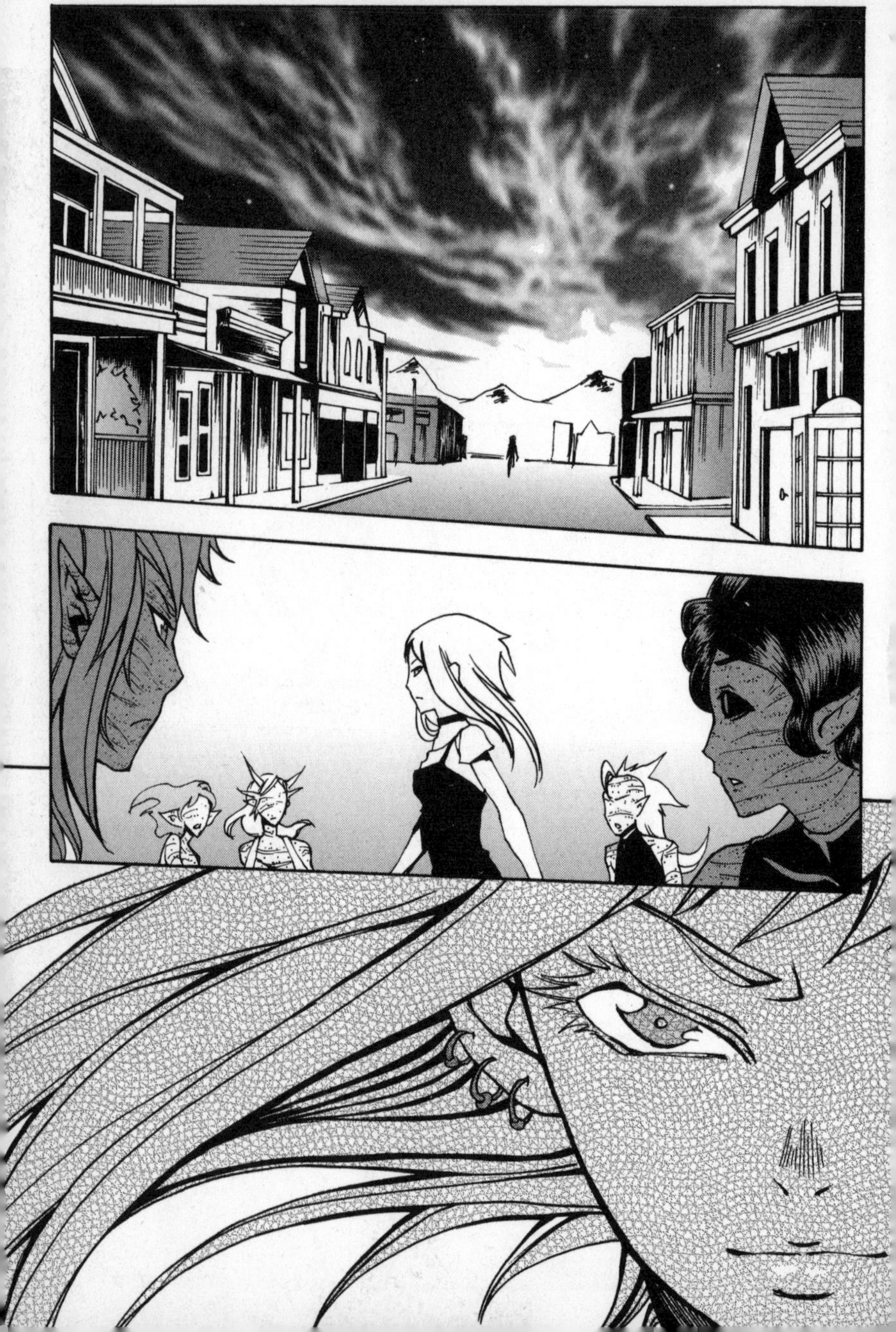

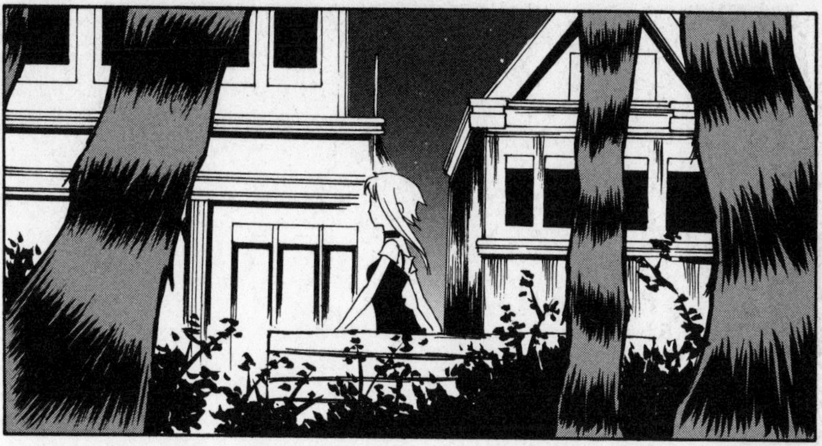
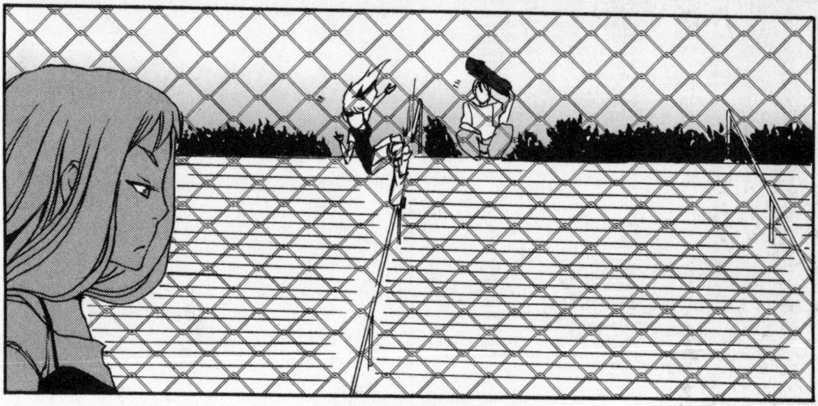
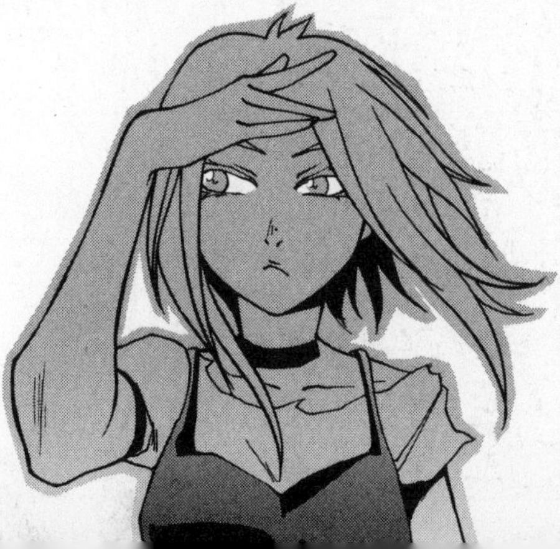

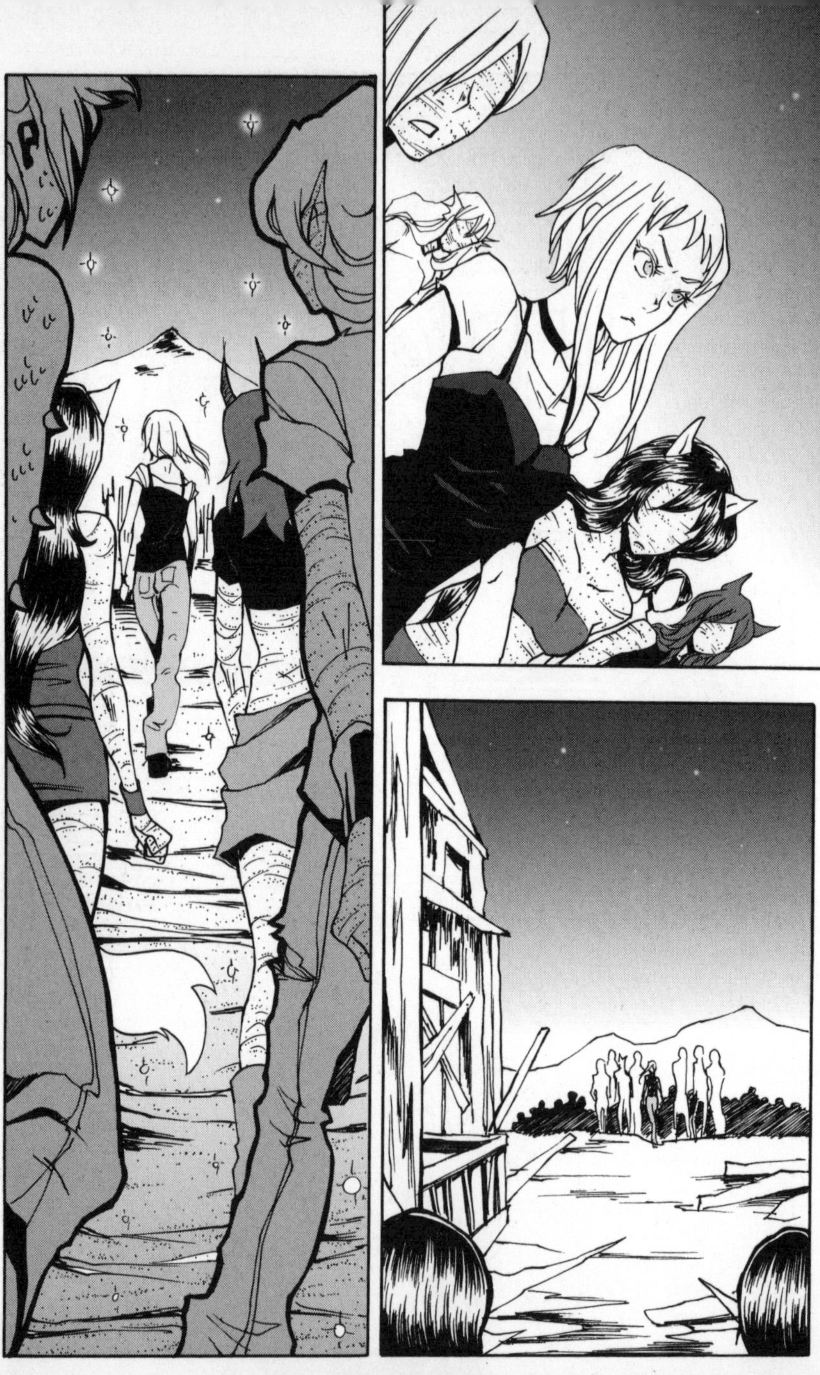

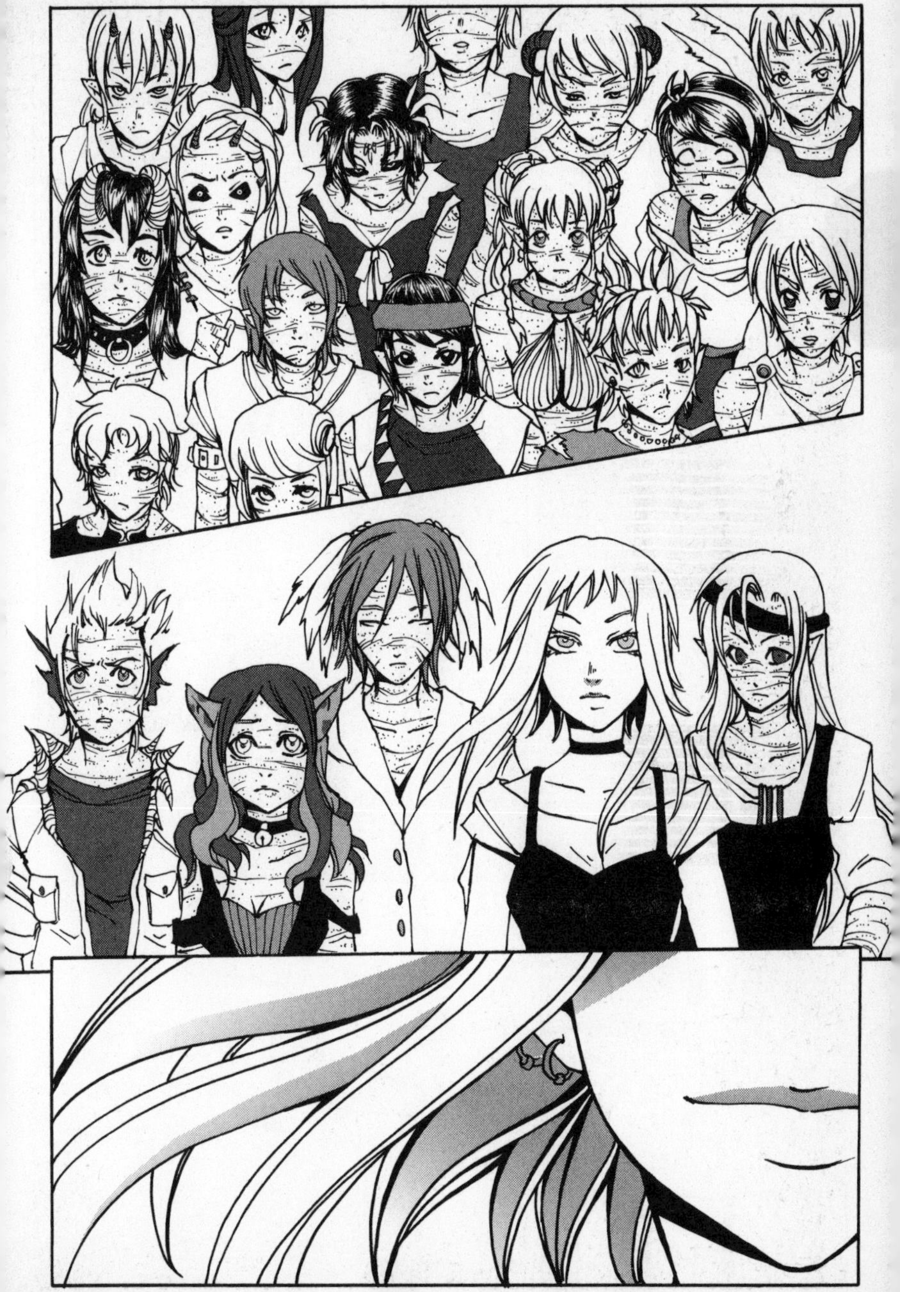

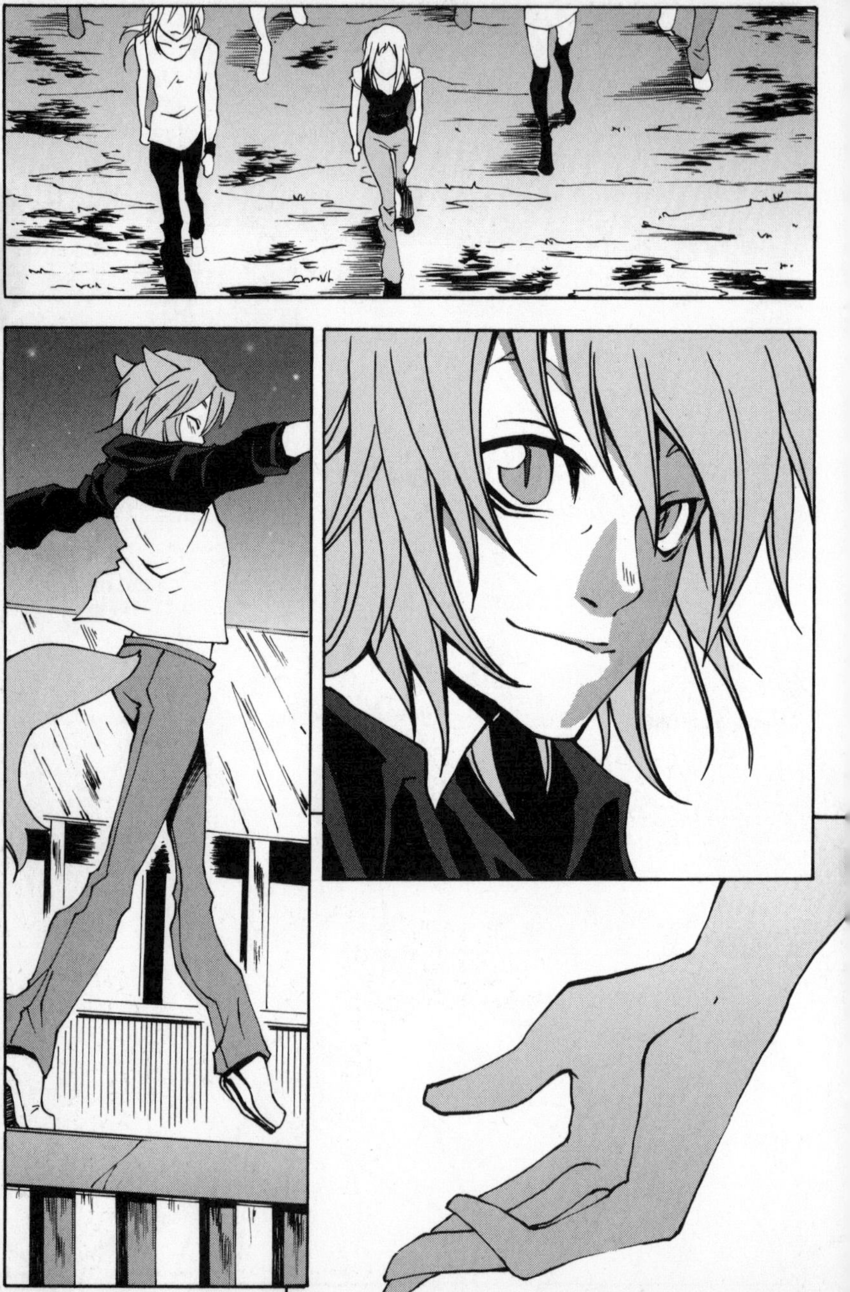

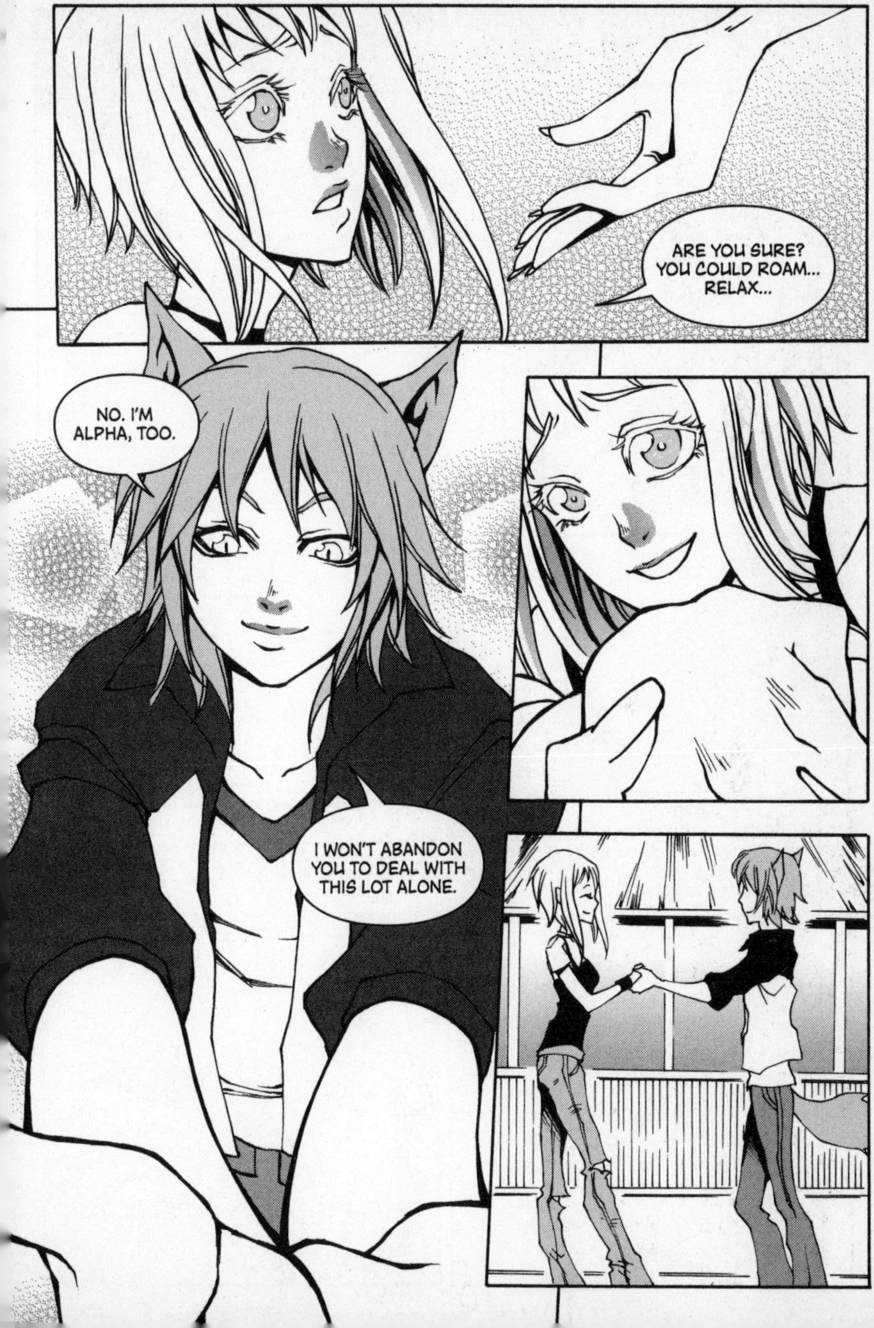
ARE YOU SURE? YOU COULD ROAM... RELAX...
NO. I'M ALPHA, TOO.
I WON'T ABANDON YOU TO DEAL WITH THIS LOT ALONE.

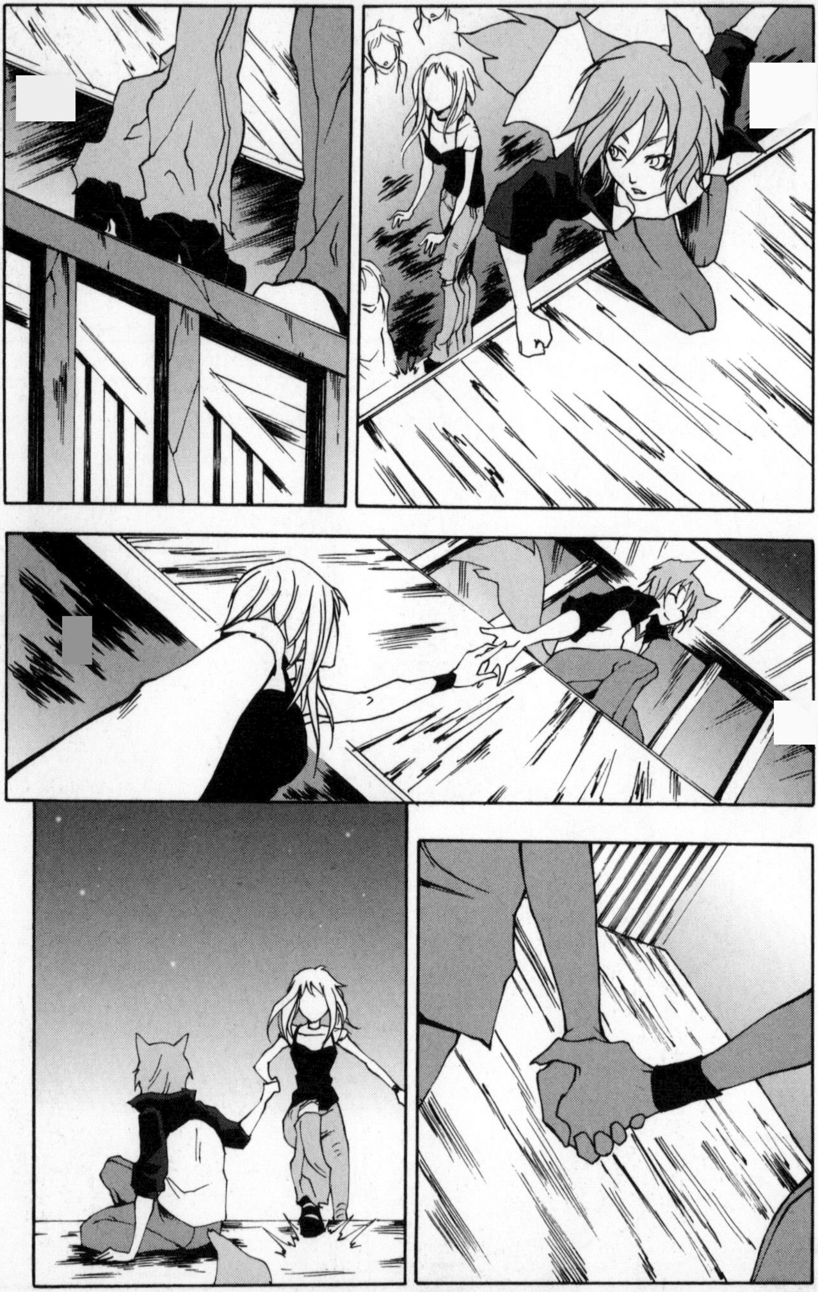

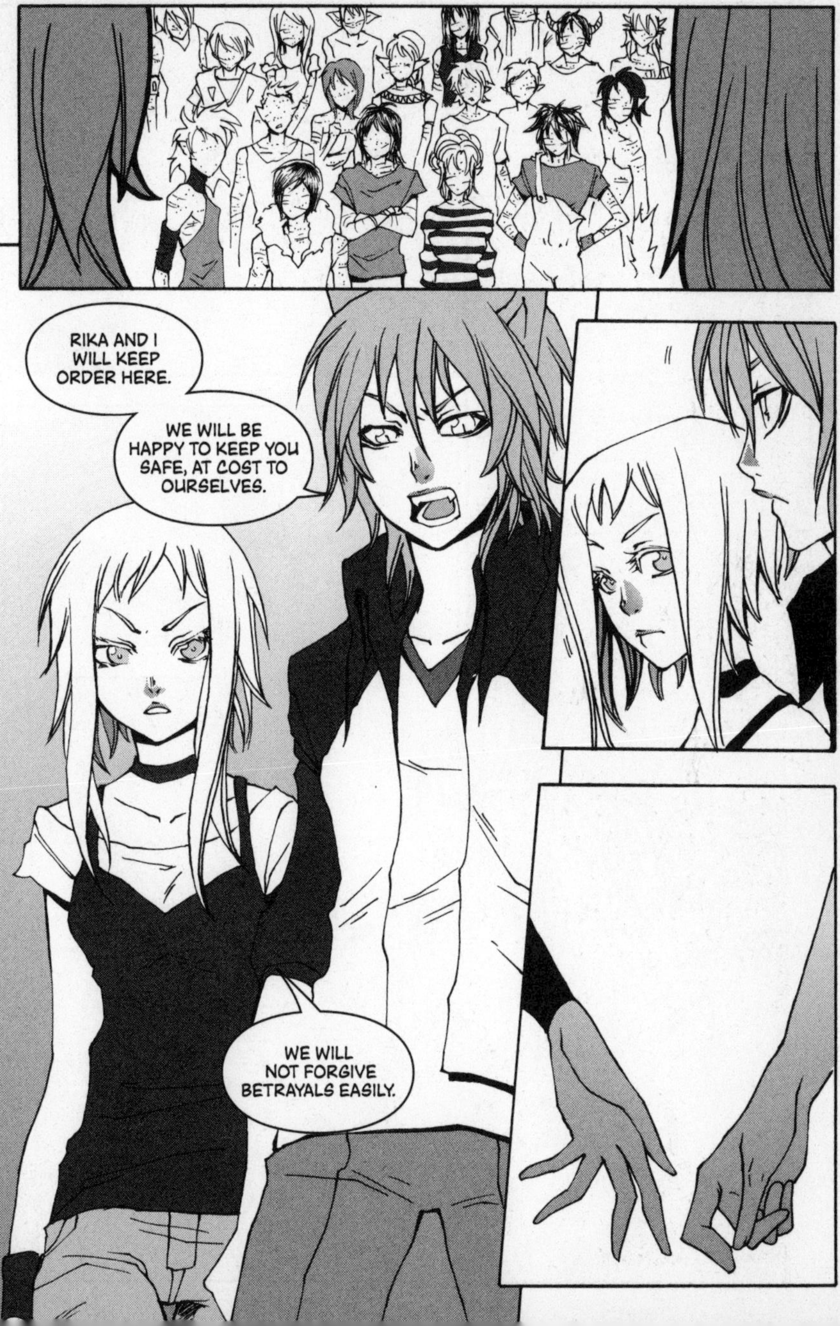
RIKA AND I WILL KEEP ORDER HERE.
WE WILL BE HAPPY TO KEEP YOU SAFE, AT COST TO OURSELVES.
WE WILL NOT FORGIVE BETRAYALS EASILY.

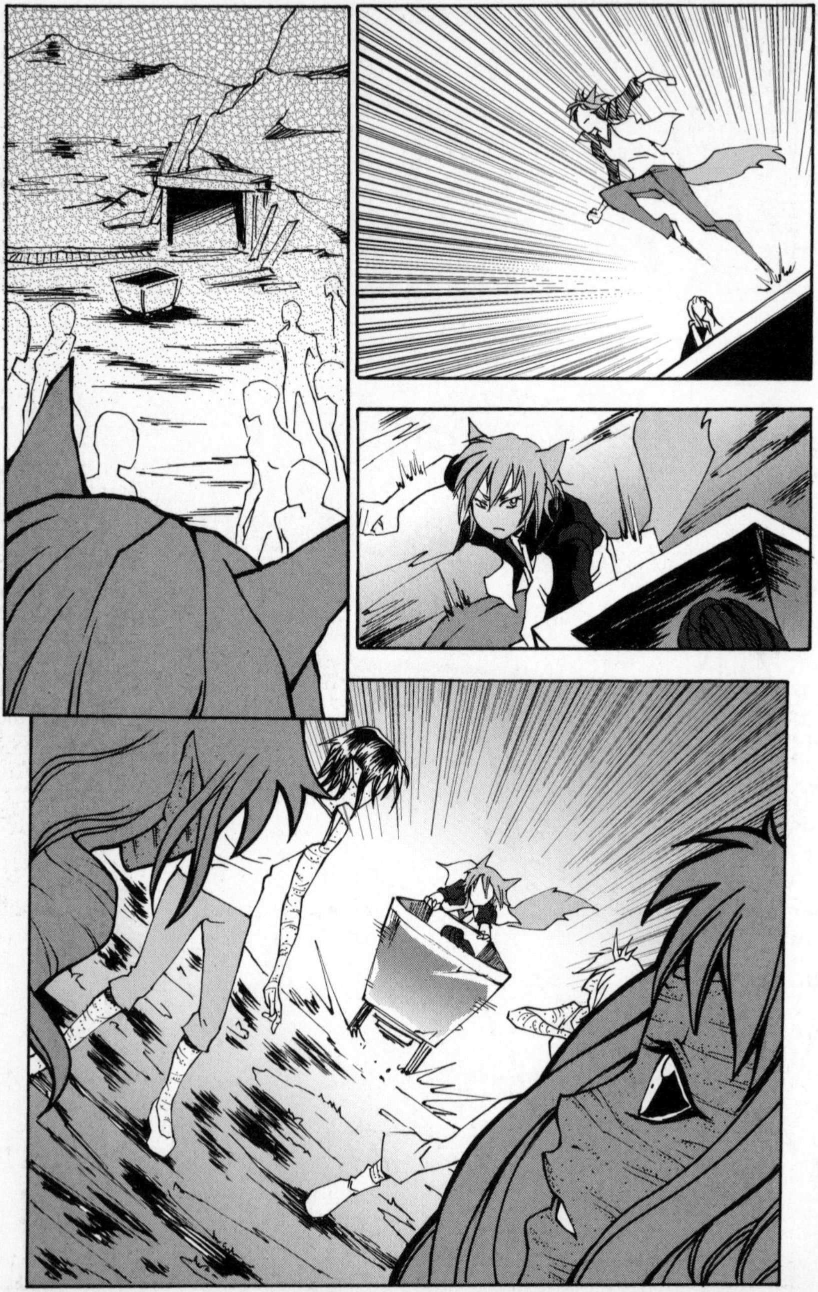

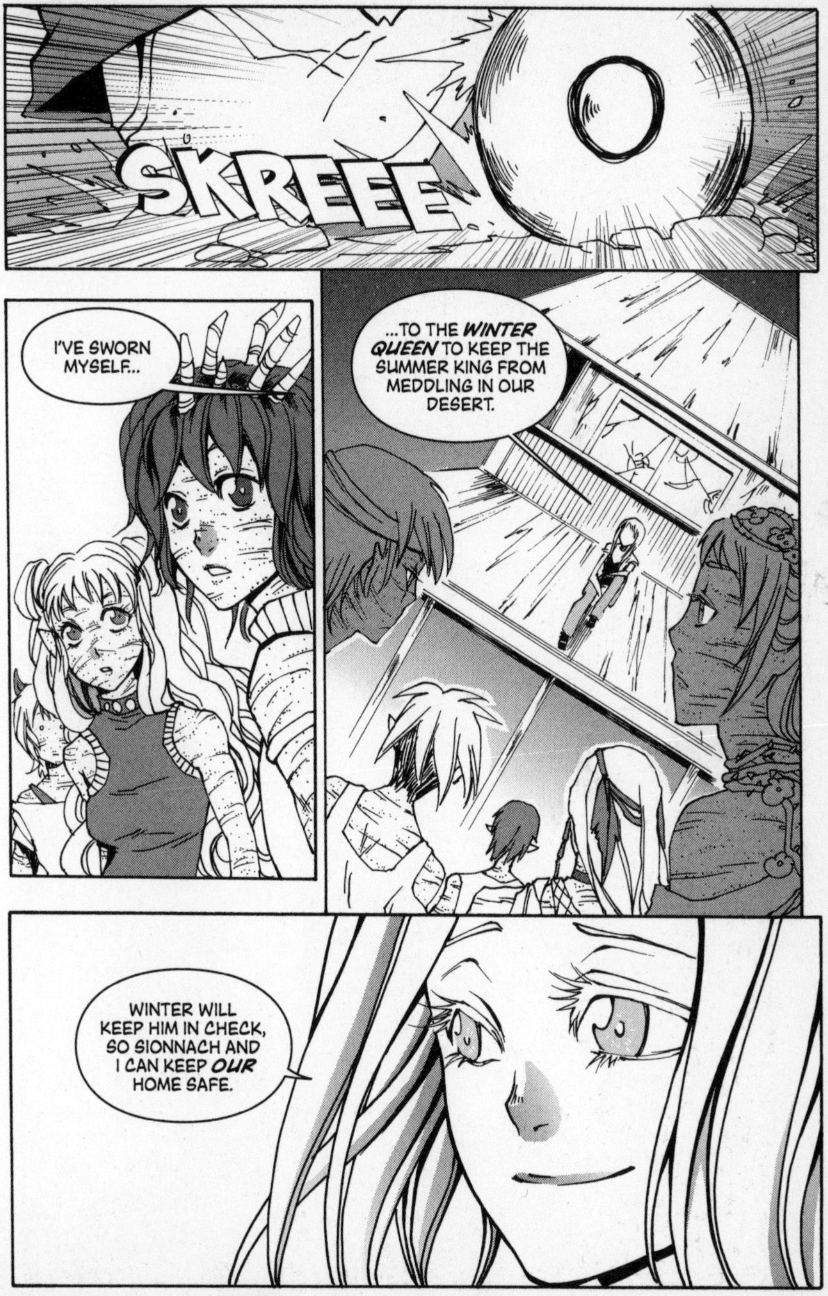
SKREEE
I'VE SWORN MYSELF...
...TO THE *WINTER QUEEN* TO KEEP THE SUMMER KING FROM MEDDLING IN OUR DESERT.
WINTER WILL KEEP HIM IN CHECK, SO SIONNACH AND I CAN KEEP *OUR* HOME SAFE.

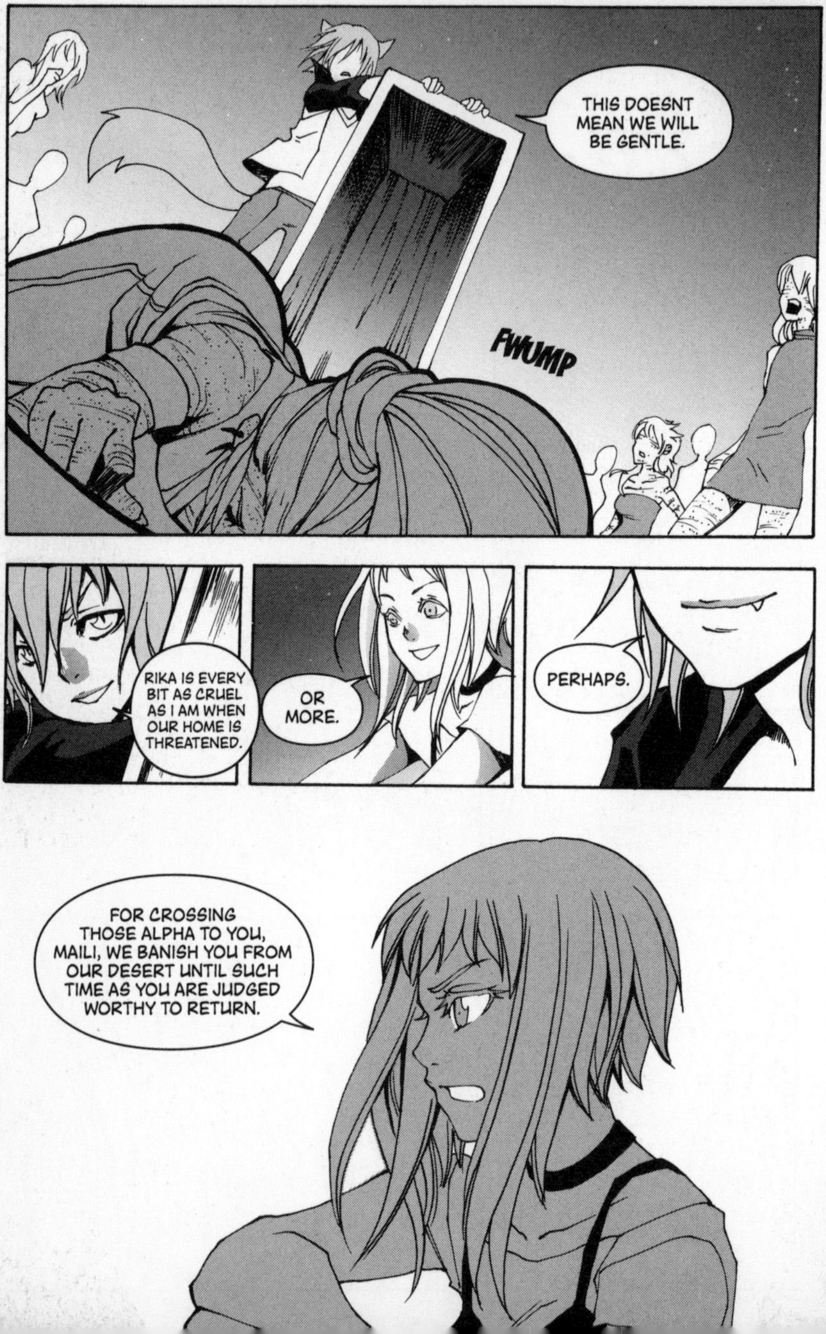
THIS DOESNT MEAN WE WILL BE GENTLE.
FWUMP
RIKA IS EVERY BIT AS CRUEL AS I AM WHEN OUR HOME IS THREATENED.
OR MORE.
PERHAPS.
FOR CROSSING THOSE ALPHA TO YOU, MAILI, WE BANISH YOU FROM OUR DESERT UNTIL SUCH TIME AS YOU ARE JUDGED WORTHY TO RETURN.

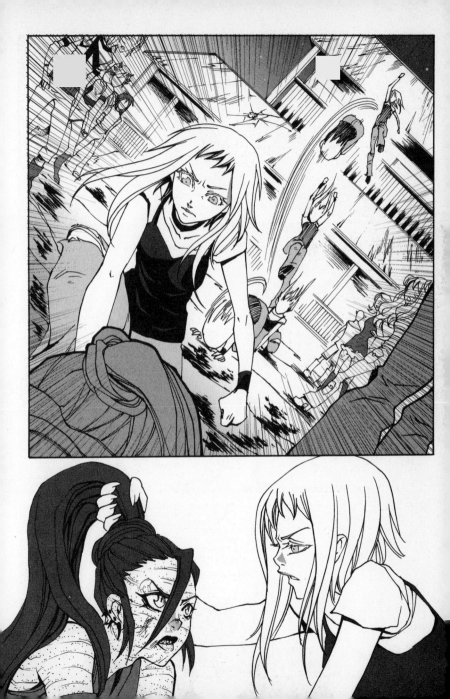

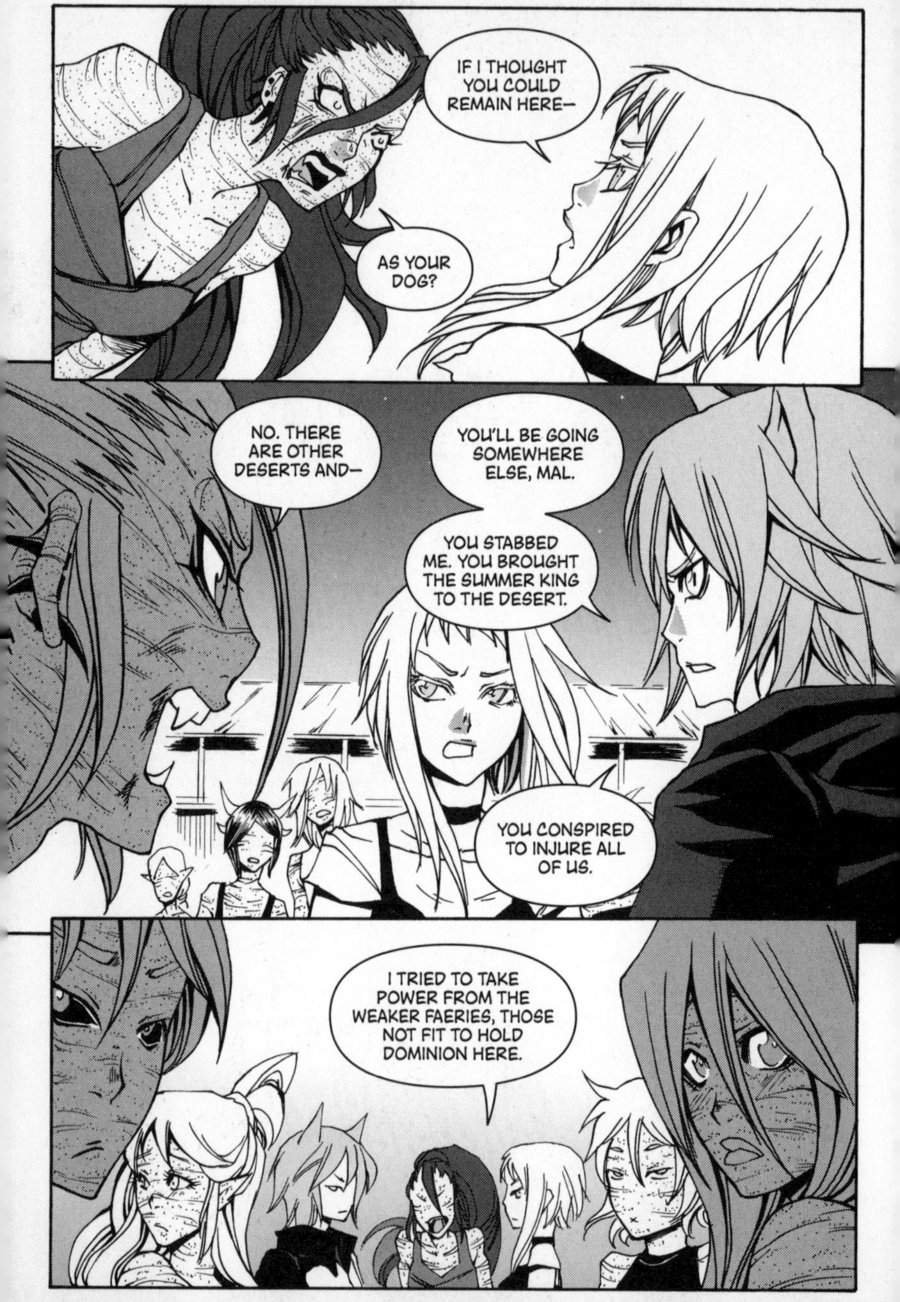
IF I THOUGHT YOU COULD REMAIN HERE—
AS YOUR DOG?
NO. THERE ARE OTHER DESERTS AND—
YOU'LL BE GOING SOMEWHERE ELSE, MAL.
YOU STABBED ME. YOU BROUGHT THE SUMMER KING TO THE DESERT.
YOU CONSPIRED TO INJURE ALL OF US.
I TRIED TO TAKE POWER FROM THE WEAKER FAERIES, THOSE NOT FIT TO HOLD DOMINION HERE.

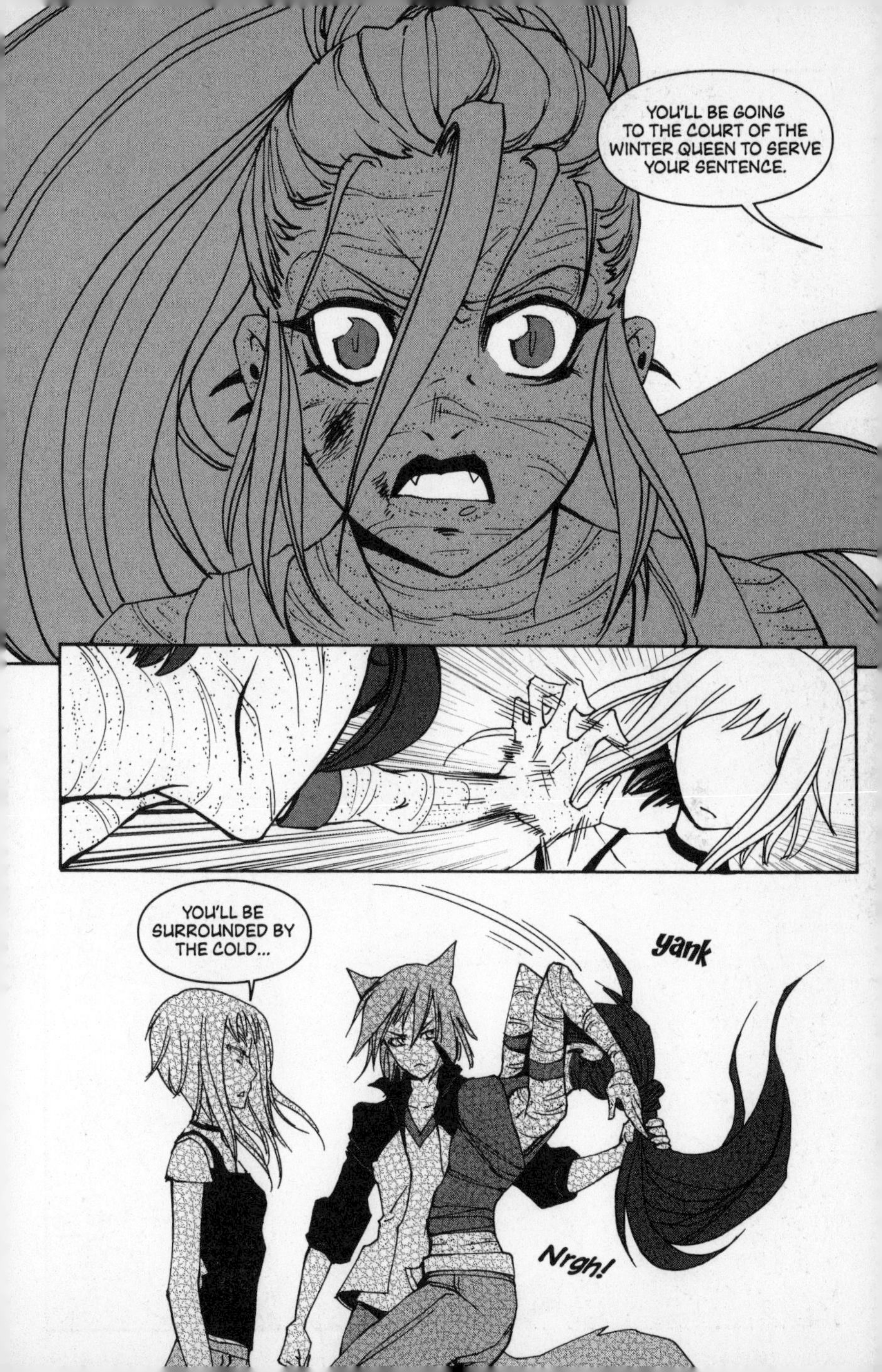
YOU'LL BE GOING TO THE COURT OF THE WINTER QUEEN TO SERVE YOUR SENTENCE.
YOU'LL BE SURROUNDED BY THE COLD...
yank
Nrgh!

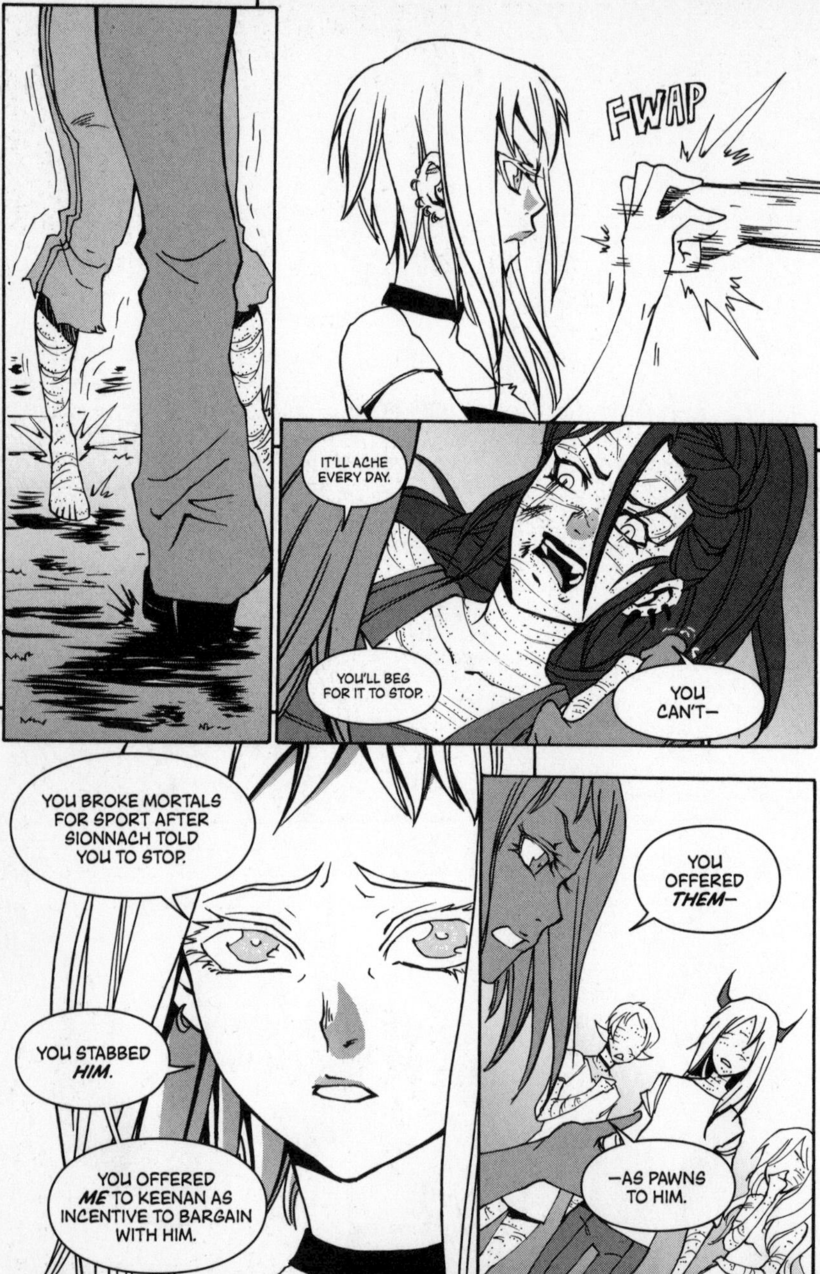
FWAP
IT'LL ACHE EVERY DAY.
YOU'LL BEG FOR IT TO STOP.
YOU CAN'T—
YOU BROKE MORTALS FOR SPORT AFTER SIONNACH TOLD YOU TO STOP.
YOU STABBED *HIM*.
YOU OFFERED *ME* TO KEENAN AS INCENTIVE TO BARGAIN WITH HIM.
YOU OFFERED *THEM*—
—AS PAWNS TO HIM.

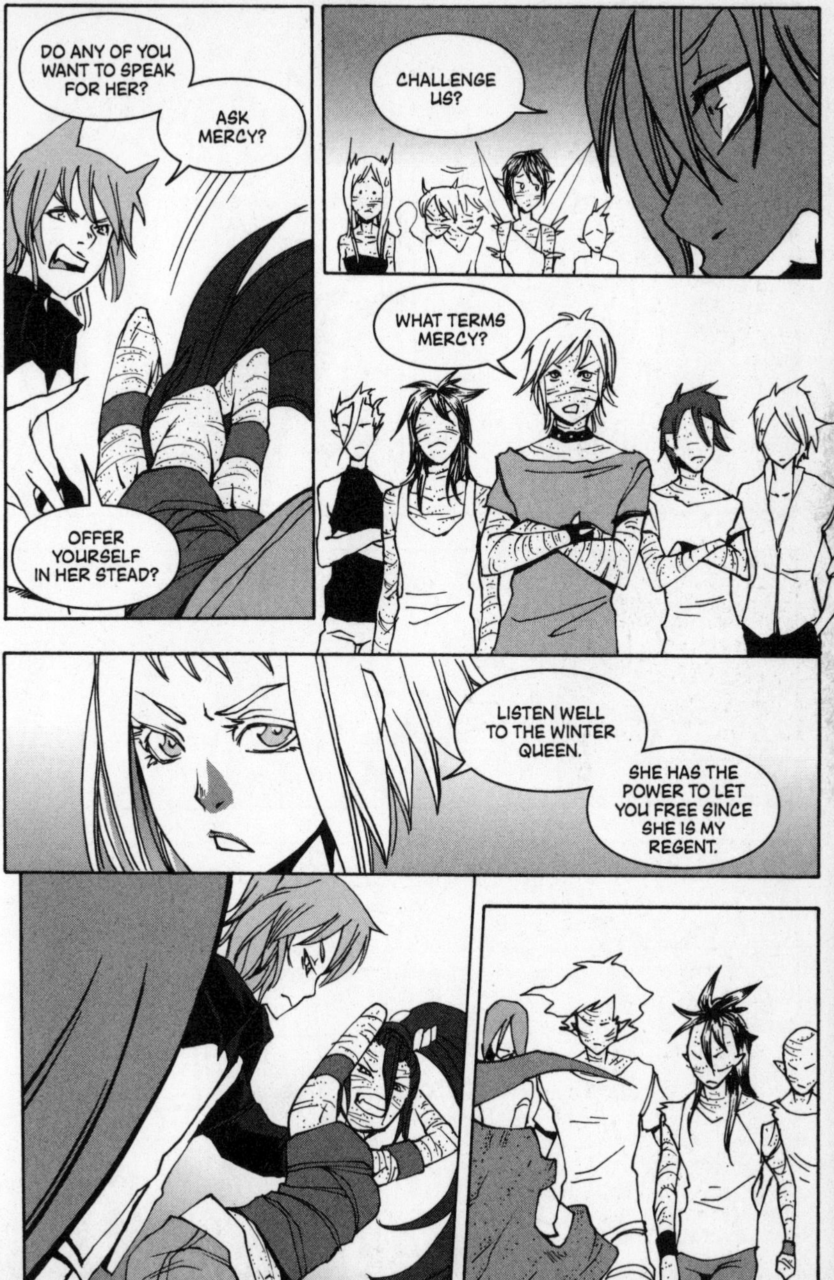
DO ANY OF YOU WANT TO SPEAK FOR HER?
ASK MERCY?
OFFER YOURSELF IN HER STEAD?
CHALLENGE US?
WHAT TERMS MERCY?
LISTEN WELL TO THE WINTER QUEEN.
SHE HAS THE POWER TO LET YOU FREE SINCE SHE IS MY REGENT.

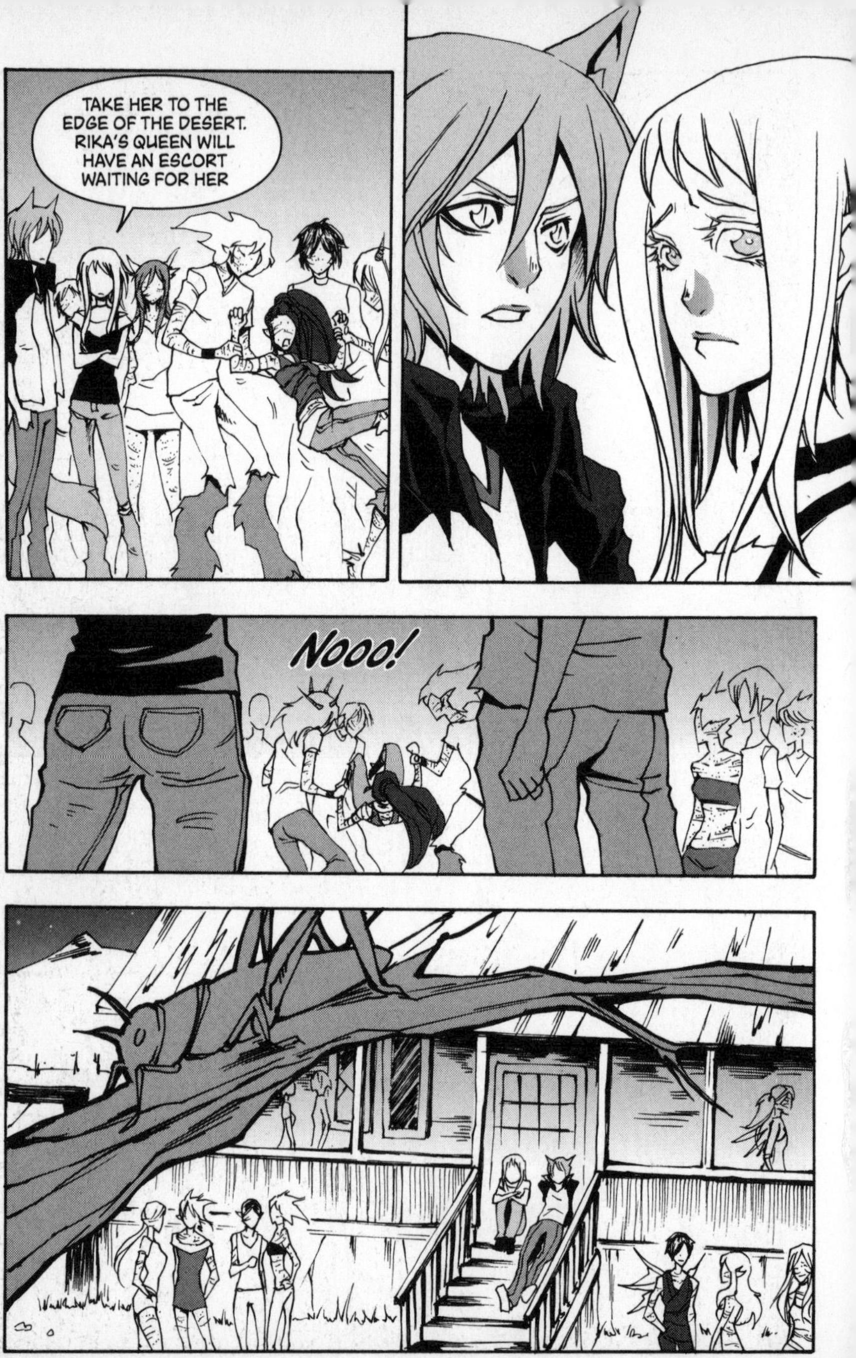
TAKE HER TO THE EDGE OF THE DESERT. RIKA'S QUEEN WILL HAVE AN ESCORT WAITING FOR HER
Nooo!

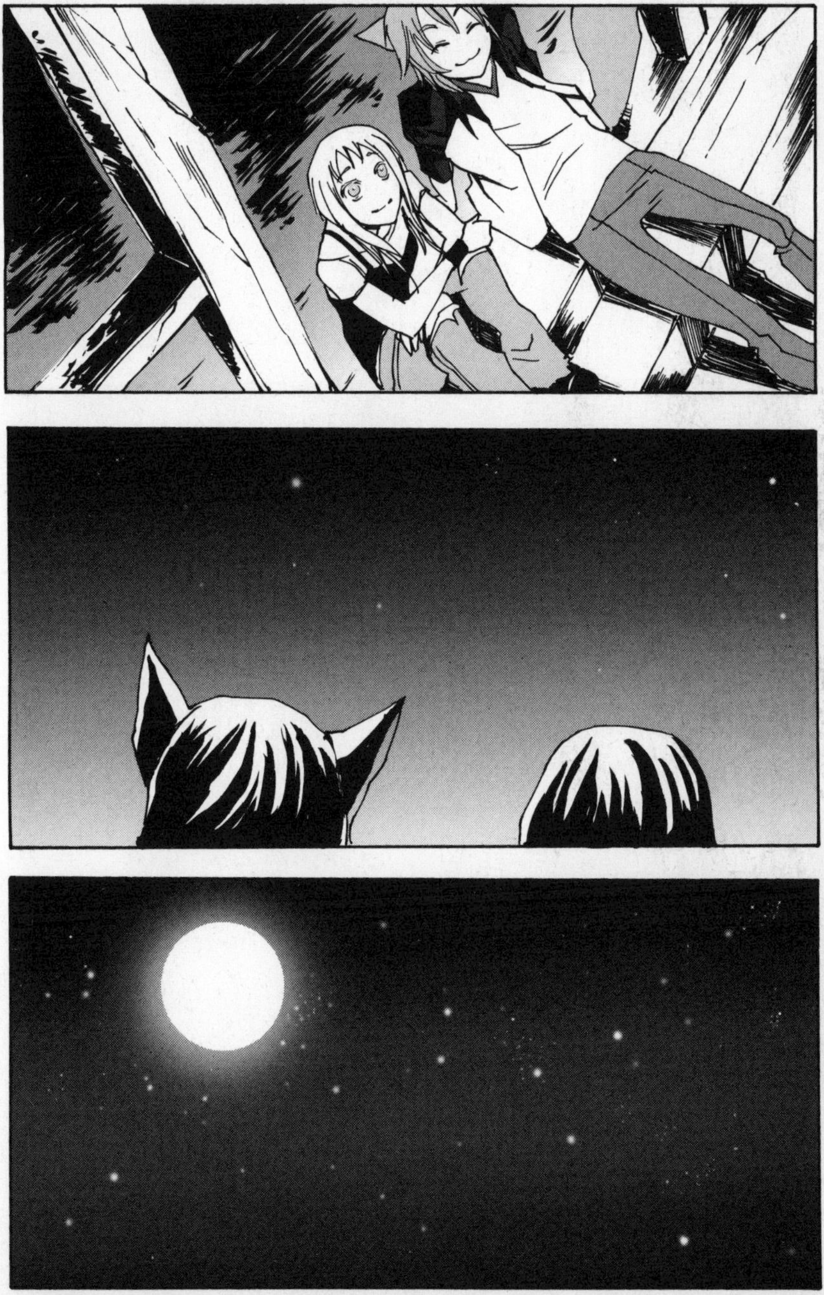

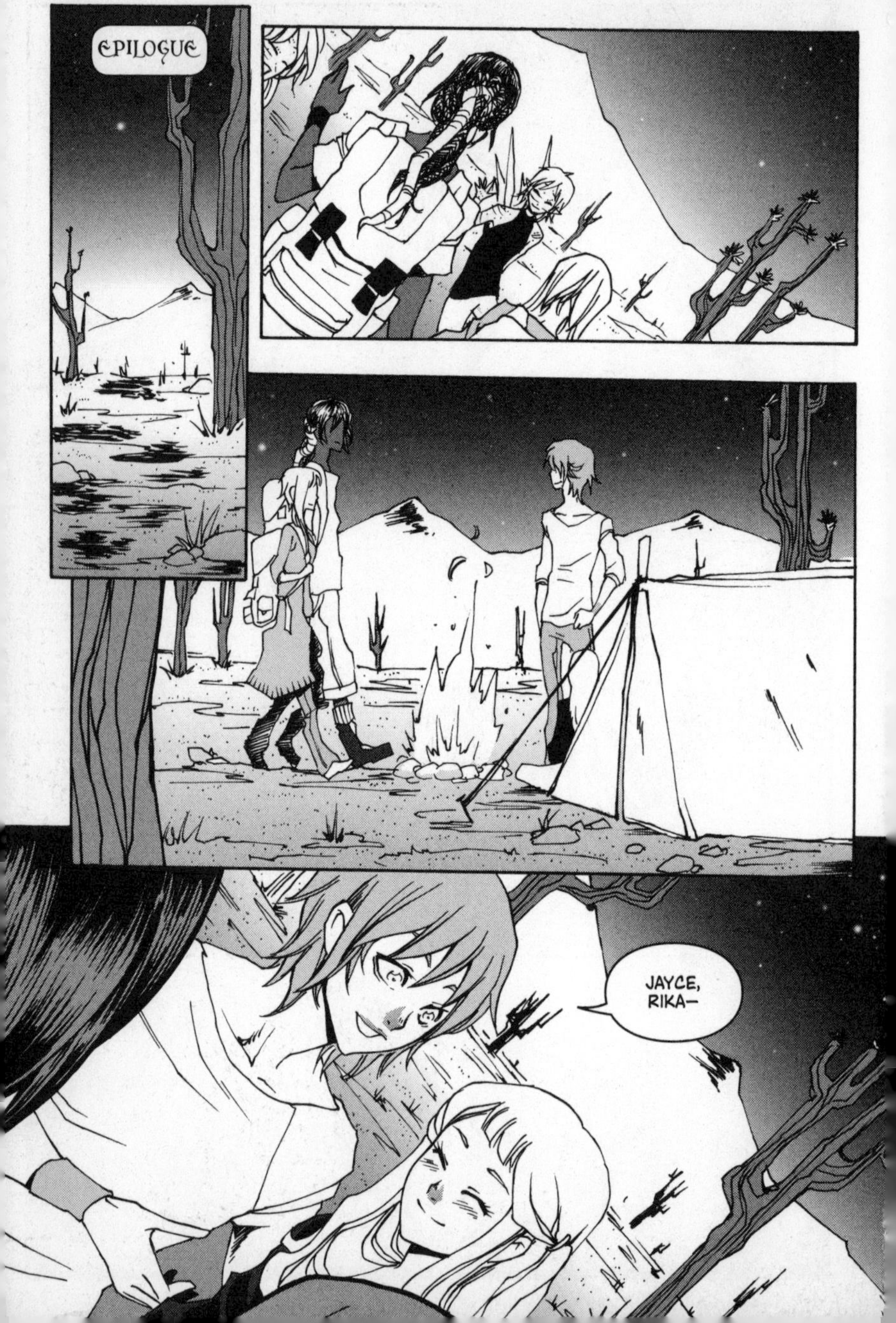
EPILOGUE
JAYCE,
RIKA—

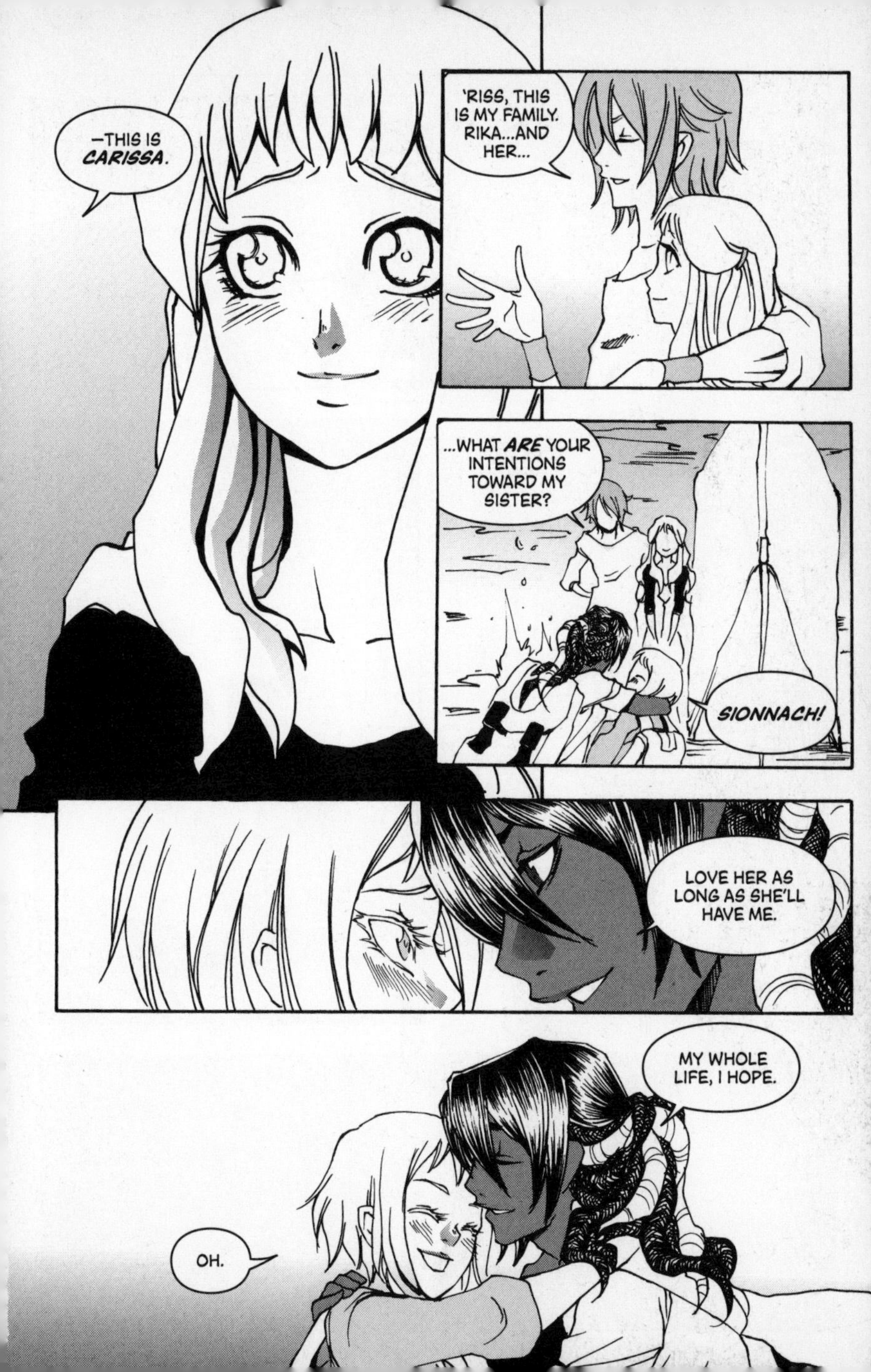

—THIS IS *CARISSA*.
'RISS, THIS IS MY FAMILY. RIKA...AND HER...
...WHAT *ARE* YOUR INTENTIONS TOWARD MY SISTER?
SIONNACH!
LOVE HER AS LONG AS SHE'LL HAVE ME.
MY WHOLE LIFE, I HOPE.
OH.

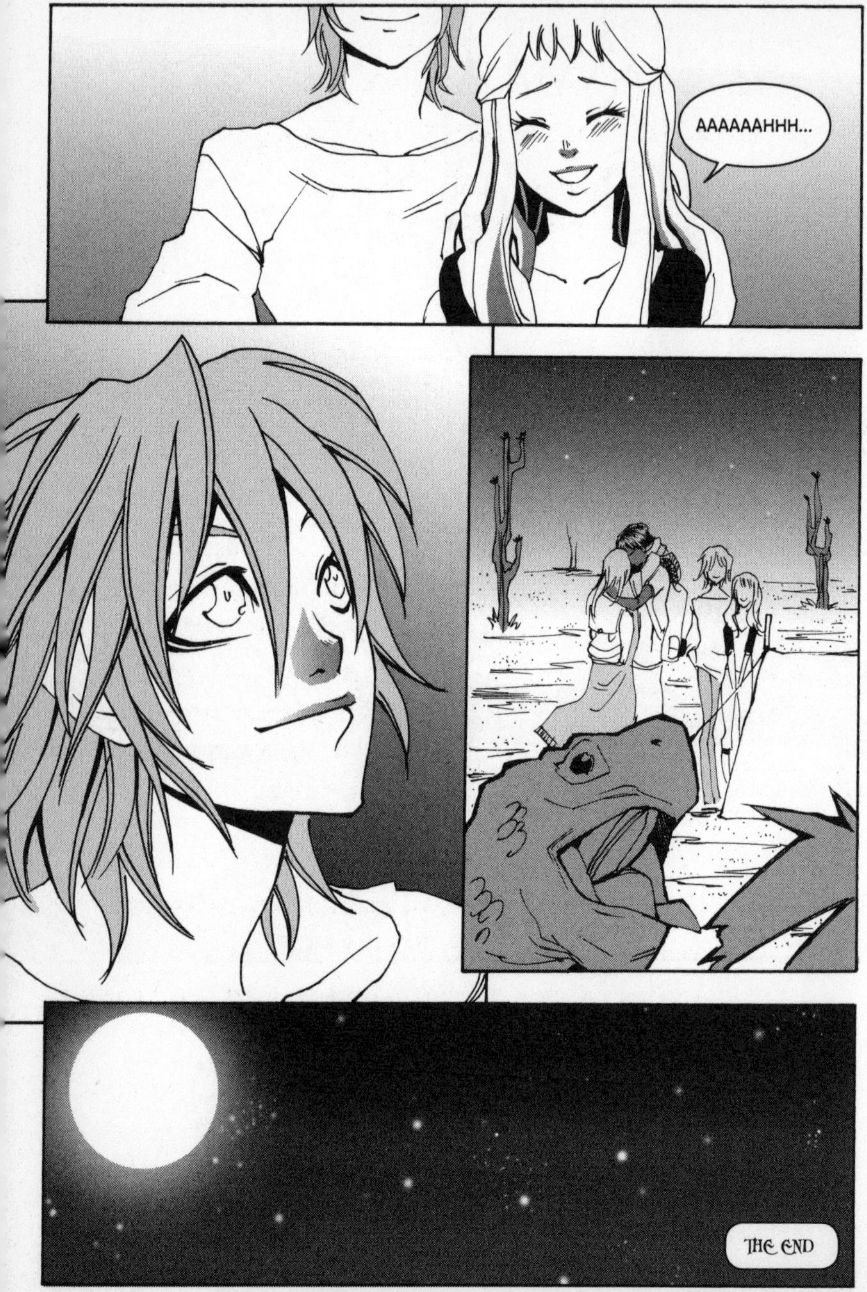
AAAAAAHHH...
THE END

Read on for a sneak peek
at Melissa Marr's final Wicked Lovely novel,

DARKEST MERCY

Donia walked aimlessly, taking comfort in the crisp bite in
the air. The promise of it made her want to draw it deeply
into her lungs. She did, releasing the cold with each breath,
letting the lingering breath of winter race free. Equinox was
fast approaching. Winter was ending, and letting loose the
frost and snow soothed her as few things could of late.

Evan, the rowan-man who headed her guard, fell in step
with her. His gray-brown skin and dark green leafy hair
made him a shadow in the not-yet-dawning day. "Donia?
You left without guards."

"I needed space."

"You should've woken me at least. There are too many
threats. . . ." His words dwindled, and he lifted his bark-clad
fingers as if to caress her face. "He is a fool."

Donia glanced away. "Keenan owes me nothing. What
we had—"

"He owes you everything," Evan corrected. "You stood
against the last queen and risked all for him."

"One's court must come first." The Winter Queen lifted
her shoulder in a small shrug, but Evan undoubtedly knew

that she was walking because she missed Keenan more and more. They didn't discuss it, and she'd not descended into foolish melancholia. She loved the absent Summer King, but she simply wasn't the sort of person to fall apart over heartbreak.

Rage, however . . . that *is another matter.*

She forced away the thought. Her temper was precisely why she couldn't settle for only half of Keenan's attention.

Or heart.

Evan motioned to the other guards he'd brought out with him, and they moved farther away, all but three disappearing into the night at his command. The three who remained, white-winged Hawthorn Girls, never wandered far from her side if at all possible. *Except for when I leave without telling anyone.* Their red eyes glowed like beacons in the poorly lit street, and Donia took a measure of comfort in their presence.

"I would be remiss if I didn't remind you that it's too dangerous for you to be out alone," Evan said.

"And I would be a weak queen if I wasn't able to handle myself for a few moments alone," Donia reminded her advisor.

"I've never found you weak, even when you weren't a queen." He shook his head. "Summer Court might not be powerful enough to injure you, but Bananach is growing stronger by the day."

"I know." Donia felt a flush of guilt.

Faeries from all of the courts had been slipping away, and Donia knew that they were joining Bananach. *Can she form her own court?* The mortality of the newer monarchs caused more than a little unease, and War had made sure to nettle to heighten the tension. Likewise, worries over the interrelations between courts caused traditionalists to rally around Bananach. Niall wasn't openly sympathetic to the Summer Court, but his centuries advising them made his faeries ill at ease. Her whatever-it-was with Keenan had a similar effect on some of her court, and Summer's attempts at imposing order on their court made faeries who were used to freedom chafe.

Donia wished that a new court was what Bananach sought, but the raven-faery was the embodiment of war and discord. The odds of her settling for a peacefully created court—if such a thing was even possible—weren't high. Mutiny and murder were far more likely goals for Bananach and her growing number of allies.

War comes.

Once the others were out of sight, Evan announced, "I have word of trouble from the Dark Court."

"More conflict?" she asked, as Evan led her around a group of junkies on the stoop of an abandoned tenement building. When she'd walked with Keenan over the years, he'd always sent a cloud of warm air to such mortals. Unlike him, she couldn't offer them any comfort.

Keenan. She felt the fool for being unable to stop thinking about him. *Even now.* Every other thought still seemed to lead to him, even though he'd been gone for almost six months. *With no contact.*

She exhaled a small flurry of snow. In almost a century, she'd never gone very long without seeing him, or hearing from him, even if it was nothing more than a letter.

"Bananach attacked the Hounds two days ago," Evan said, drawing Donia's attention back to him.

"A direct attack?"

Her guard and advisor shook his head. "Not at first. One of the Dark King's halflings was caught and killed, and while the Dark King and the rest were mourning, Bananach attacked them with her allies. The Hunt is not reacting well."

Donia paused mid-step. "Niall has *children*? Bananach killed his *child*?"

Evan's lips curved into a small smile. "No. Neither Niall nor the last king has children of his own, but the *former* Dark King always sheltered his court's halflings. His fey— *Niall's fey* now—are amorous creatures, and the Hounds mate with mortals far more than any other fey. It is an old tradition." Evan paused and flashed a faux-serious look at her. "I forget how young you are."

She rolled her eyes. "No, you don't. You've known me

most of my life. I'm just not ancient like you."

"True."

She waited, knowing he wasn't done. His patterns were a familiar rhythm by now.

"The Dark has a regard for family that is unlike the other courts." With a slight rustling of leaves he moved closer. "If Bananach is killing those dear to Irial . . . the court will be unstable. Death of our kind is never easy, and the Hounds, in particular, will not deal with pointless murder. If it were in battle, they would accept it more easily. This was before the battle."

"Murder? Why would she kill a halfling?" Donia let frost trail in her wake, giving in to the growing pressure inside. It was not yet spring, so she could justify freezing the burgeoning blossoms.

Evan's red eyes darkened until they barely glowed, like the last flare of coals in an ashy fire. He was watchful as they moved, not looking at her but at the streets and shadowed alleys they passed. "To upset Irial? To provoke the Hunt? Her machinations aren't always clear."

"The halfling—"

"A girl. More mortal than fey." He led Donia down another street, motioning for her to step around several more sleeping vagrants.

She stopped at the mouth of the alley. Five of Niall's thistle-clad fey had captured a Ly Erg.

When Donia stepped into their field of vision, one of the thistle-fey slit the Ly Erg's throat. The other four faeries turned to face her.

She formed a knife of her ice.

One of the thistle-fey grinned. "Not your business."

"Does your king know—"

"Not your business either," the same faery said.

Donia stared at the corpse on the ground. The red-palmed Ly Erg was one of those who often lingered in the company of War. They were all members of the Dark Court, but the Ly Ergs gravitated to whoever offered access to the most fresh blood.

Why are they killing their own? Or is this a result of factions in the Dark Court?

The murderous faeries turned their backs to leave.

"Stop." She froze the metal fence they were about to scale. "You will take the shell."

One of the thistle-covered faeries looked over his shoulder at her. The faery flashed teeth. "Not your business," he repeated again.

The Winter Queen advanced on him, icy blade held out to the side. It was a sad truth that the fey, especially those of the Dark Court, responded best to aggression. She raised the blade and pressed it against the dominant faery's throat. "I may not be *your* regent, but I am a regent. Do you question me?"

The faery leaned into her blade, testing her resolve. Some residual thread of mortality made her want to retract the blade before it was bloodied, but a strong faery—especially a queen—didn't fold under challenges. She willed serrated edges to form along the blade and pressed it hard to the faery's skin. Blood trickled onto the ice.

"Grab the body," the faery told the others.

She lowered the blade, and he bowed his head to her. The thistle-fey held their hands up in a placating gesture, and then one after another they scaled an unfrozen section of the aluminum fence. The rattle of the metal joined the growing din of traffic as morning broke.

The last faery heaved the corpse over the fence, and then they ambled off with the body in their hands.

Beside her, Evan said quietly, "Violence is here, and conflict is growing. Bananach will not stop until we are all destroyed. I would suggest that you speak to the Summer Queen and to the Dark Kings. Divisiveness will be to our detriment. We need to prepare."

Donia nodded. She was tired—tired of trying to bring order to a court that couldn't remember life before Beira's cruel reign, tired of trying to find a balance between discipline and mercy with them. "I am to see Aislinn soon. Without Keenan . . . *between us*, we are communicating better."

"And Niall?" Evan prompted.

"If Bananach is striking Irial's family, she is either testing for weaknesses or has found one already." Donia whistled, and Sasha came toward her, the wolf appearing from the shadows where he'd waited. "We need to find out who the girl was before I seek out the Dark King. Summon one of the Hounds."

Evan nodded, but his expression darkened.

"It is the right course of action," she said.

"It is."

"The Hunt is not all bad."

Evan snorted. The rowan had a long history of discord with the Hounds. Her advisor did not, however, object to her plan. She took comfort in that. The tranquility of Winter was pervasive in her fey. Typically, they could consider the situation, weigh the possibilities, and bury their tempers under the cold. *Most of the time.* When those tempers came screaming to the surface, the winter fey were a terrifying force.

My *terrifying force.*

As comforting as it was to have such a strong court, the pressure was daunting. She'd never thought to be sole monarch of a court. Once when she was still mortal, she'd dreamed of joining Keenan, ruling at his side. Barely a year and a half ago, she'd expected to die at Beira's hand. Now, she was trying to function in the role into which she'd been thrust. "Some days, I am not ready for what approaches."

"No one is ever ready for War," Evan said.

"I know."

"*You* hold the most powerful court. You *alone*. You can lead the way to stopping Bananach."

"And if I can't, what then?" She let her defenses drop for a moment, let her fears show in her voice.

"You can."

She nodded. She could if she didn't let her doubts get in the way. She straightened her shoulders and peered up at Evan. "If I allow another early spring, Summer will grow stronger, closer to an even balance with our court. I will speak to Aislinn. You will find out what you can about the Dark and send word to the Hounds. Sasha and the Hawthorn Girls will see me home."

"As you wish." With a fiercely proud look, Evan nodded and walked away, leaving her with the wolf and the trio of Hawthorn Girls, who were silent but for the whirring of their wings.